Praise for

The Departed

and Kathryn Mackel's other books

"As timely as today's TV Guide, Kathryn Mackel's *The Departed* offers both a chilling read and the brightness of divine Truth. This book snagged me with the first page and didn't let me go! Clear out a block of reading time because you won't be able to put this one down."

— Angela Hunt, author of
Unspoken and *The Debt*

"It was a fabulous read! Once again Kathy's profound depth of sensitivity to the heart and soul of mankind delivers a journey to the inner most being of her characters, allowing the reader to experience the story from their perspective. *The Departed* gives riveting insight to the unsettling dangers of opening a door to the occult. I can't wait for her next endeavor!"

— Kelly Neutz, VP of Development,
Namesake Entertainment

"Not for the faint of heart! *The Departed* is fast paced, deliciously creepy and unafraid to deal with the very real spiritual consequences awaiting those who dabble in the occult. Excellent!"

— DeAnna Julie Dodson, author of
In Honor Bound, By Love Redeemed
and *To Grace Surrendered*

"Christian Chiller is the only phrase to describe Kathryn Mackel's books, and *The Departed* is no exception. Mackel's new book is a testament to the power of God over any forces Satan can marshall. A gripping story I literally could not put down. Don't miss this one!"

— Colleen Coble, author of the
Aloha Reef Series and the Rock
Harbor series

"*The Departed* dives head first into dark zones that face Christians trying to live out their faith in spite of the evil they encounter. Kathy Mackel wakens us to the war we fight right here at home."

— Lois Richer, author of
Forgotten Justice

"*The Surrogate* is a fearless thriller that tackles uncharted territory with uncompromised skill and ease. It's a terrific and exciting read."

— Bill Myers, best-selling author of
Eli and *Touch the Face of God*

"*The Surrogate* drives to the heart immediately and doesn't let go. I can't wait to see what is next!"

— Ralph Winter, producer, *X-Men,*
X2: X-Men United, and *Planet of the Apes*; executive producer, *Star Trek V: Final Frontier*

"Kathy Mackel is one of my favorite writers. Her stuff is always tightly woven and sharp, cutting to the marrow. *The Surrogate* is a prime example of her best work. You'll savor every page."

— Jerry Jenkins, best-selling author
of the Left Behind Series

The Departed

The Departed

KATHRYN MACKEL

A Division of Thomas Nelson Publishers
Since 1798

visit us at www.westbowpress.com

Published in Nashville, Tennessee, by WestBow Press, a division of Thomas Nelson, Inc.

WestBow Press books may be purchased in bulk for educational, business, fund-raising, or sales promotional use. For information, please e-mail SpecialMarkets@ThomasNelson.com.

Publisher's Note: This novel is a work of fiction. Names, characters, places, and incidents are either products of the author's imagination or used fictitiously. All characters are fictional, and any similarity to people living or dead is purely coincidental.

Library of Congress Cataloging in Publication Data

Mackel, Kathryn, 1950–
The departed / Kathy Mackel.
p. cm.
ISBN 0-7852-6229-6 (trade paper)
I. Title.
PS3613.A2734D47 2005
813'.6—dc22 2004024841

Printed in the United States of America

05 06 07 08 09 RRD 6 5 4 3 2 1

To the memory of Pepperell's Dave McDowell,
who was a loving father and a great family man

And even if our gospel is veiled,
it is veiled to those who are perishing.

2 Corinthians 4:3

One

MAGGIE RACED DOWN THE STREET, CLUTCHING JOSHUA'S NOTE. Two simple words had propelled her into the night. *It's finished . . .*

They had come up from Fall River this morning after performing at a benefit. Joshua had whistled as he drove. Geneva commandeered the passenger seat of the camper, leaving Maggie to bounce around in the back. Her sister-in-law claimed to be carsick, but in truth Geneva wanted to be in control of the map. In control, period.

Joshua had dropped Maggie off at the Laundromat less than two hours ago. He was in a terrific mood, looking forward to talking to their agent. "Abner will come through for us," he had promised. "We'll be back in the big time before you know it, Princess."

And now this—*finished*.

Maggie crossed Fells Way, barely pausing as a minivan screeched and spun away from her. He had to be at the beach—the ocean always had a way of calming Joshua. They were in Lynn, Massachusetts, scheduled to perform at a dinner theater. It was early March. Off-season, which was how they had gotten the gig.

Maggie reached the public beach, deserted now that the sun had set. It was too dark for dog walkers, too early for kids making out or drinking in cars. She dashed across the parking lot and down the stairs, jumping the last three steps. Her heart pounded; the pulse in her neck felt like a rocket about to explode. She looked right, then left. The vast expanse of sand was broken by a long pier on one side and a public bathhouse to the other.

Someone was at the end of the pier. "Joshua? Joshua!"

The figure turned—an old woman. Maybe she should run up there, ask the woman if she had seen Joshua wandering on the sand. But the old woman bent back over the railing, cradling her head in her hands, her message clear. *I have my own pain. Leave me be.*

Maggie turned in a circle in the sand, unable to decide which way to go. The beach was too long. How would she find Joshua, tell him that none of it mattered, that she still believed in him?

"Oh, God," she cried. "I'll do anything—just help me find him."

Stop your blather, old woman, Julia Madsen told herself. *Marco is not coming back.*

She stood alone at the end of the pier, speaking nonsense into the night, knowing that there was more life in the oil-soaked pilings under her feet than there was in Marco. But she could sooner stop breathing than stop talking to Marco. It had been sixty years since she had gone to Hollywood to make her fortune and win the hearts of millions. Marco had been right there with her, telling her she was beautiful and talented and deserving of every bit of it.

Marco even understood when Julia had to marry Geoff Wiggin. The studio expected their leading lady to be squired around on the arm of someone photogenic and famous. Things were different these days—blond starlets were hip when they kept company with dark-skinned boys. Today Marco would be a star in his own right, an exotic mixture of the islanders and the Europeans, with that strong body and silky hair that Julia loved to run her fingers through, only a wisp on the day that his eyes closed for the last—

No. That day still tore through Julia like fire. Not that they didn't have warning. Two years of chemo and radiation had left Marco a shadow. But his will burned bright, even with his last breath. "I swear I will push through that gate and come back. Listen for me . . ."

Marco had kept up with his island religion, a sensual mythology that ascribed power and personality to the sun and wind and sea. In his illness, he clung especially to a deity named Sola, the gatekeeper between here and now and that to come. When a person was born, Sola ushered his spirit into this world. At his death, she swung the gate the other way and welcomed him into *summerland*, a place where poetry and love were eternal. It was said that, if properly approached, Sola would let the dead speak from the other side on the anniversaries of their births. Marco had spun tales of lovers reuniting on the birthday of the one who had passed.

He would have been seventy-nine today. Julia had tried every prayer and incantation she could think of, but the gate to whatever lay on the other side had remained stubbornly closed. "Come on, Sola. Open up and let my dear one pass . . ."

Julia leaned into the wind, listening to the waves struggle against the incoming tide. A plane roared overhead. Gulls squealed in constant expectation. Someone screamed from down on the sand. It was all background noise, a track laid down with no meaning.

She wrapped her fingers around the razor. The ivory handle was inlaid with silver and carved with Marco's initials. The blade was finest steel, kept sharp long after Marco switched to disposables. It would all be over in a couple of hours now. Just one more obligation.

Geoff's nephew Dane had called earlier in the day, begging Julia to come to Boston. She had no energy for dealing with city traffic and no wish to disturb this fragile peace that had settled on her now that she had come to a decision. Even so, there was something in Dane's tone that made her agree to have dinner with him. He was anxious to tell her about his latest scheme—something to do with the Internet—and no doubt looking for money to make it happen.

She should have refused and kept this night simply for herself. There was no reason for Dane to hit her up for money. He was about to inherit it all anyway. Despite her nephew's loose way with women and drugs and his incessant scheming, Julia had always had a soft spot for him. She'd wish him good luck while meaning good-bye.

Julia had suggested the Sea Breeze, telling Dane it was an easy drive from her estate in Hawthorne. But her choice had been made from sentiment—she and Marco had met there. She had been a teenage waitress, jingling with tips because of her bright beauty and pert manner. He had been a busboy, overlooked because of his dark skin.

Tonight, after she bought Dane supper and bid him good night, she would come back out here and open the razor. It would be quick and painless, her blood ebbing away on the tide. Unless Sola allowed Marco to come to her before then. "Marco, you promised me a sign . . ." But the only reply was the first star of the evening, winking in the sky like some scrambled marquee.

Show's over.

Joshua Lazarus sat in the cold shadows under the pier, trying to find courage in the sweep of the wind to tell his wife and his sister that it was now official. Abner had made that perfectly clear during their phone conversation: "Sorry, man, but we've got to face the truth. Your brand of magic is obsolete, was probably obsolete the moment I signed you. It's just . . . you had that amazing stage presence . . . but listen, I've got to move on, Josh. There's young talent, kids coming up that need my guidance."

Joshua was twenty-eight years old and finished.

How could he tell Maggie he had failed when she had given up everything for him?

I don't care about college, Joshua. I don't need it. I only need you. My husband, till death do us part. No, not even death; that's how much I love you . . .

And what could he say to Geneva? She had made his career her whole life.

I'll sell Ma's house, buy a camper so we can travel to different cities. We'll have money for props, for wardrobe, for publicity. No arguments, Josh. I'd move heaven and earth for you . . .

Four years ago, he had had it all. A contract with a top talent agent. A bride so beautiful she made his eyes ache. A smart sister who would help him navigate the tricky waters of show business. Joshua had known he would be something special, someone great.

It sounds weird, Gen, but I feel like I was born to be up there in those bright lights. And not because it's all about me—no, it's about the way I can make people feel. Even if it's just for the length of the performance, if I can make them more alive, then . . . who knows, Maggie? Maybe they'll take something away that makes their lives just a little better. All because of me . . .

Maggie would swear none of it mattered anyway as long as she had him. Geneva would try to fix him, just like she had all their lives. But this couldn't be fixed.

He would pray if he could. But God didn't exist—Geneva had told him that from the time he was a little boy, and she was always right about such things. Yet there must be some force to keep the stars in their courses and the tides coming in; some universal agreement must keep the earth from flying off its axis and spinning into the void.

He leaned against the base of the piling. Tattered seaweed swept in and out with each wave. The tide was coming in, slapping against the rocks where he sat, soaking his legs. The sharp cold was an agreeable sensation, reminding Joshua that he was still alive, that the pain gripping his chest wasn't the only pain he could feel.

I still want to shine. I would do anything, if only some god or spirit or force would tell me what I have to do!

A low moan crept over him, perhaps from the pier overhead. Was that another heartsick soul? Or was it the wind, caught in the same dead end as he was?

He buried his head under his arms and let his own tears wash him with what little warmth he had left.

When his soul felt as raw as his throat, he felt dear arms encircle him and then heard the only words that could possibly matter. "I love you."

"I love you too, Maggie." He clung to her, feeling her fingers tighten into his back, smelling the salt on her skin. They kissed and clung to each other, not wanting to move even though the surf splashed against their ankles.

"You're cold." Joshua rubbed her arms.

"It's still winter. And here we are, standing in the water. Aren't we the bright ones?"

He shook his head. "You didn't need to come out."

"Oh yes, I did. I had to make sure you're okay. I mean, of course you're not okay. But as long as we're together, we will be okay."

He brushed her cheek with his lips. Her skin was cold and damp, her breath labored. "As long as we're together . . ."

She pressed against him, squeezing him so tight his ribs ached. "Why did you pick this place, Joshua? It's so cold and dark here."

"I'm not really sure." And that was the truth. Joshua didn't know why he had been driven into this particular darkness.

Until a voice spoke from out of the night.

Two

Shopping for diamonds was tricky.

Nothing but the best would do, which was why Penn Roper had driven down to Boston. Tiffany's in New York City might have been closer from western Vermont, but the traffic was a bear. Not that Boston was any laughing matter with its unmarked streets and constant detours.

A saleswoman came to the counter. Tall and slim, she was modestly attired in an expensive gray suit. Her name tag read Annette Donaldson.

"Good evening. Is there something I can help you find?"

"Hmm . . . good question. May I call you Annette?"

She beamed. "Of course."

He extended his hand. "I'm Penn Roper. My daughter is turning eighteen next week. I want something with lasting value but something she'll think is *cool* enough to wear right now. Needless to say, I haven't the foggiest idea where to start."

"Tell me about your daughter. What's her name?"

"Tanya. She's my only child. And she's . . . well . . ."

Annette laughed. "The apple of your eye. It's written all over your face."

"That obvious?"

"It's that special father-daughter thing. I still call my father a couple times a week." Annette leaned across the counter, close enough so Penn could smell lilacs. "And I still call him 'Daddy.' Because he'll always be."

Penn smiled. "I hope Tanya will feel that way in ten years or so."

"Ten years?"

"When she's your age," Penn said.

Annette laughed again. "Either you're half-blind or you're incredibly charming."

"Not blind. And not charming. Truthful."

"Well, then . . . thank you. I accept your compliment. Okay, let's see what we can do for Tanya. How would you classify her personal style?"

"Ask me what the stock market closed at today. Or what the latest Intel chip is capable of. That I understand."

"Is she hip? Conservative? Sporty? Preppy? Retro?"

Penn shook his head. One word couldn't possible capture the wonder that was Tanya. She danced ballet and jazz. She sang folk songs and pop tunes. She climbed mountains and kayaked rivers. She cried over stupid movies and laughed at dumb jokes. She slept with her curtains open so she could gaze at the stars.

His daughter believed that life was good, and Penn would move heaven and earth to keep it that way for her.

"She's a dreamer," Penn said. "My little girl is a dreamer."

Tanya Roper was head-over-heels, crazy-as-a-loon in love. "Mrs. Jack Sanderson. How hot is that?"

Hillary made a face. "Is that how Jack got you into bed? Promising to marry you?"

"Who said he got me into bed?"

"That stupid smile on your face."

Tanya blushed. "He made love to me. There is a huge difference."

"Not to guys. They'll get it any way they can."

"Jack's not like that."

Hillary groaned. "Yeah, and Elvis is my garbageman. Okay, so when did this all happen? I can't believe *Mother* let you out of her sight long enough to do the dirty deed."

"Last month, at the lake. Mother was so busy getting ready for the convention, she never had a clue. And my father believed me when I said I'd be with you."

Hillary's mouth hung open. "You lied to your father?"

Tanya shrugged. "Had to happen sometime."

"Whoa . . . I guess so. So when is the wedding of the century going to happen?"

"After graduation."

"That's a long time away."

"Only two months."

"Months . . . ? You mean, *high school* graduation?"

Tanya grinned. "Yep."

Hillary grabbed her shoulders. "Oh my gosh. You're pregnant, aren't you?"

"Why would you say such a ridiculous thing, Hil?"

"You've got to be. Why else would you be getting married?"

"Try love."

"Right. Uh-huh. How pregnant are you?"

"Who said anything about pregnant?" Tanya was dying to tell Hillary, but she couldn't, not until Jack knew. This morning had been incredible, watching the blue dot turn into that little heart that meant yes, a baby was on the way.

Things would be different for her and Jack and their little boy. They wouldn't be like her parents, who spoke in hushed tones and measured each word, maintaining the pretense that anything but her mother's political career kept them together.

"You're getting married just to get married? You expect me to believe that?"

"No. I expect you to listen to me. I love Jack and Jack loves me."

"Does this mean you're not going to college?"

Tanya gave Hillary a quick hug. "It means I won't be going to college with you. I know I promised, but . . . you understand. I'll be going to the university with Jack." Tanya had it all planned. They'd get married, set up an apartment off campus. Papa would help with that, of course. In December, Jackson Penn Sanderson would be born. Penn for Papa, who would be the best grandfather ever. Mother, on the other hand, would probably only see the baby when she needed a photo op. And that would be fine by Tanya.

"So when are you going to tell your mother?" Hillary asked, as if reading her mind.

"Tell me what?" Joanna Roper stood in the doorway.

Tanya felt a chill settle on her. Mother was so controlling and tenacious. She'd need to tread carefully here. "Mother! I thought you were still out. We were just heading off to the library."

"I repeat: tell me what?"

Tanya bit her lip, hustling to come up with something. "Um . . . I'm dropping out of National Honor Society."

"What?!" Mother's voice was raspy from the cigarettes she swore she didn't smoke.

"The meetings are such a drag, aren't they, Hil?"

"Uh . . . they can be."

"You'll do no such thing. You made a commitment and you'll see it through."

Tanya squeezed Hillary's hand. Hillary took the cue. "I told her that, Mrs. Roper, but she wouldn't listen to me."

"Well. She *will* listen to me. Won't you, Tanya?"

Tanya hung her head, biting her lip to hide her smile. "Yes, Mother."

"Now, get off to the library. I won't tolerate sloppy behavior just because it's your last term of high school."

"No, Mother."

Hillary couldn't get out of the room fast enough. Tanya grabbed her bag and hustled out after her. She could feel Mother's eyes on her as they went down the stairs.

Tanya was hiding something. Joanna Roper had seen it in the flush of her cheeks, the shifting of her eyes. The search of her bedroom and bathroom had yielded nothing, but she was too experienced to stop at half measures.

Joanna spread a newspaper on the garage floor and emptied the contents of the trash barrel onto it. The bag from Tanya's bathroom had been shoved under the kitchen trash. Joanna ripped it open, pawing with gloved hands through tissues, cotton balls, teen magazines, and—wait, were these ashes? A love letter, perhaps? The remnants were too dense, more like charred cardboard. Joanna examined an unburned piece that was printed with a bar code and its associated numerical code.

She flipped open her cell phone and dialed her assistant. "Call Frank Emmett. I need him to check his inventory codes. I want to know what product this number is key to." Joanna read off the numbers under the bar code. "Lean on him if you need to—he owes me a favor. Call me back ASAP."

Tanya had destroyed the evidence. But of what? Was she taking some sort of over-the-counter drugs? Joanna had warned her more than once against taking those diet pills. Or maybe birth control pills. Her phone buzzed. Joanna opened it, listened for a moment, snapped it shut.

The numbers were the code for a home pregnancy kit.

Joanna went back down on her knees, this time involuntarily as her stomach went into a tailspin. *No, please. Not my daughter. She can't be pregnant.*

And yet, it all fit. Tanya's vomiting the last three mornings, blaming stress over exams for her queasy stomach. Her recent purchase of oversized T-shirts and stretch jeans. *Get with it, Mother,* she had said when Joanna questioned her taste.

The motor over her head hummed. Joanna shoveled the trash back just as the garage door opened and headlights framed her. Joanna took great gulps of air, trying to get her bearings, the color back in her face.

Penn could not know about this. He'd have some ridiculous notion of helping to rear Tanya's baby. Or worse, he'd want to adopt it and make Joanna raise this kid too. She was nearly finished with her obligation to him—she was not about to go back into the harness all over again. Nor did she want Tanya to be tied back to her papa just when she should be going off to college, making a life of her own, a life away from him.

Penn turned off the car and left it in the driveway.

"I know politics is a dirty business, Joanna—but Dumpster diving?"

"I lost an earring. One of my tourmalines."

"Oh. Sorry. Want me to help you look?"

"No."

"Really—I'd be happy to do it. You shouldn't be picking through the trash like some bum."

"I said no, didn't I?"

Penn yanked her to her feet, his fingers biting into her arm. "You only say no if I say you may."

She breathed deeply, trying to keep the pain from showing. *Don't shake. You'll get through this and get Tanya through this—just keep your head.*

Her husband's hair was short, his face clean shaven, his shirt crisp, his tie perfectly knotted. Penn Roper looked the part of a successful businessman, but she knew what was under that civilized facade. "I'm sorry, Penn. I'm just tired. Long day."

"You're sure there's nothing I can do to assist you?"

"No. Thank you."

Penn let her go, nodded, and went into the house, leaving Joanna alone with the garbage—and her daughter's secret.

She would do anything it took—*anything*—to make sure her daughter avoided her own fate. Married to a man she couldn't love, parenting a daughter she couldn't mother because Penn insisted on being mother, father, and the world to Tanya.

His devotion was bizarre for a man with his background of covert ops, of hard violence in the service of his country. For Tanya's sake Penn had stepped out of that secret life and into the role of doting papa. He had made Joanna an offer: if she had his baby and mothered it well, he would treat her kindly, give her a comfortable life, and fund her ambitions. She wanted to serve in public office; he had the smarts and contacts to make lots of money in the defense industry. It had been a devil's bargain, but Joanna had no choice.

Tanya had a choice, as long as they acted quickly and secretly. This would be an easy fix, a matter of getting Tanya to see that she had no option. And keeping it all from Penn, because what he didn't know wouldn't hurt him. But if he ever found out, then the hurt would be hers—for sure.

Three

Maggie and Joshua clung to each other, dripping water all over the floor of the camper they called home.

"That voice we heard up on the pier—should we have done something?" Maggie said. "She sounded so determined."

"She was gone when we got up there. What could we do?" Joshua kissed his wife. "You do realize who she was, don't you? I'd know that voice anywhere. Julia Madsen."

"Who?"

"Once upon a time, a famous movie star. She hasn't been seen in public for a long time."

"I just hope she's all right. That talk about the razor." Maggie buried her face into his shoulder.

"We tried to get to her, Maggie. What else could we do?"

"Nothing, I suppose."

The door to the camper opened with a bang. Geneva stormed in. "You're late. The manager is barking all over the—What the—? Your shoes are soaked! Joshua, even your pants. What happened to you two?"

Joshua squeezed Maggie playfully, then smiled at his sister. "Um. A puppy."

"A what?"

"A puppy that turned out to be a teddy bear. Probably some ticked-off teenager threw it in when she caught her boyfriend cheating."

"You jumped in the ocean to rescue a teddy bear? This time of year? Are you insane?"

Joshua laughed. "That's me, always the hero."

Geneva glared at Maggie. "You put him up to that foolishness, didn't you? Don't you care if he catches pneumonia?"

"Of course I care. You have a lot of nerve, Geneva, coming in here like this, making accusations—"

"Excuse me, your *majesty*. But this happens to be my home too. Unless you prefer I sleep on the pavement tonight—"

"Whoa, time out here!" Joshua stepped between them. "This was all my fault. Now can we get on to the business at hand? I've got a show to do."

Geneva hurried to the closet, looking for his tuxedo. Maggie tried to wedge in behind her at the table to put on her makeup. The camper was midsized but taken up with all their props and sound equipment. They had lived four years in impossibly close quarters. During the rare times when they had a little extra money, either they or Geneva would grab a motel room for a few nights. On good nights, he and Maggie would drag out the pup tent and let Geneva have the camper to herself.

Maybe it's good that it's over, Joshua thought. A chill went through him, scattering a new rash of goose bumps. After all—what good had fame and money done for Julia Madsen?

Maggie wrapped her arms around him, her warmth rushing through him. Maybe his magic was over, but Joshua would find something new for her to believe in.

"Your audience is getting restless." Geneva tapped her foot hard enough to shake the camper.

Joshua dressed quickly. Maggie slipped into her royal blue gown. Her hair—the color of spring honey—was loose around her shoulders. Joshua slipped the props into his jacket sleeves, kissed Maggie, hugged Geneva, then headed for the door.

"Okay, ladies," he said. "Let's go knock 'em dead."

Every time Joshua stepped into the spotlight, he took Maggie's breath away. Not just hers—she could feel the air being sucked in throughout the room as the women saw him emerge from the shadows. Even the men stared in veiled admiration.

Joshua was movie-star handsome with a straight nose, strong jaw, and rich black hair. But it was his eyes that captivated audiences. He seemed to look deep into each person he turned his attention to, the confidence and warmth of his gaze telling them that although he knew their dreams and their secrets, he not only accepted them but approved.

Charisma, Abner had called it when he had signed Joshua. Magic, Maggie knew. He had entranced her the moment they met and had held her under his spell since.

And yet, as fixed as the audience was on Joshua's appearance, they seemed to have no interest in his magic. The Sea Breeze—a smoky, dark dinner theater—was a poor venue for the act. People were already shifting in their seats, clinking silverware, and talking. Joshua's knuckles were white on his cane, and suddenly his silks tangled in his cuff.

"Last time I use that laundry." Joshua's chuckle was rewarded with weak laughter. This was the second blown trick. He had already tried to make Geneva disappear. But when Joshua pulled the curtain of the palanquin, Geneva was stuck in the trapdoor, swearing loudly enough for half the audience to hear.

They should have just blown off tonight. But Geneva had finally gotten someone to cash the check, and they'd need the money to get back to Maine. Beyond that, the future was dark. *Dark, but not bleak,* Maggie reminded herself, as long as she and Joshua were together.

"And now, if I can ask my lovely assistant to step forward?"

Maggie moved to center stage as Joshua went through his patter, bragging that he would lift her "up to the stars, where she belongs." She lay down on the table, and on Joshua's signal, she pressed the button to start the lift. The arm of the lift was hidden by the table leg. As it extended, raising the hidden board and Maggie, Joshua would block sight of the arm with his own body. The audience would see only Maggie suspended three feet above the table, with nothing but empty air in between.

As Maggie levitated, the applause began. She felt a rush of relief. Joshua made a few jokes while Maggie lay still, pretending to be in a trance. "And now, I'd better bring this lovely lady down before she outshines those stars."

Maggie slipped her finger onto the button and pushed. Nothing happened.

"Well, isn't that like a female? Not coming down until she's good and ready."

Joshua waved the silks in a shimmering curtain to distract the audience. "Push," he whispered.

"I am pushing! It's stuck."

Joshua reached under the board, keeping the silks moving so the audience wouldn't notice. He pressed the button. Nothing. Maggie could slide off, but she was six feet up and wearing high heels. Even if she didn't break her ankle, the board would be exposed for everyone to see. Where would the magic be then?

Joshua dropped a smoke bomb to obscure the whole stage. "If she's going to be stubborn, I'll just have to make *her* disappear," he called out to the audience.

"It might work this time," some loudmouth called out. "She ain't fat like the other chick."

"Some magician. He disappears the hot one, not the dog," someone else called out.

"I'm going to swing the board behind the curtain," Joshua whispered, his face red. He pushed hard—too hard. The board tipped, toppling her down onto him. They rolled out of the smoke, a jumble of her gown and his silks.

He jumped up, straightening his jacket. "Sorry 'bout that. A little magical malfunction."

"More like magical *malpractice*," someone yelled.

"More like they just *stink*," someone else called out.

Maggie sat there, rubbing her ankle as the audience convulsed with laughter and boos. Joshua walked to the edge of the stage and stared at the audience. "Stop that. Right now!"

His voice was so startling that the heckling instantly stopped. As he jumped off the stage, Maggie's throat clenched. Geneva was at her side now, cursing a blue streak. "What does that idiot think he's doing?"

"These are all just cheap tricks," Joshua said, his stage voice strange and hollow. "But there are those among us whose need is far beyond a night's entertainment."

Maggie hobbled to the stairs, Geneva pushing past her, both intent on stopping him. Joshua waved them back. He walked among the tables, his face fading from hot anger into something strange. Something bloodless.

As if he had just seen a ghost.

Meaningless. Every heartbeat a dull thud, every breath a sorry waste of air. Julia just wanted to be done with it all.

Dane had yapped for the past hour, going on about his latest venture, some Internet deal. Poor boy didn't have to try so hard; he would get it all anyway. Meanwhile, this show was beyond torture—a handsome magician with an act that looked like it came from his grandfather's attic. Not that any of it mattered; her heart and mind were tuned to a silent voice.

Time is running out, Marco.

Laughter erupted. The assistant had gotten stuck up in the air, then tumbled down on top of the magician. He was up now, staring at the audience with fury. *Such eyes,* Julia thought. Darker even than Marco's. Something in the magician's gaze shifted—even from the back of the room she could see it.

"Stop!" he said, and the audience obeyed. He jumped off the stage.

The air around Julia took on a strange clarity. *Those eyes . . .*

"I pretend to make magic, but sometimes—just sometimes—real magic breaks through."

Someone in the audience snorted. Someone else hushed him.

"No, you're right, sir. I've put on a miserable show tonight. Those of you who want your money back, you can have it. But first, there's something that needs attending to."

He was moving too fast now, coming her way. Julia panicked, rising from her chair. Dane pulled her back down. "We'll get our money back later, Aunt Julia. This should be a blast, seeing what trick Lazarus is going to blow now."

The magician—Lazarus—was at her side, his dark hair framed in haze and light. "You know, don't you?"

Her heart beat so hard now she thought it would crack her chest open. "I'm not sure."

He smiled. "I have a message for you. Sola has opened the gate to allow a voice to speak from the other side."

Julia gasped, felt herself rising from her seat. Dane grabbed her arm. "Julia?"

"Marco. Am I correct, Julia?" Lazarus said.

Julia pushed Dane's hand away. "Yes. Marco Campia."

Dane stood, trying to pull her away. "What're you talking about? The gardener? That Marco?"

She heard her name echoing through the room. *Julia Madsen!* Foolish people. She was just a frail moment of flesh. The magician—or whatever Lazarus was—had somehow locked into what really mattered.

"Marco says that you hid your love for all those years."

"All those years, Marco and I could have, should have been together."

"Hold it there! What's this about Marco? What about my uncle?" Dane's voice sounded far away, in another lifetime.

Lazarus tipped her chin up. "Marco refused to marry you. He said Geoff Wiggin would be good for your career."

"How do you know all this?"

"This isn't about me, dear one. It's about what Marco wants you to know."

It was hard to find breath to speak. "What does he want me to know?"

"For one thing, you are beautiful. That's from me, but Marco agrees."

"Beauty means nothing," Julia said.

"It does when it's from here." Lazarus put her hand over her heart. She was water, flowing wherever he led. "Marco wants you to know that his love for you is stronger than ever."

"Thank you," she whispered.

"There's more, lovely lady." Lazarus brushed her tears away with his fingertips. His voice was low now, his words right in her ear. "You are not to use the razor. Do you understand me? This is from Marco, and I agree."

She leaned against him. "I'm so tired; I've waited so long . . ."

"And you've wasted too much time waiting. Marco expects you to live the life you've been gifted with. He says—"

Lazarus bowed his head and closed his eyes, rocking now on his feet, so rapt that Julia feared he'd topple into that other side. Then he looked at her and smiled. "He says there's work for you to do. People need your help, so hop to it. You've left those responsibilities for too long—you need to get back to them. Do you know what he's talking about?"

"The Right Hand Foundation. To support our staffs in their old age—the folks who cleaned our houses, drove our cars. I just let it go after Marco—"

"Marco is saying it again—hop to it. And one last thing. Marco says to stop overwatering his orchids. Okay?"

"Okay," Julia said. And then she collapsed into the arms of Joshua Lazarus, seeing nothing but believing everything.

Four

Amy Howland's first impulse was to scream.

As the coven closed in on her, a raspy voice muttered, "Corner it." The rest picked up the refrain. "Corner it. Corner it. Corner it."

Every nerve in Amy's body shrieked for flight. But no—*If you make the Most High your dwelling*—this was God's work—*then no harm will befall you.*

They closed in on Amy, hell's acolytes in red hooded sweatshirts, black leather pants, biker boots, and gleaming chains. She exhaled to keep her knees still, then held her breath as the Astaroth leader pushed into the circle.

Theo's face was covered with a spider-web tattoo and dotted with the star-shaped scars that all these freaks burned into their faces. Amy dug her toes into her shoes to keep her feet from backing away—*no disaster will come near you.* No one, no matter how bizarre or insane or evil, would drive her and Safe Haven out of this house.

"How dare you come into my house?" Amy kept her voice low and firm, the same tone she used with street toughs and drug dealers.

Theo laughed, a chest-deep rattle. "The question is, how dare you stay in *my* house? You have been told to leave."

"I have a lease."

Theo stepped closer. "Leases—or lessees—can be broken."

Amy suppressed a gag. The Astaroths chewed strong tobacco and foul herbs in the belief that they could curse simply by breathing. As if reading her mind, Theo commanded his adherents, "Curse it."

The refrain deepened to a growl. "Curse it. Curse it. Curse it."

"Leave now, you jerks, and I won't have you arrested," Amy said.

"Leave now, you fool, and I won't harm you," Theo said.

They pushed in on her, black-nailed fingers hovering over every part of her body. They didn't have to touch her to snake tendrils of dread through her skin, flooding her muscles, twisting around her bones.

Theo leaned into Amy, his lips a hairsbreadth from hers. "Those we can't curse, we kill."

The refrain changed, so deep now it seemed to vibrate through her skin. "Kill it. Kill it. Kill it."

Theo framed Amy's throat with his hand, so close that she could feel the heat of his palm. She flipped the top off the pepper spray in her pocket. She needn't fear their incantations—*You will tread upon the lion and the cobra*—but she wouldn't put it past Theo to have a knife under that sweatshirt.

"He will command His angels concerning me . . ." She exhaled on each word to keep her voice from cracking.

Theo clicked his tongue—pierced with a metal bolt—against his front teeth. "Is that so?"

"To guard me in all my ways," Amy continued. "So *you* will not lay a hand on me."

Theo's eyes narrowed. Then he laughed, this time a full, throaty sound. Still gazing at Amy, he tipped his head at the hall. His followers left the room. Amy heard the door open and each adherent's steps as he or she went down the stairs.

Theo put his mouth to Amy's ear. "Soon," he whispered.

Even though they were on the front sidewalk, his Astaroths somehow picked up the chant. "Soon. Soon. Soon."

Theo left, laughing the whole way. Amy slammed the door behind him and set the alarm. Her back was soaked with perspiration even though it was March and a cold wind drove under the door.

Soon.

Yes, that much was true. God was preparing Amy for some darkness greater than the drug dealers, junkies, prostitutes, and devil-worshipers who already afflicted this hard-bitten neighborhood called the Beak. Something more was coming, something that would test her mettle and shake her faith—*I will be with you in trouble*—but, God willing, she would stand her ground.

Amy leaned against the window, letting the glass cool her fevered skin. She watched the Astaroths walking toward their various houses, disappearing into shadows that shouldn't be there in the afternoon sun.

Suddenly furious, she flung open the window and drank in cold air. But Theo's odor lingered, as did his parting words.

"We won't have to lay a hand on you. We never do."

Tanya would be thrilled. Penn couldn't wait to see her face tomorrow when she opened his present and saw the jewelry. Annette had helped him pick out three gold bangle bracelets. When he insisted Tanya have a diamond, she steered him to a solitaire pendant. She had wisely suggested that Tiffany's put safety clasps on everything.

He had come back to Boston today to pick everything up.

Traffic had been horrific, and by the time he got there, the store was closing. Annette was gracious enough to stay and wrap everything for him. It seemed only right to buy her dinner.

Penn sipped his martini and smiled. "So what do you think, Annette? Bermuda or the Bahamas?"

"What I think is that your daughter is one lucky gal."

"Am I going overboard? The jewelry *and* the vacation?"

"You'll be creating a memory that will last a lifetime."

"I was thinking she could take her best friend—Hillary Martin. Bermuda might be the best bet. They can race around on those little motorbikes while I stay out of the sun and read my journals."

"It's a vacation, Penn. You're supposed to be reading trashy novels on the beach. Not wearing sunscreen and reading . . . what kind of journals?"

"High tech. I'm one of those big bad villains—a defense contractor."

"Really? Well, I am grateful for your contribution to my safety. What do you make?"

"Optical fiber devices, mostly for communications. We do a lot of satellite work. We also have a line of miniature devices. If I tell you more than that, I'll have to kill you. Then again, if I told you more than that, I'd probably bore you to death anyway."

She laughed.

"Have you been to the Caribbean, Annette?"

"Not yet. I'm a skier—been to the Alps, Aspen, New Hampshire. Though with my creaky knees, I probably need to head to the beaches instead of the slopes."

"We've been to St. Thomas, Aruba, Curacao—any one would be a great start."

"*We*. Meaning you, Tanya . . . and Tanya's mother?"

Discreet but right to the point. Penn liked this woman. "Tanya's mother and I are somewhat separated."

"Oh. I'm sorry." She briefly touched his hand. She had beautiful nails—a soft rose color that matched her lipstick. A kind touch from a classy woman was not something that came Penn's way often. When he needed what Joanna had never shown interest in, he had discreet and expensive sources to go to. Even though he insisted on the very best, they were still not the kind of women he would be seen in public with.

"No, no. It's been years. We reside in the same house for Tanya's sake, but we are not together. I can't even call it a marriage of convenience, because it's pretty inconvenient most times, maintaining the pretense. I've been adamant on wanting Tanya to grow up believing marriage is a sacred and beautiful thing. Unfortunately, my wife and I discovered many years ago that our marriage was not."

"And your wi—Tanya's mother—goes along with this?"

"Quid pro quo. I fund Joanna's political ambitions, and she manages the home and plays mother."

Annette twirled the onion in her martini. "So it's a permanent arrangement?"

"No. Tanya will be off to college this fall, and then her mother and I will put even more distance between us. She's already got an apartment in Montpelier. She's a state rep, spends a lot of time up there. I'm sorry. I don't know why I'm boring you with all this."

She touched his hand again. "Because I want to hear it."

He put his hand over hers.

She smiled. "Tell me more about Tanya."

Tanya came home from school to find Mother in her room, packing up her new T-shirts. "What do you think you're doing? That's my stuff."

"You won't be needing these ridiculous shirts," Mother said.

"But I . . . like them."

"Well, I do not. And I will reiterate, Tanya: you will not be needing them."

Everything about Mother was sharp—the edge of her lapel, her blunt-cut bangs, her hard stare. A tiny tremble crept into the back of Tanya's knees. She took a long breath, determined not to waver. "I paid for those shirts with my own money," she said. "So you have no right—"

"I have every right. I know about the pregnancy," Mother said.

"That's Hillary—"

"Don't even try to lie to me. I heard you again this morning, throwing up."

The tremble blossomed into full-blown shaking, and Tanya sank to her bed. Mother pushed the box of T-shirts aside and sat next to her, taking her hand. Her grip was firm and her palm was like ice. "Sweetie, it's okay. It's easy enough to take care of this."

"There's nothing to take care of. Jack's going to marry me." Tanya pushed air up from her diaphragm, trying to keep her voice strong.

"I know you have some romantic notion of that happening. But it won't."

"He loves me."

Mother laughed. "All men love us when they're . . . well, never mind that. Tanya, even if he wanted to go ahead with a marriage, it wouldn't be good for you. Look how hard you've worked in school. The bright future you have. How proud Papa is."

"He'll be happy for me."

"Oh no, he will not." Mother shook her head. "Sweetie, you've got to trust me on this. I've already made the appointment. We'll go tomorrow, get it done, and won't mention this again."

"Jack will marry me. I know he will."

"He won't—and even if he would, your father wouldn't let that happen. If you care for that boy as much as you say, you'll just let me help you get out of this. Nice and quietly."

"I don't need your help on this or anything." Tanya grabbed her bag and sweater and ran out of the house. She hiked the mile to Hillary's house. This afternoon had been springlike with a warm breeze and mild sun. But sunset had brought back frigid air. Tanya welcomed the darkness, a shield from prying eyes.

I know about the pregnancy.

When she arrived at Hillary's house, she didn't bother to say hello. She simply demanded to borrow her car. "I need to see Jack right now."

"Call him."

"Face-to-face," Tanya said.

"Are you nuts? My parents would kill me!" Hillary said.

"Fine. Then I'll hitch."

Hillary pulled her back. "What's so important that you have to see Jack right now?"

Tanya couldn't tell her about the pregnancy. As much as Hillary disliked Mother, she would take her side in this—it had been Hillary's dream since eighth grade that they go to college together, be roommates, meet guys, graduate with honors. Tanya's baby would change all of that.

"I just have to. And it's got to be right now."

"Then I'll drive you."

"No. It could take all night. Please, Hil . . . I'm begging you."

Hillary tossed her keys on the table, then left the room.

Tanya made it to the university in less than an hour, then took another hour tracking down Jack. He was at a pub, knocking back beers.

"Hey, Tee! What's up?"

"We've got to talk."

He patted the bar stool next to him. "Hop up and let's talk. Want something to drink?"

"I can't."

"What—you're grounded?"

"I'm pregnant."

He stared into his beer. "Sorry to hear that. Talk about major bummer."

"I'm not bummed. I'm happy."

He looked at her, his eyes blurry from a night of drinking. "Who's the lucky guy?"

That took her breath away. "You are, of course."

He emptied his mug and motioned for another one. "Can't be. I'm the condom king."

"Condoms don't always work, Jack."

He rolled his eyes. "Oh, I got it now. You're after the signing bonus, aren't you? Hooked up with some high school stud, then try to blame the baby on me."

"I haven't been with anyone else. Ever. It's your son."

Jack looked her in the eye, blinking hard to focus. He got off the stool, took her arm, and steered her to a booth in the corner. "There's money for this. It's kept quiet, of course, but when someone on the team gets into certain trouble, an alumni slush fund pays for . . . what needs to be done."

Tanya's stomach seized. Mother had scheduled the *procedure* for tomorrow. She had to make Jack agree to marry her. Papa said marriage was sacred. If she and Jack were married, he'd forgive their mistake and help them raise the little boy. But if she came home pregnant and alone, how could she face him?

"Jack, please. I'm begging you. Just give us a chance. Me and your little boy. Everything will turn out all right."

Then Jack told her, in no uncertain terms, that it was not going to be all right and that it would never be all right. Somehow Tanya managed to drive home without killing herself. She pulled into Hillary's driveway in the middle of the night.

Mother sat on the front steps, waiting for her. Even in the dark, Tanya knew she was smiling.

The god of this age has blinded the minds of unbelievers, so that they cannot see the light of the gospel of the glory of Christ, who is the image of God.

2 Corinthians 4:4

Five

GENEVA HAD ALWAYS KNOWN HER BROTHER WOULD BE FAMOUS. In just a couple of months, they had gone from performing in a backwater dinner theater to appearing in this posh studio in New York City. Josh's success was not unexpected—she had known he would be acclaimed and adored. But Geneva had never, ever imagined that he would capture the hearts of thousands by talking to dead people.

That night in the Sea Breeze, Dane Wiggin had seen Joshua's star quality. After getting Julia Madsen settled, he tracked them down at the camper. They were still in the parking lot, trying to decide where to go. Josh and Maggie had just broken the news about Abner Fortis dropping them. No work, no home, no place to go—it had felt like the end of the world.

Dane poked his head in the door, all swagger and spunk. He made Josh a simple proposition: "I'll make you a star if you'll let me be your manager."

Geneva had bristled. "I manage my brother's career."

Dane took one look at the camper—props strewn on the floor, filthy dishes in the sink, empty soup cans—and snorted. In the end, this new act had been what Josh wanted, and whatever he wanted, Geneva made sure he would get it.

She was in the fancy hotel room now, working on a laptop, trying to get ready for tonight's show. Dane draped his arm along Geneva's, resting his chin on her shoulder. On the monitor, the cursor fluttered, then jumped out of sight. But no, there it was, smack against the top of the screen. Geneva wanted to throw the computer through the window and Dane after it.

"I can't do this," she said through clenched teeth.

"You have to do this," Dane said. "We can't bring someone in from the outside. Loose lips—"

She pushed Dane's hand off hers. "Yeah, yeah. The whole sinking ships thing."

"I could always train Maggie to do this. Maybe she's better for more than just standing around, looking hot. Though that's enough to ring my chimes."

"Keep Maggie out of this."

"Ooh . . . territorial, are we?"

"Shut up, fool."

He just laughed. "Whatever. Now, pay attention. This sweet piece of code should get you into almost every state motor vehicle database that gets you photos and social security numbers. Once you've got those, you can get into medical records, which gets you—"

"Thank you for the pep talk, but I'm already on board with this." As much as she wanted to wring his neck, Geneva had to admit that Dane was a genius. He had come up with the perfect scheme for ensuring Joshua Lazarus would speak to the dead with amazing accuracy. Instead of booking tickets through agencies, Dane and Geneva booked them directly. Once they had a name, an address, and credit card information, they used various Internet-hacking tools to research audience members. Joshua's charisma and quick thinking, combined with the profiles that they prepared, gave him what seemed to be a direct connection with the departed.

"Do you realize how big tonight is? This pilot is just the start of the money coming in."

"Trust me, Dane. I know what's at stake."

"Sorry, babe. I'm just jazzed about tonight's filming. When this show airs next Friday night, your baby brother is going to become a huge star."

Geneva felt a chill working up her arms. Call it fate, destiny, or plain dumb luck, but it paid to be wary. The universe had a cruel way of evening the score when you least expected it.

Something was wrong with Tanya.

She'd been listless and drawn for weeks now. When Penn asked if there was anything he could do—*anything*—she claimed it was the pressure of finals. Hillary had whispered to him that she had broken up with Jack. Even the week in Bermuda hadn't put the color back in her cheeks.

Hillary had talked Tanya into going to this show. They were going to take the train, but Penn had insisted on driving them. No way Tanya was going to New York City on a Saturday night. He would wait in a nearby coffee shop or a restaurant while they were in the theater.

It was a beautiful evening in June with warm breezes, flowering trees, and chirping birds, but he would not enjoy it as long as Tanya drifted in the shadow of some cloud he couldn't seem to catch.

"What did you say this guy's name was?" he asked.

"Joshua Lazarus." Hillary said.

"And he's a mind reader of some sort?"

"He's a medium."

"So am I. But no one pays a hundred bucks a ticket to see me."

"We're not talking shirt size," Hillary said, laughing.

He glanced in the rearview mirror. Hillary was so excited, she practically bounced out of her seat. Tanya stared out the window, expressionless.

"So what exactly does a medium do?"

"He talks to dead people," Hillary said.

"Do they talk back? I've got a couple of customers that had the nerve to buy the farm before settling their bills."

Hillary laughed. "Joshua Lazarus says they do."

"Nobody's going to talk to anyone," Tanya said. "It's just a stupid show."

Penn risked a glance back. "You okay, sweetheart?"

"I'm fine. Will you stop asking that?"

Penn drove on, making stupid jokes and hoping that somehow this Joshua Lazarus would bring back his daughter's smile.

The Reverend Dr. Patrick Drinas paced back and forth in the playroom, taking such long strides that Amy was tempted to open the door to the front porch so he'd have more running room. In his jeans, flannel shirt, and hiking boots, Patrick looked more like a nature guide than a well-respected psychiatrist. "Any idea how this Theo keeps getting in?"

Amy shrugged. "I changed the alarm code, but he keeps showing up in my living room. Sometimes with his freak show, sometimes without."

"What do the cops say?"

"Prove it. Maybe I need to buy a video camera or something."

Patrick stopped his pacing and studied her. "They've really got you rattled, don't they?"

Amy shook her head. "Patrick, I grew up on the mean streets of Dorchester. Theo is just a big wannabe spook with too much time on his hands."

"So what is it then? I can see it in your eyes—you're holding something back."

Her skin flushed. "Yes, I am. I should have shared this with you sooner, but I haven't because it's . . . I don't know . . . crazy? Delusional? Paranoid? You're the shrink. Pick one."

"How about you just tell me?"

She took a deep breath, let it out. "Okay. At the risk of sounding like something out of *Star Wars* . . . I feel that dark forces are gathering. Sometimes I feel it in my bones. Sometimes it sweeps right over me like a thundercloud racing in front of the sun. I get creeped out, get on my knees and pray, then the sun's back out. But that storm is still on the horizon. Moving closer."

Patrick was silent.

"So am I deranged? Or just a fool?" Amy said.

"There's nothing foolish in that notion. You are in the witchcraft capital of the world, after all. Are the Astaroths what this is about? This *gathering* that you sense?"

"Yes. No. I don't know. All I know is that I'm supposed to watch. Watch, wait, and keep working with the kids. And beyond that . . ."

Patrick opened up two folding chairs, motioned for Amy to sit. "Beyond that, we pray for the light to shine in the darkness as God's glory is revealed."

Joshua closed his eyes and let the darkness surround him. His breathing slowed; his chest relaxed. The shuffling of feet, the shifting of bodies, the whispers and not-whispers all faded into a velvet fog.

Sola, come to me now.

He had heard Julia call to Sola that night on the pier, asking her to let Marco pass. Later, she told him about summerland and how Sola was the gatekeeper for all the spirits, assigning people to this life or that, and sending the wind and sun and rain "hither and yon."

Why couldn't Sola be more than an island myth? Julia's prayer had been answered, in its own way. And so had Joshua's, bringing him to this place where he again thrilled audiences with a kind of magic.

Sola, fill me with power.

In each performance the power had been growing, sliding under Joshua's skin, tightening his muscles, making his eyes shine and his voice deep. Dane and Geneva did the research, but Joshua was the key to the other side, and now Sola was the key to Joshua.

Now, Joshua prayed. *Swing open that gate and bring your spirits to me now.*

This was a strange setup for a show, Tanya thought. There was no stage—the chairs were grouped in a semicircle. A man sat in shadow, his head bowed.

The lights came up. Joshua Lazarus stood, his gaze moving over the audience with such intensity that he had to be memorizing each face. Hillary was right—the man was handsome enough to melt stone. But Tanya didn't care about any of that, not anymore. It was all she could do to pretend she didn't want to scream at the stupidity of it all.

"Good evening." Simple words, but they seemed to charge the air like lightning. Tanya had been numb for so long that she was surprised to feel her skin prickle.

"Do you ever have that feeling? You catch something out of the corner of your eye, but when you turn, it's gone? Or you smell something that instantly transports you back to your childhood. But when you try to grasp it, it's too late. Maybe you hear a song that suddenly rocks you even though you're a grandparent.

"It's like that for me with the departed. Sometimes I see them in shimmering light, like heat mirages. Often I hear them—sometimes in whispers and sometimes in shouts. They are distinct personalities, just as they were when they lived on this side. But they now have one thing in common—they are in a better place."

He bowed his head. The silence lasted a full minute. Then Joshua opened his eyes and laughed. "Yes, they're in a better place, but that doesn't stop them from checking back now and then. They're here tonight. I ask you to make them welcome."

Some people shifted in their seats; others glanced over their shoulders. One lady stared up at the ceiling as if she expected a spirit to swoop down on her.

Hillary grabbed Tanya's arm. "He's coming this way."

Lazarus stopped at a woman with big glasses and frosted hair. "I'm hearing from someone whose first name begins with a *J*. James, maybe?"

"Jamie?"

"That's it. Jamie. Not your son but a younger relative. Your nephew."

The woman nodded, eyes wide.

"He's sorry he missed . . . I'm getting a big party. Not a wedding but some occasion related to a wedding."

"My thirtieth anniversary. Jamie died a few months before."

"His mom had been part of your wedding party. She helped plan the anniversary."

"Oh yes! She was my maid of honor." The woman was breathless now.

"There's a whole gang coming through now. They're all talking at once, all so loud, it's hard to sort them out."

The woman laughed. "Big family, big mouths."

Joshua Lazarus smiled. "And big hearts."

Hillary groaned. "I'd haunt that man in a minute."

"Shut up," Tanya said. It was one thing to enjoy a performance; it was another thing to make a spectacle of yourself. As Lazarus moved among the people, the message seemed to be always the same. *Your loved one—whether it was a father, brother, friend, wife—is in a better place.*

If only Tanya could believe that. Then maybe she could let go of the emptiness that sucked everything out of her so hard that her skin felt like it was wrapped around her bones.

"He's coming this way. Oh my gosh, he's looking right at us," Hillary said.

Let him look, Tanya thought. *There's nothing to see.*

Joshua normally didn't read teenagers. They were either too unpredictable or just didn't know anyone who had passed. But the girl with the haunted eyes fascinated him.

Dane hadn't provided background on these girls. That was okay—cold readings kept the show spontaneous. Joshua wandered down her aisle, taking a closer look. She had long auburn hair, a round face, clear skin. She glanced up at him, then down at her fingers. Her nails were bitten to nothing. The poor girl was too young and too pretty to be so sad.

Sola, show me how to help this girl.

Joshua felt the current rising in his skin. The power was coming on him, and if he could use this power to help others, then he would. That was his obligation now, his act of devotion.

He squatted down next to her seat and laid his hand on her forearm. "It's difficult to lose someone at any age. But for someone as young as you . . ." He let the phrase linger, hoping to draw a reaction.

Nothing.

"Someone has come through for you. But he's not sure if you want to hear him."

Her hands were clenched so tight that her knuckles were bloodless.

"Would you like me to leave you alone?"

She shook her head. Her friend stared at her with wide eyes.

Whom could she have lost? A parent, maybe. Tough on a kid but not something you let show. Geneva had taught him that. He needed to fish a bit. "You thought you'd have a lifetime together. But it didn't turn out that way."

A tiny nod.

Dane had grilled him silly until he knew all the statistics. Kids and cars—the leading cause of death for teenaged boys. "He's showing me metal. Shiny and bright. Too bright."

She looked up, eyes slowly focusing on his.

Oh yeah. He had it now—had to be a boyfriend. "It was a violent death."

Her friend grabbed her arm. "Tanya, what's he talking about?"

He shook his head. The friend sat back in her seat, pouting.

Joshua brushed Tanya's cheek with the back of his hand. "He understands about the promises you made that you couldn't keep. He wants you to just let it go. Get on with your life."

She grabbed his hand, so hard that he almost cried out. "Did it hurt?" she whispered.

Wrapping a car around a tree or slamming against a stone wall or bashing some poor woman on her way home from a long day's work? Had that hurt Mum, trapped in the car, her neck broken? Stupid drunken teenager, heartless hit-and-run.

"Not for long. He's let it go. He wants you to let it go too. He forgives you, Tanya. And he wants you to know that he will love you forever."

Joshua kissed the top of her head, then walked away. "Someone is speaking. The name is . . . Bill? No, it's a woman. Billie?" The man three seats down shifted suddenly in his seat. As Joshua worked the man, he couldn't shake that Tanya out of his mind.

He had absolved the girl. So why didn't she smile?

Six

LAST NIGHT TANYA HAD ASKED JOSHUA LAZARUS WHAT IT FELT like to die. Did it hurt?

Not for long.

Did he remember her?

He wants you to know that he forgives you . . . and that he will love you forever.

Were there angels on the other side who kept her baby safe? Or did he come out all grown up, the man he would have been if he hadn't been aborted? Had she robbed him of his childhood? Or was he there now, a little boy, with no one to care for him?

Surely God wouldn't allow that. But how exactly did God work? Mother had taken Tanya to church when she was a little girl. She remembered fluffy dresses, tight shoes, and important people talking politics. Their voices were hard and never seemed to match up with the kind words that Tanya heard in the service.

Papa said he worshiped the god of nature, and if she grew up to feel the same way, she would be ahead of most people. But what kind of God ran a creation that included earthquakes and hurricanes and cancer and abortions?

Even if God didn't exist, killing a baby had to be a crime against nature. Who would be held responsible for the procedure? Mother, who had browbeaten and then tranquilized Tanya into letting it be done? Or Tanya, who somehow should have found the strength to fight back?

"It's best this way," Mother had said. Mother had been sympathetic, putting Tanya into the car, handing her a carton of orange juice, speaking in soft tones, urging her to drink, telling her everything would be okay.

Mother was wrong. Nothing was okay, and nothing ever would be.

An abortion? His precious daughter . . .

That blasted Jack Sanderson. A high school girl had no business dating a college kid, especially a pampered, arrogant quarterback. But Tanya had been nuts over the kid, and Jack seemed respectable. Penn had taken great care to supervise their every encounter—so he had thought.

"Rope, you okay?"

In his shock, Penn had almost forgotten Jib was sitting across the table from him. They were meeting in a blue-collar bar far enough out of town that Penn wouldn't be recognized.

Jib was a small man with tight muscles and a quick smile. Women loved him and men dismissed him—until Jib got down to business. Then he couldn't be ignored. They had served together in Spec Ops, then moved into the covert service. Jib was a freelancer now, commanding high fees and worth every nickel. Penn had him on retainer—in the defense industry, it didn't pay to be caught by surprise.

Penn clenched his fists, then opened his fingers one by one. Center on the problem, and hold back the anger for a time when he was free to indulge it. "I need someone who can do clean work. Needless to say—"

"Then don't say it," Jib said. "Not coming back on you. The bottom line, always."

"This task will have some minor public ramifications."

"Then I'll do it myself."

"Don't know if you can, man. The kid is headed for the NFL. Outweighs you by almost a hundred pounds. A quarterback."

Jib laughed. "Then it'll be fun. Anything else, Rope?"

Joanna. He couldn't do much now, but a time would come . . .

"No. Thanks." Penn tossed Jib two envelopes. "One for the work at the clinic, the other for the quarterback. Info is inside. My daughter is fond of him, so don't kill him. Just maim him."

"Even more fun." Jib stuffed the envelopes into his jacket, downed what was left of his beer, and left.

Penn went over to the bar, bought a double bourbon, then went back to the booth to look at the medical records that Jib had lifted from the clinic.

All those years ago, Penn had paid Joanna *not* to abort her baby, to give life to the joy that was their daughter. And now this. Why hadn't Tanya come to him? Penn would have made it work—if he had been given the choice. If it hadn't been for that snafu on Joanna's credit card, he never would have found out. Someone was trying to charge a twelve-thousand-dollar motorcycle on her card. The company couldn't track down Joanna, so they called Penn. He told them to deny the charge, call the police, and fax him all the transactions for the past three months.

The charge for the clinic was in the faxed transactions. Joanna was too arrogant to pay the clinic in cash, thinking he never looked at the bills. She was right—he usually just forked over whatever she needed.

Before confronting Joanna, he had needed to get all the facts. Maybe it wasn't Tanya—maybe Hillary or another one of Tanya's friends had gotten in a bind and Joanna stepped in to help. An act of mercy, Penn had desperately hoped, though Joanna had never been long on mercy.

But the proof was right in his hands. Patient name: *Tanya Mary Roper*.

Penn studied the medical record, trying to hold back his emotions. Tanya had been eight weeks pregnant. How had she been persuaded to do this thing?

The admitting notes told the story. "Patient seems lethargic, difficult to arouse. Blood pressure normal, blood chemistries are all within normal range."

Apparently a counselor had been called in to see Tanya. "When questioned if the patient understood the procedure and agreed to it, she said yes. Mother attributes lethargy due to patient being up all night with her friends. 'Tired from too much partying,' in the mother's words. All medical work is okay. Patient denies using drugs. Quik-Tox shows no presence of street drugs. I see no reason not to proceed."

No reason? Joanna had to have drugged her. She certainly had enough Xanax and Valium in her arsenal. And who at the clinic would question the most vocal pro-choice advocate in the Vermont state house? It was in the clinic's best interest to believe that Tanya was there on her own free will.

Penn had to get home right away, tell Tanya that it was okay, that her papa would somehow make it better for her. Then he would deal with Joanna.

The gun was where Papa had put it two years ago, after having taught her to shoot. "Only for emergencies," he had warned Tanya. "In case of life and death."

Life and death—that was all she could seem to think about today. Her mind was twisted around that one thought: *What does it feel like to die?*

"What're you doing with that?"

"Mother! What are you doing here?"

"The school called, said you went home sick. Now, answer my question. What are you doing with that gun?"

"Nothing. I thought I heard something prowling around upstairs. Must have been the squirrels again." Tanya put the gun back in the box but didn't close the top.

"I told your father to take care of them. But of course, he didn't listen to me. I suppose I'll have to call someone in. Now, put that gun away. You know how I feel about firearms." Mother's tone was brisk and confident, but she kept her distance.

"Oh, I know how you feel about everything, Mother. Especially unwanted pregnancies."

Mother shook her head. "Oh, baby, you're young. I know you don't understand now, but you will. Trust me. I suppose it's not your fault, living in that protected little cocoon that your father built. Just remember—when you were in trouble, you came to me, not your papa."

"I didn't *come* to you. You invaded my privacy."

"Because I cared about you! Someone has to make sure you stay out of trouble. I know you love your father—and you should—but you must realize that he would rather play Santa Claus than father. Leaving it up to me to keep you on the straight and narrow. Even when you were a baby, I was the one who insisted you go to bed at a decent hour. Your father would have let you stay up as long as you wanted. Bouncing you on his lap, making those silly faces . . ."

"And you didn't?"

"Don't be silly. Of course I did. But love requires toughness sometimes. Right now, in fact. I told you to put that thing away, Tanya. I was always against your father teaching you how to shoot it in the first place."

Tanya took the gun out and laid it across her palm.

"What are you doing? Please, Tanya. Just put that thing away."

"I will, Mother. I'm just making sure the safety is on, that's all."

"You're making me nervous. So just get done with it, please."

Get done with it. The same thing Mother had said about Tanya's baby. The pain came then, flooding Tanya's body so she had no choice but to put the gun to her throat. The steel on her skin was surprisingly warm.

"Tanya! Baby, what are you doing? Don't, baby, don't fool around like that. Please. That is not funny."

And yet another surprise. Tanya had just reduced a lifetime of tyranny to pure panic in only a second. All it took was a gun. Yes, the gun was her god now. She could do anything with this gun in her hand.

"Stay back, Mother."

"Anything you say, baby. Just put the gun down. For Mommy. Please, darling."

Mommy? Had she ever called this woman *Mommy*? "Why did you make me do it, Mommy?"

"Darling, it had to be done. For your own good."

"Why?" Tanya tapped the gun against her temple, trying to stop the tears.

"Baby, you've got to try to understand. Please put the gun down so we can talk."

"Even if Jack wouldn't marry me, I still could have been a good mother."

"Honey, you have no idea what you are talking about. That's why I had to step in, help you through this situation."

"You're the one who has no idea."

"Don't I? You don't know what it was like for me. Why, I would have given my right arm to have had—"

Tanya went cold. "Had what?"

"A . . . college education. You know how I struggled to get where I am. I want things to go better for you. I'm sorry, Tanya. I didn't realize how painful this . . . episode . . . has been for you. If you would please—please, baby—put that gun away. We can sit down, talk this out. If you need help, I can take you to see someone."

"Mother. What were you about to say? You wish you had had . . . what?"

"I told you. I wish I had gone to college. I was so young when you were born. I missed out on so much."

"You wish you had aborted me, don't you, Mother?"

"Of course not. Why would you say such a thing? Your father and I were thrilled when we found out I was pregnant."

Tanya slid the safety off the gun. "I was thrilled too, Mother."

He's showing me metal.

"No, Tanya. Please, don't. I beg you, don't . . ."

"I'm warning you, Mother. Stay back."

But Mother didn't listen, just like she never listened. She kept coming, grabbing at Tanya, trying to stop her from what needed to be done, but no one could stop her now, because something else had ahold of Tanya, someone else from beyond the other side . . .

Shiny and bright.

. . . showing her, in one agonizing moment of clarity . . .

Too bright.

. . . of what needed to happen to show her baby how sorry she was, so terribly sorry for what they had done to him.

A violent death.

Seven

MOST MOMENTS, PENN STRUGGLED IN A BOTTOMLESS PIT OF grief, tormented at every turn by what had been lost.

Murder-suicide. Joanna, a bullet through the throat. Tanya, a bullet through her chest. She had missed her heart by half an inch, which meant it had taken an hour for her to bleed to death. An hour, lying on the cold floor, her mother dead and her papa somewhere else. An hour in which Penn could have saved her, if he had been smarter and quicker and rushed to her side.

Penn could take the same course, maybe find Tanya in some other life. If only Joanna were alive so he could kill her himself. It would be slow and exquisite, not the easy way that Tanya had given her.

He had made it through the inquest and the funerals on autopilot. Concerned friends pushed food into him, kept the reporters at bay, ensured that the lights were on at night and the drapes open to the sunlight during the day.

Penn had made the last of them go home today, promising that he'd take a shower, then a long nap. Swearing he would be okay. Instead, he sat in the basement, staring at the gun safe. Praying his anger would subside so he could just be done with it all.

The doorbell rang. Penn let it. They'd go away.

More ringing. Then footsteps in the kitchen. "Mr. Roper?"

Hillary. Her heart had been broken too. Penn brushed his hair back, rubbed his face, and went up the stairs.

"Mr. Roper. I'm sorry to bother you." Hillary's eyes were rubbed raw.

"Don't be. What can I do for you?"

She burst into tears. He made no move to comfort her—he couldn't.

"I didn't know about any of it," she said. "If I had known, I would have done something."

"I know. You told me already."

"She had talked about her wedding. Then suddenly, she and Jack had broken up and the wedding was off. She said it was no big deal, and I wanted to believe her. I should have made her tell me how desperate she was. I would have done anything . . ."

"Let it go, Hillary. There's nothing we can do."

"Remember when you took us into the show?"

"What show? Oh, that one in New York. I forgot, I guess."

"Something happened that seemed strange. She said it was nothing, but . . ."

Penn felt like this conversation was happening underwater. "Something happened?"

"It's just . . . well, you can see for yourself. The show we were at was filmed for television. They aired it last night. It creeped me out, seeing it on the night of the funeral. I taped it for you."

"I'm not following. Why would this show be significant to . . . what happened?"

"Joshua Lazarus did a reading on Tanya. Afterward, Tanya said that the guy didn't know what he was talking about and that she just went along for laughs." Hillary put a videocassette on the counter. "It's probably nothing, but at least, well—you can see her."

"Yeah. Thank you for thinking of me." Penn nodded, relieved to see Hillary head for the door.

"Mr. Roper?"

"Yeah."

"I'm sorry. Maybe if I was a better friend, there might have been something—"

"No. Don't even tell yourself that. Please."

Hillary blinked hard, then left. Something under Penn's pain and anger stirred. Gratitude, maybe, that Tanya had had such a good friend.

He took the videocassette into the family room, shoved it into the VCR. He collapsed into a chair and stared at the screen. It was black. The VCR was running, but he had forgotten to turn on the television. It would kill him to see his daughter. And yet, it would kill him not to.

Penn turned on the power. He watched fitfully for the first couple of minutes. He spotted Hillary more than once, with Tanya just a shadow slumped in the seat next to her. He fast-forwarded, then backed it up, not wanting to miss even a glance at that shadow, forcing himself to endure Joshua Lazarus's routine.

The show was little more than a carnival act. Simple mind-reading crap that any skilled psychologist, police interrogator, or con man could pull off.

Hillary sat at sudden attention. Penn leaned forward in his chair as the camera cut to Lazarus kneeling down next to Tanya. Penn hit pause—he couldn't bear to look, couldn't bear not to look, wasn't sure if his heart could take either.

It was a full minute before he started the tape moving again, and a full three minutes before he truly comprehended what Lazarus said and how Tanya must have interpreted it.

He's showing me metal. It's shiny and bright. Too bright.

Tanya's stricken face.

It was a violent death, wasn't it?

The anger in Penn surged now, a mighty river of rage, set free at last to flow where it should. He would live, at least for as long as it took to make Joshua Lazarus beg to die. But death would be too good for Joshua Lazarus.

Penn would deliver something far worse.

For we do not preach ourselves, but Jesus Christ as Lord, and ourselves as your servants for Jesus' sake.

2 Corinthians 4:5

Eight

CHARLIE MILLOY WALKED INTO SAFE HAVEN, KNAPSACK ON HIS back, Patriots hat on his head, and his face covered with a spider-web tattoo. "Like it, Amy?"

Amy wanted to rip her hair out, but she kept her voice calm. Even at nine years old, Charlie wouldn't back down if she challenged him. "Very creative. But you know that you'll have to wash that off."

"Why? You ain't cool with it?"

"No colors allowed, remember?"

"This ain't gang stuff. They were just face painting at school, that's all. At the book fair."

"The school let witches in to paint your face?"

"Who said anything 'bout witches? This was a guy who wrote a spider book. He and this lady painted my face so I could look like a spider web. Said he'd bring his spiders in sometime soon. And he gave me a book for free. Look!"

Web Magic was a picture book, with eye-catching illustrations and incredibly detailed photographs—especially of spiders in their webs, munching on their prey. The author's name was Theodore Marks—the Theo of the Astaroths. In the picture on the back cover, his face was clear, almost handsome. He must have been wearing makeup to cover the tattoos.

"Charlie, can I borrow this book for a while?"

Charlie snatched it back. "The spider dude gave it to me. It's mine."

"How about if we trade? I'll let you take that book home about motorcycles."

"Cool, the spider dude drives a motorcycle, like those Astaroth guys."

"Oops, I forgot that I misplaced it somewhere." At least she would misplace it as soon as she could. "How about that book on football that you love so much. In fact, you can keep it. And I'll keep this safe for you. I only want to check it out. Okay?"

Charlie chewed his bottom lip, thinking it over. "How 'bout I take the football book and the one about the space shuttle? They're old and this one's new, so then it'll be even."

Amy smiled. "Sure. While I'm getting them, why don't you wash that off?"

"How come I gotta wash it off? I wanted to show the kids."

"Remember the rules. No rock band T-shirts, no chains, and no colors."

"I already told you. This ain't colors. This is . . ." Charlie chewed his lip again, then brightened. "This is educational! You're always trying to get us to do smart stuff, right?"

Amy wanted to scream. It was bad enough that these kids lived lives out of *Cops,* but now the Astaroths had targeted them for exploitation too. She leaned down and whispered: "You and I know they aren't colors. But the rest of these kids won't know that you're wearing something educational. So to keep things cool in here, could you wash off that stuff? As a favor to me?"

Charlie's eyes sparkled. "Can I get an extra pudding for snack?"

"You bet." They tapped fists, and then Charlie headed for the bathroom.

Oh, Lord, Amy prayed, *they can go after me. But not the children.*

She flipped the book open and despite herself was impressed by the photographs, diagrams, and text. A flyer was stuck in the back of the book, advertising a group called "Science Scouts," for children ages seven to twelve. The first meeting was this coming Saturday at 43 Dunstable Street—the Astaroth house across the street from Safe Haven.

"Let me get this straight," Theo said. "You're the only one in this town who can help the kids?"

"You won't be helping them," Amy sputtered. "You'll be corrupting and perverting them."

"By showing them spiders and snakes and snails? Oh, I understand now—you'd rather I showed them butterflies and hummingbirds and ladybugs."

Theo had a hard time keeping a straight face. The Scouts had been a brilliant idea. If he couldn't drive Safe Haven out of his house, then he'd steal the kids away. It had been a ploy at first, a natural follow-up to his book, but Astarte had seemed to approve of his plan. His dreams had been so vivid lately, the goddess so quick to whisper in his ear, to bless him with delights.

Theo was convinced that it was Astarte who lured the children. She had her own purposes, just as this Howland cow had hers. The woman had berated him for four minutes now. He would have slit anyone else's throat for less, but if she went missing, the cops would come to him first. He let her anger flow over him, taking in all that was dark and letting the rest blow like the leaves in the gutter, tumbling to bits and pieces until they were swept away into the sewer.

Amen, great Astarte. Snatch the children out of her hands and bring them to me.

"There is cosmic symmetry to having you live in my house," Julia said.

House? It was a mansion, Joshua thought, especially to a kid raised in a four-room ranch with plywood walls and linoleum floors. Windward was coming to them rent free, with gratitude from Julia Madsen. That near-tragic night at the Sea Breeze had been turned into gold for everyone involved.

"Are you sure?" Maggie was saying. "I don't want to push you out of your home."

Julia laughed, bearing little resemblance to the broken relic whom they had encountered last March. She had gotten a discreet face-lift, had her hair colored, and resumed a life of glamour in Hollywood. She was hard at work raising funds for the Right Hand Foundation, tracking down elderly staff who had been impoverished after their employers' deaths, making sure their needs were met. There was even talk of resuming her film career—nothing crass but small roles in artful and classy productions.

Julia pressed her hand to Joshua's cheek but kept her gaze on Maggie. "My dear, your husband gave me what no one else in this life could have—my Marco. Giving Joshua a place to live as you launch your ministry is nothing compared to what I owe him—my life, my soul, my heart."

Joshua smiled warmly, hoping Julia didn't notice Maggie stiffen.

"I am eternally grateful to him," she continued. "And to you, Maggie, for sharing him with me, with all of the people who watch his show."

Joshua squeezed Maggie's hand. She forced a smile and said, "We're happy to see you so well, Miss Madsen. But shouldn't Dane be living here instead of us?"

She waved her hand in dismissal. "Dane needs glitter and noise. This place wouldn't suit my nephew's lifestyle, not one bit. I want you to have it and to enjoy it."

Joshua pulled Maggie to him as if he could will her to enjoy all of this. They stood at the French doors in one of the living rooms, peering out at the side lawn. The grass was a deep green, a sharp contrast against the pale blue of the sky and the sheen of the quiet ocean.

"It is so beautiful," Maggie finally said. "Thank you."

Julia opened the French door, letting in a crisp breeze. "Looks like Geneva is done inspecting the carriage house. Why don't I take her down to the beach, show her the steps to the sand, and warn her about the cliff. That should give you two enough time to tour the house"—she grinned—"especially the upstairs, and decide that this is a place where you can be happy."

Joshua leaned over and pressed his lips to her cheek. "You're an angel, Julia."

"No, I am not," she said. "But you, Joshua Lazarus, *are*. And for that I thank you."

Joshua pulled Maggie to him. "Too good to be true?"

"How did you know what I was thinking?"

"Haven't you heard, Princess? I'm psychic."

She wiggled her fingers at him. "That so? Then tell me where I'm going to tickle you next." She faked at his ribs, then dug into his armpits.

He danced away, laughing. "It's all over your face. As if this is just too much for us."

"Isn't it?" They had wandered into the foyer, where their voices echoed back to them off the shining marble. With a curved mahogany staircase and the three-story windows, this house was like something out of a fairy tale, Maggie thought. *Please let us have a happy ending.*

"We need this, Maggie. For the privacy and the security. Besides, Julia will be hurt if we don't accept her offer."

Ten acres of walled, oceanfront property on Hawthorne Neck would give them plenty of privacy. The safety came with a high-tech security system. Maggie wished it weren't all happening so fast. It seemed like just yesterday that she, Joshua, and Geneva shared a camper, and just a few minutes ago that Joshua was telling her that the act was dead. Now *The Other Side* was a cable sensation with growing ratings and talk of a major network buying in.

Joshua kissed the base of Maggie's throat. "You heard Julia. Let's check out the bedrooms."

She pushed him away. "They'll be back right away."

"The property is huge. It'll take a lot of walking to cover it all."

"Your sister will make sure they walk fast."

"So what? There's scads of rooms down here. Two formal living rooms, a dining room, a breakfast room, a morning parlor."

"I don't even know what you're supposed to do in a morning parlor."

"Me either, but I bet you do it in the morning."

Maggie laughed and slapped at him.

"Then there's the upstairs. Eight bedrooms. It'll take us a long time to break them in, so we'd better get started." Joshua swept Maggie up and carried her up the front stairs. There were three staircases in this house. Twelve fireplaces. Seven full baths and three half baths. Unimaginable splendor, especially for two kids from Maine.

Joshua stopped at the top landing where a huge window overlooked the ocean. "Look at that back lawn. It's a good place to raise a family, Maggie."

"It would take a pretty big family to fill this house."

"Which is why we need all the practice we can get . . ." His voice drifted off. His cheek against hers felt cool now, his skin tight.

She slid out of his arms, took his face in her hands. "What is it?"

He smiled. "What is *what*?"

"You're keeping something from me."

"Hey, who's the psychic now?"

She wrapped her arms around his waist, laying her head on his shoulder. "Tell me."

He kissed her. "Love me first. Then we'll talk."

"This is loving you, making you talk. It's been nagging at you all day. I see it in the way you just stop—talking, eating, whatever—and stare. Especially at Julia."

Joshua went to the window. The back of his neck was rigid, his shoulders hunched. "I knew Marco was Julia's gardener because I remembered seeing an article years ago about their place in Beverly Hills. He was mentioned in there. His green thumb, award-winning roses, that kind of thing."

"You've always had an amazing memory."

"It was easy enough to make the jump from what we heard under the pier, her calling out to Marco for a sign, to recognizing who it was Julia had loved."

"It wouldn't have been easy for me," Maggie said. "You've always had that intuition with people. That magician's gift of reading them on the spot."

"I said, 'Marco says to stop overwatering his orchids'? Remember that?"

"That was in the article, then?"

"I thought so. But I sent my secretary to the library yesterday to get me a copy. It took Beth a couple hours to track down the right issue. The thing was like twelve years old. I studied the whole thing. There was no mention of orchids in the article."

"None?"

"I stopped by here last night to see Julia. Pretending I was just trying to find the place before our tour today, but I wanted to talk to her face-to-face. I brought up the line about the orchids. 'Just curious,' I said. 'About what it really meant.' Apparently when Marco was dying, Julia, in an effort to take care of what was important to him, overwatered his plants. She killed all of them except the orchids. She still has them, took them back to California when she left here."

"If it wasn't in the article and we didn't hear it under the pier, how did you know?"

Joshua gazed out at the ocean. "The orchid line came into my head as if you had said it to me from across the room."

"Me? I didn't say anything." Even with the sun coming in the high windows, sparkling off the marble floor, Maggie felt a chill.

"Of course not. There's only one way I could have known about the orchids. Only if Marco told me."

"They're accusing you of child endangerment, Amy." Patrick put the document on the table between them.

A complaint had been phoned in against Safe Haven, charging that Amy was operating an illegal day-care center. No doubt Theo's work.

"I should rip this complaint into a thousand pieces," Amy said.

"I'm inclined to agree with you," Patrick said. "But it is God's command that we obey civil authorities."

"Tell that to Martin Luther. And Martin Luther King, while we're at it. Not to mention Rahab. She didn't obey the civil authorities, did she?"

"You've got a point there. But we're not talking life and death."

"Of course we are. It's us or it's the street after school. And Safe Haven is the only place many of these kids are exposed to the gospel. They're more likely to stumble over a witch than a Sunday school teacher in this neighborhood."

"Speaking of which—has that Theo been in here again?"

"A couple times. The security company swears there's nothing wrong with our alarm system."

"Did you check the basement? Maybe he's getting in through a window."

Amy shuddered. "I'm not easily creeped out, but that place is dismal. Like being in a crypt, all that stone and dirt, closing in on you, choking you . . ."

Patrick laughed. "Don't tell me I've finally stumbled on your Achilles' heel?"

"I'm not afraid of the basement. Just . . . discerning."

"Want me to go down there?"

"No, no. There's no windows, no hatch to the outside. I swear—with my heart pounding like a bass drum—I did check. It's all solid stone and brick walls. No way to slip in, not at all. It's so frustrating—by the time the cops get here, he's gone. My word against his, and he claims I'm harassing him! No doubt he's behind this challenge. We'll just have to go to court and fight it out."

"The board of directors isn't inclined to get into some lengthy legal battle. We just don't have the funds." Patrick's church sponsored Safe Haven, with Patrick as Amy's mentor.

"I'll pay for it."

"On your salary?"

Amy put her hands on her hips in mock protest. "I'll have you know that nurses get paid very well. Not to mention the respect we get, the clean working conditions, the wonderful hospital food—"

"Enough already." Patrick laughed so hard he started coughing.

Amy wagged her finger. "Don't make me do the Heimlich on you, Dr. Drinas. I'm saving that for my friend Theo. Not that I'm hoping he chokes or anything . . ."

Patrick lifted his hands in surrender. "The board doesn't want to shut you down. They're simply considering a move to Saugus or Peabody. The need is just as great there."

"It's not about need. It's about where God has planted us. *Here*—in the Beak. It's bad enough we got the drug users and sellers; now we've got these Astaroth freaks spewing their bile, body odor, and black magic in this spiritual sinkhole of a neighborhood. You can't expect me to cut and run from here."

"We won't abandon the kids. We'll bus them to the new site."

"No. Absolutely not, Patrick. We have to meet this threat head-on by answering the complaint head-on."

"It's not just the city we'd be taking on. If the health inspector decides that Safe Haven is a day-care center and not a recreational program, then since you're the only adult, you're violating state law of one adult per ten kids. You serve how many children?"

Amy shrugged. "God is bringing them in abundance. Fifteen yesterday. That should tell us that we're meant to be right here."

Patrick laughed. "You should have been a lawyer, not a nurse. I'll get a lawyer friend to research this complaint, but in the meantime make sure you always have enough volunteers so we're staffed up to code."

Amy busied herself picking up games—any excuse not to look Patrick in the eye. "They quit," she said quietly.

"Who quit?"

"The volunteers."

"All of them?"

"They're scared, Patrick. People have good intentions, but you have to have a strong calling to work in the Beak."

"That's disappointing. I would expect Christians to be made of sterner stuff."

"Don't blame them. The Astaroths harass them. Cleverly, of course, but the threat is there. A volunteer drives into the Beak, an Astaroth on a motorcycle will ride their tail the whole time. Even worse, follow them home, then drive up and down in front of their house. Or they stake themselves out on the sidewalk, whispering at my people. Ugly things but nothing they can be arrested for. No wonder they're freaked. If I knew better, I'd be scared too."

"And what about the kids? They must be terrified."

Amy laughed. "A few weirdos in hoods don't faze them."

Patrick pushed aside the complaint and reached for her hand. "I guess we'd better pray fervently for a helper who is not afraid of these Astaroths."

"Or the kids," Amy said, laughing.

Patrick laughed with her. "Amen to that."

Amy bowed her head, feeling that rush of assurance. *Amen. Lord, bring someone soon.*

Nine

"MAGGIE HAS GOT TO GO."

Joshua wanted to throttle Dane. "My sister put you up to this, didn't she?"

"Geneva agrees. But this was my idea. If we're going to sell the show to a network, we have to get rid of anything that smacks of your old magic act."

They were in the new offices of *The Other Side,* though *new* didn't describe anything in Raven Village. Once part of the legendary Salem, Raven was a crowded cluster of old houses, many of which were over three hundred years old. "Salem has been done to death. This little village has more cachet," Dane had claimed. "Plus people here are serious about their spiritualism."

Raven's other selling point was an up-to-date studio available for reasonable rates. Broadcasting live was the key to their growing success. Other mediums had done the speaking-to-the-dead thing, but their shows were heavily edited, with sappy music and fuzzy lenses. The live show kept the immediacy and excitement that made Joshua Lazarus such a hot commodity. Skeptics couldn't refute his accuracy or claim that bad readings had been edited out.

For their office suite, Dane had tried to get Joshua to buy an ancient house with a dirt basement with narrow windows, and a widow's walk. "No way," Joshua had said. "*The Other Side* is all about light and assurance. We're not spooking people." They had finally compromised on a two-hundred-year-old Georgian with high windows and a fireplace in every room. The reception room was done in Early American, with high-backed chairs and pine tables. Beeswax candles were always lit in the chandelier and sconces. The business suite, where Dane and Geneva worked their magic, was high-tech and secure.

Upstairs, Joshua's office was spacious with long windows, ornate moldings, and a marble fireplace. The walls were cream and the floors were wide pine, stripped and refinished to a natural color. Joshua's desk was polished cherry. His reading room was simple—lavender walls, cream carpet, an oak table, and two comfortable chairs. In good weather, Joshua could do readings in the garden, in a vine-covered gazebo that would allow for privacy.

"Maggie has been with me from the beginning. A key part of the act," he argued.

"This isn't an act. It's a *ministry*. We want to shed anything that looks like illusion."

Joshua laughed. "The whole thing is an illusion."

"Not when you do it, it's not."

"Maggie keeps people at ease."

"Look, kid, you're about to explode onto the entertainment scene. But it's got to be all you. Anyone else on camera is going to be a distraction, especially someone as attractive as Maggie. People need to know that this isn't a cheap mind-reading act with the assistant feeding information."

Joshua walked to the window. The massive oaks and maples were just beginning to turn to red and gold. By November, he'd be able to see the harbor. He loved the ocean. He and Maggie walked the beach at Windward as often as possible.

"Maggie needs something to do."

"We just got a pretty chunk of change. Let her *buy* something to do. Listen, Josh—I'll be the bad guy on this. I'll make her understand."

"Read my lips, Dane. She's my wife. I absolutely forbid it."

"Ah yes. I've been meaning to talk to you about that too. It's not just about her on camera. It's this whole *wife* thing. It's got to go . . ."

Maggie was stunned. "A mountain bike?"

Dane grinned. "Josh said you biked all over central Maine when you were a kid. I thought you'd enjoy having this. It's a top-of-the-line model. Go ahead, try it."

She hopped on, rode it up the driveway to the front gate, and then coasted back. "But . . . it's just . . . I don't know."

"What's there to know? It's September in New England. Best time of the year, right?"

Maggie laughed. "Spoken like a guy raised in California."

"You're outdoorsy. Josh says you walk the beach all the time, even if it's pouring rain."

Josh. Dane was in Geneva's camp to stay, then. "But where would I ride? It's not like we're out in the country."

"Come on, girl. The Neck has the most beautiful real estate on the coast. You could head south to Marblehead. Up north, you've got Manchester-by-the-Sea or really way north to New Hampshire and Maine. There's enough sightseeing to keep you busy until next Christmas."

"Thank you, Dane. I'll give it a try."

"Can we go inside? My Hollywood blood is too thin, even for Indian summer. I've got something I need to discuss with you."

Minutes later they sat in the kitchen, Maggie sipping a diet soda, Dane drinking a cup of black coffee laced with Julia's expensive whiskey.

"So, m'dear. Are you happy with this turn that Josh's career has taken?" he asked.

"Of course. We never could figure out how to make his natural charisma work in the act. We'll always be grateful that you have."

"Hey, the thanks is all mine. This is a blast, launching a show. The networks are already sniffing around because we have sewed up a very underserved demographic."

"I don't understand."

"Women. Actually, girls too. From twelve to eighty, they're going nuts over Josh."

"Oh. I guess that makes sense. Women are more . . . intuitive."

"They connect with Josh on so many levels, it's astounding. But there's one important way that we can't overlook, not if we want to give *The Other Side* every chance of success."

"What's that?"

"Women see Josh as the guy who can see deep into their hearts and—this is the key thing, Maggie—a guy they can *trust*. In other words, they see him as the perfect friend *and* lover."

Maggie went to the sink. Her hands shook as she rinsed her glass. "More coffee?"

Dane came up behind her, standing so close that she could smell the whiskey on his breath. "This is what drives show business, babe. Women's ability to make the face on the screen the man they see in the dark when they're staring at the ceiling, listening to some overweight jerk snore. Our viewers need to believe that Joshua could be that man. You know they do."

"I guess," Maggie finally said.

"Josh forbade me talk to you about this. But something needs saying, and because you love him, I know you'll agree it needs doing."

"You want him to divorce me." Her voice came from somewhere far away.

"No, Maggie, not that. Josh loves you. Poor baby, I never meant you to think that."

Dane pulled her into a hug. He was soft and sweaty, not like Joshua, who was so strong and lean and loved and, *Dear God, if you're listening, don't let me lose my husband.*

"What do you want me to do, then?"

"Nothing. That simple. You kept Deschenes as your professional name. So as long as you lay low, no one needs to know that Joshua Lazarus is married. We'll refuse to give personal details on his life. That will only add to the mystery, which is always a good thing. Just don't tell any of your new friends here in Hawthorne that you're Josh's wife."

"Who should I say I am?"

"You can be Julia's niece."

"This is what Joshua wants?"

"Absolutely not. But this is what he needs. Trust me on this."

Maggie would never trust Dane. But she believed him. "Okay. As far as the world knows, I am Marguerite Deschenes and Joshua Lazarus is available for the world to love."

Dane drained his coffee, wiped his mouth, then smiled. "They already do, Maggie. They just don't know it yet."

The wind blasted through Maggie, biting into her bones. She'd love to go inside, but this was the only time she had Joshua alone, except late at night in bed. Even then, he slept fitfully, too much on his mind.

She leaned into him. "Venus is out tonight. See? Above the moon."

He kissed her. "I thought I was the only star you gazed at."

"Venus is a planet, not a star."

"Whoops."

He pulled her into a hug. She stayed there, listening to the waves lap on the sand. "You are a star, aren't you? Four years, and then suddenly, you've made it."

"*We've* made it, Maggie."

She took a deep breath. "Joshua, I think you should do the show without me."

"What the—"

She pressed her hand to his mouth. "Let me finish. What you're doing needs to seem as genuine as possible. Understated and nuanced."

"Those are Dane's talking points coming out of your mouth. I'll wring his neck."

"No, you won't. He's only looking out for your best interest."

"This Friday is our first show on cable, and you have to be there with me."

"No. I won't."

"I need you there." Joshua pulled her closer.

"My mind is made up. I'm not going on camera anymore. If you try to make me, I'll eat a quart of strawberries and break out in hives. Or I'll eat a pound of fudge and break out in zits. Or I'll eat fudge and strawberries and pizza and Chinese food and break out in flab. Or I'll—"

"Okay, I get it. If I want you to stay the lovely girl I married, I need to give you your way—which is really Dane's way—in this."

"You got it, pal." Maggie snuggled into him.

"You're getting cold. Maybe we should go in."

"Another minute. I love being out here under the night sky." The moon was full, its light dancing on each wave, then breaking into a million points onto the sand.

"Maggie, you won't ever leave me, will you?"

"Why would you even ask me that?"

He buried his face in her hair. "I'm psychic, remember?"

"Don't joke about that now."

"I'm not joking. I have this . . . call it a feeling, that something dark and vast, like the night ocean out there, might come between us."

"Never," Maggie swore. "Never ever."

Five months of training and planning.

It had been excruciatingly hard work, of course. But the anger served Penn well, giving him an impetus to move, an edge to excel, an intelligence to plan to the smallest detail. Everything was in place now. He had what he needed and he knew how to use it.

A violent death . . .

That was far too good for the man who destroyed Tanya for the sake of a night's entertainment. Joshua Lazarus would see hell open and drink in all he held dear. Only then would Penn give him the final push.

"Rope, you paying attention?"

Penn mentally shook himself alert. "Sure. What do you have for me?"

Jib placed an item the size of a button on Penn's fingertip. "Check this out. These bad boys are so small, you'll need tweezers to implant them."

Penn swore in admiration. He had never seen a speaker this small, though he shouldn't have been surprised, what with all the commercial advances in electronics. "What kind of frequencies?"

"Up to 19 kHz. High-powered little babies, ain't they? Sensitive too. Listen up."

Jib tossed the speaker across the room.

"Hey!" Penn said.

"Just demonstrating its durability. Now listen." Jib fired up his Palm Pilot, then clicked on a music icon.

Penn was startled when music played from across the room. "Not exactly surround sound, but I sure can hear it. I'm impressed."

"Don't expect no discount. This ain't toilet paper, Rope."

Penn laughed. "You're singing that sad song to me? I made millions peddling stuff like this."

"Yeah, yeah. Here's the next bad boy I got for you."

Jib unwrapped something that looked like a pearl. Penn had to use his jeweler's loupe to see the slender threads attached to the device. "Video?"

"Yep. With fiber optic feed. The wireless ones are bigger, almost the size of a grape."

"How secure are these things?"

Jib laughed. "You know how many embassies in D.C. are loaded with them? These babies are almost impossible to pick up, even with the more sophisticated technology. You loop eight of these sweethearts on the middle of a ceiling, you got three-sixty views and no one's the wiser."

"Can I get the twenty-four I ordered?"

Jib grimaced. "I warned you, man. You're gonna break your bank if you take that many. One or two missing from an order, well—they're so tiny, inventory control expects to lose a couple. For as many as you want, I'm paying five times the going rate. I got my geek working under the radar, churning 'em out for you."

"It's only money."

Jib looked straight at him. "You gotta hold something back for yourself, Rope. Retirement or whatever."

"It'll be *whatever*."

Jib shrugged. "Your call, man. Your call."

Ten

MORNINGS WERE GETTING COLDER, BUT HILLARY HAD TO KEEP coming out here to the broken bench on the far side of the duck pond. She needed this time alone, sometimes to remember, sometimes to work hard at not remembering, and sometimes just to watch the mist rising out of the water.

Sometimes she prayed for Tanya's soul. Most times the questions nagged at her. Was there some warning sign she had missed? Some way she could have comforted Tanya after that breakup with Jack? The jerk had been headed for an NFL contract before he got mugged. Beaten to a pulp, Hillary had heard. Was that some sort of cosmic justice because of the way he had treated Tanya? Or did life just stink?

Her parents had kept on her: Not your fault. Get on with life. Enjoy college. You'll forget.

But she wasn't forgetting. She had to do something. She flipped open her cell phone, speed dialed the number she had programmed weeks ago.

"*The Other Side*, Rebecca speaking."

"Um . . . can I speak to Joshua Lazarus?" Hillary said.

"Are you calling to book a reading?"

"I guess."

"I'll need a credit card, please."

"Can I pay by check?"

"Sure. But we can't actually book the reading until we have the check in hand. The fee for a private reading is five hundred dollars."

"Oh, I just can't . . . could I come to the show instead?"

"Sure. The tickets are twenty dollars each. We have a waiting list of about ten months."

Hillary snapped the phone closed without another word.

The *glamorous* Joshua Lazarus, *StarField* magazine called him.

Not much glamour in this, he thought. Every week, memorizing faces, learning names, tracing through family connections. The preparation was pure boredom.

But the show was pure adrenaline. *StarField* called *The Other Side* a cultural phenomenon, another quest to answer what happens after death. What will happen *to me* after death?

Joshua supplied a user-friendly answer. *The departed forget the pain but not the love . . .*

Every day it felt more genuine. Maybe it was. Maybe he really did have the power.

"Jerk," he said, laughing. He shuffled his papers, then got back to work.

The phone buzzed. "It's Mr. Wiggin, with a guest."

"Okay, Beth, give me a minute." He swung the desk's false top over the profiles for Friday's show. "Okay, send them in."

Dane entered, followed by a tall man with intense blue eyes and a full dark beard. His face was lined and his longish brown hair was streaked with silver.

"Here he is. Your security guru and personal bodyguard—Ben Cord."

They shook hands. "Nice to meet you. Please, sit."

Dane went to the credenza, poured himself a scotch. Joshua would have to talk to him about that—it was too early in the day to be doing that kind of thing.

"Ben, can we offer you something?" Joshua asked.

"No, thanks."

Dane joined them, his scotch in one hand, a diet cola for Joshua in the other. "Ben's got lots of experience. Ten years in Special Operations with the Marines, ten more in the NYPD."

Joshua popped the soda. "Why did you leave?"

"Bad knee. Which has since been replaced, by the way, but the NYPD doesn't yet recognize titanium and Teflon as a suitable substitute for bone and cartilage. I was too young and frisky to retire, so I went into personal security. I'm almost ashamed to admit that it's far more rewarding."

"He's even had all those defensive driving courses," Dane said. "The kind they teach you to avoid kidnappings. He comes highly recommended."

Joshua smiled politely. He was more than satisfied to drive himself, but Geneva was increasingly alarmed by the quantity and passion of his fans. Dane had wanted a phalanx of bodyguards—more cachet—but Joshua had compromised on one full-timer.

"I've got to tell you, Mr. Cord—this whole limo thing is kind of weird," Joshua said. Dane had bought a silver Lincoln Town Car and given the leased Lexus to Geneva.

"You'll get used to it, Mr. Lazarus. And call me Ben."

"And call me Joshua."

"Thank you, but no. You'll be Mr. Lazarus. It works better that way."

"Okay, you're the boss," Joshua said automatically.

Cord laughed. Joshua liked the man. He seemed genuine, unlike Dane, who was a major bootlicker. "What else do I need to know?"

"We'll hire security for all public events and for show night of course. But anytime you're out, I will be at your side. While you're in the office, I can run errands for you or do whatever I can to help, either at home or here."

Joshua glanced over at Dane. "He could drive Maggie around, then?"

Dane poured himself another two fingers of scotch. "She's supposed to get her own car."

"She finds excuses not to. I'm not sure why."

Dane laughed. "I can't say I blame her. You Easterners complain about LA, but driving in Massachusetts is like roller-skating in a rat's nest."

Ben nodded. "I'll make sure she's taken care of. No worries there, Mr. Lazarus. I expect you to call me anytime, day or night, if either of you needs a ride. And I mean that: day *or* night."

"I can see you do. Thank you." Joshua smiled at Ben, then looked at Dane. "Are we still on for that late lunch?"

"You bet. Make sure you're ready for that reading."

Joshua laughed. "I'm the boss, but Dane is the real slave driver, Ben."

After another minute of small talk, Dane went out, still carrying the scotch. Cord followed quietly.

Joshua sank down in his chair, head in hands. He missed working with Maggie. She laughed at his dumb jokes, encouraged him when he was down, swatted him when he was arrogant. He missed having her where he could reach out for her at any moment.

Joshua hadn't made love to her in days. Maggie was willing, but he couldn't seem to muster the passion. The stress of preparing the show each week had totally drained him.

He would make it up to her. Soon.

Eleven

MAGGIE FELT LIKE THE WICKED OLD WITCH.

All she needed was a basket on the back of her bike and she would look like that crazy woman from the *Wizard of Oz* who pedals her bike out of Kansas and into a cyclone. Was the bike a dumb idea? She could have taken a cab. *Oh, darling, I was just out shopping and I thought I'd drop by. Let's do lunch, then this afternoon, I'll go pick up my Infiniti.*

Then again, Joshua Lazarus wasn't supposed to have a wife, and Maggie wouldn't know an Infiniti if one ran her down. It was better to be on a bike on a glorious day like this. The sky was so blue and clear, it seemed to go on forever. The trees blazed in yellows, golds, and reds.

Now that she'd worked the cobwebs out of her legs, she enjoyed the salt air on her face and the warm breeze at her back. She had been shut up in that mansion for too many weeks. There were just so many pans of brownies she could bake, so many suppers she could prepare and then have to toss because Joshua was late, so many hikes on the beach by herself, so many sighs of discontent and murmurs of fear at striking out on her own path. She was sick of her inaction, embarrassed by her jealousy of Joshua's success with Geneva at his side and no part for her.

Maggie needed to do something. Should she join a gym? Enroll in college? Get a job? She was determined to ride this bike until she had an answer.

Hawthorne was a cozy harbor village with sailboats bobbing at their moorings and flags stiff in the sea breeze. White churches, brick buildings, stone walls, and dignified homes clustered around the town green. The library and town hall were cut granite, while the police station was sided in weathered cedar shakes. Ancient oaks lined the streets, roots snaking under the brick sidewalks. She stopped briefly at a small graveyard that was bounded by granite posts and iron chain links. The stones were cut black granite. Maggie gasped as she read the dates—some going back to the seventeen hundreds.

The scenery changed dramatically when Maggie turned onto Route 1A and the world of strip malls, bowling alleys, and fried-clam shops. Drivers sped along like they were outracing the end of the world. She kept to the shoulder, her legs burning by the time she reached the turnoff to Raven.

Maggie had taken this route many times with Joshua, but on the bike, everything looked different. She pulled off onto the shoulder. What had she done with the map? It wasn't in her bag. Then she remembered—she had sat down at the kitchen table, sipping tea and planning her route. The map was still there.

It couldn't be too hard to find Admiral's Row. Maggie turned west and started pedaling.

"It is Sola who guides you, is it not?" the crooked little woman said. Endora Simon peered at Joshua through tangled bangs, her silver hair like wire, her gray face like leather.

Joshua nodded, his throat tight.

"I suspected as much," she was saying. "There's others out there who can ferry spirits to and fro, but Sola is the gatekeeper."

"I . . . sometimes on the show . . . we help the readings along a bit," Joshua muttered. Why was he even admitting this much? Even Dane had been uncharacteristically silent about how *The Other Side* worked its magic. He had required every employee to sign nondisclosure agreements even though only he, Geneva, and Joshua knew what went on in the computer room.

Endora smiled, showing a huge gap between her front teeth. "We all help our magic along. It's expected that we use our gifts to *enhance* what our spirit guides give us. But I look at you, Joshua Lazarus—" She grabbed his hands, her bony fingers surprisingly strong. "—I look at you, listen to you, feel you, and know that the spirits are pressing the back side of your soul. You haven't chosen Sola. She has chosen you."

Joshua felt a current between them, felt the veil behind his eyes lift, saw a darkness sparkling with its own vast nature, like velvet to wrap in, voices whispering now, telling him *to come, to walk, to be, to be one with us . . .*

Be us, an alluring voice sang, sliding into his ears, winding around his ribs, touching his heart with tender fingers, teasing him from the inside out with a cold, refreshing touch.

Joshua felt pain in his forehead, opened his eyes to see his head had fallen forward onto the oak table. Endora Simon was gone. But the candle she had brought for him burned with a steady flame. He stared into it, now knowing all of what Endora had taught him with few words, what Sola asked of him with a sweet touch, what he would offer back in his devotion.

Sola, I come to you, my patron and guide. Open your world to me now. Muster your spirits to work your will through me. I call on the spirits of wind and water and sun to light my way and guide my words.

He stared into the candle for a long moment, feeling that shift deep inside.

Sola, mistress of rain and sky and earth, help me to see beyond myself. Help me open the gate to the other side.

A sudden gust of wind blew out the candle. Joshua spooked, then laughed. This was nuts—he was just an entertainer, the wind was just the wind, and Endora Simon was just another Raven occultist who had stopped in to welcome him to their ranks.

Joshua put the candle and the matches in the bottom drawer of his desk. Time to perform his own brand of magic, which depended on his own good looks, quick thinking, and abundant charm. No need for incantations—he was in the driver's seat, not Endora Simon or Dane Wiggin or some wisp of candle smoke named Sola.

Dane Wiggin had finally hitched his wagon to the right star—a slick-haired, sweet-faced, broken-down magician who had a magical way with people. Add a little of the Wiggin hucksterism to that Lazarus charisma and you got a gold mine, baby.

Yeah, Dane was cruising big-time now. And here was the proof, this long-legged, natural-blond goddess cooling her heels in his office, waiting for Joshua Lazarus to give her a moment of his valuable time. Dane couldn't take his eyes off Cassandra Knowles; few men could. Her skin was flawless and her eyes a deep green. If her lush lips had been enhanced, he couldn't tell.

She turned her fluttering eyes to him. He took her hand, all soft and worried.

"You sure he won't mind me dropping in like this?" she asked, her voice that strange mix of husky and innocent that frenzied her fans.

"We have to limit encounters. They take a lot out of him," Dane said. "But I've vouched for you, Cassie."

"Oh, thank you," she said, squeezing his hand.

Should Dane have played harder to get? Should he have said, "No way," then let Cassie take him out for drinks and use her wiles to persuade him to get her in to see Josh? He could imagine being side by side with her on bar stools. Better yet—in a booth, sitting on the same side, leaning close so they could hear each other over the noise, her arm warm against his, her hair falling loose, brushing his cheek. These were the perks, after all, of being the executive producer for the hottest commodity in show business.

But no—*The Other Side* was still ramping up. They needed the Cassandras of the industry to keep that momentum. She was stunning, but she was only one of many. Once they went network with the show, Dane could have his pick.

Yeah baby, life was good.

His intercom buzzed. Beth's voice came through. "He'll see you now, Dane."

Dane smiled, helped Cassandra up. She steadied herself against him, a practiced move he knew, but welcome just the same.

Moments later they came into Josh's office.

"I'm delighted to meet you, Ms. Knowles." Josh held both her hands and stared straight into her eyes, just as Dane had taught him. Letting her know that she might be the star, but he was in control.

"Call me Cassie. I am such a big fan of *The Other Side.* You are so totally cramping my social life—I can't go out on Friday nights until after your show!"

Joshua smiled. "I know you've got lunch plans with Dane. But do you have time for a reading?"

Dane bit back his smile. He didn't need to be a psychic to know why she had really called him. They had prepared the research, knowing they'd be using it.

"Oh, wow, I wasn't expecting this—wow, such a privilege. Of course I'd be interested!"

Yeah, baby. Hang another star in the universe of Dane Wiggin.

Maggie couldn't believe what she was seeing, and yet, it was inevitable, wasn't it? She had just turned onto Admiral Row when she saw Dane coming out the front door. She stopped behind a huge oak tree, feeling sheepish because she hadn't called to say she was coming. Joshua came out next. His arm was around Cassandra Knowles, who made twenty million dollars per film and had won last year's Oscar for best actress. The movie star looked at Joshua like he was the only sun in her sky. Was this why their love life had faded to almost nothing?

Maggie turned the bike around and pedaled hard. Ten minutes later she was lost. Was this block of triple-deckers even in Raven? Drunks lounged in an alley. A couple of homeless women pushed shopping carts filled with plastic bags. Young toughs clustered around a boom box, making obscene remarks and explicit gestures as she rode by.

Maggie was so scared that she'd swallow her pride and call Geneva to come get her—if she hadn't left the cell phone on the table with the map. If only she could find a church or a respectable-looking house where she could ask someone to make a phone call for her. These houses all had broken windows, cracked steps, and dirty yards. Trash tumbled across the street on the gusting wind. Clouds were moving in. Was it going to rain? Maggie looked up, trying to read the weather.

A motorcycle roared out of the bushes.

Maggie yanked the handlebars, pulling a hard right. Time slowed to a crawl as she tumbled from the bike. She could see the grit on the road as it rose to meet her, feel the heat of embarrassment, then a shock as her face hit the pavement. The pain was bad, but the fear was worse. A man in a hooded sweatshirt leaned over her, his face marked with black lines and dotted with scars. His mouth was set in a wolfish smile. She rolled into a sitting position, then scooted backward, scraping her hands on the road.

"I don't bite. I'm trying to help you." The man was handsome in a hard way, but those lines on his face were frightful, and he stunk like rotted fruit.

"I don't need your help." A lump formed on Maggie's face; her vision was blurred.

"You almost ran me down, you know," he said.

"Ran *you* down! You're the one riding your motorcycle on a sidewalk!"

"I was simply pulling out of my driveway. You would have seen me if you hadn't been stargazing. What's up there anyway?" He craned his head back, grinning.

"Nothing. Storm clouds," Maggie said, suddenly dizzy.

"It is fortunate that I was not hurt." His eyes were a light hazel, so clear they were almost transparent.

She *had* almost run him down, hadn't she? "I'm sorry. I'm glad you weren't hurt."

"You need ice. Would you like me to get you some? Ice would help."

Maggie touched her cheek. A painful egg had formed. "Ice would help, wouldn't it?"

"Why don't you leave your bike here? No one will take it. Come inside with me."

The hooded man slipped his hand around her waist and helped her up.

"I don't think you should . . ." Maggie said. "But no one will take my bike."

"You're unsteady. I need to help you."

Her legs were wobbling now. "Thank you. I am unsteady and I do need help."

"I know you do. And you know you do. Which is why you—"

"Hey. Get your hands off her," someone barked.

Maggie jolted, the dizziness going right out of her. Who was this man with his arm around her? And who was yelling at them?

"I said, let her go!" It was a woman's voice, raspy but strong.

Maggie tried to push away. "Let me go."

He bent his face to Maggie's. "Is that what you want?"

The lines on his face uncoiled, coming for her now. Maggie backed away.

There was a light touch to her shoulder. "Why don't you come with me, miss? You probably want to use the phone."

The woman wore a pink T-shirt with a smiling pickle on it. Thick glasses made her big brown eyes seem enormous, and frizzy hair stuck out from under a Red Sox cap. She couldn't be much older than Maggie, but as she glared at the hooded man, he stepped back.

"Do I know you?" Maggie said.

"You do now. Amy Howland."

"Maggie. Maggie Deschenes."

"Ms. Deschenes almost ran me down," the hooded man said. "But I've forgiven her."

Forgiven sent a chill down Maggie's neck.

Amy shook her head as if the man had made a stupid joke. "Right. Talk about hell freezing over." She guided Maggie toward the other side of the street. "Come on in."

"I don't know . . ."

"It's okay. This is where I work and live. Safe Haven for Children."

"Safe Haven," Maggie repeated. She must have a concussion—she couldn't seem to form a coherent thought. Though that self-realization was coherent, wasn't it?

"We'll get some ice for that lump on your face," Amy said.

"I've already offered," the hooded man said.

"You don't want his ice. He probably makes it from toilet water. Come with me, okay?"

Maggie felt like a bone in the street that two dogs were fighting over. Except one dog looked like a wolf, and Amy . . . well, she was sure she could trust this woman, even for the simple reason that Amy smelled of bubble gum and not like the inside of someone's sneaker.

At first glance, Safe Haven looked like all the other houses on this street. The first-floor windows were barred, the shutters were cracked, and the paint was peeling. But Maggie could see what made this house different. Children crowded in the windows and at the front door. Boys and girls of all shades and shapes, waving as if Maggie were some sort of celebrity.

The man called after her, "We'll meet again."

"I hope not," Maggie and Amy said at the same time.

They looked at each other, laughed, and went into the house called Safe Haven.

Twelve

"CAN I COME AGAIN SOMETIME?" MAGGIE ASKED. "IT LOOKS LIKE you need a little help."

"You noticed, huh? Sure, you can drop in again."

Maggie swung her bike up and into the trunk of Amy's car. "I don't think the trunk will close."

"I'll tie it."

"The bike will scratch your car."

Amy laughed. "Are you kidding? This hunk of duct tape is fifteen years old. A scratch would be an improvement."

As Amy pulled out of the driveway, a motorcycle skidded to a stop behind her. The rider wore the same hooded sweatshirt that the guy who almost ran Maggie down had worn.

"Watch out!" Maggie said.

Amy kept backing up. The motorcycle peeled away. "The only way to deal with those creeps is to ignore them. And pray that someday they will go away."

"Oh." Maggie didn't see how it was possible to ignore those hulking figures with their tattooed faces and muttering lips.

"Are you serious about helping out? Or are you just feeling sorry for me?" Amy said.

"Absolutely serious. I've been . . . at loose ends lately."

"No job?"

Maggie rolled down her window, took a deep breath, then wished she hadn't. It was a lovely autumn night, but all she could smell was car exhaust. Traffic was heavy even though it was almost eight o'clock. "I don't need to work. My family has some money and . . . well . . ."

"How old are you? If you don't mind my asking—though I'm going to ask you anyway."

"I'm twenty-three. You?"

"Twenty-seven," Amy said. "So what about college?"

"I was going to go—but instead, I joined a magic act and toured the country."

"Aha! That explains how you pulled all those quarters out of Charlie's ears."

"Was that okay? The kids seemed to like the tricks."

"As Charlie would say, 'You were the bomb, dude.' Though next time, can you make them fifty dollar bills instead of loose change?"

"Are you a teacher?" Maggie asked.

"A nurse. I work eleven to seven, then go home and sleep most of the day. I try to get awake and alert before the first kid shows up. That's usually Charlie, by the way."

"He's a strange child, isn't he? Not that I'm judging or anything."

"Charlie is having a strange week. Next week it'll be someone else's turn. Which way?"

"Out to the Neck."

"Whoa. Awesome. The road out there is nasty, though. So twisty. If it's foggy, you could ride right off into the ocean and not know it until you get haddock swimming in your sinuses."

Maggie laughed. "Yeah, I almost got hit on the causeway today in full sunlight."

"So whereabouts on the Neck are we heading?"

"I'm staying at my aunt's place. Maybe you've heard of her—Julia Madsen?"

"Julia Madsen is your aunt? She must be almost eighty now. I bet she's still gorgeous."

"Absolutely." Julia had called last night to tell them she was to begin filming in a week. *A bigger role than I had imagined,* Julia had said, *but they really seem to want me.* What Joshua was doing in *The Other Side* was a good thing, though Maggie had been creeped out when Julia had asked Joshua to ask Marco if she was doing the right thing.

"So if it's okay, I'd love to come back. You don't have to pay me or anything."

"Oh, I don't think there's any danger of you getting paid. At least not in dollars. But at the risk of being serious, there's a couple of things you need to know."

"Okay . . ."

"Safe Haven is a Christian mission, supported by a large church out of Boston. Our mission is to show the love of God by ministering to what Jesus calls the 'least of us.' That neighborhood you stumbled into on your bike is one of the worst around. It's called the Beak."

"Okay. So what's the problem?"

Amy smiled. "It's just . . . it just helps when we're on the same page."

Was there something about how Maggie looked that made Amy think she *wasn't* Christian? "We didn't really go to church. But we always celebrated Christmas."

Amy squeezed her hand. "That's a great start. We can talk about it again tomorrow."

"What's the second thing?"

Amy sighed. "Well, then there's the Astaroths. They're kinda out to get me . . ."

Geneva Lazanby sat in the recliner, intent on just resting before making supper. Her neck ached. Maybe she could doze for just a few minutes. Her eyes felt so heavy . . .

Josh was curled in his bed, arms tight around his teddy bear. It was hard to be a little boy with no dad and a mom who worked all the time. Sometimes he needed something to hold on to.

A thousand teddy bears wouldn't help this, though.

The police had just left. They had wanted to stay until someone could come be with Geneva. "You must have a grandparent, an aunt, someone I can call?" the officer had said.

"No one."

Their minister arrived just as the police were leaving. "God is with you," he said. "Trust in Him and everything will work out."

"Get out of my house." She slammed the door in his face.

Then she went into Josh's room. His skin was so fair, his hair so dark. So handsome and so smart, he was the neighborhood king—storyteller, game-maker, peacekeeper. The world would be his, she knew. If they could survive the next few years. If she could survive waking him up and telling him Mum wasn't coming home ever again.

She wouldn't tell him about Mum's broken neck, of course. She had forced that out of the cop. Someone had to know—it was only fair to Mum. But not Josh, not her little brother whom she had cared for as an infant while Mum worked the overnight shift at the factory and Dad had died in jail. "Don't let anything happen to my baby," she'd whisper every day to Geneva, even as Josh began kindergarten, then Little League, then third grade.

Geneva put her face to Josh's hair. "You'll be my baby forever."

Joshua touched Maggie's shoulder. "Hey. Sleepyhead."

She rolled over in the bed, blurry eyed. "'Bout time you got in. So how was the meal?"

Joshua unbuttoned his shirt. "What meal? You mean the lobster?"

"Oh, so that's what movie stars eat?"

"What movie—oh, you mean Cassandra Knowles? She came to take Dane out to lunch. They invited me to tag along. We ran into some other people, and before you knew it, we had a business meeting. Then supper. Who told you about her?"

"The question is, why didn't you tell me about her?"

"I was going to when I got home."

"Right. Uh-huh." Maggie rolled over, burying her head in the pillow.

Joshua tickled the back of her neck. "Hey, Mags. Talk to me."

"What's there to talk about?"

"Why you won't talk to me."

"Talking about *not* talking? Isn't that kind of self-defeating?"

He kissed her cheek. "In that case, I surrender. Please tell me what's wrong."

"Nothing's wrong."

"Tell me."

She rolled over. "A trailer-park kid can't compete with Cassandra Knowles."

"Whoa, slow down there. Am I asking you to?" He brushed her hair back. "Hey, what happened to you?"

"Nothing."

"Where'd you get that bruise?"

"I fell off my bike."

"What were you doing on that bike?"

"I have to do something with my time. It's not like I'm hanging out with movie stars all day." She rolled over, her back again to him.

He slipped his arm around her, snuggled into her neck. "Hey. I would never compare any of these high-flying movie stars with you. You know why?"

She shook her head.

"Because it wouldn't be fair. Because no one can compete with you, Maggie."

"Don't," she whispered.

"Don't what? This?" He put his lips to her ear, lightly kissing her.

"I'd rather you didn't tell me everything is fine if it's not."

He worked his way down her neck. "From the moment I saw you, the moment I touched you, the moment I married you—I have always loved you. Nothing will change that, not a million dollars or a million Cassandra Knowles. Nothing."

"You'll never let me go?"

"Never. Maggie, please. I hope you don't ever let me go."

If Penn Roper were able to enjoy anything, it would be this freedom to act at will, to stroll through *The Other Side* offices as if they were his private domain. Dane Wiggin thought he had set up an impenetrable fortress here. *Fool.*

Wiggin didn't use an agency to book the tickets; they came right through this office. Once they had a name, address, and payment information, Wiggin and Geneva used various hacker's tools to access databases—social security, medical, birth, death, marriage, divorce. Even real estate transactions could be used to provide relevant information.

For celebrity readings—a high-stakes game—Wiggin used various private investigators, as well as bribery to pry secrets from staff and hangers-on. It was brilliant and it worked. Joshua Lazarus made millions pretending to speak to dead people.

Penn Roper was about to make sure they spoke back.

Thirteen

THE SIMPLE QUESTION PIERCED PENN.

"Do you have a family?" Maggie asked.

"Please, Mrs. Lazarus, call me Ben."

"Okay, but you'll have to call me Maggie."

"I'd prefer to call you Mrs. Lazarus."

"If I'm Mrs. anything, it's Mrs. Lazanby. That's Joshua's—our—real name. But only in private, as you know. So please, just call me Maggie and neither of us will hear about it from Geneva."

"Whatever you say, Maggie." Penn hoped that would be the end of it. Lazarus had asked him to drive her to the after-school program she was volunteering at. She had dragged him off to Wal-Mart, gone on a shopping spree, then had him load up the Town Car's trunk. He liked the idea of being alone with her, giving him time to figure out what kind of monster she might be. That she was a monster was not in doubt—he had seen her in the tape, standing in the background, approving—no, delighting—in every move her husband made.

He didn't like the idea of her cross-examining him. He was supposed to be the help—taken for granted and ignored.

But she was like a cat, pawing at the mouse between its claws. "Do you, Ben?"

He tried to keep his tone neutral. "Do I what?"

"Do you have a family?"

"My parents have passed on."

"I'm sorry. Mine too. How about a wife? Or kids?"

"Divorced. No kids."

"Oh. Sorry."

"I'm not. I don't miss my ex-wife one bit. So where we going today?"

"The usual. Safe Haven."

"Is that why you didn't go out west with the rest of them?" Lazarus, Geneva, and Dane had been gone for three weeks, with appearances in Las Vegas, San Francisco, and Los Angeles. It had given him ample opportunity to get his devices in place, create the necessary files, and learn the show, the business, and this area.

He had a long-distance surprise planned for Joshua. The fool thought his little candle ceremony was a secret—but there were no secrets, not with those microcameras scattered around the offices and the estate. Penn's laptop would let him know when they had checked in. Jib was in place to carry Lazarus's luggage to his room. He'd open the curtains, check the bathroom, the excellent valet doing excellent work—for Penn.

"That, and other reasons."

Other reasons. Geneva Lazanby had used Wiggin to maneuver Maggie out of the show. That didn't matter—Penn still held her responsible.

"You're doing a good deed, working at the children's center," he said.

She laughed. "More like they're doing the good deed. I'm just having a great time."

Enjoy it while it lasts, Penn thought.

"Good grief, girl! You must have robbed your piggy bank."

Maggie felt like a creep, lying. "When she heard about Safe Haven, Aunt Julia wanted to help out somehow. So she made a small donation."

"I don't know if these kids even know how to use a crayon that's not broken. And they've gotten really proficient ripping paper with their teeth."

Maggie had bought twenty tackle boxes and enough supplies—markers, scissors, paper, pencils, glue sticks, sparkles, stickers, and anything bright and shiny she could find—so each kid could customize his or her own craft kit.

Amy hugged her. "This is just so cool. Thank you. Make sure I have your aunt's address so we can send her some artwork for her fridge. She does have a fridge, doesn't she?"

Maggie laughed. "The cook needs something to store all that caviar and champagne in."

"Hey. Want to join the Scripture lesson today?"

"Um . . . let me clean up around here a little, and then maybe I'll come in." Even after a month at Safe Haven, Maggie wasn't quite ready to show off her ignorance of the Bible. There were enough paper scraps on the floor to occupy her for thirty minutes or more, and by then the kids would be working on their puzzles or playing their games.

Amy took the kids into the den, which served as a quiet room for reading, homework, and Scripture studies. The downstairs had a wide center hall and five decent-sized rooms: the den; a playroom, with games, indoor toys, and puzzles; a dining room that doubled as the art room; the kitchen; and Amy's tiny office, converted from the pantry off the kitchen. Upstairs was a three-room apartment, where Amy lived, and two storage rooms.

This house had been built long before the Civil War, with faint traces of its elegance still apparent, like the curved staircase and the mahogany banister the kids begged to use as a slide. The wallpaper was ten years out of date, the curtains were faded, and the woodwork was scratched, but Maggie felt more at home here than she did in Julia's mansion.

Maggie could hear Amy reading and the kids' occasional laughter; she could see their personalities in the craft projects still on the table; she could feel a tender sense of peace throughout all of Safe Haven, even though they were surrounded by poverty, dysfunction, lawlessness, and even witches.

Charlie came out of the back hall where the downstairs bathroom was. "There's a problem."

Maggie felt his forehead. "You sick?"

"No. Kind of nervous."

"Nervous? About what?"

"A noise."

"What kind of noise?"

"The kind of noise you should be nervous about."

"Okay, pal. I got your back. Let's go have a listen."

Ma said Charlie knew things in his bones. So when his bones told him the *whoosh* he heard under the bathroom sink was scary, he knew something needed to be done. He expected to find Amy and the kids still in the dining room. Amy was short but tough; Pedro was almost as big as her and much stronger; and Dawna could yell any bogey to bits, real or made up.

Charlie wasn't sure how much help Maggie would be. He really liked her, to be sure. The girls wanted to look like her, with sunlight hair and sky-blue eyes. The younger boys wanted her to be their mother, and cool dudes like Manny wanted her for a girlfriend.

In this moment, Charlie wanted her to be tough enough to make that *whooshing* stop.

Maggie didn't hesitate to do what Charlie wouldn't have done for a million bucks—open the door to the vanity and look inside. She pulled out a roll of toilet paper, a scrub brush, and spray bottles of glass and toilet cleaners. "Nothing here," she said.

"I heard it."

"I believe you." She got on her knees and stuck her head in.

"Not a good idea. Something was in there."

"There's a hole in the floor of the vanity. We need to check out the basement."

"Forget it. It was probably just my imagination."

Maggie smiled. "You with me, or should I send for reinforcements?"

"No, no. I got your back too." Charlie followed Maggie to the basement door. "No one goes down here, you know. Not even Amy. She says it's a thousand years old and gross."

"A thousand years old, huh? This I have to see."

They went down the stairs carefully—they were cracked and creaky. When they reached the bottom, Maggie yanked on a string. A single light came on. The foundation was brick on stone; the floor was hard-packed dirt. Maggie walked slowly, her eyes on the ceiling. Pipes ran over their heads, hung with cobwebs thicker and longer than the curtains in Charlie's kitchen.

Maggie pointed to the rear corner of the basement. "This is the pipe to the bathroom sink. This metal duct next to it is what's called the cold air return."

"How do you know all that stuff?"

"I grew up in a trailer. My parents stunk at taking care of stuff. I was always having to climb under the trailer to fix something. At least down here I'm not on my belly." She pointed between the pipes and the ducts. "Look, there's the hole. Let's be quiet for a minute."

Charlie crowded behind Maggie. This place smelled like only bad things could live here.

"Hear anything?" Maggie asked.

Charlie shook his head.

"Me either." Maggie reached up and tapped the heating duct.

Whoosh.

"That's it," Charlie said.

Maggie grabbed a wooden crate from under the stairs and set it under the duct. "It's probably a rat. I'm going to try to catch it."

"What if it bites you?"

"It won't." She climbed onto the box and stood on her tiptoes. "Uh-oh."

"What is it?"

"A snake."

"Get it out of here!" Charlie wanted to run up the stairs and lock the door, but it would be mean to leave Maggie alone with a snake.

"It's okay. I got it already. Can you get me a paper bag from the kitchen?"

"What if it's poisonous?"

"The only venomous snakes in New England are copperheads and timber rattlers. Neither one would be caught dead in a musty basement. It's probably a huge garter or maybe a black snake that crawled in through the windows down here."

"Um, Maggie, I don't see any windows down here."

"Okay, we'll worry about that later. Could you go, now? My arm's getting tired."

Charlie ran up, grabbed a bag, and ran back down. "Here."

"Open it and set it on the floor."

After he did that, Maggie slowly stepped down from the box, holding the snake right behind its head. The snake was huge—over three feet long—black with red stripes and a spotted belly.

"Charlie, go get me a craft box." Her voice was suddenly hard.

"Whose? Why?"

"Just get me one!"

He ran up, grabbed the closest box, and ran back down.

"Empty it."

He did that. "Now what?"

"Put it on the floor, the top open. That's right. Now go get Amy."

"Now?"

"Do it."

He ran back upstairs, hollering that Maggie had caught a snake. Amy came running down behind him, with all the kids following even though Amy told them to stay back. Maggie stood with her foot on the craft box.

"What's the problem?"

"No problem. Send the kids home." The way Maggie's voice broke made Charlie certain there was a problem. But before he could make anyone tell him what it was, Amy had them in their jackets and on their way home, an hour early.

All the way home, he bragged to Pedro how he helped Maggie catch a ten-foot-long snake. Pedro laughed. "Big deal. Not like it was poisonous."

"You don't know that," Charlie said, feeling only a little guilty about lying.

"You're adopted, right?" Amy said. "If you don't mind my asking."

David Drinas bent down from the ladder to look at Amy and Maggie. "I don't mind. But why would you ever ask that?"

"Because you're the *anti-Patrick*," she said, laughing.

He laughed with her, leaving Maggie to stare at them like they'd lost their minds. "Maybe I'm still snake-shocked, but I don't get the joke."

"That's because you haven't met—" Amy and David said it in unison, then laughed even harder.

"You haven't met David's father yet," Amy said. "Patrick is a great guy but definitely the Boston intellectual. He's the lean and clean type, like a marathoner. He's got the wire-rim glasses, hiking boots, and carefully cultivated beard."

"Don't forget Dad's neatly pressed flannel shirts, with the cuffs folded to perfection halfway up his arm. The closest my T-shirts come to even presentable is when I grab them off the rack at the bargain store. And the only time I run is when someone calls me for dinner." David's voice became muffled as he squirmed the ladder into a dark corner behind the vent.

Amy had called Patrick for advice on what to do with the snake. He had sent his son, a contractor who specialized in rehabbing housing for the poor. "He's chased snakes out of job sites in Costa Rica and Panama. Even faced down a nest of alligators in some shell of a house in Florida."

Short, chunky, balding, with paint-splattered clothes and dirt-crusted hands—David Drinas truly was the antithesis of his father. Yet he had been just as quick to answer a call for help.

"I found where your friends are getting in," David called out. "Come on, take a look."

"No, thanks," Amy said. The basement made her skin crawl. The only reason she had stayed down here was because Maggie insisted on being here. She stood next to Amy, clutching her hands convulsively, trying to keep the shakes away. All her adrenaline had gone into holding that snake's head until they could get it into the box. If Maggie could tough it out, Amy had to.

David came off the stepladder. "Dad says you face down those Astaroth dudes every day, Amy. You can't be afraid of a few cobwebs."

"I prioritize my battles, thank you. Though if the Astaroths begin to slither along the street, I might have second thoughts."

David grinned, showing deep dimples. "All right. Let me tell you what's going on here. This is a pretty old house—a nice one too, built almost two hundred years ago. The floor is dirt, the lower part of the foundation stone, then halfway up the builders used brick for cosmetic reasons. You sure you don't want to see for yourself, Amy? I've found something quite interesting in the corner."

Amy shook her head. "Thanks, but no thanks."

"I'll look," Maggie said.

"You don't have to—" Amy started.

Maggie cut her off. "Yes. I do."

Maggie ducked under the wide metal vent, then climbed up the stepladder. Her knees wobbled, but she went up, one step at a time, until Amy could see only her feet. "Oh my. It's a tunnel," Maggie called, her voice echoing through the vent.

"When I poked around up there, I realized the bricks in that corner were stacked, not cemented in," David said. "You wouldn't have noticed it because the vent blocks it from view. I knocked in a few bricks, found the tunnel. Now you know how that creep Theo and his biker-witch wannabes keep getting past the alarm system."

"Theo built a tunnel?" Amy said. "That's pretty drastic just to harass us."

"He didn't do it. It's pretty old. The timbers rotted out long ago, but there's some solid brickwork in there, keeping it up," David said. "Raven is an old city, you know, with a whole network of old sewers and water pipes under the roads. A lot of the older houses have old root cellars or ice rooms. I bet a lot of homeowners don't even know what they've got under their property."

"This house has an abolitionist history," Amy said. "Maybe this tunnel is left over from the Underground Railroad."

Maggie climbed back down, brushing dirt from her hands and shirt. "Massachusetts didn't have slaves, so why would they need a tunnel?"

"Before the Civil War, slave hunters could haul runaways back to their owners, even from New England. This house could have been part of the rescue network," Amy said.

David smiled again. Despite the thinning red hair and pudgy face, Amy did see Patrick in the same kind eyes and quick intelligence. "It's kind of fitting, isn't it? That this house be used for a different kind of deliverance all these years later."

"If we survive the snakes," Amy said, rubbing her arms.

"There won't be any more snakes. I'm gonna cover that hole with heavy-grade plywood so sturdy that spider-faced freak would have to bomb it to get through."

Amy closed her eyes. *I don't put a bomb past him. Oh, Lord, please send Your angels; protect Your children.*

"He was all apologetic," Amy told Patrick on the phone. "Old houses, yadda yadda, we've had rats in our basements, yadda yadda, anything I can do, yadda yadda. But Theo denied that it was his snake. He won't even admit to being Theodore Marks, the creepy-crawly guy who writes those weird books. The cops chalked our slithering intruder up to bad luck, case closed, thanks, ma'am."

"Thank God for Maggie. How did she know it was venomous?"

"She was spooked because she didn't recognize it. She said she's come face-to-face with every snake in New England, between crawling under her parents' trailer, playing in the woods, and climbing mountains. She thought this snake was too colorful to be native. David identified it as a rainbow snake, native to Florida. Maggie's instincts were right on. "

"That's a talent you didn't see coming, did you?"

Amy laughed. "No. She's so pretty, it's easy to put her on the shelf with the Barbies. I hope you'll drive up soon so you can meet her."

"I will," Patrick said. "I'm looking forward to it."

"I hear a *but* in there somewhere."

"But I'm concerned about where she stands spiritually."

"A sinner. Just like the rest of us."

"You know what I mean. Can Maggie participate fully—or appropriately—in our mission if she's not sure where she stands in her faith?"

"Maybe she's not sure. But I am."

"Um . . . Amy? Not that I want to split hairs, but I'm not sure that flies theologically. God encounters each of us in *our* hearts. Not in someone else's heart."

Amy laughed. "You know what I mean. You're just giving me a hard time."

There was silence on the line. She imagined him chewing on his fingernail, maybe pacing back and forth. "You think that Maggie is the answer to our prayer for help."

"Somehow she's a part of this—and I don't mean just Safe Haven."

"The gathering darkness? Is that still on your heart?"

"More than ever, Patrick. I know Maggie's a part of this, though I can't explain how the Lord will use her, or any of us. All I know is that I'm supposed to prepare her to . . . to *stand*."

"I guess we're supposed to keep her, then?" Patrick said.

"Yes."

"Then we will pray that God prepares Maggie for whatever is coming."

Fourteen

JOSHUA WAS CONFINED TO HIS ROOM.

"The instant we finish lunch, you hit the bed," Dane had said. "We don't want that pretty face showing one sign of wear tomorrow." They had taken a late-night flight from San Francisco after partying with some of the Forty-niners football team, then met with studio executives first thing in the morning. They would shoot a network demo tomorrow night, then meet with more executives before flying home for Friday's show.

Geneva went to the studio to check the soundstage, Dane went trolling for starlets, and Joshua was left to pace his hotel room. Back home it was forty degrees. California was warm and bright, with a breeze coming off the water. From his balcony, Joshua looked down at the pool, surrounded by palm trees and bright flowers. He picked up the phone, intent on calling Maggie and describing the scene, and then hung it up. It was late afternoon on the East Coast; she was off to volunteer at that children's program.

Dane had left the research for tomorrow's show, but Joshua couldn't bring himself to dig in. Any more memorization and his performance would be tedious rather than fired with excitement.

The truth was that sometimes his cold readings bordered on the *inspired*. Not that he would tell Dane or Geneva that; Maggie was the only person he had hinted to about having some sort of supernatural power. And yet, how could anyone believe that first meeting with Julia was simply a coincidence? It made more sense that somehow fate—or the spirits—had brought them together.

Joshua pulled the drapes and dug his candle out of his carry-on. He lit it, then closed his eyes and let the image of the flame drift.

Sola, you have brought me this far. Tell me now, what can I do to serve you?

The flame wavered then sparked into a thousand stars. Joshua counted them all, knew them all, had cast them all into the sky with his hand, so powerful now that he could hold each star in his hand and crush its light, taking it into himself so now he was the flame and all else was darkness.

Joshua opened his eyes. He must have dozed off. What was he doing on his knees? He could hear the whir of the air conditioner, a clunk of plumbing, voices in the hall. He closed his eyes and focused on his breathing. After a minute, he could hear his own pulse, a gentle *pum-pum*.

Joshua . . .

Joshua jumped up, his heart racing.

Help them, Joshua . . .

Was this a trick? He checked the bathroom, then the hall. Empty. He got a glass from the bathroom and felt sheepish as he pressed it to the wall. He knew all the tricks. Even though Geneva had made the reservations under assumed names, Dane had made sure everyone knew he'd be in Los Angeles. One of his competitors could have set up a scam.

Joshua . . .

The voice was here, in this room. He ran his hands on the walls, searching for hidden wires; tugged on the seams of the drapes to make sure nothing was sewn between the fabric and the lining; he tipped and examined lamps, the clock radio, even the coffeemaker; opened the air-conditioning vent; unplugged the television; and pulled out the minibar.

Nothing. And yet, from various angles in the room, minutes apart, he heard that voice calling his name. He debated calling security, but that might be playing into someone's hands. He could see the headline—STAR OF *THE OTHER SIDE* PANICS WHEN THE SPIRITS SPEAK BACK.

Joshua . . .

"What?!" he said, peeved. "If you've got something to say, say it. Otherwise, shut up."

Minutes passed, but the voice didn't speak again. Had the scammer given up? Or were the spirits mad at him for doubting?

"I'm so sorry. Please come back."

Amy had gone upstairs for a nap. "I'm working at eleven tonight. Sorry to leave you."

"That's okay. My ride is coming shortly. I'll just wait." Maggie sat on the front steps, listening to night in the Beak. This place no longer frightened her. Sure, it was home to druggies and drunks, but the children were the heart and hope of this place. And David had boarded up the tunnel so the snakes—reptiles or human—would not be sneaking in again.

"Cold night."

The man in the hooded sweatshirt sat next to her. How had Theo sneaked up on her? She should have smelled him a block away—he stunk like a dead fish.

"I don't smell that bad. Do I?"

Had she said that aloud? She was wrong about him stinking—his scent was rich and spicy, not foul.

"We haven't been properly introduced, Maggie. My name is Theo."

"That's a strange name."

"Thank you." The lines crisscrossing his face were intriguing, almost attractive. She couldn't stop looking at them. Deep in her chest, she knew she should get away from him, go back inside or step under a streetlight where she could be clearly seen. But the scent—she wanted another breath of it, then another.

"You really don't want to be here, do you?" he said.

"I'm leaving soon."

"You should leave and not come back."

"I will leave, but . . . I have . . . to come . . . back." Why was it so hard to say the words?

Theo stood up, blocking the porch light. "You will leave and not come back."

"I will leave . . ." A gust of wind swept over her, and suddenly she choked on her own hair.

"Only one thing you can do to make it stop. Leave and do not come back."

"I am coming back tomorrow," she croaked, trying to pull the hair out of her throat.

"Not if I don't want you to."

Theo's shadow wrapped around her, and she spun into a darkness, choking—

Then—light!

Ben Cord dragged Theo into the street. They stayed there for a long moment, Ben's hand on Theo's throat, their eyes locked. Ben whispered something, then let him go. Theo disappeared into the house across the street.

Ben dashed back to Maggie. "Are you all right?"

"Just spooked. What a creep, huh?" Her head cleared; she felt almost foolish about choking on her own hair and confused about how that could have happened since she wore a tight French braid.

Theo's words chased around in her mind. *You will leave and not come back.*

Over my dead body, Maggie thought.

Stop shaking.

Theo curled his hands into fists and pressed them together. He could allow no weakness, especially with his acolytes staring at him, waiting for worship to begin.

"Get your hands off me," Theo had told the man who had come to Maggie's rescue.

"Listen and listen good," the man had said. Something about the steel in his eyes made the lines on Theo's face tighten, like wires cutting into his skin.

"Why drive away what could be a perfect sacrifice?" the man said.

Then he walked away, an ordinary person going on with his ordinary job.

Had his Mistress Astarte sent him the help he had begged for? Or was there now competition for her favor? One thing was sure—Theo had just looked into the face of a man who had already been to hell and back.

Stop shaking.

Theo crossed his arms over his chest and stared over his acolytes. "Shall we pray?"

The Astaroths rumbled their assent. There were four minions—Korad, Leonine, Palter, and Ugueth. Each minion had two familiars; females for the most part, meant to see to their needs. Together they formed a coven, devoted to Astarte, the goddess of the underworld, whose throne had been usurped by one who was most unworthy. She waited in the darkness, longing for someone to burn away her chains and bring her out.

Theo would resurrect her in a vortex of fire. The four Astaroth houses represented the ends of the earth from which the vortex would spring.

Theo was supposed to live in the middle of the four—preparing Astarte's throne—but that cow Amy Howland refused to vacate his house. She had a lease so tight that even the sale of the house hadn't broken it.

Astarte would provide other means. How sweet it would be to put steel to Amy's throat and watch her squirm. She would cry for mercy, cry for deliverance, but the only deliverance would be the will of Astarte, the hand of Theo Marks, and he would laugh and laugh when her little lamb-god turned and ran the other way.

Fifteen

DINNER, ALLEGEDLY A QUIET MEAL AT CHANESS, HAD BECOME A whirlwind. A stream of celebrities stopped at their table: rock stars, producers, studio executives, actors, financiers, and a host of celebrities whose only claim to fame was knowing where to be when. Dane made the introductions while Joshua made the small talk. He hoped Geneva was taking notes; after almost three weeks of this, his usually phenomenal memory was giving out.

"Give me a minute. I need a break," Joshua said.

"Where are you going?" Dane said. "Colleen Patrick just came in. She's the new studio head—"

"I'm going to the bathroom. Ms. Patrick can join me there."

Moments later, Joshua was in the bar, out of sight of his handlers and, hopefully, the rest of Los Angeles's glitterati. He ordered a scotch, one of the fine single malts that Dane liked to charge to the office budget. Joshua grimaced at his first sip. He and Maggie didn't drink much—they hadn't been able to afford it in their camper days. He might have to take it up, though. The liquor felt like velvet fire in his throat.

"Wow, look who's here. Are you, like, hiding out, Josh?"

Cassandra Knowles was more beautiful than ever in a cropped top and low-cut pants that showed off a six-pack stomach and a diamond-studded navel.

"Hey, Cass. Getting a moment to myself."

"Oh. Sorry, I'll just—"

It was a split second that seemed like a lifetime of indecision—he should let her go, but he didn't want to; she smelled good, and he wanted to feel the line of her neck with his fingertips; this was a new world where apparently anything Joshua wanted, Joshua could have.

He spoke before she even finished her offer to leave him alone. "Stay. Have a drink."

No one denied these people anything. Geneva told Cassandra Knowles that Joshua was in the men's room. The woman smirked, then walked right in there. Next stop was the bar. The bimbo's instincts were better than Geneva's—she wouldn't have expected her brother to sit alone, drinking.

Geneva went back to the table. "He's in the bar, having a drink with Cassandra Knowles."

"Lucky man."

She tapped the table with her fingertips. "Dane, you must know some of these paparazzi guys."

Dane munched through a piece of fudge cake, his second helping. The more money *The Other Side* took in, the bigger his appetite got. "Sure."

"Maybe you should give somebody a call. Offer an exclusive."

Dane swallowed one last bite of chocolate, then flipped open his cell.

Annette Donaldson was a lovely woman with gray eyes, dark hair, classic features. She was cultured and demure—what a woman should be. It was a shame to have to use her, but she would require less maneuvering and offer more opportunity than a stranger would.

She picked at the shrimp on her plate. "I was surprised when you called me."

"And pleased, I hope?" Penn said.

"It depends."

"On what?"

"It's been seven months. I'm not sure why you got in touch after all this time."

"Things have changed for me," Penn said.

"Oh?"

"My wife and I are no longer together."

"Oh." The same word but now weighted with anticipation and assent. She touched the back of his hand, her eyes sympathetic.

"It happened rather suddenly. I'm living in Massachusetts now. Beverly Farms."

She lowered her eyes, but he had caught the calculation. Beverly Farms was very expensive. "And Tanya? Is she with her mother?"

Penn had prepared for this question, and yet his chest felt like a pile driver was working through it. "She's with me."

"I'd love to meet her sometime." Annette let go of his hand, as if realizing she was coming on far too strong. "To see how she enjoys the jewelry."

Tanya had been buried wearing the gold bangles and diamond pendant.

"Penn, are you all right?"

"I'm just nervous. It's been a long time since I've been on a date. I mean, if you'll agree to let this be a date. You don't have to; I'll understand. But you were so kind last spring, and—"

"Shush." Annette leaned over the table. "Your wife's loss is my gain."

"Your gain is my gain," he whispered back.

Sixteen

"I NEVER CLAIMED TO BE A GIRL SCOUT." AMY GROANED.

"And you'll never make it as a magician's assistant if you don't pay attention!" Maggie wrestled to pull the ropes off her hands. She had been trying to teach Amy how to tie slipknots, but Amy only seemed to be able to make a mess.

Teaching the kids magic had been Amy's idea. If they could learn some simple tricks, they might also learn the underlying truth—that illusion can't be trusted, that they need to look beyond what they're seeing at first glance.

"This is why you do the crafts and I do the stories. I was never any good with my hands."

Amy's dexterity was so bad that her fingers weren't even all thumbs—it was more like they were toes.

"I'm not asking you to saw me in half," Maggie was saying. "Just learn this one trick, that's all. You tie me up; I escape. How hard is that? On the other tricks, you can hand me the props and just look pretty."

Amy laughed. "Now, that would be magic, getting me to look pretty."

"You don't think you're pretty?"

"Oh, stop it. You asking me that is like, I don't know—Cassandra Knowles asking the bride of Frankenstein why she doesn't feel like a supermodel."

"Okay, Mrs. Frankenstein, I'm going to give you the lecture you give to the kids. First of all, Cassandra Knowles is—shall we say—*enhanced*?"

"I don't like telling God what to do," Amy said. "But I wouldn't have minded if he had created me taller and thinner, with fewer freckles on my nose and fewer kinks in my hair."

Maggie had one hand on her hip, the other pointing in mock lecture. "Oh. So would you rather be me? Mrs. Loose Ends?"

"*Mrs.?* I thought you were a Miss. Or Ms., if you choose."

"Figure of speech. As the kids would say, you got it goin' on, Amy. Heart, head, and talent for this mission. And, as *you* would say, God looks at the heart, not the packaging."

"Well. I guess you do listen."

"Yeah, well, how about you listen right now? This is not rocket science—the rope comes through like this . . ." Maggie tied Amy up in a flash.

"Hey, I can't get out," Amy complained. "I thought this was the quick-release thing."

"Pull that little end right there."

Amy hooked her index finger around a rope end and tugged. The knots seemed to melt away, freeing her.

"Okay, okay. I'm going to pay better attention," Amy said.

"You'd better, or I'll pull that duck out of your nose."

Amy threw up her hands. "Oh no! Not the duck again . . ."

Lots of the kids wanted out of the Beak. Dawna and Pedro liked to pretend they lived in one of the snooty towns like Manchester-by-the-Sea. They daydreamed about mansions with high stone walls and private beaches and wished for parents who came to teacher conferences instead of working the second shift or hanging out at the neighborhood bar. They wanted servants who served steak and salad instead of having to make their own macaroni and cheese out of a box.

Manny dreamed about being a superstar basketball player for the Celtics and living at the Ritz, right in the middle of Boston. He would have guys they called valets doing his laundry and have breakfast delivered to his door every morning. He'd have models and actresses hanging off his arm, at least when he didn't have some goon from the Knicks hanging off his arm and keeping him from the hoop.

Charlie didn't mind living here; the Beak had its advantages. No one looked twice at a kid out after dark, though the older Charlie got, the more he realized it wasn't a good idea to get too far from his own stoop.

He had learned to show respect for the hard-eyed teenagers who wore loose jackets, even in the summer, to hide their hardware and their stash. Even so, if someone gave Charlie a hard time at school, he reminded them that he was from the Beak, and he knew plenty of dudes who wouldn't mind teaching a big-mouthed kid a sharp-knuckled lesson.

The best thing about the Beak was Safe Haven. Some kids teased him and the others for going there every day. "Sissy" was the nicest thing they said; all the other taunts were too ugly to give head space to. Those kids were too stupid to know how much fun they had, how good the treats were, and how terrific Amy was. Even so, some days Charlie hung out at home, gambling with pennies or running lookout for the dudes who owned his corner. Days like that he was cool, but the cool never lasted long enough to make up for the muddy feeling in his mind.

Charlie's head was a problem. There was a war going on between being cool and being a Jesus dude. He used to be able to leave the Jesus thing at the Haven, but lately Jesus followed him home, so running lookout didn't seem so much fun anymore. In fact, it was starting to seem like a really bad thing to do.

The real power in the Beak was the Astaroths. Everyone wanted a piece of their action. It was just—no one was sure exactly *what* their action was. They had this thing that—well, the only thing that seemed more together was this Jesus dude.

But Jesus didn't have tattoos or wear a hood. And He was dead, except—He was alive. When Charlie had those nasty dreams in the middle of the night, it was Jesus who whispered him back to sleep. Ma would be there if she could. But since she couldn't, well, Jesus wasn't a bad dude to have around—even if He didn't ride a Harley.

The kids were cleaning up after crafts. Maggie watched Charlie slip out, his face cloudy like something was on his mind. She followed him into the den and sat down on the floor next to him. "You okay?"

"Yeah."

"Bzz. Wrong answer. Try again."

"Just thinking about some bad dreams I had."

"You too? I've had some real losers in my time."

"What do you do when you can't wake up out of them?"

She laughed. "I scream until someone wakes me."

"Oh." He sounded disappointed.

"You can tell me. I won't tell Manny. Or Dawna."

"Oh man, she's worse than television, the way her mouth goes off."

Maggie crossed her heart. "I won't tell Miss Public Broadcasting, I swear."

He whispered into her ear: "I don't have anyone at home to wake me up when I scream."

"What do you mean, Charlie?"

"Don't tell the school, okay? Or even Amy." His voice was tight.

"I swear. What am I not telling?"

"Ma's at work all night. No one's there if I have a bad dream."

Maggie silently blessed Amy, realizing even more fully what Safe Haven meant to these kids. "I'm sorry, Charlie. That's a real bummer."

He nodded. "It stinks, big-time. But it beats starving; that's what Ma says, and she's right."

Maggie was trying to frame an answer when the rest of the kids came rushing in. Amy followed, her hair in a thousand directions but her eyes focused impossibly on every kid at once.

"Okay, okay, grab a seat," Amy said. "I see Maggie took the best one, but there's plenty more where that came from."

The kids laughed. The den consisted of one sofa, which the oldest kids had claim to, lots of floor space, and a pile of Bibles.

"Okay, before we begin . . . does anyone have any questions?" Amy asked.

Charlie poked Maggie. "Yeah, I do," she said. "I've been having some wicked bad dreams. I don't know what to do . . ."

"Anyone else have bad dreams?" Amy asked. Kids looked at each other, kept their hands down. "That's what I thought. *All* of us. Okay, grab a Bible and turn to Philippians."

Maggie fluttered her pages helplessly. "General Electric Power Company," Charlie whispered.

"Huh?"

"Galatians Ephesians Philippians Colossians," Dawna said. "In the New Testament—the little books after Corinthians."

Charlie paged through Maggie's Bible, then handed it back.

Maggie glanced up at Amy to see if she had witnessed Maggie's display of ignorance. Gratefully, Amy was helping Ryan, who was only in the second grade and could barely read.

"Fourth chapter," Amy said. "Who wants to read, starting at verse 8?" Most of the hands went up. Amy surveyed the crowd. "Natalia. You haven't read for a while."

Natalia beamed. "Finally, brothers, whatever is true, whatever is noble . . ."

Maggie's skin tingled, suddenly hot. She glanced around, wondering if she was the only one sweating or if maybe she should open a window.

" . . . excellent or praiseworthy—think about such things."

"That's great. Thank you, Natalia," Amy said. "Okay. Anyone want to venture a guess about what this has to do with bad dreams?"

Charlie suddenly straightened. "I know! It's all about the head space, right? If you've got good things going 'round in there, you're gonna take them to bed with you. But if you're watching nasty stuff on television or listening to ugly CDs, then that goes to bed with you."

Amy nodded. "There are things in life you can't change. Life isn't always so hot in the Beak, huh?"

The kids were silent. *They either won't admit how ugly this place is, or they don't realize it,* Maggie thought.

"So we control what we can—like the books we read, the people we hang with, the activities we choose—and we ask Jesus to help with the rest," Amy said.

What if "the rest" was too long a list? Geneva. Cassandra Knowles. Being excluded from the show and from Joshua's public persona. A childhood of neglect. A marriage that never had time to put down roots. Her own heart, torn between Joshua seeing his dreams come true and herself *being* that dream. Her own soul—something Maggie had never given much thought to before that night when she saw her husband under the pier and feared that she would lose him to the cold ocean. In that moment, she would have traded all that she was for all that Joshua could be. And yet, where was her heart now? Was it tumbling after her soul, not much good for anything?

Oh, God, is there anything true and noble and right about me that You can use?

Seventeen

MAGGIE OPENED HER EYES TO THE SUNRISE AND HER HUSBAND. "Joshua!"

He kissed her forehead, rubbing his face in her hair. "I'm back."

"I thought your plane wasn't due in until tonight."

"I took the red-eye, left Dane and Geneva to work with the lawyers and accountants."

She sat up in bed. "What time is it?"

"Six thirty. Which means *you* don't need to get out of bed yet." He yanked off his shirt, then climbed into bed.

"I've got to get up," Maggie said.

"But I just got here, Mags."

"I'm sorry. I have to be out of here in less than an hour."

"Whatever for? The stores don't open until ten."

She whacked him with a pillow. "Is that how you think I spend my time? Shopping?"

"I was just kidding. Where do you have to go so early? If it's a doctor's appointment, you can reschedule. You're not sick, right?"

She sat up. "No, I'm not sick."

"Stay with me, then. I missed you. It's been almost three weeks."

It had seemed like forever. When they had left for the West Coast trip, the leaves were still gold and red; now the trees were almost barren, the morning dew a steady frost.

Maggie kissed his nose. "I promised to do something, and I have to keep my promise." She went into the bathroom and started the shower.

He pulled off his pants and followed her in. "Want me to wash your back?"

"I'd rather you washed my hair."

He rubbed the shampoo in, working his fingers into her scalp. "I love you, Princess."

"Love you too. Hand me the conditioner."

"No, let me do it. So where are you going?"

"There's this little boy that comes to the Haven. Charlie Milloy. They're having story time at his school. His mother can't go, so he asked me to come and read to him."

Maggie turned to face him, shampooing his hair now. Even soaked from head to toe, she was beautiful. No surgical enhancements. No makeup, no contact lenses, no hair color.

"Can't you go to this kid's school some other day?"

"If I had known you were going to be home, I wouldn't have promised."

"What if I beg . . ."

"Joshua. Don't."

"I'm just kidding. I understand."

"These kids are so used to having promises broken. I want to keep this one."

"I said I understand, Maggie."

"I'll be home by lunchtime."

He turned off the shower and handed her a towel. "Go see your Charlie. Tell him I said hi."

She shook her hair out, struggling to get the comb through it. "I can't. Remember? I'm no relation to you. I'm not sure if I'm even supposed to know you. I'll have to ask Dane."

He took the comb and worked through her tangles. "All that stuff Dane is pushing on us is going to change. I promise, Maggie. And I keep my promises."

She went to get dressed. He turned the shower back on and stood under it for a long time.

Maggie read about the football player jumping out of the spaceship on the back of a bird that was really an alien. "Wasn't that brave? Risking his life to save all the people on the planet?"

"That wasn't brave. It was stupid," Charlie said.

"Why do you say that?"

"Because he shoulda known he'd get smashed to bits."

"You can't ride a bird up to a spaceship," a red-haired boy named Robbie said.

"He didn't ride it up. He rode it down," a little girl named Madelyn said.

"Those bad aliens want to take over earth, they gotta come through me first," Charlie said. "I'll get a gun and I'll shoot—"

"Wait a minute, Charlie. Hold it right there. Guns don't solve problems. Look at this story. Our hero isn't using a gun. He's depending on his intelligence and creativity and the support of his friends. Not violence."

Charlie turned away, pouting. Had she spoken too quickly and embarrassed him? Guns were a reality on his street, not something to be dismissed with a wave of her hand.

Maggie touched his shoulder. "Charlie. If aliens come calling, I'll want you by my side. We'll support each other, okay?"

He gave her just enough of a nod to let her know that she was forgiven.

"Okay, let's see if our hero makes it to earth—"

Robbie jumped up, pointing. "The creepy-crawly man is here!"

They were all up, running for the door.

"Back to your seats, please." Mrs. Grimaldi held her hands up. The kids quieted almost immediately. "Class, let's give our parents and friends a big thank-you for reading to us today."

The kids clapped. Charlie whistled his approval. Maggie felt her face go red. She'd been applauded for years and never blushed once.

"Parents and friends, I hope you'll feel free to stay and listen. Theodore Marks is a local author and has become a good friend of the Tapley School."

Charlie grabbed Maggie's hand. "Can you stay?"

"Sure, for a little while."

The kids carried their chairs to the front of the room where the creepy-crawly man was busy setting up his exhibits. Maggie sat down behind the kids.

"Good morning," Theodore Marks said in a familiar voice.

His eyes were pale, the color of a shallow tidal pool. His face was clear of tattoos. Was this really Theo, transformed somehow? She had spent enough time onstage to know how makeup could cover the deepest scars—and the darkest tattoos.

If Theo was a friend to children, why was he trying to evict Safe Haven?

He smiled directly at Maggie, as if reading her mind. "Perhaps we could get one of the parents—or *friends*—to come assist today's lesson."

Charlie turned around in his chair, squirming with excitement. "Maggie, you do it."

"I don't know—"

"Please, Maggie?" Marks extended his hand.

Before she realized it, the man had Maggie's hand. "Maggie, meet . . . Midnight."

Midnight was a spider, bigger and hairier than any she had ever found under her parents' trailer. It slowly walked across her palm, up her wrist, and would put its poison into her in an instant if she didn't swat it away or crush it or stomp it. *Dear God, I don't want to frighten the children, but I can't have this thing on me.*

And then she saw it for what it was—a helpless creature with incredible grace. "Thank you, Mr. Marks. I'm pleased to meet Midnight, but I've got an appointment to get to."

"I'm sure we'll meet again," he said.

"Probably not." She headed for the door, remembering to squeeze Charlie's hand on the way out.

The bedroom came alive. The curtains quivered in the wind even though the windows were closed. A soft light seeped up from the molding like a sunrise on every side.

Joshua . . .

"Who are you?" Joshua said, sitting up in bed.

Voices, like a whispered chorus, came from all sides. *Sola, the gatekeeper. Sending you the spirits of wind and sea and sky . . .*

He covered his head with the pillow. Too much Hollywood, not enough sleep.

Ten minutes later, he swung his legs to the floor, comforted by the feeling of cold oak under his feet.

Joshua . . .

No, he wouldn't fall for it again. This had to be a scam or a joke—something Dane might pull for a laugh. Certainly Joshua had no competitor powerful enough to reach into his bedroom to entice him. And yet, even a hundred years ago, mediums and psychics had used simple, low-tech ways to simulate voices that fooled thousands. He unplugged the television, stereo, DVD player, even his razor. Maybe it was a stray transmission. Maybe he was just hearing his name because he was grossly egocentric.

Joshua . . .

Joshua lifted cushions, rummaged through Maggie's vanity, tore through the closets. Electronics were tiny these days. If a camera could be put into a cigarette lighter, a speaker didn't need to be much bigger.

Why do you doubt us? This was a woman's voice, higher than Maggie's.

"I don't know you," Joshua said.

A thick purple film like motor oil crossed the ceiling. Joshua put his hands to his ears, then pulled them away just as quickly. If these spirits were real, denial might have severe consequences.

"Okay, you've got my attention. What do you want?"

Speak for the lost ones . . . The sound was so vibrant, it seemed to come from all around him.

"I don't understand. What lost ones?"

The ones who can't reach the light . . .

"Please, if you'd only tell me who you are, maybe I'd know what to do to help."

Believe . . .

He listened with all his being now. The only answer was the pounding of his own heart.

Eighteen

Joshua Lazarus stood in the middle of his bedroom, looking like he'd seen a ghost.

"What can I do for you?" Penn said.

"CIA and special-ops–type things—didn't I see that stuff on your resume?"

"You sure did." And that was the truth—ten years of it. Then Tanya was born and Penn broke off to start his own electronics firm, making millions in the defense industry. He had kept up his contacts and his expertise, which was why Ben Cord had been an easy sell.

"Can you sweep this room for bugs?"

"Do you suspect someone is eavesdropping?"

"We had an incident in Los Angeles with some of the paparazzi planting microphones. You know, trying to expose me as a fraud."

Penn had to force himself to keep a straight face. "But you're not a fraud."

"Of course not. Anyway, I thought I heard a buzzing up here, like electronic feedback. Thought I'd better get it checked out. If this is outside your job description—"

"Absolutely not. Let me pick up Maggie, and then I'll sweep the room. Actually, I should probably do a walk-through of the whole house, if you wouldn't mind."

"Yes, that would be great. Thank you."

Twenty minutes later, Penn was back at Tapley School. "How was third grade?" he asked.

"Fine. Except . . ."

"Except what?"

"Nothing," Maggie said.

Except their friend Theo was in attendance. Penn had seen him arrive on a motorcycle as he had been leaving to respond to Joshua's emergency call. The spook wore some sort of makeup over the tattoos, but there was no mistaking that hungry look as he approached the school. Was the spook a con artist or a true believer? Didn't matter—Penn would play him like the others.

"Mr. Lazarus asked me to pick up some coffee and rolls. I'll come in and unpack that stuff. Then, if you don't need me, I need to run to my place and pick up some tools, because Mr. Lazarus has some work he needs me to—"

"Whoa. Slow down there. I'll take the groceries in. And just let me know by two o'clock if you can't drive me to the Haven. If it's still nice, I'll ride my bike. Otherwise, I'll call a cab."

"Thanks, Maggie." The surprise he had stuck in with the groceries was going to make very interesting reading in the Lazarus household.

Maggie unpacked the groceries, feeling guilty that Joshua had to send Ben out to get him something to eat. But she hadn't known he'd take the red-eye home, had she? She dug out English muffins, eggs, butter, even some ham. Ben took good care of her husband—for that she was very grateful.

At the bottom of the bag she found a *StarField*. Joshua would want that with his coffee.

He was on the cover! She flipped through until she found the article, her hands shaking with excitement. She laughed at the picture of Joshua when he was a little boy, pulling a rabbit out of a top hat. Both Dane and Geneva had been interviewed. There was no mention of her, only that Joshua Lazarus kept his personal life just that—'personal.'

"Hey there." Joshua wrapped his arms around her.

"Hey, back. Look at this—you're famous now."

He reached for the magazine. "Let me see."

She danced away, moving to the other side of the island. "No way. I got it first. I want to see what the world thinks of my handsome, talented, sexy husband."

Joshua caught up to her and slipped his arm around her waist. "Not a bad description. Maybe I should hire you to do my PR."

"Maybe you should," Maggie said. She leaned against the sink so she could catch the sunlight coming in through the window. She flipped the page, looking now at a picture of Joshua counseling an elderly woman during the show. The woman's hands were on his shoulders, her tearful eyes obviously grateful. In each shot, Joshua looked solemn but attractive. The article itself was long with no hint of skepticism—Dane would be pleased to have this much publicity at no cost.

Joshua nibbled her earlobe. "Why don't we pour some coffee, then go read this upstairs?"

"You big stars are all alike," Maggie teased. "Always trying to get some unsuspecting woman into—"

"Into what? Say the word and I'm right there for you."

But Maggie was struck silent by what she saw on the page. Joshua's lips, so tender and familiar—pressed against lips not Maggie's, against lips that had no right to receive his kiss, *Oh, God, please, not this,* his love.

"Maggie?"

She backed away from him blindly until she bumped into the refrigerator. The shock flowed into rage now, a river about to burst its dam.

Joshua followed her, a puzzled look on his face. "Hey, I was only teasing. I didn't mean to make you mad."

She pushed him away. "Get your hands off me!"

"What's the matter?"

"So you were really worn out in California, huh?"

"What are you talking about?" Joshua said.

"Business 24/7. That's what you said. Couldn't wait to get home."

"I couldn't. I missed you." He reached for her again.

She moved sideways, along the counter. "You liar."

"What? What has gotten into you all of a sudden?"

"This." She turned the magazine toward him.

He lost his grin. "Oh."

"Oh?"

"It's not—"

"Shut up! I know what you're going to say. 'It's not what it looks like.' You're going to tell me this is a doctored photo, that you really weren't kissing Cassandra Knowles. You'll say that they pasted your image in. Oh, I know! You can say that it was all Dane's idea, or maybe Geneva's. She must love this; you playing kissy-face with a famous Hollywood tramp."

"Maggie, please let—"

"A normal sister-in-law welcomes a good wife, but Geneva has resented me from the beginning. There's something wrong with her that she can't get herself her own life—"

"You are so overreacting. You need to calm down, right now."

"Or what? You'll use my little rebellion as an excuse to get rid of me? I'm halfway out the door anyway, with Geneva's foot on my backside and Dane holding the door open. Why don't you just finish the job so you—and your precious sister—can move this plastic-faced, silicone-stuffed movie star into this ridiculous movie-star mansion."

"Just let me expla—"

"Go ahead, kiss the little tramp." Maggie mashed the magazine against Joshua's face.

"Stop that. You're irrational."

"I am not irrational; I am furious." She pushed it harder.

"Give me that." Joshua tried to pull it away from her, but she wouldn't let go. It was a ridiculous tug-of-war, but Maggie was fighting her husband and her jealousy and a woman she would never be and a sister who would never love her and a world that was too big for her and—

Rip!

The magazine tore in half. Maggie stumbled against the counter, lost her footing, and fell against the cupboard. As she banged her cheek on a knob, she cried out, anger mixing with her sudden pain.

Joshua rushed to her. "Are you all right?"

"Leave me alone," she said, scooting backward on the floor away from him.

Joshua grabbed a piece of ice from the freezer and pressed it against her face. "Maggie, oh baby, I'm so sorry."

"Get away from me."

"Please, please forgive me. It was an accident."

"Like this?" She threw what was left of the magazine at him.

"Dane was driving me nuts, so I couldn't even eat supper in peace. I went into the bar. Next thing I know, Cassie was there, leaning against me. I moved away, but . . . she came on so strong, and I'm not used to drinking, and I got confused and—"

The back door opened. "Maggie?"

Maggie stood up and shoved the magazine into the trash. "In here, Ben."

"Is Mr. Lazarus—oh, hi. I got the tools. Where did you want me to start?"

"Can we do that later? Maggie's going up to the bedroom for a nap."

"No, I'm not. I'm going out." Maggie just had to get away from him, away from the trappings of his fame. Magazines and movie stars and drivers and limos were choking her marriage and choking her.

"Where you going?"

"What do you care?"

"Do you want Ben to drive you? Or give me a minute to change, and I can take you."

"I'm taking my bike."

"It's forty degrees out."

"So I'll wear a jacket."

"Maggie, what happened to your face? Is that another bike accident?" Ben said.

She glared at Joshua. "I slipped against a cupboard. Stupid me."

"That looks raw. I think you need me to drive you."

"No offense, Ben, but I don't need you or anyone."

She slammed the door on her way out, wishing with her whole heart that that was true.

Nineteen

HILLARY COULDN'T MAKE IT GO AWAY.

She had tried for months, of course. Studying hard at college, deliberately overwhelming herself with chemistry, physics, and advanced calculus in her first semester. She was dating a skinny kid who danced hip-hop and programmed computers. She had even tried out for the drama department's production of *The Music Man,* surprising herself that she could sing.

Every time Hillary made her bed in the dorm, she straightened the sheets and comforter Tanya had picked out last February. No one had even told the college that Tanya was dead. Hillary had arrived in September and found a placard with her name and Tanya's on it, merrily welcoming them. Tanya's comforter set was packed away under Hillary's bed. She couldn't bear to offer it to the roommate the college assigned her, some mousy girl from New York.

Mom and Dad had suggested Hillary go to either church or a therapist, but neither one could undo what had happened, could they? She had asked for money for a private investigator to find Mr. Roper, make sure he was okay. "You're obsessed," Mom had said. "Sweetheart, let it go." But she couldn't, at least not until she made some sense of it.

Oh, God, don't let Tanya's death be for nothing.

Amy sat on the front step, nursing a cup of coffee. November had crept in on silent feet. The few trees on this street were barren now, the leaves clogging the gutters or blowing across the scant yards. She had slept only a few hours this morning after a tough night working the ER. Something had driven her out of bed and outside to the brisk air to pray, though she wasn't sure exactly what she should be praying about.

The kids, of course. Always the kids. Praying that they would navigate tough childhoods. Praising God as she saw them hang tough. Amy knew where they were coming from—she had grown up on the streets of Dorchester, a working-class neighborhood of Boston. Her father was unknown, her mother a hardworking nurse's aide. Her older sister was always off with some guy or another; her younger brother had been adopted out to an aunt in New Jersey. By the time she was ten, Amy ran lookout for the local drug dealers. It was a quick way to make money, and cops didn't suspect a pudgy white girl with a head full of curls.

The day the turf war started, Amy ended up on the front porch of a house where the Holy Roller lived; at least that's what her friends called the old lady who ran the after-school program. Kids who went there were babies, everyone said.

But the front hall smelled like chocolate, and as scared as Amy was, she was hungry too. She went in, ate a brownie, watched the kids play a game that wasn't totally uncool, heard a story about a kid named David who was totally cool, and kept coming.

In high school, she did her homework in the Holy Roller's office—Corinne Suarez was her real name—and then helped when the younger kids arrived. She went to church and wept when she felt God squeeze her heart dry and then fill it with Himself. She went to nursing school on full scholarship and the beaming approval of her mother and Corinne. It was a tough road, and she had setbacks, but when Amy couldn't find God, He held her tight.

Amy fell in love, then let her love go when God called him to Bosnia to build schools. Jonathan wanted her to go too, but she knew God wanted to bring her to another place. She was still young, and God was always good—someday she might find love again and have her own children. But even now He filled her life with His kids, and His joy.

Thank You, Lord. But there's something nagging at me . . .

Maggie. A lovely spirit, but Amy could sense turmoil. "Loose ends" was how Maggie described it. A soul up for grabs was how Amy saw it.

Then there were the Astaroths. What insane, foul purpose was driving them? There was still almost a year left on Safe Haven's lease. Would Theo wait, or as implied in every grim leer, would he resort to other means to drive them out? Was the snake only the first of many deadly threats?

The least of them—the children—and the lowest of places—the Beak—seemed to be at some sort of spiritual cyclone that swirled far beyond what Amy could see.

Dearest Father, keep us from this vortex. Or if You will not, then meet us there.

Theo loved the feel of earth all around him. The silence of the tomb, some might say, but he saw it as the shelter of a womb. He lay on his back, drinking in the damp solitude, feeling the heart of his world beating over him, the heart of his Mistress rising under him.

No one knew, nor would they ever know, where he went when he disappeared. This was a privilege for only him, this dirt-covered haven where the blood of the true ones still flowed. They had been the first to establish a throne for Astarte, but the early settlers of Plymouth Bay had consigned them and their efforts to death. This very ground had received the blood of their opened throats. Theo could feel them calling to him, but only here, under the ground, did he feel their blood flow through him, the true ones who had failed. He would be the true one who called the goddess of the underworld into this world until all worlds were hers.

The vortex was in place, and Theo would not fail. Let Amy Howland think she could stand against the Astaroths. Let her believe that a barrier of plywood would keep him away. When the time came, she would be the first to consecrate the altar of Astarte. And when the sacrifices were complete, the door would open and the Mistress would step through and claim Theo's seed.

I am here to do your will, Mistress. Make me strong. And make me ruthless.

Dear God, are You there?

Maggie pedaled hard, flying to the one place that might possibly hold an answer. And if not, she was racing to little arms that would at least welcome her. Seeking her own safe haven.

I love Joshua. I thought he loved me. He did, but now does he love all this more, this fame and success and the beautiful people that are his for the taking? Is there room for me in this life? I don't even know if I want there to be. I feel like a stupid kid, kicked out of kindergarten into a big world I don't understand and was never prepared for. Hanging on to Joshua, and now that he's pulling out of my hands, I'm lost.

Can I hang on to You, God? How do I know if You're real? People think Joshua is real. They long for a word from him, believe him, go away with their hearts filled, their lives somehow better. Can something that's built on lies be a good thing?

How can I know that You're real when I know that my husband is not? I'm lost, God. I know the way to Safe Haven, but that's about it.

Can You meet me there?

Twenty

"YOU AIN'T DRINKING, ROPE?" JIB SAID.

"I'm on duty." Penn had told Lazarus he had to go into the city and return the equipment. A lie, of course, since the "equipment" was a placebo, but it gave him time to examine Jib's latest shipment. "Watch how you use the name. I'm undercover here—"

Jib laughed. "I figured that. Back in the day, you couldn't grow a beard. Now you look like a flippin' Santa Claus."

Penn tossed Jib another beer. He'd love to sit back, swap stories about the old days, and drink himself into oblivion. But he was always on call for Joshua Lazarus, in more ways than that fool could even imagine. His laptop and his desktop computer took in data all the time. Letting him know of the man's whereabouts. Listening when he spoke. Speaking back as needed. Oblivion would have to wait.

"So what's the story on that lump of chaw I sent you?" Penn asked.

"Like you thought. Five-methoxy-DMT and bufotenine."

"Epena."

"You want someone to believe they've got two heads, give them a whiff of that stuff—"

"—and they're off buying an extra hat. Yeah, yeah."

"So who's chewin' it?"

"That's my problem, not yours," Penn snapped. "You got all new stuff?"

"You understand why this took some time, don't you?"

"Holoprojection without a light source is unheard of, at least in the journals and trades."

"But we got ways 'round that." Jib opened a cardboard tube, shook out what looked like Mylar sheets. "You lay these over the windows wherever you want to play your games. No one's even gonna notice if you take time to get them flat. Even the adhesive they gave me is transparent. You set up your transmitters outside—you only need four, but you gotta get the engineering right when you set them up."

"No narrow foci. I can't have my subject able to track a beam back."

"That's where the lasers come in. The sheets act like a computer monitor in the sense that the lasers will excite the electrons, but they also act like projectors." Jib played roughneck, but he had a deep technical background that had served his customers well.

"The light will be visible, then. I can't have that, Jib."

"Chill, man. Let me finish. As the laser comes through the sheets, it might shimmer a bit, but you really won't see anything until the focus reaches the distance that the computer specifies. This won't be a true hologram, you understand. You'd need a flippin' Cray supercomputer to be making that happen. Working from a laptop, you can't get the true depth."

"Doesn't have to be. Only has to be fairly recognizable."

"The image will waver too. The distance of the projection and the refresh capability of the laptop won't allow the image to hold steady. It'll look like a ghost."

For the first time that day, Penn smiled.

When Amy got off the phone, she heard the rumble of the vacuum. She came out of the office to find Maggie cleaning the playroom. "Hey, I'll do that," Amy said. "Isn't your ride due here?"

"I rode my bike today."

"Oh. Let me drive you home, then."

Maggie burst out crying.

Amy handed her a tissue. "You gonna tell me what happened to your face, or do I get to make it up?"

"It's nothing, really. I tripped in the kitchen, hit a knob on the cupboard." Maggie walked to the window. "Is Theo out there?"

"No doubt. Where else would that freak go?"

"What does he want?"

"What we all want at one time or another. To be God."

"Even you, Amy?"

"I became a nurse to heal the world. What a shock to realize I needed healing first."

"I never wanted to be God," Maggie said. "I just wanted to belong."

"And you do. You just don't know it. Yet."

"You're always so sure. Like you have a pipeline to heaven or something."

Amy laughed. "I do. It's called the Holy Spirit."

"How do you know any of it's even real?"

"Because God proves His love, over and over. Let me tell you how He's done that for me . . ."

Annette was sleek and velvet in his arms. They had started the evening in a restaurant. Then there was a movie—a romantic comedy that Penn forced himself to chuckle at while she laughed aloud. Then back to her condo for a brandy and a make-out session on her sofa.

"You're tense," she whispered. "Let me rub those knots out of your neck for you."

"You don't have to—"

Annette kissed his forehead. "I know I don't have to. Sit up. I'll massage your shoulders."

He slid to the floor, sitting so his back was to Annette. "Excited about the trip?"

"A month in the Caribbean? Who wouldn't be?"

"Tiffany's didn't put up too much of a fuss, I hope."

"I've been there so long, I could take a year off and not use up my vacation time." She worked her fingers into his neck. "You're strong. Well built."

"Lots of hard work." Months of training, rousing muscles and skills from long ago, had changed him almost completely. A hard body to go with the hard heart—there must be some poetic justice there somewhere.

She slowed the massage, her hands brushing the back of his neck. He realized she was waiting for a return compliment. "Whereas you come by your beauty naturally."

Annette leaned over, kissed Penn behind his ear. "You said I'd meet Tanya before we left. When is that going to happen?"

"Soon," he said. "Maybe even tonight."

Twenty-one

MAGGIE COULDN'T FACE JOSHUA. NOT UNTIL SHE HAD A CHANCE to think things through. "Amy, is it okay if I spend the night here?"

"Sure. You take the bed."

"I thought you had tonight off."

"I do, but you're the guest—"

"No way! I'll sack out down here, on the sofa. Is that okay?"

"If you don't mind the cracker crumbs, stickers, puzzle pieces . . ."

"The joy of my life." Maggie's laugh came out as a sob.

"Hey. Can I help?"

Maggie shrugged.

"Is this a boyfriend problem? Family? Has someone hurt you? Maggie, I'd love to help."

"No . . . I just need some space, time to think some stuff through."

"Okay. But if you run into a wall, try sticking a little prayer in."

Maggie *had* been praying steadily. If God had something to say, He was being awfully quiet about it.

"He'll answer, Maggie," Amy said, her voice suddenly soft.

"You reading my mind now?"

"It's written all over your face."

"I'm trying to make that connection, I really am."

"Don't try. Let God come to you. Your job is just to listen."

Amy went upstairs and came back with a blanket and pillow. "If you have any more questions, come upstairs and get me."

Maggie smiled. *She's so sure, God. If only I could be too . . .*

Amy got down on her knees.

There's so much in this place that abhors Your Spirit, dear Father. So many around us that want to hurt—destroy—Your children. And Maggie's one of yours, I'm sure of that. So I ask You to command Your angels to hold her up, to guard her in all her ways.

Cold air brushed the back of Amy's neck. She pulled on a sweatshirt, got back on her knees. The cold intensified, working into her legs. She got up, checked the window. The once magnificent house was now little more than a wreck—the windows were loose, air leaking in around all the sashes. She couldn't turn up the heat—Safe Haven couldn't afford it.

Amy slipped her hands under her sleeves. She tried to rub out the rash of goose bumps, but her hands were like ice. She grabbed the phone and dialed a familiar number.

After a mumbled hello and a sheepish apology, Amy got to the heart of the matter. "Patrick, we need to pray."

Listen, Amy had said. How could Maggie do that with the tag-team match going on in her head? Joshua, Geneva, Amy, Dane, Charlie, Theo. Tumbling around, coming up again. Joshua, Dawna, Manny, Charlie. Even Ben was in the mix, turning over and over.

Maybe she should go outside, walk around the block a few times. No, she wasn't that stupid. She grabbed a Bible. That lesson on everything that was *true and right* had helped with Charlie's bad dreams. If nothing else, reading might help her sleep.

Maggie's note was crumpled on the seat.

> *Joshua—I just don't know you, and I don't even know me anymore. I need some time to think, so I'm going to stay at Safe Haven for a while. I'll call Ben when I'm ready to be picked up.*
>
> *—Maggie*

A while? Was that hours? Days? Or indefinitely? Joshua had borrowed Geneva's Lexus to try to track Maggie down. He could have called Ben to take him; the man certainly knew the way. But he didn't want everyone knowing that Maggie had run away from him.

Calling this neighborhood the Beak was a compliment. Hookers cruised up and down, miniskirted despite the cold. Drug dealers nodded, assuming he was here to score. Bikers in hoods roared up one street, then down another in a mindless circle.

Maggie had no business coming to a place like this. It wasn't like she could change the world, or even change this corner of it. It was up to these people to work hard, make something of themselves. They needed to watch out for their own children and not expect his wife to do it.

Finally, Safe Haven. The house at 42 Dunstable Street was almost as rundown as the rest of the houses on the block. At least there were bars on the windows and a steel front door.

He pulled to a stop, entertaining some notion about banging on the door and demanding that Maggie come home. What if she refused? He couldn't throw her over his shoulder and force her.

Joshua loved her so much. He didn't mean to be a jerk, didn't think he was being a jerk, but she had been so hurt. Wounded by what was simply an innocent moment. He hated to see her hurt—hated to hurt Maggie. But if she wanted to support his career, she'd have to develop a thicker skin.

He needed her so much. Why couldn't it be like it used to, Maggie always at his side?

Joshua opened the window and let the night air soothe his frayed nerves.

Sola . . . show me what I need to know.

A cloud passed in front of the moon. The wind picked up, howling through the car window. Joshua turned on the heater at full blast, but his hands were suddenly frozen. What was he thinking? Maggie would come home when she realized what a fool she'd been.

Thank you, he breathed. He pulled away from the curb and headed for home.

The sun stung Maggie's eyes. Morning already? She blinked hard, trying to fight the bright light. She had thought reading would quiet her. Instead, the Bible had created a fury inside her—every hope, fear, hurt, and disappointment and beauty, wonder, and love had been pulled out of her bones and tossed into the chaos of her mind.

Jesus had made all these claims: *I am the light of the world. I am the way and the truth and the life. I am the gate for the sheep.* And in one section, just *I am.*

Jesus knew who He was. But who was Maggie? At their best, her parents had no interest in her. At their worst, she was a prime target for insults and slaps. She had worked hard to get out of that trailer, saving money for college, resolving to make something of herself.

The summer after high school, she met Joshua Lazanby. Met him, knew him, loved him, married him. Joshua became her husband and her idol. But the truth was coming clear—this man, whom she loved with her whole being, was just as human as she was. And right now, human meant confused, lost, frightened, alone, knowing she was not right inside and yet not being able to make anything right herself.

The Bible said that God knew every hair on Maggie's head and that He sent the most precious part of Himself to die for her—because she was just as precious to him.

Maggie slid off the sofa and onto her knees. *Oh, God, is this really true?*

LET ME LOVE YOU, AND YOU WILL KNOW IT IS.

She buried her face in her hands. *I don't know—*

LET ME LOVE YOU.

I don't know how—

LET ME.

Okay.

For God, who said, "Let light shine out of darkness," made his light shine in our hearts to give us the light of the knowledge of the glory of God in the face of Christ.

2 Corinthians 4:6

Twenty-two

"I'M GONNA BE RICH!" DAWNA DANCED IN HER CHAIR, EYES bright and hair bouncing.

"You won't be rich if you don't hold still," Maggie said. Four years as Joshua's assistant had given her a lot of skills, but performing illusions on a squirming nine-year-old wasn't one of them.

Maggie pulled a coin from Dawna's nose, bringing gales of laughter from the boys.

"Boogies!" Pedro shouted.

"Oh, gross." Maggie held the quarter in her palm like it was radioactive. "I guess we don't want this one." She closed her fingers over it, waved a silk, then opened her hand and it was gone.

"Hey, I would have taken it," Charlie protested.

Maggie widened her eyes. "Really?"

"Yeah, I could just wash it— Gross!" Charlie looked cross-eyed at the quarter Maggie had just pulled from his nose.

"Is that the one that was in Dawna's nose?" Manny asked, gagging dramatically.

"I don't know," Maggie said. "Smell it and tell me."

Before he could jump away, she had "disappeared" it into Manny's nose. He grabbed a tissue and blew his nose until his face turned red.

"Okay, enough. Go eat your snacks while I cut the ropes. Then I'll teach you that trick."

Amy was in the front room, talking on the phone to Natalia's social worker. It seemed like all these kids had professional support of one kind or another—social workers, psychologists, teacher's aides. "It's all meaningless without Jesus," Amy said.

Now Maggie knew what Amy meant. She hadn't had a chance to talk to her yet—she had fallen asleep at dawn and slept until the kids arrived. Maybe Amy already knew—the love that filled Maggie was so immense that it had to be leaking out of her skin.

Maggie was cutting rope in the kitchen, keeping one eye on the kids eating their snacks, when the doorbell chimed. "I'll get it," Amy called out.

Maggie heard the door open, muted speaking, and then, as the visitors came down the hall, a voice she knew as well as her own.

"Thanks for showing me around. I've heard so much about the good work you do."

Joshua! They were in the dining room now. Too late for her to close the door to the kitchen. Maggie went to the fridge and pretended to be busy with shaking ice cubes into a pitcher of juice.

"Listen up, guys and gals. You know Mr. Freeman," Amy said. "The mayor of Raven? He came to visit us last Halloween and brought those doughnuts and apple cider. Remember?"

"Hi, Mr. Freeman," Dawna called out. "Did you bring doughnuts today?"

"Just a bag of bubble gum. Is that okay?"

"Bummer, man," Pedro said.

"You'll survive," Amy said. "And this is Mr. Lazarus. He's new to Raven."

"Hi, Mr. Lazarus," Charlie yelled out, not to be outdone by Dawna.

"Hey. I saw you on TV on *The Other Side* show, right?" Manny said.

"That's me."

"Wow. That show is so cool. Especially when you talk—"

"Thank you, Manny. Mayor, Mr. Lazarus, I'd like to introduce our volunteer. If I can persuade her to come out of that refrigerator."

Maggie turned, holding two pitchers of juice like a shield.

"Maggie Deschenes," Amy said.

Maggie smiled at the mayor. She nodded in Joshua's direction.

"Nice to meet you," Joshua said.

"You too." It felt like a sheet of ice separated them.

"Listen, Amy, I've got to run," the mayor said. "Would you mind giving Joshua a tour? He's really interested in the work you do here."

"Sure." Amy showed Joshua the downstairs and then took him out into the backyard. Maggie watched as they inspected the rotted weeping willow tree. Safe Haven couldn't afford to bring in the tree experts necessary to cut it down. Joshua saw Maggie in the window and smiled.

She turned around, found Dawna, and hugged her.

"What's that for, Maggie?"

"Just for being you."

Dawna hugged her back.

"What's that for, Dawna?"

"Amy said she prayed and God sent you. So I better be nice to you if God's on your side."

"She said that?"

"Yep."

"Well, then," Maggie said. "If Amy said it, it must be true."

Money like this was always a temptation, especially with the Astaroths mounting one legal challenge after another to evict them. And there was always more they could be doing for the kids. Even so, Amy knew what had to be done.

"I'm sorry, Mr. Lazarus, but we can't accept this."

"Why not? You obviously need the money. This could pay for the cleanup of the backyard. Bring in some swings and slides, maybe put in a basketball court."

Amy handed the check back to him. "May I suggest a donation to the North Shore Children's Hospital? Or perhaps the Raven Food Bank. There are many fine charities in this area who would appreciate such generosity."

"I don't understand why you won't take the check."

Maggie stood wide-eyed, watching the exchange. Amy needed to choose her words carefully. "As a Christian mission, we are selective about how we fund our work. I'm sure you understand."

"No. I am afraid I don't understand, Miss Howland."

"Amy, it's ten thousand dollars," Maggie said. "We could do so much with it."

Amy took Lazarus's arm, trying to guide him into the front hall. "It's been a pleasure meeting you. Our kids are finishing their snacks and they'll be looking for us. Maggie, could you go check on them, please?"

Lazarus pulled his arm away. "I'd appreciate an answer to my question."

Amy sighed. Most people got the hint by now. "Tell me about your show, Mr. Lazarus."

"What does that have to do with my donation?"

"It's the source of your wealth, isn't it?"

He crossed his arms over his chest. "I thought you were familiar with *The Other Side.* That's what you said."

"I know how I see it. I'm curious as to how *you* characterize what you're doing."

Maggie came back in, apparently determined to watch the exchange.

"Like you, my ministry involves helping people. People may come to me with heavy hearts, wanting to be assured their dear one is at peace. Or maybe they've had a great joy like a wedding or a birth and they want to make sure that their loved ones on the other side know."

"Is it always one or the other reaction?" Maggie said.

"No, no. We've got our skeptics—perhaps like you, Miss Howland—who come expecting to prove me a fraud. They always go away believers. Always." His eyes burned with a dark passion. "They believe because I am *not* a fraud. I do speak to those on the other side of this life, and I bring back words of comfort and assurance and, yes—love. These are scarce commodities in this world. You know that, Amy."

Shifting into the familiar, his voice was warm, intimate. Amy glanced at Maggie to see if he was working his magic on her. She had an odd look on her face, as if confusion was chasing belief. The question was—belief in what?

Lazarus continued. "You do great work here, Amy. But the truth is that even if you raise one or two of these children out of this neighborhood, they will still face the one certainty of this life."

"That's right. We all have to give an accounting to God for what we've done with the gift of life that He's given us," Amy said softly.

Lazarus smiled. "I'm not here to disrespect your religion. But you know that there's only one way out of this life. Whether a child is from the Beak or Hawthorne Neck, we *all* face death. And unless one is an absolute fool, he or she will face death with a certain amount of fear."

Sweat pooled in the small of Amy's back; self-restraint was exhausting. "A Christian faces death with joy and anticipation."

"We all have a point of view. I offer the bridge that allows everyone—not just people of one religion or another—a way to see past the uncertainty that lies at the end of this life. My viewers know they have nothing to fear from death because what lies on the other side is good. So I ask you again, Amy. Tell me what in your religion forbids you to take my money."

"I'd rather tell you what riches God offers *you*."

"Not the subject at hand; therefore, I am not interested."

"You should be."

"Oh, really? It's all coming clear now. You're one of *those*—you get little kids in here and scare them into submission. You don't want them coming to me, because with me they have nothing to fear. Once they realize that, you lose your hold on them."

Amy held up her hand, trying to manage her anger. "They do have something to fear—and that is you, Mr. Lazarus. *You* are not the bridge to the other side, and it is despicable of you to say so. Jesus Christ is, and by standing in His place, you not only blaspheme Him but you deceive thousands, maybe millions of people, if your press releases about your ratings are to be believed."

Maggie touched her arm. "You're being a bit harsh."

Lazarus ignored Maggie and kept his gaze on Amy. "Aha, so you are familiar with the show! I bet you watch just so you can hate me."

"I pray for you every Friday night and not because I hate you. Because I *fear* for you," Amy said.

"Pray all you want—but you have no right to tell me that I'm deceiving anyone."

"But you are! You package a devilish lie as entertainment. You practice deception—don't think I believe for a second that what you do is genuine—and you do it to make money and gain fame. I pray with all my heart that you turn away before it's too late."

Lazarus turned to Maggie. "Are you going to stand there and let her talk to me like that?"

"Don't bring my volunteer into this," Amy snapped.

"What? She can't speak for herself? Is that not allowed here? What do you say, volunteer? Do you think it's *Christian* for Amy to talk to me like this?"

Maggie's face flushed.

The air seemed to spark between Lazarus and Maggie. More than just some initial attraction, Amy realized. "Maggie, do you know this guy?"

"Your boss is asking you a question, Maggie. Amy wants to know if you know me."

Maggie looked down at the floor. "He's my husband."

The three simple words slammed Amy like a cement truck.

Tears streaked Maggie's face as she reached out for Amy. "Say something."

"I honestly don't know what to say."

Lazarus whistled. "Bet that's a first."

"Shut up, Joshua," Maggie said.

Amy felt her heart skipping beats. "I don't . . . I'd better get back to the kids. We'll talk tomorrow, okay?"

Lazarus grabbed Maggie's bag from the top of the refrigerator and pushed it at her. "Let's go, Maggie."

Maggie hugged her bag like a shield, frozen with indecision.

"I said we're going," Lazarus said. "Ben's outside waiting."

Maggie looked at him, then to Amy. "I'm so sorry. I should have told you, but as you can see, my situation is . . . complicated."

Lazarus took her arm and steered her toward the hall. "It's not complicated at all. You're my wife; your loyalty is with me. Period."

Maggie shook him off, her eyes still fixed on Amy. "Can you forgive me for . . . not telling you?"

A strange peace came over Amy and a gentleness that she heard in her own voice. "Maggie, it's done. But I need to ask you this: Is he why you came here last night?"

She nodded. "We had a fight."

"It's over, Maggie. I apologized," Lazarus said.

Amy held up her hand. "Leave the room now, Mr. Lazarus. I need to speak with Maggie without you butting in."

Lazarus scowled, but the resistance seemed to have gone out of him. "Maggie, I'll be in the hall. Waiting to take you home."

"Mr. Lazarus, I would prefer that you wait outside, on the front porch, if you'd please."

"Maggie, we don't have time for any more of this religious chatter. I've got work to do, a phone conference."

"Joshua, you can wait five minutes for me. Now, go outside."

He turned and walked out. Maggie came to Amy, her face a deep red now. "You see—it is complicated. He does that show, everyone knows him, he's—"

"Hey, none of that is important right now. It's you I need to think about." Amy took Maggie's hand and rubbed it between hers. "Tell me the truth. Is he a danger to you? Abusive in any way, physically or mentally?"

Maggie's eyes widened. "No. Of course not."

"Do you swear that? I can't let you go home with that guy if he might hurt you."

"Joshua has an attitude sometimes, but really, he's gentle. He wouldn't hurt me in any way . . . or at least in the way you're saying."

"No? Then how did you get this?" Amy gently touched the bruise that was coming clear as Maggie's tears washed away her makeup.

"Honest truth—I was yelling at him, stumbled, and fell against a cupboard in the kitchen."

"He didn't push you?"

"No!"

"So if you go home with him, you will not be in any immediate danger?"

"Why do you keep saying that? Do I need to swear it on a Bible or something? Joshua wouldn't hurt me."

Amy wanted to shake Maggie and tell her about the spiritual danger her husband represented. *Lord, You're holding me back because You're working; I can feel it. But please don't let me be doing the wrong thing here by letting her go. Please protect her.*

"Maggie, you coming?" Lazarus was in the doorway, tapping the wall with his fingers.

Amy hugged her. "Go home and try to work through whatever needs your attention. Let's talk tomorrow morning."

Maggie nodded to Amy, then followed him out.

Moments later the door slammed, and as if in unison, something crashed in the dining room, Dawna screamed, Manny cursed, Charlie laughed.

Lord, here we go. All hell is breaking loose . . .

twenty-three

JOSHUA PACED THE BEDROOM LIKE A CAGED TIGER.

"So that's who you've been spending time with? A pasty-faced, acid-mouthed religious fanatic! I swear, Maggie, if she's been brainwashing you, I'll sue the living daylights out of her. What did she do to you last night? Beat you with the Bible? Or drag you off to some prayer meeting where they could heal you by destroying our marriage?"

Last night. It seemed like an eternity ago that Maggie had wrestled with herself and ended up in God's loving arms. To have this blowup before she even had a chance to tell Amy seemed cruel. What happened to her safe haven? And yet, this wasn't just about her—Joshua was her husband, and she needed to deal with the growing gap between them.

"Joshua, I need to know something. Have those spirits talked to you again?"

He went rigid.

"Joshua . . ."

"Who said they did?"

"No one. I'm just asking."

"What do you care?"

Maggie trailed her fingertips along his jaw. "I care because I love you."

"You left me and ran to that woman? She accused me of being the devil incarnate."

"She can get carried away, can't she?" Maggie laughed, amazed at the peace flooding her. "I'm sorry, Joshua. I should have stopped the . . . um . . . discussion a lot sooner. I was caught short by you showing up there."

"I was scared, Mags. You promised you'd never leave me, and then . . . you left me. On your bike, of all things."

"I just had to get away for the night. I needed time to think. But look, I'm here now." She took his face in her hands, kissed his forehead.

He flushed. "I practically dragged you out of there, didn't I?"

"I would have come without the theatrics. I really would have."

"I'm not so sure."

"Joshua, I mean it. I love you." As soon as the words left her lips, her heart soared. This was a surprise—somehow loving God meant her love for Joshua was stronger, despite everything that had come between them.

"Even though your friend thinks I'm a deceiver and blasphemer?"

"Yes."

"Do you think that?"

"Joshua, I know your heart is good. The rest we'll worry about later."

Suddenly he was holding her so tight she could barely breathe. "I'm such a jerk, trying to buy you back with ten thousand dollars. Can you forgive me?"

Another surprise—she could forgive as easily as she had been forgiven. "It's done. Done and forgotten."

"Maggie, don't leave me."

"I have no intention of leaving you." That was *her* truth.

But she didn't know where God's truth might lead her.

Maggie and Joshua snuggled at the edge of the back lawn. They had dragged quilts off the bed and made a nest of satin to watch the night from. They were at the highest point on the property, where the wind swept over them like a cold, clean hand. To the north, a cliff face looked down over a rockfall and crashing surf. To the east and south, the lawn eased down into scrub pine, then a narrow beach.

"Maggie, I've made a decision."

"To go inside?"

"Not until we count all the stars in that beautiful sky up there."

"You're either a romantic or an idiot."

"Guilty to both," he said, kissing her cheek. "You can throw *jerk* in there if you'd like."

"I've let it go. You need to."

"Is that what Amy is teaching you down at the Safe Haven? To turn the other cheek?"

Maggie laughed. "You mean that pasty-faced—what did you call her?"

"I thought we were letting this go."

"I just want you to know, Mr. Salon Tan, that Amy Howland is pasty-faced because she works the overnight shift at the hospital. She sleeps most of the day, then works with the kids. Doesn't leave much time for going to the beach."

"Saint Amy, huh?" Jealousy edged his voice.

"It's a good thing she does. That we do."

"That's why I tried to give her money! Isn't pride a sin? Because she is so proud she's outright rude," Joshua said.

"It's not pride you saw. It's conviction."

"Yeah—well, there's a fine line there."

Maggie's newborn faith bubbled up. "I need to tell you something."

"Go ahead, Princess."

Suddenly the sky was too big. A chill worked between her and Joshua even though she could feel his breath on her face, his heart beating against hers.

"You go first. You wanted to tell me about some decision."

"On this Friday's show, I'm going to explain that the picture of Cassie and me was something completely innocent. Honestly, Maggie, we had just had a drink, then she was leaving, leaned over to kiss me, and—"

"Please spare me the details. I believe you already."

"I want you there with me so everyone will understand how there's only one woman for me. They'll have no trouble believing that when they see my wife."

The wind picked up. Maggie had to bury deep into the quilts. November was half over—soon the snow and icy surf would keep them inside. "I don't want to offend your demographic."

"Honestly, I think the only reason Dane wants me to act like I'm single is so he can meet all the cool chicks that come around."

"He's not the only one."

"What do you mean?"

"Geneva. She wants you to really be single. You know that."

"Geneva's not the one you need to worry about. If you appear on the show as my wife, Amy might make you leave Safe Haven. She won't want you leading those kids astray now, will she? It's your call, Mags. What do you want to do?"

"I don't know . . ." She didn't know *anything*—what she had just heard in her heart, how to obey God's call on her life, how to love the children of Safe Haven the way they deserved and her husband the way she wanted to.

"I don't like that Amy's attitude, but you guys do good work. If you want to keep us quiet and stay there, I can learn to live with it. As long as she's not bad-mouthing me all the time."

"Bad-mouthing is not in Amy's nature."

Joshua laughed. "Are you kidding? I'm still pulling out her darts. Do you need time to think it out?"

Oh, God, forgive me, Maggie prayed. *I don't have a clue what I'm doing.*

"I want to stay at Safe Haven . . . but I'm your wife. That comes first. So if you're ready to introduce me to the world, I would be proud."

twenty-four

JOSHUA HAD MET AMY HOWLAND FOR ONLY TEN MINUTES, BUT her words seemed stuck to the front side of his brain. *You not only blaspheme Him but you deceive thousands, maybe millions . . .*

Under it all, another voice, whispering, *Joshua . . .*

He would love to wake Maggie, talk this out with her. But he didn't dare rock their already shaky boat. He needed to get away where he could think. No matter how big this mansion was, it wasn't his space. Not like his office was.

Joshua should just drive there now—except they still hadn't gotten a car for their personal use. He could wake Geneva up to borrow the Lexus, but she'd want to go with him, defeating the whole purpose of getting away. Then there was the camper, but who knew if it would even start?

He called Ben. This was what they paid him for, after all.

His voice was thick with sleep. "No problem. Just give me a little time . . ."

"Never mind, Ben. You don't have to—"

"Yes, I do. I can hear it in your voice. Give me a few minutes to shower, get dressed, have some coffee. I'll be there before you know it, Mr. Lazarus."

Penn shimmied down from the tree, trying not to laugh. He had set up over half a million dollars of top-secret, ultra-high-tech toys up here a few days back. It had just been a matter of climbing up and turning on the power. The windows were coated, the sound checked, the lasers fired up, the files loaded on his laptop and ready to transmit. All systems go.

Time to resurrect the dearly departed.

Joshua stared into the candle, trying to empty his mind. He didn't even know how this litany had started. But the words came so fluently that he knew he prayed as he should. "Sola, open your gates, grant your secrets, guide my hand, send your spirits to speak . . ."

Joshua . . .

This was the moment of truth, the moment when he either turned his back on this or grasped it for all it was worth.

Joshua . . .

"I'm here."

And I am here . . .

He scanned the room. The desk, sofa, two chairs, credenza were all solid in the candlelight. The only other light was moonlight, dappling the floor with silver.

"Who are you?"

I had a violent passing . . .

"I'm sorry. Did someone hurt you?"

Too afraid. He lingers nearby . . .

Joshua sat on his hands to stop them from shaking. His feet started then, a rapid *tap-tap-tap.* "What can I do to help you?"

I can't reach the other side . . .

"I don't understand." He trembled so hard his chair rattled. "Tell me your name."

Annette . . .

"Annette." He said it again, letting it sink in.

Don't leave me . . .

"I'm staying right here, Annette. Can you tell me your last name?"

I can't . . . don't . . . nothing to be known here, in the dark . . .

"If you're not on the other side, then where are you?"

Under the bridge. Over temptation.

"What bridge?"

Over temptation.

"I don't understand."

Dark. Waiting for the tide . . .

"If I go to the police, will they know you?"

Cold. Tell the ones who believe . . .

"The police must be looking for you."

They don't believe. Tell the real believers.

Of course—his viewers, numbering in the millions now. Someone might know this Annette. He could do it at the end of the show.

I want to rest . . .

Something clanked against the window. Joshua jumped, his heart punched with a rush of adrenaline.

This could not be. Simply could not be.

An image pressed against and then through the glass. It took shape in the middle of the room, little more than a splash of color and dust motes that resolved into an elegant woman in a business suit. Her hair and eyes were dark, but her smile was bright.

Look what he did . . .

The image blurred, and now she was naked and lifeless, her head slumped to one side. Her eyes were open but empty.

Tell tell tell . . .

He felt rather than saw the wisp of colors wrapping around him, red leaking through his eyelids even though he was squeezing them shut.

Tell tell tell . . .

Then she was gone.

twenty-five

AMY DIDN'T KNOW WHETHER TO CRY, "GLORY HALLELUJAH!" OR to tear her hair out.

Maggie had come to her on Friday morning with simple words—"Jesus came to me, and I said yes"—that made everything wonderful and everything complicated. They had been talking for an hour now, with Amy rejoicing and yet absolutely confounded. How could she let the wife of an occult entertainer volunteer at Safe Haven? And yet, could she turn away someone God had called?

"Why didn't you tell me you were married to him?"

Maggie chewed her thumbnail. "The producers wanted people to think he was single. To keep the female fans on the edge of their seats, I guess."

"Maggie, you know you could have told me. Right?"

She nodded.

"What's the real reason, then?" Amy kept her voice soft—she had come on too strong yesterday. Maggie needed a gentler hand than the one she had whacked Lazarus with.

"I feel terrible about lying to you, but even early on, I felt that part of my life and this just didn't mix. Maybe you can explain why—I kind of know it in my gut, but I don't know how to explain it to Joshua."

"As a Christian mission, we can't have anything to do with the occult."

"Occult? But that's devil stuff, right? Joshua doesn't do any of that stuff."

"Anything that has to do with the supernatural—outside of the God of the Bible, the God revealed in Jesus—falls into the occult. People get involved in a lot of stuff just for fun. Like Ouija boards. Crystal balls."

"Astrology?" Maggie asked.

"A great example! Horoscopes sometimes seem right on, but—"

"—they're often so vague they could apply to almost anything, if you wanted them to."

"Exactly. Then you've got all these folks here in Raven who practice witchcraft as a commercial venture. They don't want to be accused of Satanism, so they adopt this Wicca stuff. Worshiping the things of nature and pretending to have power that is as old as the earth itself."

Maggie nodded slowly. "What about the Astaroths? What kind of freaks are they?"

"Astaroth is an ancient name for some demon. If I had the time, I'd do the research, but I'm betting Theo is making up his own mythology."

Maggie put her hand to her mouth. "You're not putting Joshua in the same class as Theo!"

"All of us are in the same class—Joshua, Theo, you, me, even Charlie or Dawna. Joshua is a sinner, but so am I. The difference is that you and I have been saved by grace, while your Joshua is still treading some very dangerous waters—and wackos like Theo are feeding the sharks."

Maggie was very still.

"That's enough for now," Amy said. "This is too much, too soon for you to take in."

Maggie slammed her hand down on the table. "Stop treating me like a baby! Everyone does that, and I'm sick of it. Tell me all of it."

"One condition, then—we pray. Right now. I want to make sure God is guiding this conversation and not my frustrations. You up for that?"

Maggie reached for Amy's hand. "You go, girl."

They bowed their heads.

The dead have spoken.

Would the fool believe?

Penn shook his head. The question was rhetorical: of course Lazarus would believe. His ego was voracious, swallowing anything in its path that pointed to his glory. Sure, he'd dance around, playing hard to get, making sure he would look like a prophet and not an idiot. Lazarus was a fish nosing the bait, waiting for one more jiggle before he was hooked.

The fool thought that Penn was in Boston right now, visiting his FBI pals to borrow more sophisticated equipment to scan Lazarus's office. Instead, he was in his apartment, working at his laptop, encrypting the images of Annette so it would take a miracle to open them.

Annette. Blushing when Penn said he wanted a picture of her to put in his office. Posing with dignity once he got her to agree.

Annette. Still able to be posed because rigor hadn't yet set in. Eyes glued open, head taped so it wouldn't loll, hands arranged on transparent Plexiglas so they extended toward the camera. A lovely woman, somewhat sad, sweetly genteel, and subtly sophisticated. A dead woman, a righteous sacrifice for the cause.

The fool would believe.

Penn tapped the keys and sent the last gasp of Annette into cyber-oblivion.

"Joshua misleads people when he makes it seem that their loved ones have come back from the grave to say hi," Amy said.

"But what if people come away feeling so much better? Joshua certainly changed Julia Madsen's life. She was about to commit suicide. Now she's back in Hollywood, working and helping others."

"This stuff is like cocaine—it may make you feel like a million bucks, but eventually it'll destroy you."

"What if Joshua really can look into heaven? Wouldn't that mean God approved?"

"He can't."

"How can you—how can *we*—be so sure that this isn't something God has given Joshua to do for Him?"

"He can't be speaking to dead people because Scripture says so. Jesus tells a parable about a beggar named Lazarus—"

"You're kidding, right? That's his name?"

Amy fidgeted with her spoon, stirring tea that had long ago gone cold. "That's his name. In this parable, Lazarus begged at the gate of this rich guy. Every day, the rich guy walked right by, as if Lazarus meant no more to him than the stones under his feet. The only comfort the beggar received was when the dogs would lick his sores."

"Gross. That didn't really happen, right?"

"It's a parable. An illustration of a real truth. In the story, both Lazarus and the rich guy died. The rich guy was in torment in hell when he looked up at heaven and saw Abraham. Do you know who Abraham is?"

"I know the God of Abraham, Isaac, and Jacob. But exactly who Abraham was . . ."

"He was a patriarch of the Old Testament. A very faithful man. God built the nation of Israel from him and his descendents. Anyway, the rich man saw the beggar Lazarus in heaven, being comforted at the side of Abraham. He begged Abraham to send Lazarus with just one drop of water to cool his tongue. But Abraham refused."

"Why? I mean, God is supposed to be merciful and kind, right? Shouldn't Abraham jump at the chance to help the rich man?"

"Even God has a limit, and this rich man had surpassed it. When the rich man begged Abraham to send Lazarus to warn his brothers who were still alive, Abraham says he couldn't because . . . wait, let me get my Bible so I can quote it correctly." Amy read, "' . . . between us and you a great chasm has been fixed, so that those who want to go from here to you cannot, nor can anyone cross over from there to us.'"

"What does that mean?"

"That God does not allow people to cross over between heaven, hell, and this life."

"But angels come to earth. So isn't Lazarus an angel?"

Amy smiled. "Angels are not men and women, and we do not become angels when we die."

"So are angels better than us?"

"Nope, just different. In fact, only humans—you and me and Charlie and even Theo—are created in God's image."

"So what does this story prove?"

"That your husband cannot speak to the dead."

Maggie's insides twisted. "But what if he is? I mean, what if he actually hears voices?"

Amy covered her face with her hands.

"Don't hold back, Amy. You swore you'd tell me everything."

Amy looked up, her eyes solemn. "If he hears voices, he's in serious trouble."

"Why?"

"Because he's either insane or . . ." Amy took a deep breath, let it out.

"The thing is this, Maggie: if Joshua really hears voices that give him genuine information, then he's hearing demons. And that is a very dangerous thing."

Maggie couldn't bear this feeling of being ripped apart for a second longer. "Oh. Okay. Thank you for your time, Amy. And tell the kids I was asking for them."

She grabbed her bag, got up, and walked out of Safe Haven.

twenty-six

MAGGIE DIDN'T SAY A WORD THE WHOLE WAY BACK TO THE estate. Ben glanced at her a couple of times but respected her silence. Her insides churned—wanting to believe her husband, having to believe this Spirit now moving through her.

Ben dropped her off at the front door. "I need to run over to the office. They keep me busy on show days."

"Sure." Maggie tried to muster a smile. She was inside and punching in the code to disable the alarm when Ben drove back down the driveway.

"These were just delivered," he said. He handed Maggie a long white box, decorated with a silver ribbon and huge bow.

"Thanks."

Ben waved, then drove off.

Maggie carried the box into the kitchen. Inside were at least three dozen long-stemmed roses. The petals were a rich cream tinged with pink. The stems were deep green with finely shaped leaves.

This was like something out of a Hollywood movie, Maggie thought. So typical of Joshua to be this dramatic.

Maggie found a vase in the dining-room closet. She had become accustomed to the massive bathrooms, the two living rooms, even the library with its dark mahogany shelves and Persian rugs. But the dining room still intimidated her. Maybe it was the thought of dropping a dish on the buffet and scratching the cherry, so highly polished she could see herself. The crystal chandelier cost more than her parents' trailer.

Maggie went back to the kitchen, filled the vase with water. She pulled the roses out of the box and dug through the tissue paper until she found a card, printed in a calligraphic script with one word: *Sorry.*

Maggie buried her face in the roses and breathed deeply. The scent reminded her of hot summer days in Maine, stopping play long enough to run across the street and smell Mrs. Overhiser's roses. She would rub her cheeks against their velvet petals, dreaming that she lived in a white house with rosebushes and cherry trees and not a trailer surrounded by weeds and broken-down cars.

Something feathery brushed her eyebrow. Had a petal gotten caught in her hair? She reached up to brush it away.

It moved. She slapped at her cheek, then looked at her hand. A black mass was spread across her fingers—the remains of a huge spider.

Maggie stuffed the roses back into the box, then ran into the bathroom. She studied her face. No marks, and she hadn't felt a pinch. The thing hadn't bit her, then.

Something moved on top of her head. She stopped herself before she slapped it—she might drive the creature straight into her scalp.

Chances were that it wasn't poisonous.

No, chance didn't play a part in this at all. These flowers were not from her husband but from a warped man who delighted in snakes and spiders, especially the poisonous variety.

God, steady my hand.

She grabbed a tissue and draped it over the spider. Her hand shook. She took a deep breath; if she didn't do this right, she might cause the spider to bite. Too slow—the creature had worked under her hair. She could feel its legs against her scalp, sheltering deeper under her hair. She'd never get it out if she didn't act—

Now!

She pinched hard, wincing as she pulled out hair with the tissue. Black legs moved in the crumpled ball that she dropped into the toilet. She flushed, then flushed twice more to rid herself of the insane thought that it would climb out when she least expected.

What if there were more? They could be crawling all over the house by now.

Back in the kitchen, she wrapped a tablecloth over the flowers, the box, the ribbon, and hopefully all the spiders. She ran out the back door, across the lawn, heading for the ocean.

Joshua wanted her out of Safe Haven, and now it was obvious that Theo did too.

Where do You want me, God? And if I go there, will You protect me?

Maggie ran to the cliff and flung the roses—box and all—into the roiling ocean.

Ben had swept Joshua's office from top to bottom and again proclaimed it free of bugging or broadcasting devices. *It has to be real,* Joshua told himself as he stared into the flame. If Sola was opening the gate and letting the dead come to him, then he had to listen.

Joshua . . . A man's voice this time. Deep, authoritative.

"Who are you?"

Sola knows.

"What do you want?"

For you to believe.

"I . . . I do! Sola knows that."

Then you must tell.

"Where is Annette?"

Under the bridge over temptation . . .

"Why didn't she come back to me again?" Joshua asked, his stomach twisting as he realized he didn't want to see her again, that broken body, those lifeless eyes.

Bound by the tide now. She needs your help. Someone will hear if you will tell . . .

Joshua waited another twenty minutes, then blew out the candle.

Maggie stood at the edge of the cliff, staring down at the water. She lifted her face, trying to absorb what little warmth the sun gave this time of year. God had righted her world two days ago. Why was He now tipping her sideways and shaking her? Spirits, spooks, and spiders—it sounded like a bad movie, and yet, it was her life.

Someone poked her.

Maggie startled, then stumbled toward the edge. She would crash at the bottom—*Oh, God*—if she couldn't stop. Her feet scrambled and she stopped right at the edge.

"Geneva! You gave me a heart attack."

Geneva grabbed Maggie's shoulders. "I only tapped you, for Pete's sake. You need to be more careful."

"*I* need to be careful?"

"Absolutely. Did you tell anyone you'd be out here?"

"Why would I do that?"

"Let's say you tripped. Let's say you broke . . . oh, I don't know. An ankle, maybe. Who would know?"

Maggie wanted to yank out of her sister-in-law's grip, but an abrupt movement could send her tumbling again. "Forget it. I'm going inside. It's cold out here."

"You bet it's cold. The rocks are icy, the wind hard. You could go off balance, and *bam!*"

Maggie shifted sideways. "Let go."

Geneva tightened her grip. "Don't fight me."

"What do you want?"

"The question is, what do you want? Other than to destroy everything we worked for?"

"I have no idea what you're talking about."

"Josh wants to use tonight's closing segment to introduce you as his wife. It's a horrible career move. Not that you care, of course."

Maggie clamped her hands over Geneva's wrists. "I would do anything for him. I wish you would believe how much I love him."

Geneva leaned into her, her face so close to Maggie's that she could smell the coffee under the breath mints. "You don't know what love is."

"Do you, Geneva?"

"I love my brother so much that I would die for him. Can you say the same?" Geneva let go abruptly and walked away.

Dane and Joshua were going over the schedule with the show's director, Bruce Tanis. "We're talking about the last segment. I'm planning to set two stools up so Josh and Maggie can be side by side," Bruce said. "What color is she wearing?"

"I . . . don't know," Joshua said. He couldn't think straight. It was always like this on the show day. Decisions to be made, one more run through the audience profiles, wardrobe checks, sponsors calling. People coming at him from all directions. *Spirits* coming at him from all directions.

"Can we spring an extra two minutes out of the audience segment for introducing Maggie? I don't want to do away with the 'Messages for Home' segment," Joshua said. "I have something that needs saying."

That segment came at the end of the show, with Joshua giving messages from the other side for the viewing audience. The readings—allegedly spontaneous—were based on research involving e-mailers and letter-writers. With creative planning, they threw messages out there blind, knowing that more than one viewer would swear the reading was meant just for her or him.

Dane shook his head. "If we shortcut the audience readings, people will be ticked off."

"In that case, I'm going to reverse myself."

"Josh, we can't keep changing things around," Dane said.

"I'm not changing anything. We'll keep the 'Messages' segment. Save Maggie's introduction for some other time. Maybe around Christmastime, or when we go to the network."

Geneva smiled. "Smart thinking. But we don't have a script for the 'Messages' segment."

"Don't worry about that," Joshua said. "I've got one prepared."

Geneva gave him a strange look. "I expect to see it."

"You don't have to."

"Yes, I do."

Joshua slapped the table. "I said *no*!"

Geneva leaned back in her chair, studying him.

"Sorry, Gen. I'm stressed—but it's all under control. Listen, I've got to call Maggie," Joshua said. "She's going to be disappointed."

Dane laughed. "Disappointed? She's gonna rip your skin off, man."

"No, she will not. Your princess will survive," Geneva said. "She always does."

Dane pushed his chair back. "No time now for a long apology. We've got Gerald Remy coming in from Web-Dawg. You've got to do your thing, Josh. There's huge potential here for sponsorship."

"Ben is supposed to pick her up in half an hour," Joshua said. "I've got to let her know."

"I'll notify Ben. And I'll call Maggie for you," Geneva said.

"Tell her I'm sorry. And I'll explain later tonight. Ask her to come to the show and get her a seat in the front row. And be nice about it, okay, Gen?"

Geneva smiled. "Of course."

Maggie's fingers trembled as she applied her makeup. Joshua had promised to send Ben back to get her around six. The show started at eight, showing live on the East Coast, on tape for the rest of the country.

She finished her makeup, ate a piece of toast with a cup of tea, then sat down and waited. She wanted to ask Ben to check the house for spiders, but he was so busy on show night. And she wanted to make sure he got her to the studio on time. If she were at Safe Haven right now, she'd be starting to clean up, maybe walking some of the kids home. David Drinas had come up from Boston to help out until a decision had been made about Maggie continuing.

When she appeared on television tonight, the decision would make itself. Maggie had read enough of the Bible to know God wanted her to honor her husband. What better way than to support his calling? And yet, why was she so drawn to Safe Haven—to the children, to Amy, to God's calling?

Maggie had read and reread the passage in the Bible that they had discussed this morning. She understood what it said, but she also understood that Joshua was a wonderful man. Jesus worked through people; wasn't that what the Holy Spirit was about? Why couldn't God be working through Joshua to give people comfort and make them feel better about their departed?

Twenty minutes after six. It wasn't like Ben to be late. Maggie glanced at the alarm panel. The front gate was still closed. Traffic could be nasty on a Friday night. He was probably caught in a mess on Route 1A, or maybe there'd been another accident on the causeway out to the Neck.

Maggie made the circle of the downstairs, going from the hall to the formal living room, the dining room, back into the kitchen, out again to the other side of the downstairs, the library, the media room, the morning room, back to the front hall and the alarm panel.

Where was Ben? Six twenty-five now. Joshua wanted her at the studio by six thirty so she could have her makeup touched up. Maggie grabbed the hall phone. No answer on Ben's car phone or his cell. She tried his home phone.

No answer there. She didn't even know where he lived. She had asked, but Ben had a way of steering the conversation away from his personal life.

He must be in the studio somewhere. She should have just taken the camper over and given Dane a heart attack when the honored guest climbed out of a junk box. It wasn't too late to do that—but if Ben were on his way, she didn't want to waste his time.

She dialed Joshua's cell phone. It went straight to voice mail. He must have shut it off or left it in his dressing room. She rang the office. Beth answered. "May I ask what this is in regard to?"

"It's urgent."

"If you could state the nature of your call, ma'am?"

"This is Maggie Deschenes. I mean, Maggie Lazanby."

"Which is it?"

"Lazarus. Maggie Lazarus. It's in regard to my husband."

"Right, and I'm Cleopatra." The woman hung up before Maggie could explain. He hadn't even told his secretary that they were married?

Her stomach did a flip-flop. Had he changed his mind?

She dialed Dane. No answer. She took a deep breath and dialed Geneva.

"What?" It sounded more like a bark than a greeting.

"Joshua was supposed to send Ben to come and get me."

"What for?"

"You know what for. You yelled at me about it a few hours ago."

"Oh, that. You're not on the call sheet anymore. He came to his senses and decided against this whole stupid thing."

"You're lying."

"No, I'm not. You've been scratched for tonight."

"Send Ben to get me."

"He's busy. Useful guy, you know. Unlike some people . . ."

"Fine. I'll take the camper over."

"Go ahead. You won't get in without a ticket."

"You'll get me in or I'll stand on the sidewalk and scream that I'm Joshua's wife."

Geneva laughed. "We get two of those a week, minimum. Now get off my phone. I've got a show to run." Geneva clicked off.

Maggie threw the phone, shattering a crystal vase. Her anger dissolved into shame. How trashy, destroying someone else's property. What was wrong with her? That was the question, wasn't it? What was wrong with *her* that Joshua had forgotten—or gone back on—his promise?

twenty-seven

"GOOD THING HE CANCELED MAGGIE, HUH?" DANE WHISPERED. "I've gotten calls from some of the hottest talent in the biz, wanting intros to him. A few photos like that one with Cassie Knowles will broaden his exposure."

Geneva nodded, intent on Josh as he did a cold reading on a bearded man at the back of the audience.

"I see a uniform," Joshua was saying. "Military, perhaps?"

She looked for that subtle body language. There—that turn of the head that was a negative indicator. Joshua saw it too.

"No, that's not it. I'm seeing blue," Joshua said before the man could reply.

Eyebrows up.

"Fireman . . ."

Dead stare.

"No, a policeman. Close but not your brother . . ."

There was no pain in the man's eyes—even from the control room Geneva could tell that. What Joshua was putting into the guy's mind had to be a more distant relative, or an acquaintance.

"A cousin."

Bingo. The man straightened up and nodded. "My wife's cousin."

"A violent death."

Geneva winced. She hated it when her brother pulled that garbage. Unless they had prepared a profile, guessing how a departed had died was going way too far. Her brother claimed that the risk of error kept him fresh. Tonight he was almost frenetic in the way he went from mark to mark, doing too many cold readings and hitting more head-on than ever before. His feverish look captivated the women and intrigued the men; even Geneva felt the current of excitement in the show.

"Got run down when he stopped to help change a tire," the man said.

Josh had nailed it again.

"Counting down," Bruce said. "Ten-nine-eight . . ."

As they moved to commercial, Joshua continued speaking with the man and his wife. It wouldn't do to be too abrupt. He had a minute to counsel, then another sixty seconds to get set up for the closing segment. Why had he refused to tell Geneva what he had planned for "Messages"?

"So, Gen, this thing with Maggie," Dane said. "Who did you have to kill to make that happen?"

Geneva cursed him out. Dane just laughed. Everything was a joke for him, Geneva thought. He'd better watch it. Someday he'd laugh at the wrong guy and be sorry.

Maggie burned with anger as she watched the show. No call, nothing—Joshua had just blown her off. The commercial messages closed out and the show promo came on. The camera cut to Joshua, sitting on the stool.

He looked scared.

Spirits of Sola, spirits of flesh and bone and blood, guide my words . . .

Joshua looked straight into the camera. "Welcome back. I usually use this time to impart messages for our home viewers. Thank you for letting me know that these messages hit the mark. If they bring you comfort and assurance, then I am grateful to be able to help.

"Tonight's message will be startling to you. It certainly was to me. If you have children in the room with you, I'd ask that you'd send them out now." Joshua closed his eyes and counted a slow ten. Still time to back out.

Tell tell tell . . .

He looked up at the camera. Geneva was at stage left, whispering to Dane.

"If you have any understanding of what I'm about to reveal, please contact the proper authorities. Do not contact us here at *The Other Side.* I'm just the messenger—if this message means something to you, then you'll know how to act on it."

"Last night I received a strange and very heartrending visit from the other side. My visitor was a woman named Annette. She had shoulder-length dark hair, dark eyes, and was dressed in a business suit. She told me that she had been murdered."

Joshua ignored Geneva's gasp.

"She says that no one has found her body and that she was lost 'under the bridge over temptation.' I'll say it again: 'under the bridge over temptation.'"

Geneva waved frantically, giving him the cut sign. He shook his head. She glared, then reached for the camera feed.

"No. Please. Don't cut the transmission. I said no!"

Joshua looked back at the camera.

"I'm sorry, folks. This encounter has been upsetting to all of us, even my technical staff. And yet, I promised I'd bring Annette's message to you in hopes of helping this lovely lady. No one should die like she did and then be left . . ."

He cleared his throat, trying to work past the sob. "I'm sorry. So sorry."

Joshua got up and walked off camera.

Twenty-eight

Amy answered the door armed with a baseball bat. "Oh, Maggie. Are you okay?"

Maggie turned to leave. "Oh. Sorry. I didn't realize you were in bed."

Amy pulled her back. "Do I look like I'm in bed? Well, okay, maybe I do."

"I'm so embarrassed, walking out on you this morning, then crawling back tonight."

"I'm the one who should be embarrassed, being caught in public wearing pink elephants on my feet. Are you coming in, or should I tell the Astaroths we're having a pajama party?"

"I shouldn't have bothered you. There's nothing anyone can do . . ."

"I saw the show, Maggie."

"Then you know."

"I don't know what I know . . . except that you'd better get your backside in here before Theo shows up with the popcorn."

Moments later, Amy made hot chocolate while Maggie paced the kitchen. It took Maggie four turns of the kitchen to realize Amy was singing a chorus over and over:

> For love has found the meaning
> of the deepest magic before the dawn of time,
> for your life and for mine,
> for the art of love.

"What's that song you're singing?"

Amy glanced over from the stove. "Huh?"

"That song. Something about the art of love."

"Oh, that. Just a song I heard."

"Where?"

"I went to a concert last weekend."

Maggie came to the side of the stove so she could look at Amy. Her neck was flushed. "With whom?"

"Some friends."

Maggie laughed, the first note of something other than dread in this long day. "You went with David Drinas, didn't you?"

Amy shrugged. "He makes a good friend."

"Sing the song for me."

"The hot cocoa's almost ready."

"There's something about it . . . I want to hear it."

Amy stirred the cocoa while she sang.

For love has found the meaning
of the deepest magic before the dawn of time,
for your life and for mine,
for the art of love.

And when you go to the other side,
do you see? Do you hear how I've cried
for our love, for our love?
I've asked for truth that I'd understand.
and though you've slipped out of my hands
I found love. I found love.

Where do we go from here?
Where do we go from here?
Tell me, where do we go from here?

Maggie started to cry. Amy wrapped an arm around her shoulder. "Hey, my singing's not that bad, is it?"

She shook her head. "Don't you see? I found *love*. So where do we—Joshua and me—go from here?"

Amy guided her to the table, then brought two mugs of cocoa over. They sat in silence for a minute, the words of the song running through Maggie's mind. *When you go to the other side, do you see?*

She felt Amy's hand close over hers. "Talk. What's going on?"

"He's gone over the edge. This thing about a murder victim coming to him is insane."

"Is it possible that someone is feeding him information without him knowing it?"

"He knows all the tricks. He says no. I don't know what to do. Amy, I don't know what God is doing."

Amy squeezed her hand. "He doesn't consult me as often as I would like either. So we're going to pray. And then . . ."

"Then what?"

"You're in a position no one should be in, especially a brand-new Christian. Caught between your husband whom you need to love and honor, and his career, which you need to reject. It's a precarious place, emotionally and spiritually. You have every right to step back from Joshua, if that's where God is leading you."

"I'm okay—for now."

"Are you sure of that?" Amy watched Maggie's eyes, looking for any indication that she was coming apart.

"I'm sure."

"Then you may go to your husband and stay by him until God tells you otherwise."

Geneva paced like she'd rip the wallpaper off the walls. "Are you insane?"

"He's not insane. He's a genius," Dane said. "It's brilliant, Josh. Just brilliant."

Joshua stared into the mirror, removing his makeup. "Yeah. Something like that."

"You can't just be making up stuff about murder victims," Geneva said. "Where did you find this woman, anyway?"

"I didn't find her. She found me."

"That's my man! Stick to the story no matter what." Dane rubbed his hands together, gleeful. "What's planned for next week? I got it—a dismembered body! You can say that a hand reached out for you . . ."

Joshua glared at him.

"Just kidding. I swear. But how 'bout this? Jimmy Hoffa's never been found—what a media storm we could cause on that one. Gen, we've got to research missing people, especially famous ones. We could have a gold mine here."

"We already do have a gold mine," Geneva said. "We don't need to be messing with the format. What got into you, Josh? Did Maggie put you up to this with all that religion nonsense?"

Maggie. She had gone totally out of his head, so consumed he had been by Annette. "You called her—right, Gen? And broke it gently that we had to delay the announcement?"

Geneva shrugged in mock innocence.

Joshua speed dialed the house, then Maggie's cell. No answer. "Where is she?"

"Forget Maggie," Dane said. "We've got to work out where we're going with this."

Bruce stuck his head in. "Beth called from the office. The phone is ringing off the hook over there. People with leads on this Annette, wanting more information."

"What are we, Scotland Yard? They were told to call their local authorities," Geneva said.

"Wait!" Dane said. "Hold it. What if we actually get a hit on this gig? Bruce, get Jennifer and Catherine over there to work the phones with Beth. We'll take information, see if there's anything of value, and then refer them to the local authorities. Wait, I'll come with you. I want to take some of these calls, get a handle on this." He followed Bruce out.

Geneva stayed behind, staring at Joshua. "It's not real. You know that," she said.

"Sometimes you've just got to go with the gut. So I went with it." Joshua got up, slipped on his overcoat. "Now I've got to get home, explain all this to Maggie. Because I'm sure you handled her with your usual kid gloves made out of cement."

Geneva laughed.

"She won't find this very humorous. Neither do I."

Geneva kissed both his cheeks. "That's okay. I'm laughing enough for all three of us."

"Do I need to ask her to leave Safe Haven?" Amy asked Patrick.

"What do you think?"

She took the phone away from her mouth and screamed.

"Ouch!"

"Sorry, Patrick. But you drive me nuts when you pull that shrink stuff."

"I don't have all the answers. Nor am I supposed to."

"I know. I'm sorry."

"So what do you think, Amy?"

"I think that she's a sweet, naive young woman who has been shuffled around all her life. Her parents were alcoholics and drug addicts. Her husband is seven years older than she is, married her out of high school. She's stayed in his shadow so her mean old sister-in-law wouldn't eat her alive. So this is what I think—I think she's got a tough road ahead of her."

"Then we'll thank God she's no longer walking it on her own."

Joshua followed Ben out the back door of the studio. Staff parking was fenced and guarded by a uniformed cop, but even so, Ben walked the perimeter, then checked the Lincoln. After a minute, he waved Joshua over.

The night was cold, the sky sprinkled with stars. *Life going on,* Joshua thought. People putting children to bed, truckers driving the highways, women giving birth, people living and dying. How had he gotten swept up in something so strange?

Ben nodded to the guard as they drove out of the gate. Someone waited in the street, flashing headlights and laying on the horn. The cop came running out, hand on his holster.

Joshua jumped out, ignoring Ben's protests. "No! Tell him to back off. It's the camper!"

Maggie sat at the wheel. "Hey."

"Hey. Nice ride you got here."

She grinned. "Want to check it out?"

He climbed in, waving Ben back to the Lincoln.

"I saw the show," she said. "You okay?"

"No. Are *we* okay?"

"God willing—yes, we're okay."

Twenty-nine

Maggie slept in the sunlight, her hair like spun gold. Joshua kissed her lightly. Then he pulled on his jeans and stumbled downstairs to start the coffee.

The front gate intercom buzzed. Joshua glanced at the screen. A dark-eyed, heavy-browed man looked back at him. "Police," he said, showing his badge and ID to the camera.

Joshua waited at the front door, cold air blasting in, while the unmarked cruiser drove down the driveway. An older man with wispy gray hair got out of the passenger side. The dark-haired driver was short and stocky, his jacket tight on his shoulders.

Joshua nodded for the men to come in. The stocky one showed his shield again. "I'm Detective Terrio. This is Detective Bowse. State police, Salem barracks."

Joshua led them into the formal living room. For all its elegance, the room was cold and uninviting with highly polished oak floors and ceiling-to-floor windows. It was decorated with Oriental carpets, crystal lamps, and straight-backed chairs. The two men sat on the sofa, one at each end. Joshua perched on a chair across from them.

Maggie came in, wiping sleep from her eyes and tightening her robe. "Who's—oh, excuse me." He introduced her to the detectives. She sat down next to him, linking her fingers through his.

"I thought you were single," Bowse said. "That's what my wife said. She's a big fan."

"That's a whole PR thing. We've been married four—no, five years now. Maggie was supposed to be on the show last night, but I had to bump her because . . ." Joshua stopped. "Is that why you're here? Because of what I said at the end of the show?"

Bowse cleared his throat. "I understand you gave some fairly specific information last night about a woman you identified as Annette. Can you tell me how you came by it?"

"Did you see the show?"

Bowse nodded. "My wife tapes it. I watched it early this morning."

"Did you find her?"

"Could you answer the question, please?" Bowse's tone was brisk.

Joshua got up, paced. "It was like I said—she came to me, asking for my help."

Terrio rubbed his face. Covering a smile, Joshua knew. "I know, you think it's a scam. There's some guesswork, and knowing how to read people. But I do have this *gift* of speaking to the departed. Two nights ago I was in my office, and Annette came to me."

"She visited in your office?" Bowse's tone was incredulous.

"That's what he said." Maggie tightened her grip on his hand.

"Her spirit visited me," Joshua said. "Which means that the poor lady had already passed."

Terrio wrote it all down. "What time did her *spirit* come by?"

"Around four AM, I'd say. I didn't check the time."

"How'd she get in?" Terrio said. "I assume your offices are locked up at that hour."

"You're either not listening or you think this is all a joke. She came to me as a spirit."

Bowse raised his eyebrows. "Okay, so where did she come from exactly? And what did she look like?"

"I was in my office when I heard someone call my name. I asked who was there. She told me she was lost. All the stuff that I said on the show. She was afraid, couldn't make the passing."

"Afraid of what?" Terrio asked.

Joshua rubbed his neck—he felt like a rubber ball getting bounced against a hard wall. "Him. Whoever killed her. She said he lingered nearby."

"So what did you do to . . . alleviate her fears?"

Joshua shook his head. "Nothing. Not then. I was too scared. Especially when she appeared."

"You saw her too?"

"In a wisp of light, an image that wavered i[illegible]
her features."

"What happened then?" Bowse said.

"She told me to tell. 'Tell tell tell.'"

"Why didn't you call us and report this cri[illegible]

"Alleged crime," Bowse said. Terrio shot hi[illegible]

Maggie lay her other hand over his and n[illegible]
"She said you wouldn't believe me. Said I had to tell the true believers."

Terrio looked up from his pad. "True believers?"

"My audience. I know it sounds insane—"

Footsteps boomed across the marble floor in the foyer. Geneva roared in, taking in the men with one furious glance. "Not another word. We're calling a lawyer."

Joshua looked at the detectives. "Do I need a lawyer?"

"Your choice," Terrio said.

Bowse just smiled.

Penn had driven them all to the state police barracks, then stood back and watched the drama unfold. Cord was invisible to these people until they needed an errand run or a fear soothed.

Dane chatted up the desk sergeant while Geneva paced. Maggie reached up, tried to take her hand. "Gen . . ."

Geneva yanked away. Penn suppressed a smile.

"I think Joshua's in serious trouble," Maggie said. "We need to work together, don't you think?"

"I'll take care of him. I always have; I always will."

Maggie stood, resting her hand on Geneva's shoulder. "The best thing we can do for him is to present a unified front."

Geneva walked to the squadroom door, trying to spot Josh among the maze of desks. "When's that lawyer getting here? Josh shouldn't be in there without him."

Lazarus insisted on going ahead with the sketch. *Foolishly overconfident, as usual,* Penn thought. Terrio and Bowse would chew through Joshua Lazarus like a buzz saw.

Geneva went back to her seat. Maggie's head was bowed, her eyes closed.

"What are you doing?" Geneva snapped. "Taking a nap?"

ooked up, smiling. "Praying."

, that's just peachy. I swear, Maggie, if I find out that you put this nse in my brother's—"

"Gen, I didn't."

"Shut up, just shut up. If you do anything to hurt him, I swear—"

Dane and the desk sergeant were staring at her.

Only Penn heard Geneva's words as she leaned into Maggie. "I swear, I'll kill you."

Peter Muir, the Boston lawyer whom Julia Madsen had recommended, sat at Joshua's side. Small and dapper, Muir nevertheless had the presence to keep Terrio and Bowse from pressing too hard. Joshua's patience was beyond its limit. "Why don't you just take me to see her?"

"We want to get the sketch done first. Once you actually see the woman, her face may supplant the memory of what you, um . . . think you saw Thursday night," Terrio said.

"The subconscious can play some dirty tricks on a guy," Bowse added.

The process of recalling Annette's face had been painful. Joshua could describe the color of her hair, the line of her cheek, but no sketch artist could capture her anguish and fear.

Afraid. He lingers nearby . . .

She hadn't told Joshua who *he* was. Maybe she didn't know. Maybe the woman who had been discovered this morning by a clam digger wasn't even the same as his Annette. But the location had to be more than just a ghastly coincidence—under a bridge, in the mudflats of the Temptation River.

"Okay, I made those changes. How's this?" The sketch artist turned the pad to Joshua.

The image was close—same dark hair, similar downturn at the corners of her eyes. "That's pretty much her," Joshua said.

"Let's get on with the identification, if we may," Peter said. "Mr. Lazarus is a busy man."

Bowse nodded. "Sure. We'll run over to Salem Union now."

"The hospital?" Joshua said.

"You don't think we keep the bodies here, do you?" Terrio said.

"I don't know. How would I know?" Joshua said, peeved.

Bowse shrugged. "You're in the business, right?"

"You don't have to do this," Joshua whispered.

Maggie tightened her grasp on his hand. "Yes, I do."

A tall man in blue jeans and a UCONN sweatshirt greeted them. "I'm the pathologist, Dr. Hagstrom. Come on in."

The morgue was smaller than Maggie expected. There was a lift in the middle of the room but no table under it, only a drain in the tiled floor. A microphone hung from the ceiling, not quite square with the drain. Next to the lift was a hanging scale. A side table was stacked with basins and plastic containers.

A refrigerated locker lined the far wall. The heavy steel doors were three feet square.

"Ready?" Terrio said.

Maggie rubbed the back of Joshua's hand. He nodded.

Dr. Hagstrom opened one of the locker doors, pulled out a metal tray with a black vinyl bag on it. He unzipped the bag, then motioned Joshua to take a look.

His face drained of color. "That's the woman whose spirit came to me in my office. That's Annette."

Thirty

By Sunday morning, crews from all the cable-news outlets were parked outside the gate. Dane had made sure of that. Ben did his best to keep them at bay. Beth had called Rebecca into the office to take calls, especially those rerouted from the home numbers.

All Joshua could do was lie on his bed, trying to block the memory of Annette's bloodless face.

Afraid. He lingers . . .

"Maggie." He pushed up on the pillows.

"I'm here." She sat nearby on the lounge, reading a book.

"I saw her, Mags. She came right into my—"

"You need to forget all that for a little while. You were up all night again. Get some rest."

He turned onto his side, closed his eyes, and there was Annette, with her dark hair and kind smile. Reaching out to him. Expecting him to rescue her, but all he had done was bring a media circus down on them both.

"Maggie," he whispered. "She keeps coming."

She sat next to him, smoothing his hair, touching his face. "Try to sleep."

He sat up. "I need to tell you something else."

"We'll talk later this afternoon. You're exhausted."

"I need to tell you this now. Do you know the patter I do at the beginning of the show? 'The spirits are here with us tonight; let's make them welcome.' That stuff?"

"Sure."

"Before each show, and sometimes just when I'm in my office—I've been doing a ritual. I light a candle and stare at it. Emptying my mind, calling on Sola."

"Who?"

"We heard about Sola that night in Lynn. Since then I've done a lot of research. She's well-known . . ." Joshua paused, realizing how far-fetched it must all sound. But it was real, and Maggie would just have to stretch her mind to accept that fact. "Anyway, then I ask Sola to open the gate and let the spirits come to me."

"You mean the people who . . . have passed on? The departed?"

"The first time they talked to me was in Los Angeles, of all places. I thought it was jet lag. Then I heard them here at home. I had Ben check it all out to make sure that there wasn't someone scamming me. Some competitor or tabloid out to expose me." He laughed. "That's ironic, huh? Conning the con man. Ben even checked this room."

"Our bedroom? You heard these spirits in here?"

He buried his face in her shoulder. "Yes."

She pushed him away. "You didn't see that Annette in here, right?"

"No, I've only heard voices in here. Here and the office. The first time I actually saw a spirit was Thursday night, when Annette appeared to me. And it was really her—I proved it, didn't I? The sketch matched the poor woman in the morgue. The cops have to believe me now."

Maggie blinked back tears. "Why did you do something like that? Your show was successful enough. You didn't need to do anything beyond what you have been doing. Contacting spirits, not even knowing who or what they are . . . it just feels dirty somehow."

"Dirty? That's an *Amy* word. Don't let her poison your mind—I'm only trying to do something good, to help people through my performance. Back when we were doing magic, we talked about that, remember? If we could send people away happy after a show, then we would have done something good. Something we could be proud of."

"Joshua, this estate, the limo, the clothes, all that money—this isn't about helping people."

"I'm entitled to a career. And if I help people in the course of it—that's awesome. I don't want you to think this was all about the money. Like I entered into some bargain with the devil."

"I don't know what to think, except that I'm afraid for you."

"I have to believe that this will turn out like it's supposed to, with Annette's murderer brought to justice. It's already done some good—that poor woman has been taken out of the mudflats. Now she can have a proper burial."

Joshua felt like a little kid, sent to bed and pleading his case from under the blankets. "It's a good thing. Right, Mags?"

She leaned down to him and kissed his cheek. "I'll pray it is, I guess."

She pulled the drapes and left him to sleep. He stayed in the dark for a long time, staring at the ceiling, trying *not* to see Annette.

Maggie knocked at the door of the carriage house.

Geneva answered, already dressed in a business suit. "What are you doing here?"

"Can we talk?"

"I'm not in the mood." Geneva started to close the door.

Maggie pressed her hand against the door. "Would you rather I apologize?"

Geneva snorted.

"I mean it," Maggie said. "I've come to apologize."

"And I mean it—I don't have time for your foolishness."

"If you can't make time for me, do it for Joshua."

Geneva took her hand off the door. "What does this have to do with Josh?"

"He's played peacemaker for almost five years now. But he hasn't been able to make peace. The best he could do has been to stand between us, keep us from going at each other. I'm only now realizing what that must have cost him."

"'Bout time you realized what a liability you've been."

"I have been," Maggie said. "Perhaps not for the reasons you're seeing, but yes, I have not been the wife I could have been. That's going to change."

Geneva stepped out onto the landing. "You've got sixty seconds to explain. Then I've got to tangle with those media buzzards out at the front gate."

"From the moment we met, we've been at odds. We drew lines and fought to keep those boundaries."

"That's psychobabble. The truth is, you were far too young to marry my brother, and he's carried you like dead weight ever since."

"I was young. I don't know if *carry* is the right term, but yes, I followed in his wake. Doing what he wanted me to do. Being what he wanted me to be. And it was never good enough for you."

Geneva shook her head. "Here we go—the accusations. Mean, overprotective, and overbearing—"

"No! Please, let me get this out. You're right in this one thing: I wasn't good enough for your brother—and therefore, for you—because I was trying too hard to figure out who everyone wanted me to be. *Lightweight* as you've called me more than once." Maggie smiled, trying to keep Geneva calm.

"Maybe you could have Ben take you to some drive-through shrink, get it all sorted out for you."

"That's not necessary. It's all been sorted out already."

Geneva raised her eyebrows. "I can't wait to hear this one."

"God has found me, and I've found Jesus, and all manner of stuff is getting cleaned out. I know what I need to make right is our relationship."

Geneva laughed. "So Jesus told you to talk to me, huh? I suppose it's no more ridiculous than what my brother's got going on. And you remember what I said—if you had anything to do with that, you'll be sorry."

Maggie closed her eyes. What had she expected? That Geneva would fall into her arms?

"Geneva, I just want you to know how sorry I am for all the times I yelled at you, whined about you, bad-talked you, wouldn't listen to you, wished that you would just go home to Maine and leave me and Joshua alone. I know that you love him with everything in you, and I hope someday soon I can convince you that I do too. I'm praying that you will believe that I will try to love you as a sister instead of down you as a rival."

Maggie was breathless when she stopped, her heart hammering so loud that Geneva had to hear it.

Geneva stepped back into the house. "You and Jesus have a nice day. I've got to finish getting ready so I can take care of my brother."

She slammed the door in Maggie's face.

Maggie stood at the edge of the cliff, looking down at the surf pounding the rocks.

The line of her neck was graceful and long, her skin creamy and smooth. Penn extended his fingers, close enough to feel the heat of her anger, sense the rush of her blood. She hadn't heard him come up behind her, not with his stalking skills and the roar of the ocean.

One good shove would be all it took.

Mr. Lazarus! Joshua! Geneva! Someone—call 911; there's been a horrible accident! Poor Maggie, I don't know what happened; she must have slipped. I need to get a rope, get down there, see if there's anything to be done . . .

Lazarus would race out after him. Penn would hold him back from the edge of the cliff, pretending not to want him to look, enjoying the anticipation of what he would see when Penn let him break away and look over the cliffs, see the lovely but broken body sprawled on the rocks, the waves slapping at her limp arm, the water coming in clean and going out red with blood.

One good shove. No, this wasn't the time, not with the plan just getting rolling. And yet, that neck was so exposed, like Tanya's soul had been exposed to Joshua Lazarus that night in New York City.

A violent death . . . but Maggie deserved so much worse.

"Good morning," Penn called out.

Maggie turned, startled. She tried to muster a smile. "Morning is all I can handle. Good is still up for debate."

"You seem to be taking this . . . *development* . . . awfully well, Maggie."

"I'm sorry for that poor woman. I hope they catch the monster that did this to her."

"Monster? That's a harsh word."

"I saw her, Ben. A beautiful woman with the marks of his fingers on her throat. Only a monster could do that."

Monster. Annette had been a righteous sacrifice. Joshua Lazarus was the true monster, feeding on children. And Maggie was right at his side, telling him how wonderful he was.

"Everyone's asking if Joshua is all right. But how about you, Ben? Are you okay?"

"Why wouldn't I be?"

"You got grilled pretty good by the police too. That's what Peter Muir said."

He laughed. "That was nothing."

"Oh?" She raised her eyebrows at him. "You've never said much about what you did before you joined us. Do you have some dark history I should know about?"

"I kept busy chasing down bad guys—overseas when I was younger, then in New York."

"You're a good man."

"I don't know about that."

She reached out, squeezed his shoulder. "I do."

He hated her touch, that soft hand that felt too much like another.

Papa, can I stay up an extra half hour tonight? Papa, can we go to the movies by ourselves? Papa, Hillary's parents are letting her buy a car.

Papa, I will love you forever.

"Don't stay out too long," Penn muttered. "The wind is rising. Those rocks are slippery."

Maggie smiled. "You take good care of us. Thank you."

He nodded and turned to leave.

"Ben, wait! Can I ask you a question?"

He turned back, raised his eyebrows at her.

"Do you believe in God?"

Penn would love for God to be real so he could spit in His face. "Let's say . . . I believe in justice," he finally said.

"What about mercy?"

"It's a waste of time thinking about mercy."

"But surely you must—"

"It's a hard world," Penn snapped. Then he walked away.

Thirty-one

THIS COULD END BADLY, GENEVA THOUGHT.

It was clear that Josh was a suspect in the murder. The cops had all but laughed outright at his claim of spirit visitations. She couldn't blame them—she despised psychics and astrologers, and put preachers and psychiatrists in the same mumbo-jumbo category. What was she supposed to make of these visitations? The thought that people actually could cross over from the other side—or that there was another side at all—terrified Geneva.

Her brother must be having stress-induced hallucinations or maybe waking nightmares. Whatever it was, it couldn't be good. Josh's world had been turned upside down, and she didn't know how she was going to make it right again.

Josh, Dane, and she were huddled over soup and sandwiches, trying to figure out where to take Friday night's show. Her brother was still spouting nonsense; she wanted to shake him silly. "It's just an act, Josh. Don't make so much of it."

"It's not just an act. Even before this spirit came—"

"Shut up about that spirit. Just shut up."

"No, let him talk," Dane said.

Geneva could see Dane's mind clicking away, considering all the angles. But this wasn't a business matter—a woman was dead.

"What I was going to say before I was so rudely interrupted—" Josh glared at Geneva. "Even before this latest manifestation, I had a lot of right guesses on the cold readings."

"Luck and intuition," Geneva grumbled.

"Maybe. Or maybe I do have a gift. Maybe we didn't stumble into an act. Maybe we were led into a *ministry.*"

Geneva threw up her hands. "Mediums have been scamming people for a hundred years. Shaking tables, conjuring up ghostly faces, calling forth howling voices. The biggest factor has always been the practitioner's ability to manipulate and persuade his mark that it's real."

"So what're you saying, Gen? That someone is scamming Josh?" Dane asked.

"Yes."

"No," Joshua said. "I would know if this wasn't real. And to be sure, I had Ben check the places that I heard the voices. He even borrowed sophisticated equipment from the FBI."

"So we're depending on Ben's word, are we?" Geneva said.

"He's solid. I checked him out before I hired him," Dane said.

Geneva slapped the table. "So we're depending on *your* word, then."

"I know what I'm doing," Dane said.

"Famous last words," Geneva said. "Especially coming from you."

Terrio and Bowse were pleased with Geneva's request.

"It had occurred to us," Bowse had said. "But we don't have the funds for that kind of sweep. Since you're willing to pay for it . . ."

Joshua, Geneva, and Dane met the detectives at *The Other Side* offices. Peter Muir was furious because Geneva had not consulted with him. "You should have waited for me. What was the big hurry that you had to do this on a Sunday?"

"This is the quickest way," Geneva argued. "We'll find out how Joshua was scammed, get the fingerprints or whatever, and put an end to this. If we wait any longer, we'll be accused of tampering with evidence or planting something."

Muir glowered. "I have a mind to walk right out of here. All the work I went to, arguing against the search warrant, and you turn around and invite the police in."

Joshua stepped in. "Peter, don't leave. My sister has my best interest at heart. None of us have any experience with this. We should have kept you in the loop."

"Where's your security man? Mr. Cord? He couldn't have approved this stunt."

Geneva steered Muir away from the group and explained that she had sent Ben into Boston on a bogus errand. She wanted to keep him out of the way in case they uncovered something that proved he had been incompetent—or worse.

The whole thing made Joshua sick. If he had been conned, then he was a fool and a party to a horrible crime. If the spirits were real, then what might they ask of him?

The woman under the bridge had been identified as Annette Donaldson. She had been thirty-six years old, a certified gemologist employed by Tiffany's in Boston. She had no husband or children, just an elderly father who had a stroke when they broke the news about her death.

Bowse snorted when he saw the false top to Joshua's desk, but Peter stayed on the cops and the experts, threatening lawsuits and worse if any *Other Side* secrets were leaked to the press.

"Hey, people want to be suckers; who are we to stop 'em?" Terrio muttered.

"Just don't tell my old lady," Bowse said, laughing. "*The Other Side* is her favorite show."

One expert examined every inch of the office with a magnifying videocamera while the other scanned with a sensor.

"Where's Maggie?" Dane asked.

"Off on her bike somewhere," Geneva said.

"It's too cold for riding," Joshua said. "I hope she's all right."

"That all you can think about? She's off gallivanting while I'm here, trying to get you out of this mess. You should be grateful for those of us who are sticking by you," Geneva said.

"Let up on the girl. Not everyone can take this kind of pressure," Dane said. He and Geneva had been at odds lately. As Geneva learned how television worked and developed relationships, Dane felt his power slipping away. Add to that her constant nagging about his drinking and her suspicions about possible drug use—their partnership was fractious at best.

Joshua tipped his head back and closed his eyes. He just wanted to climb back into bed and have Maggie massage his shoulders. He hadn't slept much since Thursday, when Annette came calling.

Awhile later, he jolted awake. Equipment was being packed. "What happened?"

Geneva looked at Dane, her face gray. Bowse chewed his lip.

"Clean," Peter Muir said. "This place is clean as a whistle."

Joshua closed his eyes. *Sola, forgive my doubt. Just tell me what to do.*

Jack Sanderson was a shadow of his former self.

"I didn't finish college," he mumbled. "What was the use?"

"Sorry." Hillary wanted to say more, but she was still getting over the shock. No one had told her how badly Jack had been hurt in the mugging. Maybe no one knew that he was confined to a wheelchair.

Jack peered up at her through a tangle of hair. "Who did you say you were?"

"Hillary Martin. Tanya Roper's best friend."

"Oh. Yeah." He started to cry.

"I'm sorry. I didn't mean to upset you." She wanted to touch his shoulder but was terrified of hurting him. He was little more than a bag of bones.

"Brain damage. I cry when I don't mean to, though I do mean to now. For Tanya, that is."

"What happened?"

"Coming out of the pub, some guy jumps me. I remember thinking how light he was, maybe it's a girl. But he took me down fast. Choke hold. Then he whales on me. A baseball bat. I see it coming, feel it. Go out. Wake up and he's waiting to take the next hit. This went on all night it seemed, until I just couldn't wake up anymore."

"I'm so sorry. Did they ever catch him?"

"No. But if I ever do, I'll break his neck." The tears came even more profusely—they both knew how untrue that was.

"Why did you and Tanya break up?"

"You know why."

"No, I don't."

"I wouldn't marry her. Wish I had, now. Maybe somehow this wouldn't have happened. She would have kept me out of the pubs, for sure. And if she didn't, then the baby would have."

Hillary gasped. "The baby . . . what baby?"

"Oh, come on. You must have known she was pregnant."

"I . . . didn't . . ." Hillary thought back to that afternoon when Tanya had danced around, declaring she and Jack would be getting married. *How pregnant are you?* Hillary had demanded to know.

Who said anything about pregnant? Tanya had said, never really denying it.

Jack sobbed outright now. "I told her to get an abortion. My own kid. Look at me now. Do you think I'll ever get another chance to be a father?"

Penn knew the experts whom the cops had called in, had done business with them for years. He knew how they worked, just as he knew they would never bother to look in the trees outside of *The Other Side* offices for his remote equipment. Once they swept the office and declared it clean, Penn would reinstall his toys and wait for the curtain to rise again on the drama.

He felt no joy in his superiority—joy was buried with his daughter.

His personal cell phone rang. Only one person had this number. "What's up, Jib?"

"Some Mass state cops reached out to NYPD. Checking your references."

"The Big Apple sang in tune, I trust?"

"Practically melted the phone with your praises."

"What about the Corps? Any calls there?"

"Not yet."

"Okay. Make sure our friends in New York get what's due."

"It's on its way now."

"What about the wireless Tasers? Am I going to see them soon?" Penn asked.

"I'll get them there tonight. They cost a fortune, you know. Homeland Security is tracking them now—they don't want them showing up in airplanes."

"What's the range?"

"A good six feet, maybe more if you only want to hurt and not put down," Jib said.

Penn laughed. "Hurt is good."

"Hey, Rope—how're your toys doing?"

"Let's just say that they're performing to spec."

"Those are some tight specs."

"Amen," Penn said.

Thirty-two

MAGGIE STARED OUT THE WINDOW. IT WAS EARLY MONDAY MORNING, with sunrise still an hour away. The ocean was painted with a faint orange blush, a wavering line against the brightening sky.

Joshua wrapped his arms around her, nibbled the back of her neck. "You're up early."

"Too cold to sleep."

"We can turn up the heat."

She leaned back and kissed his cheek. "No, I mean it's too cold to keep the window open. The surf soothes me. I miss listening to it."

"You're strangely calm about all of this mess, Mags. Is it from the bike riding? Getting you into some Zen zone?"

"Not the bike. And certainly not *Zen*, whatever that is."

Joshua traced his fingertips on her neck. "So you going to tell me what's keeping you from chewing the walls?"

"Jesus called me."

"What?"

"Jesus called me, and I said yes."

Joshua stared at himself in the steamy mirror as he shaved, trying to absorb what Maggie claimed had happened to her.

In the sixties they were Jesus freaks. In the seventies they were born-agains. The next decade saw the rise of the Moral Majority, which morphed into the religious right. These days, the smarmy talking heads called them small-minded and intolerant, dismissing them as irrelevant to the new century and new age.

And now they had a hold on his wife.

What sort of trickery had happened to Maggie? How had Amy seduced Maggie into believing something they had never even discussed, let alone entertained?

"Jesus called me," she said.

Annette had called him.

Joshua knew Annette was real—he had seen her lifeless body, first in spirit form, then lying in the morgue. The cross and all that other blather happened two thousand years ago.

There was illusion, and there was truth. People lived for more and died for less.

Joshua nicked himself. He cursed as blood trickled down his neck. *Now, this is real,* he thought. *Cut me, I bleed. As for the rest—who knows?*

A store this fancy made Bowse feel like Colombo. He played his shuffling shabbiness to the max—the dumb, underpaid cop with the Irish face, living on doughnuts and coffee. People naturally let their guard down.

Like this Margo MacArthur, chatting away from behind the diamond counter like they were old friends. "Annette had been through this bad breakup a couple years back. She dated some afterwards, but at her age . . . you know."

"I'm too far past that age to know," Bowse said.

"It's hard for a thirty-something woman to find an eligible guy who's not recycled lunch meat. The ones who still haven't married are out there hustling the younger talent, passing over a lovely, accomplished woman to bag themselves a trophy wife. Guys in their fifties just want someone around to wipe the drool off their chins when the time comes—no offense."

"None taken," Bowse said. Terrio choked back laughter.

"So Annette took art lessons, danced ballet, volunteered at a woman's shelter. Kept busy."

"So no guy," Terrio said, taking over the role of straight man.

Margo looked over to her supervisor. He was busy showing a diamond choker to a sixtyish man wearing a full-length fur coat. Colombo would vomit, Bowse decided.

Margo leaned closer. "Some time back, Annette took on a new look. Shorter skirts, glossier lips, that kind of thing. She starting taking half vacation days so she could leave early."

"We talking a lot of time?" Terrio asked.

"Nothing obvious, unless you knew Annette. I've worked with her for twelve years. I still can't believe . . ." The tears welled up. "I asked her outright if she was seeing someone. She smiled and said, 'I'll let you know when I know.' Strange answer, huh? I assume it meant that she had met someone, but she was too unsure to tell anyone yet. Then she announces she's taking a full month off. We thought she was in the Caribbean, due back at the end of this week. But now . . ."

Miss MacArthur wiped under her eye with one delicate finger, steering clear of her tastefully applied mascara. "I'm sorry I can't be of more help."

"You've been wonderful," Bowse said.

She sniffed, then drifted away, closing in on a potential customer who pored over the diamond rings that cost more than Bowse's yearly take-home.

"Think Lazarus is the mystery lover?" Terrio said.

"You seen his wife? He'd have to be crazy."

"We've seen crazier."

"How old is the wife?"

"Barely out of kindergarten." Terrio checked his notes. "Twenty-three."

Bowse shook his head. "How does it play out? Lazarus kills her for a ratings stunt?"

"We've seen slimier."

"Yeah, yeah. But they gotta be smarter than that."

"Smart has nothing to do with it. The guy is on the verge of a big network deal. What better way to make the suits sit up and take notice?"

They were out on the street now. Bowse barely registered the gray sky and scattered snowflakes. "Let's put Lazarus batting first, then. But who else can we put into play?"

"Close second, someone kills the vic to make Lazarus look good. The sister, for example. She'd chew the whiskers off a rat if it would promote the guy," Terrio said.

"Or it could play like this—someone else kills Donaldson, but somehow Lazarus finds out. Instead of reporting the homicide, he uses it for his show."

Terrio nodded. "A possibility. But he'd have to have some sort of contact with her. Well, he knew what she looked like, her first name."

"Far-fetched, I suppose."

"Not as far-fetched as the final option," Terrio said.

"Hit me."

"What if what Lazarus says is true? What if Annette Donaldson did come to him from the other side?"

Bowse laughed. "You prove that, and *I'll* chew the whiskers off a rat."

Thirty-three

On Tuesday, Penn was sent to retrieve Raven's most notorious—and thus revered—citizens.

Ryne Kubich, astrologer to the superstars, was lean and crusty, with sharp eyes under eyebrows broad enough to serve as a sunshade.

Laureen Saunders was the self-crowned maven of Raven's witches. Her coal-black hair was teased to ridiculous heights. Her eyes were heavily lined, her skin was powder white, and her voice was impossibly shrill. On Halloween, she appeared on the national talk shows, espousing the joys of paganism and explaining that witches performed only white magic, were gifted by God, and by the way, don't forget to dial 1-900-make-me-vomit.

Quite the hustle these fools had going, Penn thought. Movie stars, sports heroes, rock divas, and even new-age politicians flocked to Raven to do the celebrity witching circle—meeting with Saunders for love and virility charms, seeing Kubich to get their charts done, and then chatting with Joshua Lazarus and their dearly departed.

Penn glanced in the rearview—Saunders babbled while Kubich sat silently, his face fixed in a scowl.

Saunders tapped on the glass. "Driver! You passed it!"

All Penn saw was an acre of bramble, brush, and scrub pine. "Where is it?"

"Look for the dirt driveway," she said. "You may have to pick your way through the thorns to get to our dear Endora."

Penn left the car running at the curb and walked a good hundred feet before he could see the house through the tangle of brush and trees. The saltbox was ancient—probably from the late 1600s. The center chimney was bowed, the roof shingled with cedar shakes instead of asphalt. Endora Simon had no media presence, nor did she have a 900 number or a book deal. Even so, Lazarus had been told that all spirit councils of any import had to include her.

The door was hidden behind a wall of high, dried hedgerow. A wizened old woman peered out, so bent that she had to look up through her mass of white hair to see his face.

"Miss Simon?"

"Who are you?"

"I drive for Joshua Laz—"

"I know what you do, fool. Who are you?"

"My name is Ben Cord, ma'am."

She was the ugliest woman Penn had seen who still breathed. "Who are you?" she asked.

"Mr. Lazarus's driver. Ben Cord."

"I said: who are you?"

He closed his hand, then opened it, one finger at a time, trying to dissipate his annoyance. "My name is Ben Cord. Mr. Lazarus asked me to drive you to his office."

Endora bowed her head and studied her gnarled hands. Her spine was so bent that Penn could look down on the back of her neck. Her balding scalp was flaked with eczema.

"Ma'am?"

She raised her hand, motioning him to wait as she mumbled some nonsensical blabber. Then she looked up again, her eyes burning. "You are not who you say you are."

"Are you coming with me, or should I tell Mr. Lazarus that you were indisposed?"

Something shifted in her eyes. Her hands trembled now. "Yes, please tell Lazarus that I'm not feeling well."

Penn glanced toward the road—he couldn't see past the bramble, which meant no one could see in.

The woman started to close the door. Penn blocked it with his foot.

"I won't say anything," she said, backing into her house.

Penn shoved her. He could hear her skull crack as she hit the stone floor. He wrapped one arm around the woman, straitjacketing her. He pressed his other hand over her face, taking care to exert steady pressure with the heel of his palm so as not to leave finger marks.

She didn't struggle for long.

He felt for a pulse and then studied her face, ensuring that he had left no obvious marks. A lump had formed on the back of her head. Penn kicked a throw rug so it was ruffled opposite Endora Simon's inert foot. This would be open and shut—an old biddy takes a fall and dies. Happens all the time. No need for an autopsy, inquest, nothing. Just shovel the dirt and say good-bye.

Penn backed out of the house, using his jacket to wipe the spot on the door where he had forced it open. When he returned to the limo, Saunders was chatting away while Kubich glared at nothing in particular. Once inside the Lincoln, Penn could barely hear traffic noise, let alone anything that may have happened on the far side of the bramble.

"Where's Endora?" Saunders asked.

"I rang and rang, but no one came to the door," Penn said. "I went all around, knocking at the front and back. Looked in the one window that I could get at. No sign of life, I'm afraid."

Saunders flipped open her cell phone and pressed speed dial. She listened for a few seconds. "She's not answering her phone."

"Should I call the cops?" Penn's voice registered appropriate concern.

"We're wasting time, and I'm a busy man," Kubich said. "She probably took a cab."

Penn started up the car and drove away, whistling as he went.

The press was insane, Geneva decided.

Dane had suggested this media conference as the best way to control the spin. They needed to deflect suspicious innuendo, spawned either by rival telepsychics, the cable experts, or even the cops.

Dane was in the middle of the madness, his chest puffed out, smiling like a game-show host. He reveled in dispensing favors to the elite, powerful, and sexy. They had decided Joshua would do *one* full-length news show if they were allowed to supply edited tapes of *The Other Side*. So far one network—the one negotiating to pick up the show for their summer lineup—had agreed to the terms. Geneva was tempted to stop there. Exclusivity was as precious as exposure.

To satisfy the other newshounds, Dane appeared as *The Other Side* spokesman, mostly on news shows like Fox and CNN. He was going from one outlet to the next, changing his tie and shirt for each interview. Geneva fielded questions from print media. Newspaper giants like *The New York Times* and *Washington Post* had learned from the Lewinski, Jackson, and Bryant scandals that it was in their best interest not to leave stories like this to the tabloids.

Julia Madsen had appeared on the weekend news shows. Her charming and heartfelt testimony was a huge factor in whipping up this media frenzy. Various celebrities, including Cassandra Knowles, publicly praised Joshua, swearing to his accuracy and honesty.

Beth, Jennifer, and Catherine moved through the crowd. The staff had been prepped on the talking points: Annette Donaldson's spirit had come to Joshua unbidden; he did not know Annette Donaldson, nor was he a suspect in her murder; they had contacted her family with their deepest sympathies; they were cooperating fully with police; the show will be broadcast live and unedited this coming Friday.

Fear gnawed deep in Geneva's gut. What if *they* were the ones being spun?

"Excuse me." A young woman touched Geneva's arm.

She yanked away. "Why aren't you wearing a press badge? Who're you with?"

"Um, no one. Just myself."

"We're not working with freelancers. Leave your card with one of the admins, and we'll let you know if that policy changes."

"I'm not a reporter. I drove down from Vermont. My name is Hillary Martin."

One of them. The hangers-on skulked around after each show, claiming to want Josh to contact their dead but really just wanting Josh—period.

"This is for media only," Geneva said. "You'll have to leave."

"That lady over there—" The girl nodded toward Catherine. "She said that you were Mr. Lazarus's sister. I was hoping you could help me. I can't afford a private reading—"

"Then buy a ticket to the show. Our ticket office is open Monday through Friday, nine to five."

"You're sold out for over a year. I can't wait that long."

"You need to head for that door, right now. Otherwise, I'll have security take you out." Geneva motioned for one of the rent-a-cops whom Ben had hired.

"Don't make me go! I need help—my friend's father is missing."

"Escort this lady out, please," Geneva said to the security cop. "Carefully. We don't need a lawsuit."

"No, please don't," the girl cried. "Tanya would want me to find him, but I don't know what to do, because I think he killed himself. His name is Penn Roper, and—"

"Get her out of here," Geneva said.

What was that old saying about the one-armed paperhanger? That's what Penn felt like, though a more appropriate term might be a one-armed grave digger. Running Lazarus's errands, keeping his own multiple systems going and under control. Then there was the little matter of the old bat, Endora Simon. This evening, he'd suggest they send the police over there—anything could happen to an elderly lady who lived alone.

Laureen Saunders and Ryne Kubich were in a regular tizzy when they got to the office and realized Endora Simon wasn't there. "We need a fourth," the Saunders woman said. "East, west, north, and south. We do a spirit council in thirds, and we'll be unbalanced."

Like you're not unbalanced now? Penn thought.

"There must be someone else you could call here in Raven," Lazarus suggested.

Saunders glanced at Kubich. His face soured. "Quacks," he said, spitting out the word.

Saunders sighed. "Ryne is right. We righteous practitioners are rare, even here in Raven. There's so many wannabes. They bring us bad vibes."

"And bad press," Kubich said.

"There must be someone, maybe in Salem?" Lazarus tried to suppress his desperation.

Saunders listed off three names.

"Dante is a fool, Edwards is a fake, and Belossi is having plastic surgery," Kubich said.

Saunders circled the office, her hair bouncing with each step. "I suppose we could call Carr in Montreal. If you don't mind paying for a private plane, Joshua. He is such a prima donna. But even if he's available, we won't get the council in place until tomorrow. Ryne, do we have anyone in New York City who could jump on a shuttle?"

"No one I'd want to be in the same room with," the astrologer said.

"If I might make a suggestion . . ." Penn said.

The three of them looked at him with varying degrees of surprise, having automatically consigned him to wallpaper status.

"I've only met this guy in passing, but there's a strong spiritual presence about him. Same presence as you have, Mr. Lazarus. And your guests." He bowed to Saunders. She smiled, looking him up and down.

"I didn't know you noticed any of that, Ben," Lazarus said.

"Hard to ignore when it's this strong. This office rings with unseen power right now."

"Tell me something I don't know," Kubich said with an audible sniff. "Like the identity of this mystery shaman."

"His name is Theo. He's over in the—"

"The Beak. Nasty neighborhood. There was some talk of bulldozing it all under before his group bought those properties," Saunders said.

"Right. The Astaroth coven. Rather elitist," Kubich said.

Saunders shook her head. "They keep to themselves, which shows they're serious about the craft. Not running off to the media whenever they want free publicity to sell their silly spells and charms. I've met Theo. He definitely has spiritual gravitas. You'd like him, Ryne."

"*Like* is irrelevant. I either respect or dismiss. If you'll vouch for him, Laureen, I suppose I can sit council with him."

"Let's bring him in," Lazarus said. "Ben, do you know where to find him?"

"Sure do. I'll get right on it."

Penn waited until he was out of the room before he smiled.

Theo sat in the front seat of the limo, savoring the irony of being chauffeured by the same man who had dared put a hand to his throat a month ago. Cord had come to him in a posture of humility, with regards from the famous Joshua Lazarus.

Interesting, Theo had thought. *He drives Maggie and Joshua Lazarus?* He gladly agreed to come to *The Other Side* offices, see what the ruling elite of Raven were brewing. Perhaps Astarte had even decreed all this.

"Have you met these people before?" Cord asked.

"Flies, feeding on the carrion of weak minds."

"While you do the real work?"

"We keep to ourselves. It is therefore not anyone's business what we do."

"Except that Safe Haven is right in the middle of your business."

Cord was deliberately provoking him, but to what end? Certainly not idle conversation. "What do you want?" Theo asked.

"Me? To deliver you to Mr. Lazarus." Cord's voice was neutral.

Theo leaned across the seat. "What do you really want?"

Cord touched a switch, opening all the windows in the car. Cold air cascaded in. "Nice try, Theo, but I know about the epena chaw."

Theo fought to keep his face composed. Epena was so rare to be almost unknown.

"It's a marvelous substance—intensely intoxicating but extoxicating as well, when blown or puffed on a subject," Cord said. "You get a short-acting high in which the subject is malleable to any suggestion."

"Where are we going?" Theo said. "You missed the turn."

"Just a little side trip."

Cord pulled into the Raven Marina parking lot. This time of year, the sailboats and powerboats were shrink-wrapped and in dry dock. The harbor was gray; the morning mist had lingered past noon. Empty moorings bobbed in the mild swells.

"This is the point in the movie where the good guy lectures the bad guy," Theo said wryly. "But I can't decide whether you're the bad guy or I am."

Cord smiled. "Amusing. But let's skip the drama. I've got an agenda. You've got an agenda. There's some common ground here."

"What do you want?" Theo asked.

"For starters, enough epena chaw to make someone happy. A bag should do for a start."

"Hmm. I would expect more subtlety from a narc."

Cord laughed. "Epena is not a controlled substance. Though, if it were readily available, it certainly would need to be. The implications for controlled hallucinations are staggering—though you already know that, don't you, Theo?"

"If you're not a narc, then what do you want with a product like that? I doubt happiness is in your nature."

"My own purposes that have nothing to do with you. And I can guarantee that they won't come back on you. We've both got something to gain here."

Theo stared at a lone seagull picking through scattered trash. He had been like that once, pecking his way through the dregs of life. Three years ago, he had stumbled on epena during a surveying trip to the Brazilian jungle. A secret ceremony had opened his heart and mind like he had never dreamed possible. He stayed an extra month, learning the glory of epena and the wonder of the goddess Astarte, from whose breast had flowed the mighty Amazon River and from whose lips had puffed the breath of all life. She had been banished to the underworld by a jealous god, bound there by that hypocritical liar from Nazareth. Throughout eons, worshipers had tried to free her, including the true ones of early Raven Village. But they had all failed.

So Astarte still waited, longing for the fire to melt her chains, the sacrifice to feed her hunger, and the mate to bring her race into being.

Theo left the jungle and returned to his job as an ecological consultant to a major oil company. Astarte followed him, coming to him in glorious dreams and visions. He had divorced his yuppie wife, sold their expensive house, and dissolved his 401K so he could buy the houses on the ground where the true ones had been executed. Then he had recruited and trained acolytes so they would be a coven, though they were no more witches than the fakes who operated storefronts in Raven and Salem were. They were Theo's slaves, entrenched by an addiction to epena and any other drugs they could score in their free time.

Let them enjoy it all while they could.

In the fullness of time, Theo would trigger the vortex of fire that would free his goddess. Astarte would come to him in the fullness of flesh, and he would offer himself as her consort. Soon enough, the rest of the world would kneel to her—and him.

"What do I get in return?" Theo said.

"Access to the hottest show in town. Lazarus and his clown friends."

Theo laughed. "That is meaningless to me. I'm only here out of curiosity."

"More about me than Joshua Lazarus, I take it."

"Is that a question or a statement?"

"A fact. What do you really want, Theo?"

"Don't play coy. You know what I want."

"Safe Haven out of that house."

"*My* house."

"Except for the fact that their lease has precedence over your ownership."

"Unfortunately, yes. I can't evict them. The Board of Health won't close them down. Apparently I can't use my considerable powers of persuasion to charm them out."

Now it was Cord who leaned across the front seat. "I've already provided you the answer. When it comes down to it, you just don't have the guts, do you?"

Time slowed for Theo. Not the epena—he was immune to that. Astarte's cold fingers, digging into his brain, teasing him and testing him.

Why drive away what could be a perfect sacrifice?

If he failed, he would be less than worm food for Astarte's minions. If he succeeded, she would take his seed, bear his child, and rule with him forever.

He smiled back at Cord. "Just try me."

Thirty-four

THEO WAS A STRANGE SPOOK WITH HIS TATTOOED FACE, HOODED sweatshirt, and leather pants. But who was Joshua to call anyone strange? He was sitting around a table with an astrologer, a witch, and a devil-worshiper, about to embark on a spirit council.

"Just so I'm clear—we're contacting the spirit world to make sure that I'm . . . ?"

Laureen Saunders squeezed his hand. "Playing in the right ballpark. There's a lot of nasties banging around that you want to avoid. We'll take a look, maybe put up a couple of spiritual guide rails that will stabilize you while your gift is being honed." She turned to Theo, her eyes glittering. "You do have experience in this sort of thing, I understand?"

Theo smiled with chilling confidence. "My people spend a lot of time in prayer and meditation, communing with and drawing power from the various spirits. I fully agree that there's some shark-infested spiritual waters that Mr. Lazarus may want to steer clear of."

"Let's get started," Kubich grumbled. "I've got a racquetball game at five."

"No. Wait. I have a question," Joshua said. "I should have raised this earlier, but Theo just reminded me of it when he talked about prayer. My wife has recently become—"

"Your *wife*? I thought you were single," Laureen said.

Joshua smiled sheepishly. "That's what my PR *implies*. We've never said one way or the other."

Kubich nodded. "Good move for a media-based practice like yours."

"What's your wife's name?" Theo asked.

"You're from the Beak—you may know her. She volunteers at Safe Haven, which is on Dunstable Street. Her name is Maggie Deschenes."

"So what did your wife just *become*?" Kubich asked, tapping his fingers. "We talking a pregnancy here? I suppose you'll want me to run a chart for the fetus."

"No, she's not pregnant. Forget it. It's not important."

"Oh, but it is. I can feel the undercurrent. Can't you?" Theo turned to Laureen for confirmation.

She laid her hand over Theo's. "I can. So go ahead, Joshua. Tell us."

"Maggie recently became one of those born-again Christians. She argues that the occult is—"

Laureen laughed. "Oh, *that* old slam. We're evil, dabbling in black arts, calling up demons. Deluded and disgraced. Blah, blah, blah. We've heard it all, haven't we, Ryne?"

Kubich cleared his throat dramatically. "The evangelicals are the worst. Claiming to have the one answer, stuffing it down the throats of the rest of us. Like we're too wicked to have any integrity."

"As if God could be so limited as to place His power in one guy," Laureen said. "We are quite confident our power is God-given. I wish these small-minded Christians would open their hearts to the larger possibilities of the universe and leave the rancor for those who deserve it."

"Like the Psychic Network," Kubich said, his voice dry.

Laureen ignored him. "For example, how many hundreds—or perhaps thousands—of people have you brought comfort to in the course of your ministry?"

"It's our hope that many people have been blessed by the show," Joshua said.

"Stop with that PR crap," Kubich snapped. "What's the bottom line here?"

"We've had over a thousand testimonials. Even people who haven't had private readings or been on the show have come forward with accounts of being touched and comforted."

"That's wonderful! We're always seeking to inform and liberate people—you should be proud to count yourself among us," Laureen said.

"These religious bigots want to enslave people," Kubich said. "They accuse us of using old texts and practices. Meanwhile, they rely on one source, some parts of which are over six thousand years old. Furthermore, they indulge in rituals that, examined in the light of common sense, are offensive."

"Bread and wine, the body and the blood," Laureen said.

"Primitive," Kubich said. "It makes me shudder."

"Like I said, *limited*," Laureen added, her mouth in a lemon-sour grimace.

Joshua turned to Theo. "What do you think?"

Theo took a long look around the table. "I think we've each been called to our own work by powers far greater than ourselves. It's not anyone's business what we believe or do, as long as we do it faithfully."

"Here, here," Kubich said. Laureen echoed him.

Here, here, Joshua thought. If only Maggie were as broad-minded as these people.

Bowse slammed down the phone. "I hate it when one of these do-gooders is murdered."

Terrio dug deep into a pile of papers on his desk. "And that is because the world has lost a good person?"

"Oh, please. No one's good—you know that. Sure, there's the rapists and murderers. But then there's the rest of us, cheating on our taxes—"

"Or wives," Terrio said, laughing.

Bowse held up his hands. "Not me, man. My old lady and me got a routine, and we're sticking to it."

"Since I'm playing straight man, why do you hate it when a do-gooder gets murdered?"

"Because they leave a trail that's so flippin' complicated. This Donaldson chick spent Monday nights at the Boylston Food Bank. Don't need to tell you, Terrio, that there's a boatful of potential suspects in that stew pot. On Thursday nights, she was over at Brigham's Shelter."

"Where ticked-off boyfriends and husbands break down the door with tearful apologies in one hand and sawed-off shotguns in the other."

"Exactly. So without digging into her personal life, we've already got a stable full of potential bad actors."

Terrio took a huge gulp of coffee. It was cold and bitter, but it was free. "I'm not buying that. She was too clean. No trace, no defensive injuries that would imply an incompetent or enraged killer. This perp knew exactly how to get it done without her even seeing it coming."

"You see Lazarus fitting that picture?"

Terrio shook his head. "That pretty face? No. But they could have hired a pro."

"Hey, look at this." Bowse passed his partner a credit-card receipt. "A month ago she bought gas and condoms. Talk about a full-service market, huh?"

"Salem. Interesting. Right next door to Raven."

"So we've got her coming out of Boston and up to the North Shore for a romantic rendezvous."

"We gotta do better than this, or we're gonna get laughed out of town," Terrio said.

"Thank you, Joshua Lazarus," Bowse said.

Laureen's intonations pulsed with each beat of Joshua's heart, driving him inward until he was moving outward, into a world that was tremendously strange and yet very familiar. This was a place where a soul could linger for a long time, soaking up the quiet and serenity. The sky here was gray, like the eastern horizon before the dawn begins to take hold. There was comfort to be found in its blandness, as if the sky were as small as Joshua was and thus easily grasped. The ground was a darker gray and crunched under his feet like charcoal as he walked.

The wind *whooshed* around him, a tender breath with a distinct invitation: *Come along, Joshua. Come and be known. Come and know.*

Joshua discovered that he could fly simply by willing it. The ground gave way to twisted and intricate trees that had long ago refused to spring leaves so their branches could reach full glory. There were no seasons here—time was uncounted and nature subservient to his will alone.

Joshua soared now. The sea rose up to meet him in a swell of green mystery. *How amazing,* he thought, and then he was in it and under it, breathing fluid that was too thick to be water. The primitive stew nurtured him, then birthed him, spitting him out so he alone soared with the power that the whole world lusted for.

You are all, the ocean roared, and the sky echoed it, shaking Joshua like a leaf in that mighty wind, except he remembered now that the trees here had no leaves, which meant there was no need to die because death had no meaning because this was death and *you are god.*

Was that true? Hadn't he just been Joshua Mark Lazanby, the baby cradled by a father, then bruised and shook because he wouldn't stop screaming screaming SCREAMING? Hadn't he just been son Josh, held by a mum who gave all her energy and all her hopes to raise him and Gennie? Hadn't he just been brother Josh, rocked by a sister who was stone as she said Mum is dead and God died with her? Hadn't he just been cool Josh, amusing the guys, loving the girls, charming the teachers? Hadn't he just been the Amazing Lazarus, his hands flying too fast for the naked eye, making doves disappear and skunks appear, waving silk until the whole world was simply an illusion?

The sky wrapped him in a silver embrace. *You are god.*

He struggled to return the embrace, confused by the other world he walked in where he was Joshua Lazanby, lover of the tender Maggie, who gave her heart and her body and her soul and now ripped it all back so she could give it to some God who couldn't get off His own cross.

No, he was Joshua Lazarus, and he would bury himself in this ocean of green and gray, stir it and stew it until he remade it in his image, because Gennie was wrong—there was a god and he was Josh—and because Maggie was wrong—she belonged to god but that god must be Joshua, the Amazing Lazarus, Joshua Lazanby, brother Josh, son Josh, the boy-magician-man-lover reborn now.

Will you take yourself as the center of this universe?

"I have, I do, I will," Joshua cried.

Forsaking all else?

"I have, I do, I will."

Go forth and love and serve thyself.

Theo had had some profound experiences, but this had knocked the air out of him. And he wasn't the only one—Laureen Saunders shook like a mad woman while Ryne Kubich stared openmouthed. Lazarus was unseeing, still in the trance Theo had induced with a gift in the man's tea as Cord had suggested.

He grabbed Lazarus's arm. "Open up, man. Look!"

His eyes fluttered open, then widened in shock as he saw the wisp of light by the window.

"It's a head in a noose," Laureen said.

"It's a trick." Kubich got up and walked through the image. It disappeared instantly. "See?"

"Fool." Laureen pointed to the opposite wall. The head and the noose had reappeared there.

"Everyone, hush," Theo said. "Joshua, it's your apparition. What should we do?"

Lazarus slowly stood, his hands outstretched. "How can we help?"

Stop me . . .

The voice was so ghostly that Theo shuddered.

"From what?" Lazarus said.

Stop me . . .

"Ridiculous," Kubich said. "I told you we shouldn't get involved with these television people. None of them are serious about the craft."

"Shut up," Laureen snapped. "Sit down, Ryne."

Lazarus waved the astrologer back to his seat. "I assure you that this place has been swept three times. There are no electronic devices here. This is what it appears. Please don't discourage this spirit from seeking help with your negative talk, Mr. Kubich. He came here because we can help him."

Theo knew the magnitude of power that came from other worlds, as well as the little games that people could play. This was beyond his experience. Was it a hoax? Or had they sprung open another door to the unseen? This was one reason he had come today—to see if there were other powers at work in Raven, be them rival or friend.

The hanged man was on the move, passing slowly over the table.

"That's a tie around his neck," Theo said.

"A designer tie," Saunders said. "See the letters? The YSL stands for Yves St. Laurent."

"Duh," Kubich said.

"What do you want?" Lazarus asked.

Stop me . . .

"That's got to be a recording. Lazarus, if I find out you had anything to do with this sham, I'll expose you from here to China and—augh!" Ryne's back arched, flinging his head back. His mouth and eyes were frozen open in a silent scream.

Lazarus pushed out of his chair.

"No, don't touch him," Theo said. "If the spirits are administering correction, it's best not to be involved."

"Correction!" Lazarus said. "Surely they wouldn't—"

"They would," Saunders said. "They would and they do."

Theo had never seen punishment administered without using a human hand. If this was genuine, it was amazing. If it were somehow orchestrated by Lazarus, it was still amazing.

Kubich's body fell forward, his face thudding on the table. Theo steadied him in his chair. "He's okay, breathing and all."

Theo ran his hand on the underside of Kubich's chair, then inside the legs. The event had looked like an electric shock, but there seemed to be nothing involved in the chair that could administer such a thing. It was hard wood with no metal parts whatsoever, no wires.

"What should we do?" Lazarus said.

"It's gone. I think . . ." Laureen shifted but stayed in her chair. Theo almost laughed aloud. The big bad witch was terrified to get out of her seat.

Kubich slowly raised his head up and looked around. "What happened?"

"You, of all people, should know better than to shoot your mouth off during a council," Laureen snapped. "The spirit seized you, fool."

Lazarus poured a glass of water for Kubich. The astrologer downed it, then looked at Lazarus. "I could sue you for this."

"You came of your own free will."

"If I find any evidence . . ." Kubich got on his knees and examined the chair.

"I already looked," Theo said. "Nothing there."

"You're too cynical, Ryne," Laureen said. "Too quick to question. No wonder the spirits don't like you."

Lazarus smiled at Theo. He let a tiny wink suffice as a response. If there was true power here, some sort of portal to what the Lazarus people called the other side, then he would need to cultivate a relationship with this man.

Kubich got up, rubbing his neck. "Call your man. I'm ready to go home."

Laureen sighed. "I'm exhausted, myself." She squeezed Lazarus's arm. "Let us know how this develops. And please call on me anytime."

Theo nodded. "I, as well."

Lazarus grasped his hand and shook it firmly. "Thank you. It's been great meeting you, meeting the spirits with you."

Thirty-five

MAGGIE COVERED HER FACE WITH HER HANDS. "DON'T TELL ME anymore. I can't hear this."

Joshua pulled on his jeans. "You go on and on about how you want to share every part of my life, but when I try to tell you something very significant—not to mention, amazing—you don't want to hear it. Nice, Maggie. Really nice."

The fire was roaring now, but Maggie shivered.

She had returned to Safe Haven that afternoon. Amy had agreed that she could continue volunteering as long as the kids didn't know she was married to Joshua. Maggie had come home energized by the kids. She had run to Joshua, eager to share the warmth and hope. They had made a nest of quilts in front of the fire, making love and sharing tender words.

Then he had sprung this whole noose apparition on her.

Joshua tossed another log on the fire. "I have witnesses, if that means anything. Or is it only *your* spiritual experiences that are valid?"

"I'm scared for you."

"For me? That's crazy. The spirits are coming to me because they can trust me."

"What do you mean—trust you?"

"They know that I believe them and that I'll get the message out."

"What is the message? A man and a noose is not inspirational. It's frightening."

"Not if it's a warning. Not if I can . . . maybe stop someone from committing suicide."

Maggie pulled on her robe and went to her dressing table. "I'm not sure I'm following this—are you telling me that you can tell the future now?"

"I don't know what I can do. I just know that I've got some sort of power to go where no one else can. Even those people that were with me today hadn't ever experienced anything like this apparition. And they've been in the business for a long time."

Maggie brushed her hair in hard, angry strokes. "What people?"

"Laureen Saunders, for one."

"That witch who is in the newspaper all the time?"

"She's considered the leading . . . practitioner . . . in this country."

"She's a media hog. Always on the news shows."

"Whose words are coming out of your mouth now, Maggie?"

"What?"

"*Media hog*? That's not something you would say."

"What? I'm too stupid to know what a media hog is?"

"Not stupid. Brainwashed."

"I'm brainwashed? What about the people you associate with? Who else was at your séance?"

"It wasn't a séance. It was a spirit council."

"Oh, excuse me. And who are your counselors, Joshua?"

"Why should I tell you if you're going to rip them? You have no respect for me, do you?"

Lord, I'm making a mess here. "I'm sorry," Maggie said. "I'll shut up so you can explain."

"No, I'll shut up."

"Joshua, please. You're trying to communicate, and I'm being a jerk. Go ahead and tell me the rest of it. I swear I won't interrupt."

"Fine. Laureen Saunders. Ryne Kubich, a well-known astrologer. He's made star charts for people all over the world, including people in our government."

Maggie forced a smile. "Was that it?"

"Then there was this guy with a real unique look."

The back of Maggie's neck prickled. She knew what Joshua was going to say before he said it.

"Goes by the name Theo. He's an Astaroth."

"Joshua, do you know what an Astaroth is?"

Joshua shook his head. "Not really. I've kind of . . . forgotten, I guess."

"They worship a goddess of the underworld called Astarte."

He gave her a wry smile. "How would you know that?"

"Because it's Theo and the Astaroths who are trying to force Safe Haven out of the house we rent."

Joshua's smile faded. "So it's come to this. Me against you, Maggie?"

She grabbed him. "Not you against me. I'm so afraid that you're setting yourself up so it's you against God."

He closed his eyes. When he spoke, his voice was faint. "Maggie, can't you just be a good wife and let me get about my business?"

She leaned into him. The body that had minutes ago molded so perfectly to hers was now rigid, unyielding. "I don't know what a good wife is supposed to do when her husband is talking to dead people. I have to pray and find out."

"So your God is the final authority now, huh? Not me?"

She took his face in her hands, trying to caress away the knots in his jaw. His eyes were so sad, so tired.

"Baby, I understand. I've left you alone too much, and now you found something to keep you . . . occupied."

"Joshua, it's more than—"

"Hush. Let me finish. It's my fault. I did let you get shoved aside. No more, Maggie. I swear. No more."

"Joshua, I don't know what to say."

They stood there, holding each other at arm's length. Finally, Joshua grinned. "How 'bout—you'll make me a fried-egg sandwich?"

"You want me to cook?"

"That's the only way them eggs gonna get fried, kid."

As they went down to the kitchen, Maggie struggled to keep her voice light and her smile warm. But a chill grew inside her, as if a shadow had soaked through her skin.

Joshua felt better, now that his stomach was filled. Maggie had made fried eggs over easy, melted a slice of Jarlsberg over them, then served the whole mess on a chunk of wheat bread. He had set the dining room table for two, using the Wedgwood china. He lit the candles, long tapers in sparkling crystal holders.

As they ate in the flickering light, they looked at their food and not each other.

Maggie got up to clear the dishes. "Can I get you some decaf coffee?"

"How about a big mug of cocoa?"

She came around the table and kissed him. "Just like bedtime in the camper. You with your cocoa, me with my tea."

Joshua watched as she pushed through the swinging doors. Her silky nightgown clung to her in the best places. He should be the happiest man alive; happy to be alive, period. Poor Annette. Not all that much older than him, and someone had strangled the life out of her, then pressed her into that cold mud.

What did the noose mean? Joshua pulled a candle closer and stared into it. Time slowed—each flicker of flame seemed to last a lifetime. *Sola . . .*

Crash!

Maggie stood in the door to the kitchen, a tray of dishes shattered at her feet. Her hand shook as she pointed up to the corner of the room.

A noose hung in the air.

Joshua . . .

He stood, faced it. "I'm here. What do you want?"

Maggie slapped at him. "No! Don't talk to it."

"That's my job, Maggie. That's why it's here."

The noose disappeared.

"It's in the hall now." Maggie trembled so hard, her nightgown seemed windblown.

The noose was suspended over the stairs.

"What can I do for you?" Joshua said.

Stop me . . .

"Tell it to leave," Maggie said.

"For Pete's sake, you refuse to believe what you can see right in front of you?"

Maggie fell to her knees, her head bowed.

"Get up," he snapped. "What do you think you're doing?"

"Praying," she whispered.

Joshua walked into the living room. Maggie stayed behind in the hall, her face bowed to the floor. Thoughts peppered him: *She must be freezing; that marble is cold. Gennie is right; she is too unsophisticated for all this. Why won't she acknowledge my power? Why has she chosen a God she can't see over a husband she can?*

The living room was empty. "Are you still here?" Joshua whispered.

The glass in the picture window shook suddenly, as if slapped by a gust of wind. A face appeared, flattened against the glass.

"It's okay. This is my house and I *invite* you in."

The image melted through the glass, reappearing near the fireplace. It was definitely a man, but his face was fuzzy.

"Is there something you need me to do for you?"

Stop me . . .

"Who are you?"

The tie-noose appeared on the window, then through it, flying around the room like a trapped bird. All the while, the spirit-man stood near the fireplace, his head tipped drunkenly to one side, calling out, *Stop me . . . stop me . . . stop me . . .*

"Sola, if this is one of yours, show me how to help," Joshua whispered.

Maggie rushed in, screaming. "Get out of here. Get out of this house!"

"Maggie, shut up."

"I won't shut up. This is my house too, and I don't want any of this in here. I don't want them near you. I want them to go back to whatever pit they came from."

The spirit disappeared, then reappeared in a flash at the back of the room.

Joshua reached for it. "What can I do to help you?"

Maggie slapped his hands down. "No. Absolutely not!"

"Stop it!"

"I won't stop it, Joshua. Either these spirits go, or I go."

He glanced at her, afraid to take his eyes off the spirit.

"I mean it, Joshua."

Joshua . . .

He'd have to worry about Maggie later. This spirit needed him now.

"What should I do?" he said, reaching again for the spirit.

When the front door slammed, Joshua paid it no mind.

thirty-six

TERRIO HAD A HARD TIME CONTAINING HIS LAUGHTER. *MURDER,* he reminded himself. *Not amusing at all.* But Joshua Lazarus's freak show certainly was.

The state cops and the locals were very familiar with Laureen Saunders. The witch dispensed hexes like candy: cursing a lady in the express checkout who had the nerve to unload twelve items instead of ten; placing a hex in the mailbox of the *Salem News* because they had the gall to refer to her as an "alleged" practitioner; chalking jinxes on cars that took her favorite parking spot at her beauty parlor. Saunders had even appeared on national television, trying to undo the curses on the Boston Red Sox and the Chicago Cubs.

Bowse stared at Ryne Kubich like he was a dead fly in his soup. "You see this thing too?"

Kubich nodded. At least the astrologer kept his mouth shut and the sidewalk in front of his office clean.

Terrio wasn't so sure about the third freak. The Astaroths poured money into the Beak, buying up condemned houses and refurbishing them; that was a good thing. They had also poured cash into the mayor's campaign chest, which was business as usual. Beat cops were reminded not to be stringent in enforcing noise laws in regard to their motorcycles, but beyond that, the Astaroths were an unknown.

Why anyone would tattoo his face was far beyond Terrio. Then again, boxer Mike Tyson had done it, and look at the money and chicks that loser scored.

"And you too, Mr. . . ." Bowse cleared his throat. " . . . um, Theodore, is it?"

"Theo. No mister necessary. And yes, I saw it too."

"So you see, Detectives, I wasn't hallucinating when Annette came to me," Lazarus said.

Terrio laughed. "You understand that this ghost stuff won't hold up as an alibi?"

"Does he need an alibi?" Theo's tone was rich and deep. The man had a strange odor to him—foul at first, then somehow pleasing. Even so, Terrio kept his distance.

Saunders narrowed her eyes at Terrio. "I don't know why we should have to prove anything to your kind. You are not only unbelievers; you outright hinder our efforts."

Bowse had had enough. "A woman died. Your little sideshow just wasted an hour of our time that could have been spent finding her murderer."

Lazarus shook his head, his smile rueful. "We want the same thing. I wish you would give us the opportunity to work with you. Do what we can for Annette."

Geneva Lazanby stormed into the room, cursing a blue streak. "Who let them in?"

Lazarus stepped in front of her before she could climb down Terrio's throat. "We're explaining to Detectives Terrio and Bowse about yesterday—"

"Fool. You don't even ask them what time it is without Peter Muir present." She glared at Terrio, then Bowse. "Get out."

"We're invited guests," Terrio said.

"Right. Like cockroaches. Now, get out."

"Who are you?" Laureen asked.

"You get out too."

"Gennie, this is Ms. Saunders. She's helping—"

Geneva Lazanby turned on her brother. "I heard about the garbage you pulled while Dane and I were at the media circus yesterday." She waved her arm so forcefully, Terrio almost ducked. "All of you, get out."

Theo nodded, courtly despite the biker getup. "I'm sorry we've disturbed you."

"Ingrate." Kubich took Laureen's arm. "Come on."

The witch tweaked Lazarus's cheek. "Don't worry, sweetheart. We'll be in touch."

Terrio and Bowse didn't move.

"I told you to get out, didn't I?" Geneva Lazanby looked like she'd take an ax to them.

Terrio ignored her. "Mr. Lazarus, do you have anything to add to this statement?"

"No. Just that—we saw the noose again last night. This time it was here at the house. My wife—"

"Enough!" Geneva Lazanby inserted herself between them and her brother.

"What about your wife?" Bowse asked.

"It's not important. Thank you for coming out."

"Don't come here again," Geneva Lazanby said.

Bowse didn't laugh until they were driving away. Terrio, on the other hand, was no longer amused. He didn't have any fancy psychic power, but he knew trouble when he smelled it.

Lazarus reeked with it.

"I'm not going back to Julia's house. Not with those spirit things there," Maggie said.

"That's probably a good idea," Amy said.

"And I'm going to tell Theo to stay away from my husband."

"That is definitely a bad idea," Amy said.

Too furious to listen, Maggie stormed out of the house and down the sidewalk.

"They sleep during the day," Amy said, chasing her up the steps to Theo's house.

"So do you. But you're up." Maggie pounded the door. No answer. She hammered again, and then again.

Someone tapped Amy on the shoulder. She yelped.

Theo laughed. "How nice. A neighborly visit. Why have you waited so long, Ms. Howland?"

"When you took the Bible I brought over last spring and burned it in the middle of the street, I got the message," Amy said.

"And Ms. Deschenes. To what do I owe this pleasure?"

"Stay away from my husband, you freak."

"Your husband?"

"You know quite well who my husband is."

Theo looked at Amy. "Do you know what she's talking about? Because I surely don't."

"Joshua Lazarus," Amy said. "Apparently you've been messing with him."

"You stay away from him," Maggie said.

Theo smiled. Amy backed away, not wanting to breathe in the foul odor that emanated from him. She suspected the stuff they chewed had some sort of mind-altering properties and had warned Maggie and the kids never to get too close to any of the Astaroths.

"What will you do to me if I don't obey?"

Maggie wagged her finger at him. "If you don't leave Joshua alone, I will do something that you will find absolutely despicable."

"Really? I can't imagine finding anything that you would do *despicable*."

Maggie grinned slyly. "I will pray for you."

"I'm not afraid," Theo said.

Amy laughed. "You should be. 'It is a dreadful thing to fall in the hands of the living God.'"

"Yeah. What she said," Maggie said.

They linked arms and walked back to Safe Haven.

"This stuff tastes like goat puke. But man, is it sweet afterwards." Dane Wiggin lay on the floor, staring at a white ceiling—seeing stars or fish or fireworks or fruit, Penn mused.

He sat on Dane's leather sofa, enjoying the show. "You don't have to inhale or inject. It's non-habit-forming. Won't show up in routine tox screen."

Dane laughed a full minute before stopping to breathe. "I'm the exec producer—I do the testing, not get tested upon. Or tested in. Or whatever. You sure you're not a narc, Cord?"

"Do I look like a narc? Besides, what narc deals in stuff this fine?"

Dane rolled to his side and rose up on his elbow. His eyes were red-rimmed and unfocused. "I can't believe how hi-dee-hi-dee-high I am."

"It can get even better," Penn said.

Dane sat up, pulling his knees to his chest. "Spill, dude."

"You can intensify the experience by holding your breath. Go ahead, try it. Just hold your breath as long as you can and watch the high bust you through the roof." No such thing would happen, but that wasn't the point—epena chaw made a subject tremendously vulnerable to suggestion and manipulation.

Dane closed his eyes, took a deep breath, and held it. He looked like a moronic child, inflating his cheeks. After about thirty seconds, he let the air out in a huge *whoosh,* then collapsed backward. "Man, oh man . . ."

"Amazing, isn't it?"

"Incredible."

"There's another way to—no, never mind. We're being too daring as it is."

Dane looked up at him. "Hey, man, you ain't holding out on me now. Let's have all of it."

Penn studied his fingernails, pretending to hesitate. "Well, there's some element of danger."

"Danger, my foot." Dane struggled back into a sitting position. "Tell me or I'll fire you."

Penn laughed. "No. You won't."

"Tell me and I'll give you a raise."

Penn rubbed his face. He'd deserve an Oscar by the time this was over. Too bad he wouldn't be around to collect it. "Well . . . no, I'd better not."

"Tell me!"

"Okay. But make sure someone's here when you do it. We can try it tonight, if you'd like."

"Yeah, man. Let's do it."

"Yeah, man. You got a tie handy?"

Thirty-seven

"JUST BECAUSE I MOVED OUT TO THE CAMPER DOESN'T MEAN I don't love my husband," Maggie said.

Patrick Drinas smiled. "What does it mean?"

"It means . . . I'm scared."

"You're honest."

"I'm not honest. I'm desperate."

"What are you afraid of?"

She shifted in her seat, unable to get comfortable, even though Dr. Drinas had done his best to make her feel at home. His office was stately yet warm. A gas log burned in the fireplace. Books were scattered everywhere. "Amy told you all this stuff, right?"

"Amy only told me what you gave her permission to tell me. And you need to know that what we talk about in here is confidential between us. You can tell Amy whatever you want, but I cannot."

"I don't have any secrets."

"It's not about secrets. It's about giving you a place to feel safe."

How could anyone *not* feel safe in this place? Maggie had instantly loved the church where Patrick had his office—the rich stone walls, the majestic spire, the bells ringing on the hour. The windows looked out on an ancient cemetery that was only about as big as the living room of Julia's estate. Snow flurries spun out of the sky, melting as soon as they hit the ground. In a couple of weeks, winter would move in and the snow would stay.

"How old are those gravestones?" Maggie asked.

"They date back to the American Revolution. People from all over come to honor the patriots buried there."

"I know so little about so much . . ."

"Humility brings its own wisdom."

"I just turned twenty-three. I barely feel adult sometimes, let alone wise."

He laughed. "I can't even remember what twenty-three felt like."

"For me, it feels like I've hid away all my life. It wasn't until I met Joshua that I had a purpose. He was my world until God called me."

"Any confusion about your calling? Even doubt is part of the process; nothing to sidestep."

She shook her head. "Way back in elementary school, we saw a video about how plants grow. A tiny seedling pushed through the shell, then snaked up out of the earth, vibrating the grains of dirt around it. That's how I feel—like my shell has been pierced and nothing will stop me from opening my leaves to the sun."

"Praise God."

"But I'm worried that I'm betraying my faith by being so fearful."

Patrick smiled. "Fear is healthy when it keeps you out of danger. Can you be more specific about what concerns you?"

"Joshua is involved in some creepy stuff and getting in deeper by the moment. I know you've heard about Annette Donaldson. It's all over the news."

Patrick leaned forward. "This will be a hard question, but the situation is too serious to back away from it. Maggie, do you think your husband had anything to do with her murder?"

"Absolutely not. He's gentle, Patrick, and so convinced in what he's been hearing and seeing. I don't believe in any of these spirits for a minute."

"Even though you saw something? A noose, correct?"

She shrugged. "Almost any illusion can be created. Even a master can be fooled, if he wants to be. Apparently my husband does. Tell me something—is it sinful to speculate about someone if I don't have any proof?"

"Tell me and we'll decide together if we should nurture the speculation or just leave it right here."

"I'm scared that my sister-in-law is involved in this."

"Is that your husband's sister?"

Maggie nodded. "Geneva Lazanby. I'm afraid that she killed Annette, then set everything up to persuade Joshua he was actually communicating with her."

"What makes you think that she could have done this?"

"First, she'd do anything to promote his career, And second, a few days back . . . this is totally stupid. Forget I mentioned it."

"You can't keep hiding behind that, Maggie."

"Behind what?"

"I think you know. Don't you?"

Maggie bit her lip. "It's easier to admit I'm stupid than to have someone scream it at me or beat it into me," she finally said.

"You're far more perceptive than you let on—which is why I know you're not speculating about your sister-in-law without basis. Can you finish that line of thought for me?"

Maggie went to the window. The sun was setting even though it wasn't even five o'clock yet. The days were so short this time of year. Now that she had moved out on Joshua, the nights seemed endless.

"She tried to kill me, Patrick. And I don't put it past her to try again."

"Nice of you to show up for work," Joshua said. "Now that the day's almost over."

Dane's eyes were red-rimmed. "What? I'm on a time clock now?" He went to the credenza, searching the liquor cabinet. "Where's my Johnnie W.?"

"Down the sink," Geneva said. "You want to get looped, you do it on your time."

Dane laughed. "You're a hard woman, Gennie."

"Sit down," Joshua said. "What do we do about this latest vision?"

"Flush it," Geneva said.

"Flaunt it," Dane said. "You're a psychic. You're supposed to see these things."

"I'm not a psychic. I'm a medium."

"You're a magician," Geneva said. "That's it. The rest of this . . . I want to bring someone else in to check out this office. Someone is scamming you."

"Three other people saw it with me, all experienced practitioners. They swore to the cops that it was genuine."

She folded her arms over her chest. "Flush it."

Joshua looked at Dane.

"You got it, you got people to say you got it, you gotta flaunt it, Josh."

"Even if it gets me arrested?"

"Did you kill that Annette chick?"

"No! Of course not."

"Then what are you worried about?"

"Okay," Joshua said. "Okay."

Dane laughed. "And you think I'm rattlebrained? *Okay* what?"

"We're tabling this until it either goes away or we can't ignore it. Agreed?"

"No," Geneva said.

"For once, I agree with the lady," Dane said. "No."

"Meeting's over," Joshua said.

His sister and his producer bickered their way out of the room and down the stairs.

Joshua locked the door, went to his bathroom, and lit his candle. "Sola, open the door for me . . ."

Meeting called to order.

Later that night, Maggie and Joshua sat in the foyer, side by side on the majestic staircase. She refused to get any farther into the house.

Witness to what you know. Tell why you believe. Be clear and passionate. Do not accuse, but do be firm. Patrick's words to Maggie.

"I've never felt so alive," she said.

"I could say the same thing. My nerve endings feel like they're on the outside of my skin."

"Alive and hopeful."

"Hopeful? Is this what you were hoping for? That we'd separate?"

"Remember Utah, Joshua?"

"We played three resorts and then had to blow all our money on getting the transmission rebuilt. That was then; this is now."

She rubbed his arm. "Stay with me for a minute. We lived on cereal and powdered milk—all we could afford until the next gig. You had to grow a beard because you ran out of razors and we couldn't afford new ones. Geneva made us use the same plastic forks and cups over and over again."

"Yeah. So?"

Maggie twined her arm through his, pressing against him. "We couldn't afford a campsite, so we hiked out into the desert. No electricity and all our water coming out of the town spigot. My hair turned green from the copper in the pipes. Geneva slapped my hand when she caught me using dish soap to wash my hair. 'We're not eating off your head,' she growled."

"That was a long time ago."

Maggie snuggled into him. "It was the happiest time of my life."

"Are you nuts? The three of us spent almost two weeks in that stupid tent."

"*Geneva* slept in the tent. Don't tell me you forgot? She snored so much, we moved our sleeping bags outside. Every night we lay out there, surrounded by the mountains on the western horizon, serenaded by the calls of the prairie dogs and those funny lizards."

He closed his eyes, finally relaxing against her. "I never knew the sky could get so black and the stars so . . . alive."

"Night to night they were unchanging. And night to night they took our breath away. We wrapped up in each other and let the night sky cover us like a blanket."

Joshua shook his head. "Penniless, exposed to the elements, no home, few prospects . . ."

"But we were so happy that week."

He put his arm around her, his face to her hair. "I was happy because I was with you. That's never gone away, Maggie. You have to believe me."

"Every night we felt the presence of a power far greater than ourselves. A power so vast that the beauty around us seemed to make our hearts beat stronger. A presence so real that it made our love *sacred*. You were the one who used that word. Remember?"

Joshua nodded. His eyes were closed, his lashes damp.

"I'm not denying God."

"Then I beg you, Joshua. Turn to His truth now."

He pulled away and leaned forward, his elbows on his knees. "Oh, Maggie. Everyone's version of the truth differs."

"God's truth is absolute. He made us and loves us and wants us so badly that Jesus died for us."

"Platitudes, Maggie. Can't take that to the bank."

"But you can take it to heart. In the darkest night inside me, when the stars wouldn't shine and I felt myself dissolving into nothing, Jesus made me alive in a way I never could have imagined, and nothing—nothing—will make that go away. He wants to love you so much, Joshua. All you need to do is open your heart."

Joshua wrapped himself around her so tightly that she could feel the pulse in his neck. His breath came in ragged gasps, and she found herself thinking random thoughts like *He needs a haircut* and *He's been drinking coffee* and *His sweater is scratchy.*

The whole time, she prayed so hard her heart seemed to turn inside out.

" . . . wants to love you so much . . ."

Penn pulled the earpiece out of his ear. He looked at the flesh on his forearm. Goose bumps. He rubbed his arm, cursing. Maggie's words had pricked him, as if God were the cosmic neurologist, sticking needles in Penn's heart to see if it was still hardened to his purpose.

I will not feel because the pain is too vast.

I will not hear because the confusion is too great.

I will not believe because the possibility of opening to love again is too horrible to even consider.

Play your silly word games, Jesus or Astarte or Sola.

I will be God before this is over.

That Ben Cord was one generous guy.

He had left Dane a bunch of presents. A tin of chaw. A case of Johnny Walker. A mighty fine woman. Not to mention all the time in the world.

That was the thing about the chaw—it made time slow. He felt like he had been asleep for hours and hours, but the chick said no, it was still the middle of the night. He rubbed his face, half expecting to find stubble to prove her wrong, but he was still clean shaven.

Girls liked a slick face. Sure, all those young studs in Hollywood were going 'round with that day-old stubble, but they weren't getting the ladies—except maybe ladies of the night. Hollywood was one big harlot, and very shortly she'd be at Dane's door, begging to get in.

But there was a woman here now who needed attending to. This friend of Ben's—what was her name again? Dizzy? No, that was him, stumbling out of bed and into the bathroom, then back again. He was so happy that it wasn't time to get to work yet.

Too much playing still to do. Too much higher still to go.

Thirty-eight

GENEVA SLAMMED DOWN THE PHONE.

"What did he say?" Joshua asked, looking up from tonight's profiles.

"He didn't say anything. *She* said he was in no shape to come to the phone."

"She who?"

"Some bimbo he picked up out of the bimbo gutter."

Joshua laughed. "Come on, now. Dane is a creep, but he's got better taste than that."

"You mean he has more expensive taste than that. I suspect he's spending his money on something other than women these days. All we need is for Dane Wiggin to get so deep into coke or heroin he'll do anything to get his fix—including selling you out. You want that, Josh?"

Joshua raised his hands in surrender. "So what do you want me to do? Call Dane back and ream him out?"

Geneva smiled. "No. That will be my pleasure." At the rate Dane was going through the booze and women and who knew what else, he might not be around much longer. And that would suit her just fine.

The hooker had been paid in cash without ever seeing Penn's face.

The idiot was sleeping like a baby. Misty had been ordered to slip him the draught at exactly midnight, with the promise of great reward if she did and the threat of bodily harm if she screwed up. The timing would be tight, but Penn knew he could depend on Dane's greed and appetite to make it all come down the way he envisioned it.

This week's rehearsals had gone well, though Dane had no idea that it was a practice run. All Penn had to do was tell Dane that the high was intensified by their little game, and indeed, Dane had gotten so high, Penn almost had to reel him off the ceiling. But not until he had videotaped the images he needed.

The Other Side was in its third segment now. Once they broke for the final commercial set before "Messages for Home," Penn would put everything in motion. It was all programmed into his laptop, even the phone call to Dane. All he had to do was literally lift one finger, press enter, and the next step to Joshua Lazarus's doom would be sealed.

"I feel dirty, making you watch this," Maggie said.

"You didn't make me watch this. I volunteered," Amy said.

"But it's the occult. And you said we're not supposed to have anything do with it."

"Do you see me in that studio audience, asking your husband to contact the hamster I lost when I was four?"

"No, but . . ."

"So shut up and let me watch."

Maggie ran her hands through her hair.

"I did it again, didn't I?" Amy said. "Some teacher and counselor I am. Confusing you at a moment's notice."

"So it's okay for Christians to read horoscopes and visit psychics, as long as we know it's not real?"

"No. It's not okay. And if this wasn't about you and that hardheaded husband of yours, it would be wrong for us to be watching *The Other Side.*"

"So we're back to you having to watch this because I put you up to it?"

"No. We're watching this because God put you up to me. And God put Joshua up to you."

Maggie laughed. "You're a piece of work, Amy Howland."

"Now *you* sound like Patrick."

"He kinda rubs off on people."

"Don't get too rubbed off on—I might have to start yelling at you on a regular basis."

"Yeah, he told me about that too. 'Shrink-induced screaming,' I think he called it."

"Speaking of my favorite tormentor," Amy said. "You do know that everyone on the prayer team at Patrick's church plus at my church are watching *The Other Side* tonight. They've been asked to pray for the people who are at the show and watching from home—that they won't believe what they're seeing. And that God touches Joshua's heart and turns him away from this . . . this . . ."

"Say it, Amy. It's a scam."

"Okay. We're praying that God turns him away from this scam and to what's real and wonderful."

"That's why I'm not going nuts, isn't it? I'm protected by all those prayers. I can feel it, like it's not up to me to save Joshua."

Amy squeezed her hand. "It never was, Maggie. Now shut up and pass the popcorn."

Was it just a few minutes ago that he and Cord had done this? All Dane could remember was feeling incredibly . . . happy. People had sex and sports and religion and power, but when you came down to it, it was all in the chaw.

Somewhere, a woman had come into the picture. Then a little nap and . . . it was still night. One long sweet night. *May it never end.*

Cord was on the phone now. Dane hadn't really noticed him missing, but yes, now he saw that he didn't see him. "I ran out to grab some more chaw. I'm having trouble tracking it down, but go ahead and dig into what's left."

Dane giggled. "I already did."

"You gonna do the tie thing again?"

Dane eyed the setup they had made, just a few minutes ago it seemed. "Should I? I mean, if you're not here?"

"Well, if I can't score any more tonight, you gotta make the high you're on last, man. But it's up to you. I do it all the time on my own. You've practiced enough that you'll be cool with it. It's an even better high because there's no one between you and that heaven, man."

Truth. Yes, Dane knew it when he heard it, and that's what Cord was preaching at him. Nothing better than stepping up on that stool and slipping into what would be his next step to heaven. Especially with the chaw hot in his blood.

He let the phone drop from his hand. Had he clicked off? Who cared? Cord would be here in a minute, but this was his moment minute hour lifetime to shine.

Yeah, man. Going up high to get higher. Oh yeah.

Joshua took a deep breath, collecting his thoughts before the on-air light came on. The text for the script was being fed into the TelePrompTer, but he wanted to be fresh, put the best face on the "Messages for Home" segment.

He needed to forget the noose.

Nooses. They'd been everywhere in the past two days, always with that head but no face. Strange, both his sister and his wife were united in their desire for him to put this spirit thing behind him. Geneva thought it could lead to career or even legal suicide, while Maggie feared spiritual suicide.

Maggie had slept out in the camper again last night. She had gone off to Safe Haven this afternoon—he had sent Ben to drive her, but since discovering the camper still ran, she had declared her independence from any trappings of the show.

Was she watching tonight? He had debated with Geneva about telling his audience that he was married, but she steered him off that course, arguing that after last week, telling people about having a wife would seem bizarre. They could save that for the network debut, assuming Maggie hadn't divorced him by them.

Where was Dane? This erratic behavior had to stop. As usual, Geneva was correct in that assessment too; an out-of-control Dane Wiggin could endanger everything the show was built on.

There was movement behind the camera. Bruce raised his fingers, mouthing the count. Five-four-three-two-one . . .

"Hello again. Before we sign off, I've got a few messages for you at home. Brian is coming through to me now . . . a musician of some sort. I'm hearing something like a marching band. Sure, I'm seeing shiny brass. Can't tell if it's a trumpet or trombone . . ."

Chuckle the TelePrompTer said, and Joshua did.

"He wants Annie to know that the music he's making now is so awesome . . . and he . . ."

Joshua looked off into the distance, his usual trick for making it seem like he was receiving further communication.

A noose swung over Bruce's head. Joshua gasped.

Geneva's voice barked through his earpiece. "Stick to the cues."

She was in the control room, couldn't possibly see what he did; nor could Bruce or the cameraman.

"Dead air, Josh. Come on!" Geneva hissed.

"Sorry, that band on the other side threw me for a loop."

He averted his eyes, focusing directly on the TelePrompTer. The noose was there now, taking shape around the neck of a man. Unlike earlier visions where the man was vague and fuzzy, this image was clear.

"Read the TelePrompTer," Geneva said.

Joshua took a deep breath. "I'm hearing from Sally. She had a falling out with a loved one before she passed, and she's so sorry. She wanted . . ."

The man's body slowly turned. Joshua could see the profile, so familiar and yet . . .

Dane.

"Gennie, call the cops! It's Dane . . . get them over there . . ."

Dane's eyes were open, his hands grasping for his throat.

"Get the cops! Hurry! He can't last much longer!"

Thirty-nine

"It's a nasty scene," was all Detective Bowse would say to Peter Muir.

Joshua glared at Geneva. "The spirits tried to tell me he was in danger, but no . . . you wouldn't hear it. Maggie wouldn't hear it. These moron cops wouldn't hear it. And now Dane is dead."

"Don't be ridiculous. It's not your fault," Geneva said.

"Isn't it? All week, they've been trying to warn me. But I didn't believe in them enough to take a stand."

"Keep your voice down," Muir said. "This place is crawling with press."

They sat in the manager's office of Dane's condo complex. When Joshua had seen Dane swinging in the noose, he had rushed out of the studio, telling Ben they had to get over here. The EMTs and cops had gotten here before them and had blocked off the condo.

Trying to push through them, Joshua and Ben saw Dane hanging from the closet, his tie noosed around his neck. Anyone could tell he was dead, and that he had died hard.

Joshua grabbed the phone.

"Who are you calling?" Geneva asked.

"Maggie."

Geneva slammed his hand down. "Are you *crazy*? We don't need any more complications."

Muir stepped in to referee. "We'll talk to Mrs. Lazarus in a while. We don't know what to tell her yet."

Joshua looked back at Ben. "Could you get out to the estate? If she's home or on her way there, I don't want the reporters crawling all over her. I'll come home with Geneva."

"Sure."

"Thanks."

Geneva whispered something to Peter Muir. He nodded, then followed Ben out.

"What? You want to ream me out again?" Joshua asked.

"Of course not." She came to him where he sat and brushed back his hair. "It'll be okay. I'll make it okay."

"Gennie . . ." He wrapped his arms around her waist and hugged her, the years dissolving until he was that little boy holding on for dear life to his sister because there was no one else left.

"Baby, it's okay. Shush."

"It's not okay. People are dying, Gen. The spirits keep trying to warn me—"

"None of that now."

He looked up at her. "We can't ignore it."

She mustered a brave smile. "No, but we can do something about it. If someone is screwing with your head, I will kill them with my bare hands."

"You can't kill a spirit."

"It is not a spirit."

"How do you know that? You've never seen one of these things."

She disengaged from his hug, started pacing the office. "Remember the night Mum died?"

"Don't remind me."

"You were still in bed when Pastor Whatchamacallit—I've blocked out his name—barged in. 'Nothing happens without a reason,' he said. 'God knows what he's doing.'"

Geneva slapped the desk. "I decided right then and there that God couldn't exist."

"I don't get it."

"The thing is this, Josh: If He did exist, then He didn't know what He was doing, because He let Mum die. And if He didn't know what He was doing, then He couldn't be God."

Joshua smiled. "I didn't know you were capable of such flawless logic."

"So it follows that if God doesn't exist, these spirits *can't* exist. Because people are just here and then gone. It's always been like that, always will until we blow this stupid planet up."

"Is that what you think, that Mum is just . . . dust?"

The tears came, huge drops. "No. I don't."

Joshua's head ached. "Then what do you think?"

She kneeled down next to his chair. "It's you. You're Mum's legacy, her hope, her dream, and how she lives on. Which is why it's up to me to keep you safe."

Joshua held his sister for as long as it took for both of them to stop crying.

"This could explain a lot," Bowse said.

Terrio snorted. "Or we could be expected to think that it explains a lot."

"You think this stuff is planted? Underwear in Wiggin's drawer that's the same expensive French brand Donaldson wore?"

"You take good notes, Bowse."

"Learn from the master, youngster."

"I have. Which is why this whole thing stinks. You saw Wiggin last week. The guy pranced around like the master of the universe. Did he strike you as strong enough to kill a woman with one hand, then man enough to off himself out of guilt?"

"We've worked enough suicides to know that these people are sometimes manic before they pop that final pill."

"Manic, maybe. But that guy was so full of himself, it was coming out his ears. Not the kind to do the deed on himself."

"So you're not buying the guilt angle? He accidentally killed his girlfriend, then hung himself because of remorse?"

"That motive and five bucks won't even get you into a bad Hollywood movie."

"You still like the Lazarus crowd for this? Knocking people off in a play for ratings?"

Terrio shook his head. "I don't know. I just can't see anyone going this far just to get famous. Besides, everyone I've talked to has said that the network deal is just a matter of time."

"Maybe we're looking at a psycho fan, trying to make his or her fantasy a reality."

"I just don't know. I don't even know where to start looking."

Bowse slapped him on the shoulder and laughed. "We could always ask Joshua Lazarus. He talks to dead people, right?"

Terrio rolled his eyes. "You may have to take me out and shoot me, Bowse, because I'm beginning to worry that that may be true."

Forty

FEAR.

Maggie reeked with it, a sharp, salty odor. Lazarus trembled with it, his hands shaking as if he had Parkinson's. Geneva's eyes darted back and forth, not knowing where the danger would come from next.

Only Penn knew that.

The day after Wiggin's demise found them gathered in the living room of Julia Madsen's estate. Peter Muir had joined them, with Terrio and Bowse expected at any moment. Without experience in this sort of thing, the two cops would be a long time in tracking what really had gone down in Dane Wiggin's apartment.

No doubt forensics had vacuumed up the fine, white powder from various places around the condo. Even if testing showed silicon and plastic, it would take a wizard to discern that the powder was all that remained of Penn's self-destructing microcameras. A toxicology screen would show coke in Wiggin's blood, but labs in this country wouldn't be able to backtrack the metabolites to the epena.

Misty had been paid handsomely to forget she had ever even been in the apartment. Wiggin was a known user of prostitutes, so she would be only one of many whose prints would show up. Annette's prints would show up as well, on the items that Penn had strategically arranged. He had already anonymously tipped off the media that Dane was being linked to her death. He would leave it up to the vultures to decide if Joshua Lazarus was a prophet or an accomplice in the whole sordid matter.

Meanwhile, Ben Cord had become a trusted confidant of Joshua Lazarus. He stood silent, admiring the drama that played out before him.

"I beg you. Stop the show." Maggie sat next to her husband on the sofa, practically wringing his arm off.

"You may not have a choice," Muir said. "The district attorney is making noises about getting an injunction to stop you from broadcasting until they confirm that Dane Wiggin murdered Miss Donaldson."

"He was a creep," Maggie said. "But I just don't see him as a murderer."

Muir shook his head. "We all have it in us, Ms. Deschenes. Except for the grace of God, it could be me. Or you."

Maggie has gotten that old-time religion, and now she's found a friend in this rat's hole, Penn realized. *So be it—true believers are usually the easiest to fool.*

"What about the First Amendment?" Geneva said. "Can the government stop my brother from speaking freely? Or from making a living?"

"The DA can convene a grand jury and bring down a charge of conspiracy," Muir said. "The contracts with your affiliates carry a clause that allows them to shut you down. Sue you, even."

"A conspiracy?" Maggie asked. "A conspiracy to do what?"

Lazarus laughed bitterly. "Come on, Maggie. The cops think I'm paying someone to knock off people to make the show look good."

"Then shut the show down. That will prove you're not doing that," Maggie said.

"Shut up," Geneva barked.

"Peter, what should we be doing now?" Lazarus asked.

"Write an account of all your movements in the past week. And I mean everything, from a haircut to a staff meeting. Think back to whatever you know about Dane, what he did in his free time, and who he did it with. Whatever you can tell the police about him may shed some light on all of this."

"Do you think I'm involved in his death?" Joshua asked.

"That's not the issue at hand."

"Yes, it is." Maggie got up and grasped Muir's shoulders, stopping short of actually shaking the man. "You need to believe that Joshua isn't involved in either of these deaths. He would never do anything like this."

Muir was spared answering by the front gate buzzer. "I'll let them in," Penn said.

He was surprised to see it wasn't Terrio and Bowse. He should have expected this—and was quite disappointed with himself that he hadn't.

It was below freezing, with a harsh wind roaring off the water. Even so, Julia Madsen insisted that Maggie and Joshua go down to the beach with her. They bundled in down jackets, wool caps, and ski mittens. Julia simply raised the hood of her mink, staring across the ocean as if she could see clear to England.

"I've come to claim his body," she said.

Maggie squeezed Julia's hand. "I'm so sorry. He's been a good friend."

"We all know my nephew was a scamp. To be honest, a two-bit hustler."

"He was kind to me, Miss Madsen. Even bought me a mountain bike," Maggie said.

Julia smiled. Her famous green eyes swam with tears. "Geoff indulged him. We never had any, you know. If I were to have had children . . ."

" . . . they would have been Marco's," Maggie said. Why wasn't Joshua saying anything to help?

"The thing is, I was consumed by my own interests. I had Marco, my career, the Right Hand Foundation. When Dane was a teenager and the most impressionable, I left him to Geoff. I really should have been more involved. His parents were alive back then but useless. It was dismal how they ignored the boy to indulge their decadent lifestyles. Geoff tried to pick up the slack; he was a good man but not much more than that handsome face. I just let the years slip away, with so many things left undone. I'm working hard, trying to make up for all that, thanks to you, Joshua."

He forced a smile but didn't answer. Dane had never told Julia that *The Other Side* was just a well-crafted scam.

Julia sat down on a flat boulder at the base of the rockfall. She patted the rock and smiled up at Maggie. "Sit here with me, dear."

Maggie did, instinctively linking her arm through Julia's.

"As for you . . ." Julia looked up at Joshua.

"I am so sorry," he said, tears coming now. "Dane was a friend. He really was. I never wanted this to happen to him, Julia."

"Shush. I know you didn't have anything to do with this. But one thing I'm going to ask . . ."

"What's that?" Joshua asked, but Maggie knew.

"No . . ." she said, but her protest was lost in the rising wind.

"See if he can tell us why he would do such a thing."

Maggie got up, grabbed Joshua's arm. "I don't think that's proper."

"Sit down! I am not speaking to you." Julia's voice was commanding.

"Please," Maggie begged. "It's not right. He just died."

Joshua stepped past Maggie, his eyes fixed on Julia. "I'll try. Just give me a minute."

He fell to his knees in the sand and bowed his head.

"Joshua, don't," Maggie said, but either he couldn't hear her or he refused to. She kneeled next to him, bowing her head in her own prayer.

Joshua had failed.

If he hadn't given in to Geneva's derision or Maggie's fears, maybe Dane would still be alive. If Dane had been the one who killed Annette Donaldson, they could have gotten him help. If someone else was behind all this, Joshua had blown off the warning and Dane had paid the price.

Sola, open the gate, dear one.

He let the wind take him, blowing over him and then through him, a force so magnificent that it surely had its own mind and soul, a power so eternal as to form mountains and move oceans. He listened to the water coming and going, the mighty lifegiver of this planet, from which he and Dane and all had sprung. He felt the sand under his knees, the cushion of Mother Earth, the foundation on which man stood and the spirits still moved, their mysteries unfolding to those who opened their souls to that which lay on the other side.

Dane. Are you there, buddy?

Joshua suddenly felt himself rising, higher and higher even though his knees were cold and wet in the sand. He soared, flying strong and tight, the world all his, nothing could stop him, everything loved him, so good and so fine and so right he was. There was music, rocking through his blood, making his heart beat with a steady thump that felt like the step of the mighty man that he was. There had been a woman, but she had long since faded away, and he didn't need her even though she prayed on the sand. No, wait, no woman he knew prayed; they all partied. He didn't need anyone except for that little pinch of chaw that went into his mouth and took him even higher and higher; oh, what a friend we have in chaw.

He put on his tie, but no, he wasn't going to work now; he was going higher just as his friend had taught him. What a friend to bring him this high and always give him what he needed; his friend was his god, but no, the chaw was his god and he would make it do his bidding, tying the tie around the knob of his closet, standing on the stool, leaning forward and bending his knees like his friend had showed him so he could go higher and higher, not wasting air but cutting off the blood to his brain so only the chaw ruled there, and he was now so high, so high, so high, but it was time to breathe again, so he straightened up his legs, but the stool—what happened to the stool?—it broke away and now he couldn't breathe and he wasn't high but he couldn't get down; he kicked his legs and the closet door just swung and he couldn't think anymore but oh how to end like this, not high but going low, too low; he was so scared, too scared, no god now to save him and the black was rushing to take him and he was so scared but no air, nothing to scream, no one to help, to save, no god no; he was going into the dark and he was so scared . . .

"Joshua! Stop it!" Someone slapped him, then slapped him again.

He went facedown in the sand, feeling the water now surging around him, but he didn't care, couldn't care because he couldn't get out of the darkness. He would die, go down with Dane into the darkness that had no bottom—

"Joshua!"

Maggie. Joshua Lazarus had loved her once, but the darkness had sucked in that love, and now it was spinning away, a thread of light in a deep pit that knew no light—

"Take me if you must. But bring him back." Maggie, her light coming clear now, except it wasn't her light but something calm and beautiful that brought him enough warmth to know that he was freezing in the surf and had better get up.

He tried to call back to her, but his tongue was twisted into his gut, and that tie still bound him so tightly he had no air to speak.

"Please, Father God, bring him back."

More warmth. Maggie's tears on the back of his neck, and he realized that she lay on top of him, the surf now coming over both of them, and she wouldn't leave him to the darkness, because somehow she had found a way out. And now, that thread of her love, silver and sweet, twined with a golden thread, true and strong. He reached out, brushing it with his fingers, feeling the heat, holding it until he could lift his head and—

"Maggie?"

"Here, sweetheart." She slid off his back and helped him out of the water. He was numb—the pain would come shortly, but now all he felt was her arms around him, her face near his as she guided him across the sand.

Joshua stumbled forward, his eyes closed, trying to find that thread of light in the darkness that would keep him from falling. He couldn't see it or hear it or feel it, but somehow it kept him on his feet, and maybe that would be enough for now.

Forty-one

"ALL YOUR LIFE, THIS IS WHAT I WORKED FOR. WHAT WE WORKED for." Geneva's plain face was transformed with triumph as she waved the fax at Joshua.

"Don't do it," Maggie begged. "Stop the show. We'll go back to magic. I'll work in a factory. Anything. Just don't do this."

Joshua's head pounded.

Yesterday, after that episode on the beach, Julia Madsen had left the estate without another word and went back to California. Dane's body would be shipped out when the coroner released it. Maggie had taken Joshua upstairs, helped him into a hot shower, then made him go to bed. He refused to speak to the police, Peter Muir, or even Geneva. Somehow he had slept the rest of the day and all night.

This was a new day, cold and bright but with no more clarity than the last few weeks had had.

"I need time to think it out," Joshua said, more to himself than Geneva or Maggie. Why wouldn't his head stop hammering? It was this tug-of-war—Maggie made sense, Geneva made sense, no one made sense. Only the spirits that Sola sent seemed to bring him peace.

"Think it out? We've been working on this for months! The money is so huge, it'll be its own sensation."

Geneva loved him so much. Could she have somehow engineered all this? He couldn't even think that; it was too cruel, too disloyal to consider.

"They want an answer, Josh. I want an answer. At the very least, think of Dane. He worked as hard for this as you and I did. Doesn't he deserve to be honored by you graciously accepting?"

"What did Peter say?" Joshua said. They had an entertainment attorney to handle the contracts, but with the legal complications, he had asked Geneva to follow up with Muir.

She turned away.

"Gennie?"

"I'm sure he said for you to keep a low profile," Maggie said. "This is not the time to announce a network deal. Two people are dead, Joshua."

"Don't you think I know that? They came to me, after all."

"No," Maggie and Geneva said together. They looked at each other, startled.

"At last we agree," Geneva said wryly.

"Don't you think I've gone over it a thousand times in my head?" Joshua said. "I know all the tricks—the tipping tables, ghostly knockings, spooky ectoplasm, spirit writing. All shams that have been exposed over and over."

"As this could be," Geneva said. "If David Copperfield could make the Statue of Liberty disappear, then certainly someone could make Annette Donaldson appear in your office."

"The experts say the office is clean."

"Maybe they aren't expert enough," Maggie said.

"Penn has that special-ops training. The guys we brought in without him knowing—they couldn't find anything. And Maggie, what happened on the beach—" Joshua broke off, feeling that sob in his voice.

"Exactly what did happen on the beach? Julia said you had a seizure, couldn't get out of the water. Your beloved wife wouldn't let me call a doctor. For Pete's sake, maybe someone is drugging you." Geneva looked pointedly at Maggie. "Maybe a religious fanatic or something."

"You call on spirits, eventually Satan will answer," Maggie said.

Geneva laughed. "You're a blooming idiot, Maggie. The devil's making Josh do it now?"

"Geneva, I haven't been a good sister to you, but I want to learn, I swear I do. But Joshua is our concern now. He needs to stop the show and get away from all of this. The three of us can go back to Maine. Get jobs. Do something that's not so . . . tainted."

"There's nothing for us in Maine," Joshua said.

Maggie grasped his hand. "God will meet us there."

Geneva laughed again. "Thank you, Maggie, for that comic relief."

"Gennie, she's only trying to help."

"Oh yeah, she's lots of help. Josh, the network's expecting an answer. As are our cable outlets—they want to know if we're running this Friday's show. Not to mention that pile of work I have to do down at the office, going through the audience, making the profiles . . ."

"Okay, okay. How about this? We'll do Friday's show. Just play it straight, using profiles and cold readings. No mention of anything except maybe a dedication to Dane at the end of the show. Tell the network they'll have an answer next Monday."

"The offer is only good for forty-eight hours."

Joshua smiled. "Work your magic on them, Gen."

Geneva threw up her hands in high drama. "Fine. Whatever. It's your life."

The only remedy was hard work.

That had been the truth of Geneva's life. Pops beats up on Mum; he goes to jail; Mum goes to work; Geneva learns to keep house and take care of baby brother.

Mum dies; Geneva quits school and gets a full-time job.

Josh shows amazing abilities to entertain people, great dexterity, interest in magic. Geneva adds Saturdays to her workweek so she can pay for props and lessons from a local magician. Josh plays birthday parties, progresses to lodges, then small resorts in Maine and New Hampshire. People like him and like the magic.

Abner Fortis vacations in the White Mountains, sees the act, likes it. Josh balks—he's fallen in love with an eighteen-year-old right out of high school. Won't leave her, so Geneva has to agree to them getting married. She sells Mum's house, buys the camper, and off they go.

Hard work, hurting sometimes to her bones but never to her heart.

Geneva refused to believe in a world beyond what she could touch—and work through. Someone was out to either discredit the show or—and this made her shudder—personally go after her brother.

"Over my dead body," she muttered.

"Huh?" Catherine looked up, startled. She sat at Geneva's computer, hands on the keyboard, confusion on her face.

"Nothing. How're you coming with those profiles?"

"Pretty good, I think. This stuff is so cool. I had no idea."

"And no one else can have any idea either. You signed that confidentiality agreement."

"You remind me every twenty minutes. I'm not about to blow my shot at being a producer. Nor would I do anything to hurt Joshua, ever. Or you," Catherine added as an afterthought.

Geneva bent back to her work. She had to check Catherine's profiles, stall the network, make sure the promos for Friday's show had been sent down the line, and return a call from Cassandra Knowles. She had sent Josh to a ritzy spa in Beverly Hills. He looked terrible, his face full of dark shadows, his hair shot with gray. She ordered the spa to deal with that, plus give an extended massage, full facial, manicure, and pedicure. He couldn't look like something that the garbage truck had run over when he went before the camera tomorrow night.

Jennifer buzzed her. "Bruce wants you at the studio."

"I told you 'no calls.'"

"He's really freaked out, Gen. You'd better go over there."

Ten minutes later she was on the Salem side of Raven, tromping into the editing suite. Bruce sat at the console, head in hands.

"What?" she barked.

He jumped. "Jeepers, Gen. You give a guy a heart attack."

"What did you drag me over here fo—" Her voice caught in her throat when she saw the close-up of Josh on the screen.

"That moment when he called out Dane's name was so dramatic, I wanted to get some stills of his face, see if we could make a real cool promo," Bruce said. "I zoomed in because there seemed to be a glitch in the pixels of his eyes. And there—"

"I see it," Geneva said, her voice a mere whisper as she stared at the reflection caught in her brother's eyes.

It looked like a man in a noose.

Forty-two

"CHARLIE'S MOTHER DIED. HEART ATTACK AT WORK," AMY SAID.

Maggie's throat seized. "Awful," was the only word she could get out.

"He's asking for you."

"I'll be right there."

She found him on the sofa, curled in a tight ball. "Charlie?"

He didn't stir.

"I think he's asleep," Amy whispered.

"What do we do?"

"We pray. And then we let God lead us."

She and Amy sat in the kitchen, hands clasped. Amy did the praying while Maggie muttered, "Yes, Lord," and "Please," not sure she was connected to God. Where was He in the midst of such turmoil? Dane's death. Joshua's darkness. And now, the grief and loss that had come upon a little boy.

Lord, I've only known You a few weeks, but You seem hard. Too holy or too far away for me, or maybe I'm just not good enough. What can I do for this poor little boy?

LET ME LOVE YOU AND HIM.

Amy had said her amen, but Maggie couldn't raise her eyes. Not yet, not until she was sure she had heard correctly.

LET ME.

"Yes," she said and felt it rush through her—the mercy of a great and mighty God who would not let her be lost and would help her so Charlie wouldn't be lost.

Amy had dealt with the worst the Beak could throw at her: the drug pushers, number runners, gang bangers, and assorted other thugs. She had worked through issues with the kids learning how to behave properly, respect each other, and open their hearts to the God who loved them so. She had even faced down the Astaroths and all the legal and psychological challenges Theo had thrown at her.

Now this. Maggie, whom God had brought to Safe Haven, shadows looming even after she had stepped into the light. Charlie, fragile at best, now orphaned.

Lord, I am not able. So You must.

She felt a strong hand on her shoulder. Patrick.

"How is he doing?" she asked.

Patrick shook his head. "This is never easy. Maggie's reading a book with him. She's far better medicine than anything I could do. Did social services come by?"

Amy nodded. "They'll let him stay here for a couple of days. But after that . . ."

"No family?"

"None that you'd entrust a child to. The social worker is talking foster care. I want him, Patrick."

"I'll speak to her."

"I've offered to switch to the day shift so I can be home overnight with him. But she's concerned about the fact that I am a missionary. She knows the good work we do at Safe Haven, but she's worried about what she called the 'use the rod, don't spoil the child' system of discipline that her boss thinks Christians use."

"Whereas unmarried couples, even Wiccans, are allowed to take in children."

"They're warm and fuzzy. The world sees us as—"

"Dangerous to children," Patrick said, without his usual laughter. "On to the next matter: our Maggie is in quite the stew, isn't she?"

"Joshua wants her back in the house with him. She asked me what I thought."

Patrick smiled. "And did you tell her?"

"How can I? Half the time I think she should kick his backside on her way out the door. The other half I think she should smother him with love and prayer."

"She can't do both?"

Amy shrugged. "You have to admit that this situation really wasn't fair to spring on a brand-new Christian."

"Would you rather she be going through this without God?"

"Patrick, just shut up already! I'm sorry, but I can't take any more wisdom." The tears flowed now. The whole thing stunk, the chaos and cruelty of this life, and the impossibility of being God's person every minute of every day.

Patrick stood behind her and put his hands on her shoulders. Amy could feel the prayer almost instantly, washing not one speck of trouble away but taking all the doubt and fear. After a few minutes, she said, "Amen."

Patrick laughed. "How did you know?"

"I know you, Patrick. I'm sorry I said to shut up."

"No, I probably need to hear that more often, especially if it saves *me* from getting a kick in the backside. So thank you. Are you going to be all right?"

Amy stood. "No. Not at all. But I'm going to be blessed, and you know what? Maggie and Charlie will be as well. So there."

"Too neat," Terrio said.

"No fooling." Bowse swigged his coffee, then took a huge bite of apple.

"That's un-American. Coffee and fruit."

"Hey, you have angina and see how fast you swear off the doughnuts."

They struggled over the latest forensics report on the Wiggin hanging. "What's silicon?" Bowse asked.

"Glass. Like sand."

"Sand isn't glass."

"It is, sorta. Haven't you ever heard of Silicon Valley?"

"Out in Montana somewhere?"

"Cut the Colombo—you ain't going to Hollywood, Bowse."

"Home of the overpriced, geek-faced billionaires. California, and used to be our own 128 Belt. So you saying these little piles of white powder ain't cocaine—they're computer chips?"

"I'm not saying anything," Terrio said. "When you get to the bottom of all this nerd speak, the overpaid laboratory that the captain is on my tail about is saying they're electronic components."

"Wiggin was only in that condo a few months. Maybe there was a computer jock there before him."

"He had a cleaning service. They'd been in on Monday. This stuff was fresh."

"But what does it mean?" Bowse said.

"Beats me."

"Me too. Why do we care? We could close the case now and get the DA off our back. Word is *The Other Side* is hooking up with the network. Lots of jobs coming to town."

"Especially in the service industry," Terrio said, laughing. "The streetwalkers will be raking it in."

"Who's got a bad attitude now?"

"You like anything about the Lazarus crowd and what they're doing?"

"Other than keeping my wife occupied on Friday nights—nope."

"Wiggin was a pawn in some ugly scheme, is my thinking," Terrio said.

"Probably."

"But I can't get a handle on it."

"Nope."

"So what next?"

"Pass me a doughnut," Bowse said. "Maybe then I'll be able to think straight."

Amy had given Charlie the option of staying up in her apartment while the kids were there. He asked if Dawna and Pedro could come up to her living room—he had discovered her video games. "We need to let them know about your mother. But after that . . . you bet," she said.

Maggie hugged each of the kids as they came in. They thought she was crazy—until Patrick sat with them to explain about Charlie's mother.

"She's in heaven, right?" Dawna asked.

"Jesus was right there, ready to take her home."

"Heaven's cool, right?" Manny asked.

"So cool that even I can't imagine it," Amy said.

Maggie wandered behind the kids, giving a reassuring squeeze or a quick whisper. Natalia's mother had died from cancer three years ago; her father had since remarried. These kids knew various degrees of loss—life was no picnic in the Beak.

"Is Charlie going to a home?" Pedro asked.

Amy and Patrick shared a quick glance. "He's staying here for tonight," Amy said. "After that, the arrangements aren't firm. But the answer is that I will take care of him, Maggie will, Dr. Drinas will. And all of you will. Because that's what God asks of us and helps us to do."

"Cool with me," Pedro said.

Forty-three

JOSHUA GOT BACK TO THE HOUSE MIDAFTERNOON TO FIND THAT Maggie had been called away on some sort of emergency at Safe Haven. Her note didn't say what. Amy probably wanted to lecture her some more about being married to an evildoer.

She should be here, with him. He sent Ben to go get her. A minute later he changed his mind. "Come back. Maggie can stay there. I want to head over to the office."

"Be there in ten," Ben said, not even questioning the reversal.

He went into the closet and pulled out a white Egyptian cotton shirt, gray slacks, and the Giorgio Santo blazer Dane had picked up for him in New York.

Dane. He hadn't given him much thought today, except how his death had caused chaos for the rest of them. No way was the guy a murderer. If he had killed Annette, it had to have been an accident, maybe some sort of role-playing thing that turned bad. But why not just tell the cops? Dane was slick and sure of himself—he could have explained it away. Why hang himself?

Why go into that darkness willingly?

Joshua was on his knees again, not knowing how he got there. He was going insane, surely.

Out of nowhere came a mighty crash, metal on metal, glass shattering, an engine revving. Had some fool reporter crashed through the gate? Joshua moved into one of the front rooms so he could see the gate.

It was intact. Beyond the high stone wall, he could see the microwave dishes on the news vans. All seemed quiet. But there was no mistaking what he had heard. A plane, maybe? Wouldn't that have gotten the news guys going? Maybe not, if it happened at the back of the house or in the cove.

Sola, sending another message? But no, she had never been this loud, this—earthbound. It must be an accident outside. This was too real, too shocking. Sola spoke in whispers.

But not all spirits were at peace.

No, he wouldn't think like this. He'd find the source of the crash; do what he could to help.

Joshua ran to the end of the hall, looked inland where the coast bowed to form a quiet bay. Nothing. At the other end of the hall, he saw nothing to the south beyond the carriage house. He went into his bedroom to look out over the back lawn. He couldn't see the beach from here, but the surf must be vicious today—he could see the white foam splashing up over the rocks.

Forget this—he had to get to the office.

Joshua pulled on a new undershirt, then buttoned up the dress shirt. Another crash shattered the air around him.

"What is it? What do you want?"

Joshua . . .

"I can hear you! Just tell me what you want me to do. Please . . ."

The room was alive with the crash now, metal grinding, brakes screeching, tires spinning, glass shattering, going again and again until Joshua begged, "Please. Just tell me. Please."

It stopped.

"What do you want?"

Help her help her . . .

"I don't know who she is."

Help her help her . . .

It came to him in a flash. Maybe the crashing was so he would know it was really her. Did he dare . . . ?

"Mum?"

The sudden silence pressed down on him, a fist closing on him, with the ticking of a clock and the faraway slap of ocean waves the only thing leaking through its heartless fingers.

Mum? No, he wasn't ready to believe that. Not yet.

He kicked off his running shoes, stripped off his jeans, and finished dressing for work. He heard the *beep-beep,* which meant the front gate was opening. Good, Ben was back from the grocery store. Joshua would go to the office, memorize this week's profiles, joke with Rebecca, speak sympathetically about Dane, snap at Geneva. Life needed to go on.

If Mum needed to come to him, she would know where to find him. Sola would make sure of that.

At Geneva's request, Bruce sent the DVD of Friday's show out to some expert he knew in Los Angeles. She didn't know what else to do or what to think. Had the noose appeared in the TelePrompTer? Bruce said that he had already checked the file Jennifer had prepared—just text. He scanned the computer—there were no graphic files with nooses anywhere.

"I should burn down the stupid studio and the office and move us all out of this cursed town," she mumbled as she climbed out of her Lexus. She had been so rattled that she almost had an accident on her way back to the office. Now that she was the sole executive producer, she'd have to get her own driver. Maybe Ben could recommend someone.

If Mum could see her kids now—making millions of dollars, living on an oceanfront estate, getting chauffeured—she'd have to be proud. Then again, getting harassed by psychos or spirits was nothing to write home about. "God help me," Geneva mumbled, locking her car.

"Excuse me."

Geneva turned fast and bumped right into some girl. One of Josh's fans—they were always coming around. This one looked familiar. "I'm not getting you in to see him," Geneva snapped. "So get lost."

"Wait. No. I need to talk to you," the girl sputtered as she followed Geneva to the employee's gate. Ben had suggested the fence around the property—good thing he had. These girls would be climbing the drainpipes so they could slobber over Josh.

She waited for the girl to back off so she could key in her code. Ben was able to drive the Lincoln right into the yard, but there was only enough parking for one car in there. The rest of them parked in the street or in the small lot outside the fence.

"I told you about my friend, Tanya Roper?"

Geneva turned and gave her a long look. "Who are you?"

"Hillary Martin. From Vermont. My friend Tanya Roper killed herself, and her father, Penn, is missing—"

"Who?"

"Penn. Penn Roper."

"I don't know any Penn Roper. Now get lost."

No way would Geneva let this girl watch as she tapped in the code. She went back toward the front of the house. She'd have Rebecca buzz her into the lobby, then call the cops or Ben to chase this girl off.

The girl tugged at her sleeve. "Please, I need your help!"

"Look. We're not shrinks or priests. We're just entertainers. You need help, call a doctor. But leave my brother alone."

"Wait! Here, here's the information. Ask Mr. Lazarus; maybe he'll know something." The girl pushed a piece of paper at her.

Geneva snatched the paper, crumpled it, and stuck it in her pocket. "Fine. Now get out of here."

"It's all on the paper. Just ask him. Please."

Geneva pushed through the front door. "Ben here yet?"

"On his way in with Mr. Lazarus," Rebecca said.

"Call the cops then. Tell them we got a stalker that needs arresting."

Rebecca took the phone with her as she looked out the front door. "What stalker?"

Geneva swore and disappeared down the hall.

"Amy's gonna kill us," Pedro said.

"Shut up about being dead," Charlie said. "Besides, she ain't killin' no one. Not today."

"She's gonna be rippin'."

"She won't find out. Dawna will say I'm sleeping and you went home." Charlie hated to lie, but he figured today was a special occasion. A bad special occasion because Ma had died sometime in the middle of the night. Charlie had known something was wrong when Ma wasn't there to make his breakfast. Overtime, he told himself. Making money for Christmas. But his stomach felt so squirmy that he couldn't eat his toast, and he went to school hungry. Even so, when Amy showed up at school, he almost puked even before she said anything.

He believed all that stuff that Dr. Drinas said about heaven and Ma being there. He was relieved to hear that it was okay—actually *good*—if Charlie felt really sad and cried a lot and got very mad. Charlie felt all of that, but deep down inside, he just needed to make sure that Ma made it to heaven all right. She'd be scared, thinking he was still home in bed, waiting for her, so he wanted her to know that Amy was going to watch out for him for a while.

Charlie wanted Ma to know that he was okay and that he loved her and she could just relax and hang out with Jesus. He could pray to God to tell her, but God had all those millions of dead people to deal with, plus the angels, plus all the people on earth, plus keeping the earth turning and the sun hot and the stars hanging up there in space. God had to be one busy dude, and Ma, being polite and all, would wait her turn to have a chat.

Charlie couldn't bear the thought of her worrying that he was still alone at home. That's why he had pleaded and cried and played baby until Dawna and Pedro agreed to make this trip happen. Dawna was supposed to tell everyone at Safe Haven that Charlie was upstairs sleeping while Pedro showed Charlie where *The Other Side* office was.

They were there now, leaning their bikes against the fence. "Nice house," Charlie said. "Why ain't there a sign out front?"

"They don't want people bothering them. Not that we're a bother," Pedro said quickly.

"He might think we are. Remember when he came by a few weeks ago? He didn't even talk to us, and he never came back."

Pedro shrugged. "He's busy. Probably got a private jet and a supermodel girlfriend."

"Now what?"

"I guess we—whoa, look!" Pedro pointed down the street. A silver Lincoln Town Car headed their way. Sure enough, its blinker went on right before the driveway.

"That gate's opening!" Charlie knew how that worked; the car would disappear behind the high fence and they'd never get to talk to Joshua Lazarus.

"No problema." Quicker than a flash, Pedro jumped into the middle of the driveway. The limousine skidded to a stop.

The driver got out, red faced. "Not funny, young man. I almost hit you."

"Sorry, man. But my friend here, he's got to speak to Mr. Lazarus. It's really important."

The driver looked at Charlie. He had cold blue eyes and lots of lines in his face. "I'm sorry, but you'll have to make an appointment. Go around to the front and our receptionist will help you."

The back window opened. Charlie's heart leaped when he recognized Joshua Lazarus. "Something wrong, Ben?"

"Just a misunderstanding."

Pedro ran to the window before the driver could grab him. "Charlie's mother died last night, and he needs your help, so don't go blowing smoke about us making appointments."

Joshua Lazarus got out of the car, walked over to Charlie. "Your mom died?"

He nodded. It hurt too much to say it aloud, though he knew sooner or later he'd have to get used to telling people.

Joshua Lazarus bent down so they were face-to-face. "How old are you?"

"Nine. You?"

"Twenty-nine. I was eight when my mum died."

"Sucks, huh?"

"Big-time. Your friend was brave to jump in front of the car like that."

Charlie shrugged.

"You guys want to come in, look around? We can hang out for a while."

Charlie nodded. "Yeah."

"Cool. Come on, let's go right through the front door here, okay? I don't get to do that often."

"Cool," Charlie said.

Joshua Lazarus smiled and motioned for both of them to follow him. Just as they went into the house, Pedro turned around and stuck out his tongue at the driver.

"Oh yeah, that'll teach him," Charlie whispered to Pedro.

"It's the thought that counts," Pedro said, and for the first time in that miserable day, Charlie laughed.

Forty-four

MAGGIE WANTED TO RIP THE WALLPAPER RIGHT OFF THE WALLS. "You tell him to get down here. Right now."

"He's not available, so you can stop shouting at me."

"Listen, you little—"

"Maggie." Patrick's hand on her arm restrained her from grabbing the girl and shaking her.

"Call Geneva, then."

The receptionist regained her professional demeanor. "Miss Deschenes, is it?"

"No. It is Mrs. Lazanby."

"Oh. You're related to Miss Lazanby?"

"Yes."

The receptionist was frantically pushing buttons. "Catherine, where's Geneva? Her . . . um . . . sister is out here."

Maggie leaned over the counter. "Sister-in-law. As in Joshua Lazarus's wife."

The receptionist stared, openmouthed. "But he's . . . he's . . ."

"A liar? Yes, he is. But single, he is not. Not anymore."

Patrick steered her toward a sofa. "This lady is trying to do her job, and we're in the way. Why don't we sit down and wait for Miss Lazanby."

"I can't believe this. Poor Charlie . . ." Maggie shook her head, wanting to hold on to this incredible rage. She'd had enough of tears, enough of excuses, enough of being patient and kind. She was sick of herself, and now she was sick of Joshua. What had they become simply for the sake of fame?

Joshua came down the stairs. "I was about to call you."

Maggie got up, but Patrick stepped between them. "Mr. Lazarus, I'm pleased to meet you. I'm Patrick Drinas, advisor to Safe Haven."

"Oh yeah. Sure." Joshua shook Patrick's hand, his eyes on Maggie the whole time.

"Where is he, Joshua?"

"Upstairs."

"Take me up there right now, or I swear I'll call the cops and have you arrested for kidnapping and brainwashing and—"

"Keep your voice down." Joshua cursed, then reddened as he looked at Patrick.

"Thank you for taking him in," Patrick said, his tone mild. "This is a tough day for Charlie; I'm sure you understand."

"Of course I do," Joshua said.

They followed him up the stairs and past his secretary, who pretended to be busy. Charlie and Pedro sat at the table, munching pizza and downing milk shakes.

"Oops," Pedro said. "Busted."

"I made him do it," Charlie said.

Maggie hugged Charlie and reached out to squeeze Pedro's hand. "We're not mad, Pedro. You're a very good friend. You ready to go back?"

Charlie looked at Joshua questioningly.

"It's okay, guys. Take the pizza with you," Joshua said.

"I'm not that hungry," Charlie said.

"I bet your friends are, though. Tell you what—I'll have a bunch of pizzas delivered over to Safe Haven. Along with some ice cream. Okay?"

Charlie shrugged.

"Works for me, Mr. Lazarus," Pedro said.

"Patrick?" Maggie looked at him.

"I'll take the boys back. I'm sure you two have things to discuss," Patrick said.

"Thanks for the pizza. Nice meeting you, Mr. Lazarus." Pedro shook his hand.

Joshua grinned. "The pleasure was mine. Charlie, you hang in there."

Charlie ran to Joshua and hugged him. Patrick grabbed the pizza, then ushered the boys out. They had decided that he would take the boys back and debrief Charlie gently, hoping that Joshua hadn't done any damage.

"Is there nothing you will not stoop to?" Maggie said.

"They were here when I got here. Did you want me just to turn them away?"

"You should have called me to come get them right away."

Joshua shook his head at her. "It all begins and ends with you, huh? I can't do a good deed?"

"A good deed? Do you realize how much damage you may have done? He is so vulnerable right now. Did you give him some warm and fuzzy message from the other side from his poor mother? That's what he was here for, you know."

"*Me?* What about you? You and your precious Amy and your high-and-mighty doctor pal there? I'd bet my right arm that you had a message for the little guy, that his mommy was safe and happy in heaven with Jesus." Joshua circled her, his eyes bright. "Aha. It's true, isn't it? That's exactly what you told him. That she's in heaven with Jesus."

"She was a believer. So we were telling him the truth."

"You tell him his mum is alive with Jesus; I tell him she's safe and sound on the other side. Different words, same message. And what the blazes does it matter anyway, because she's not coming back from there. Another little boy having to make do without his mother."

"Joshua." She reached for him. "I'm sorry, I didn't even think . . ."

"No, you didn't. You just assumed I was so starstruck with myself that I wouldn't know how to handle Charlie on the worst day of his life. At least I had Geneva to hold on to. He's got no one."

"He has Amy. Me. His friends . . ." Maggie's voice weakened with each word.

Joshua took her by the shoulders. "Look at me."

She looked into those dark eyes that once knew all her secrets, though there were so few to know, and all her dreams, of which there had been only one from the time she met him—that he would be her moon and stars and love forever.

"Do you think so little of me, Maggie?" he whispered.

"I love you." It sounded automatic, even to her.

"I don't know about any of the rest of it, the spirits and your Jesus. But

I'm real and I'm right here. If you can't believe in me, then where does that leave us?"

She rested her head against his chest. His heart raced, and she thought strangely of Charlie's mother, dead at thirty-five from a heart attack. Joshua was almost thirty. What if she lost him?

What if she had *already* lost him?

Theo's relationship with Ben Cord was odd, to be sure, and yet apparently advantageous to both. Theo had given Cord a fair amount of processed epena, though since the middle of last week, the man had stopped asking for it.

In return, Cord had given Theo plastique, timers, detonators, and wires. The man was like a superstore of death and destruction. It became clearer and clearer that Astarte must have sent Cord to fill Theo's needs. He had been wary at first, but Cord's interests were clearly independent of his own. If they could help each other along, so be it.

Theo loved coming down here during the day when the acolytes slept, when cars moved overhead, people went about their business—what little of it there was in the Beak. If Amy Howland had an ounce of sense, she would have understood that little slab of plywood would not keep him out, not when he had a true purpose. But she was all bluster and no bite, much like that little lamb she prayed to.

Astarte would come in fire and consume Amy Howland along with all the others.

Why drive away what could be a perfect sacrifice?

Cord's words, whether inspired or mocking, had taken root. The plan was coming clear—the perfect offering for his beloved mistress would well be a trinity of innocence, faith, and beauty.

"If you love me, you'll be at my side," Joshua had said. He had begged Maggie to be at Friday's show, told her that he needed her.

If we claim to have fellowship with him yet walk in the darkness, we lie and do not live by the truth. The Scripture ran through Maggie's mind over and over again.

Joshua was her husband. That God had only made her love for him burn brighter seemed sometimes cruel. If Maggie could just walk away, she could follow Jesus on a clear and steady path, without these vast shadows looming over her.

"You can't save him," Patrick had said.

"You can only love him," Amy had said. "Love him and pray for him."

Maggie didn't know how to do either. Her marriage was a puddle in the noonday sun—shining but shallow, any light a reflection that was swallowed up by night. Her relationship with Joshua had been built on adoration, intense physical attraction, and dependence.

She could no longer adore what she despised, nor depend on what she knew was rooted in darkness. The physical part was meaningless and ugly without the bond of affection and respect. Walk away, then. Leave him to the darkness he had chosen. But had Joshua really made a choice? Or had he just grabbed on to the nearest hand, not comprehending that he grasped a shifting shadow?

She could not save him. She hadn't saved herself, but God had seen fit to let her tumble in front of Safe Haven—even using Theo to make that happen. Jesus took the tattered cloth of her life and gave her back a glittering robe. All He asked in return was that she walk among the lost, shining His light. It was easy to shine a light among Dawna and Natalia and Charlie. They were sweet and funny and fresh.

It was a challenge to shine a light near Geneva, who sucked in all kindness and spit it back as spite. Difficult to shine a light for Joshua, who was tossed by spirits and dreams and his own ego. Impossible to shine a light on these horrible deaths and ugly suspicions and rising ambitions.

I just can't do it, dear Jesus.

THEN LET ME.

But we have this treasure in jars of clay to show that this all-surpassing power is from God and not from us.

2 Corinthians 4:7

Forty-five

Amy ruffled Charlie's hair. "You really like spaghetti, huh?" He nodded, his mouth stuffed with pasta, his face red with sauce.

"Cool. Listen, I'm going to sit on the front porch for a minute, okay?"

"To pray, right?"

She grinned. "What makes you think that? I might be out there just watching the motorcycles whiz by."

"You got this thing on your face."

"*Thing*? What, a zit or something?"

"Gross. No. Just this . . . nice look. That's all."

"Well, thanks, Charlie."

He dug back into the spaghetti. Amy pulled on her coat and mittens, took her mug of tea, and went out.

What a week. Charlie losing his mother. This latest death involving *The Other Side* show. Maggie being pulled in all directions. After much prayer and discussion, Maggie had agreed to Joshua's request that she be at tonight's show. Amy couldn't stop her, nor did she try. Maggie was his wife, after all. But she was also an infant in Christ, tossed into the raging river of darkness.

"The light shines in the darkness, but the darkness has not understood it," Amy said into the night.

"Amen," Charlie said.

"Hey, what's up?"

"I thought you might need my help out here."

"I do," Amy said. "Zip that jacket and pull the hood up, because I need a lot of help."

"I'm your man." He sat down next to her, and they looked into the night. After a minute, Charlie slipped his hand into hers.

The Other Side staff was all smiles and sweet words, pretending to be thrilled to be meeting their boss's wife. Geneva had reserved a seat for Maggie at the back of the audience, but Maggie had asked to be near the set where Joshua did his "Messages from Home."

He had wanted to introduce her on-camera, but she refused to allow that. She understood now that it was not proper for the wife of a man publicly—or privately—involved in the occult to serve in a Christian ministry with children. But for tonight, she would be by Joshua's side and pray against all the powers of darkness, even the ones that made this show a hit.

When she took her seat, Maggie felt conspicuous with her expensive clothes and professionally done makeup. This was a lifestyle they had dreamed, but now that it was here, it felt false and ugly.

Bruce Tanis, the show's director, hustled around like a crazy man, Jennifer at his side to keep his lunacy to a dull roar. Ben Cord stood at the back of the studio, eyes scanning the audience.

Maggie was dismayed to see Detective Bowse smack in the middle, talking to a chunky woman with brassy red hair. Dane probably had comped them tickets.

Dane—who was still alive at this time last week.

Two spirit visitations and two dead. Maggie shuddered, wanting to get away from it all. But she had promised Joshua she would be here for him. She had promised herself that she would pray.

She raised her eyes in time to see her husband step into the spotlight.

Oh, dear God, he takes my breath away—even now.

Amy felt movement at her side again. "Charlie, I asked you to go to—"

"You won't be telling him for long," a slick voice said.

Amy jumped while her stomach plunged. "What do you want, Theo?"

"Same thing you do."

She slid away from him, leaning her back against the post so she could see him clearly. "Really?"

He smiled slowly but remained silent. Trying to lure her, Amy knew, but she couldn't resist: she had to make a wisecrack. "So you're telling me that you're leaving the Beak? Is that it, Theo?"

He stood, towering over her from the top step. "What I am telling you is that I have applied to the Division of Youth Services for the guardianship of Charles Milloy."

Amy jumped to her feet, slamming against Theo, not caring that they both were tumbling off the steps, hitting the pavement hard.

He grabbed the nape of her neck and pulled her face to his, pressing his lips to her mouth, puffing his noxious breath into her lungs. She squirmed, bringing her knee up to his groin, but he rolled, now on top of her, pinning her arms with his knees, laughing like a ghoul.

"Get off me," she hissed.

"Self-defense," he said, bringing his face down to hers.

"I'll bite your nose off if you get any closer."

He jumped up, brushing his pants off. "And so you prove my point. You are an unfit candidate for foster parent, whereas I am—"

Amy pushed up on her knees, hating that she was humiliated at his feet, hating that she had not turned the other cheek, hating that God had allowed this veil of darkness to be pulled over her neighborhood, hating that she wanted to kill this man right here and now.

Hating that she *hated*.

"Go now," she whispered.

He laughed.

"Go now. And may God have mercy on your soul."

"You got good instincts, woman." Bruce's voice came through Geneva's earpiece as she stood in the back of the auditorium. She looked up at the control booth, eyes wide.

"My bud from the left coast called. According to the angle of the reflection, where Josh was sitting, he agrees it had to be on the TelePrompTer."

Geneva gave him a thumbs-up, then hustled off to find Jennifer. "Show me the text for tonight's 'Messages for Home,'" she said.

Jennifer clicked on the laptop, opened the prepared spiel. "It's fine—nothing added."

"Virus check it."

"Why? It hasn't been anywhere but this computer."

"Don't argue—just do it! Run it through Norton or whatever you got on there."

Jennifer sighed dramatically. "You want me to do the whole computer?"

"Start with that file."

A second later the program pinged. Jennifer looked at Geneva, eyes wide. "It's contaminated. Unknown virus."

"Save it to disk. Right now. Then delete the file and scrub that whole computer."

"What about the script for tonight's 'Messages'?"

"Handwrite it on cue cards."

"But there's only one segment left—"

"Then you'd better shut up and get started. I don't want that file anywhere near the TelePrompTer. You hear me?"

Jennifer nodded.

Geneva went back to the floor. Joshua was okay tonight, not great. It might be better that he was lackluster—people were at the edge of their seats, expecting something to break loose any moment. Hungry for someone else to die just to get their thrills. Beth had told her about that little boy from where Maggie worked. Charlie, orphaned a year older than Josh had been. Life stunk and then you died. It made Geneva sick and it made her sad.

She caught Ben's eye, motioned for him to follow her out of the studio.

"What's up?" he asked.

Geneva opened her mouth, then coughed. "Wait," she said. The back of her throat tickled mercilessly. The air out here was dry and filled with motes. All these people coming in, who knew what they brought with them? Ben keyed himself into the green room, came back with a bottle of water. She waved her thanks as she gulped some down.

She'd give him the file, let his experts in the CIA or wherever he came from figure it out. Obviously her brother had a very dangerous and very tech-savvy stalker. They were out there—jealous rivals who put curses on him; crazed women who thought he was married to them; bitter viewers who didn't get the message they wanted from the other side; everyday psychotics and sociopaths.

"Gen, it's almost time for 'Messages.' I need to be in there," Ben said, his hand pressed to his earpiece.

"I want you to—" She coughed again, feeling like she had swallowed a feather pillow. Why couldn't she stop? She wanted to talk to Ben about her fears and concerns, about too many people having access to too many places. Like that girl who tried to follow her inside the security fence. Hillary whatever from Vermont. Her friend Tanya a suicide victim. Looking for someone's father, thinking he had killed himself too.

Ben took her arm. "I'm going in. We'll talk later, when you're done choking."

Geneva nodded. Why had she doubted Ben Cord? He seemed the only genuine guy around. She started back into the studio. Someone tapped her back. She turned, but no one was there.

She looked down the hall, empty now. The studio and the office were as familiar to her as the carriage house was, as the camper had been. And yet, she felt those fingers again, tapping her shoulder as if trying to turn her to look at something.

This was insane. First coughing her lungs out, now imaginary fingers on her back. Must be stress bringing this all on. No one was out here—they were all inside, watching the show.

Inside.

Of course! This had to be an *inside* job—who else would have access to their computers? Katherine, Jennifer, Beth—could they be trusted, really? Or could it be Bruce? Sure, he'd found the noose—but maybe he was one of those fiendish types who took delight in playing cat-and-mouse with his victims.

What did she really know about these people, anyway? Dane had hired all of them, and she had allowed that. It had all been too new, too much of a whirlwind back then. She was no hick Maine girl now—she knew her way around this business and certainly around this show. She would have to take a close look at everyone who worked for *The Other Side* who had access—no matter how incidental—to their computers.

This couldn't wait. She'd make sure Josh got safely home, and then she would get to work.

Forty-six

Someone knew something. Bruce had turned off the TelePrompTer for "Messages for Home"; Jennifer brought in handwritten cue cards. Penn had seen Geneva shove a diskette into her pocket. He'd bet anything the file with his attached surprise was on there. If she hadn't figured out what it was and where it came from, some computer jock would soon enough.

No matter. He would make *this* Geneva Lazanby's big night. The transponder in her car would trigger a huge surprise, and Penn would be miles away, with plenty of witnesses, when that all happened.

Lazarus and Maggie sat in the backseat, holding hands but not speaking or even looking at each other. Penn had whisked them out immediately at the end of the show, telling them he was alarmed by the restlessness of the audience.

He'd get them home, and then he'd see to Geneva. He had wanted a few more days of playing with Lazarus, but maybe this was destiny—an ice storm was coming off the water, as if Mother Nature were adding her blessing to his planned event.

Joshua nuzzled Maggie's ear. "Spend the night with me. You can't imagine how I miss you." They had come in the back door and gotten no farther than the kitchen. Maggie stirred eggs for an omelet, looking so beautiful that he couldn't keep away from her.

"I would love to sleep with you. In the camper."

"Maggie. Come on."

"I will not spend the night in this house. I told you that." She looped her arms around his neck. "We can pretend it's like old times."

He laughed. "You want me to invite Geneva in, or should I set up the pup tent out on the lawn?"

"Okay. Not quite *that* old."

Something clattered from the living room, startling Maggie. "What's that?"

"Probably a bird flying into the window or something."

Her eyes were wide. "You sure it's not someone trying to get in? Ben was worried tonight."

"The alarm is set. Probably some crazy seagull, losing his way in the fog." He kissed her, thrilled to feel her responding. Man and wife—one flesh—just as they should be.

Something crashed against the house.

Maggie pulled away. He caught up to her in the foyer. She peered out the door, looking bewildered. "Nothing's out here."

He drew her inside, unable to meet her eyes.

She breathed in, then let the air out in a *whoosh*. "This isn't the first one, is it?"

"I swear, Maggie, I did not ask for this."

Something slammed against the upstairs picture window. A pair of headlights flickered on high, three stories up.

He pulled away from her and ran up the stairs.

She raced up behind him. "Ignore it!"

"I can't! It's Mum's car." Framed in that upper window, tilted on its side, was the shimmering image of the old blue Pontiac station wagon. If Joshua looked more closely, would he see his mother? Or could he call her out from there, bring her to him like he had Annette?

"Mum?"

"It's not real, Joshua. Just ignore it."

"Are you crazy? You pray to a God you can't see but tell me to deny this? You've got eyes in your head—use them!"

"Come to the camper with me now. We'll drive away, put all this behind us."

"I'm not leaving her."

Maggie pulled on his arm. "I don't know if this is a trick or demons or whatever, but it's not from God and it's not good and you need to walk away from it right now."

He clung to her. "Maggie, what's happening to me?"

"You can get out. You have to, Joshua, before it's too late. I beg you . . ."

Something crashed from upstairs and kept crashing.

"Mum needs me!" Joshua raced into their bedroom. He had to shield his eyes as a hundred headlights spun into the window, some coming straight on, some turning to the side and blinking on and off, some rolling over and over. Like a drumbeat, the crash came at intervals, so loud that the headboard on their bed rattled.

Maggie ran in after him. "Stop!" she cried. The noise stopped suddenly, and Maggie jumped back, startled. "Thank God," she breathed.

"Don't make Mum go away!"

Maggie shook him. "It's over now. Come with me, Joshua."

"Shush," Joshua said.

"Please, come—"

"Maggie, I said shut up!"

Then came a sound so chilling that he could feel every inch of his skin break out into goose bumps.

Help me. Baby, help me . . .

He numbly opened the window. Outside was the blackest night he had ever experienced. And that voice—trapped in his head like a razor slicing away every ounce of sense.

"We need to get out of here," Maggie said.

"Shut up, Maggie. Shut up. You are keeping me from Mum, so shut up."

She grabbed his shoulders. "Look at me. Look at me right now!"

Maggie didn't know him, didn't know that this had been his deepest wish from the time he was a little boy, that Mum would come back and tell him she was okay, that it was all a dream, that he was okay and that it was time to wake up—

"You need to choose. Right now. This is not real. I am. Are you coming?"

"No."

"Joshua, please."

He knocked her hands away. "Walk away."

"I beg you—"

"I said: walk away."

She leaned into him and kissed his cheek. "God save you, my love. Because I cannot."

She turned and walked down the stairs.

He let her go. The crashing started up again, metal and glass exploding, tires screeching, brakes squealing, brush ripping.

He started to cover his ears, but no, he owed it to Mum to listen.

After Geneva had made sure the offices were all empty and the outside alarm was on, she ripped the police tape off Dane's office. They had six full-time office employees and eight production staff members, plus a bunch of part-timers. She'd shake out every single one of them, track every line on their applications and résumés until she found the snake in her garden.

Didn't matter that it was past midnight on a Friday night. Didn't matter that all the schools and businesses were closed. She didn't need a voice on the other end of the line. All she needed was a way to get into their computers. She fired up Dane's workstation, loaded in every hacker's tool that he had bought or stolen, and went to work.

Thank you, Dane. You taught me well.

Three hours later she had gone through almost every employee résumé with little to show for it. She now knew that Bruce was on his third wife, that the kid who ran the camera had been convicted of misdemeanor drug possession, and that Beth had lied on her résumé. She had an advanced degree in theater arts in addition to the secretarial courses she had taken at her college—probably thought no one would hire her if they knew.

Geneva had not yet discovered anything that would make someone a murderer.

Ben Cord, on the other hand, was a mystery. The NYPD files were ridiculously easy to get in. Sure enough, Detective Benjamin Cord had a record of meritorious service. But Dane's system was set up to alarm if their hacking was being hacked back, and this contact was. Same thing happened when she tried to get into Ben's college files. What was on the résumé matched what was in the official transcript, and yet another alarm was triggered as she brought it up.

She photocopied his college record, then shut down Dane's system. Her PC was almost as sophisticated and well equipped as Dane's, so she'd go there, just in case someone was tracking back.

She'd never be able to break into the Department of Defense computers to track Ben's military records, but Dane had taught her a way around that. Rather than going to the Marines, she could go to some of their vendors, especially for their standard boot camp lab tests, to see if she could score a soldier's ID that way. Once they had an ID number, they could then query the DOD with some authority.

It took her half an hour, but she found a way into Reliable, Inc.—the independent lab that had done drug screens for new recruits. In a five-year period on either side of the date Ben claimed to have entered the military, there were seventeen Cords. None was Ben or Benjamin for either the first or middle name.

Geneva dropped her head to the keyboard. It was long past midnight—her skin felt like it was going to explode. Maybe she should shut down, go home, and sleep it off. Peter Muir could recommend a private investigator who could take this over. She was probably going about this all backwards anyway. Old coot she was—not even forty but so set in her ways, she wouldn't trust anyone to do anything for her.

No. Not for her. For her little brother, her Josh.

Ben Cord—Mr. FBI-CIA-NYPD knight in shining armor. Why were his contacts setting off alarms? Maybe because he was so well connected. Or maybe because he was so slick.

She couldn't give up, but she didn't know what to do next. She lay her head back down, wishing Maggie was right, that she could pray to God and He would guide her.

"Okay, God, what do I do?" she said, not sure if it was a prayer or a curse.

She coughed, then couldn't stop. Blast it all—she must have some cough drops somewhere. Her jacket, that was it. Still thrown over her chair from yesterday. She grabbed it and patted down the pockets. No cough drops, just that stupid paper that stupid girl had pressed into her hand.

Geneva stopped coughing and unfolded the paper.

Hillary Martin, Townsend, Vermont. Worried about Tanya's father, Penn Roper. Missing since Tanya's suicide. Please ask Mr. Lazarus to help.

Fingers, tapping on her back, tapping on her forehead. Geneva sat down, went back into the Reliable database, typed in "Penn Roper."

Not the same year as Ben Cord, but close enough. When she Googled "Penn Roper," she found enough to chill her to the bone.

"My God," she breathed. "My God, what do I do?"

Forty-seven

A NICE KETTLE OF FISH, MUM WOULD HAVE SAID.

Even though it was the middle of the night, Geneva had called Hillary Martin. Her college roommate was still up and, by the sound of the drunken laughter, partying. Hillary was home for the weekend, she had said and given Geneva the number.

The Martins were not happy to receive a call in the middle of the night and less happy when Geneva tried to explain she was from *The Other Side* show. "That show is a crock of baloney," Mr. Martin said and slammed down the phone. Geneva tried to call back, but they had disconnected the line.

She then put in a call to Peter Muir; his answering service refused to put her through. Terrio and Bowse were off duty, the cop at the police station said, refusing to give her their home numbers. He offered to help, but Geneva couldn't trust information like this to someone she didn't know. It could end up plastered all over the tabloids or worse—maybe Ben Cord had the local cops in his pocket too.

She had called the estate over and over. No answer. Ben had taken Josh and Maggie home after the show. What if he had . . . no, that wasn't his game. Not yet at least. Maybe she should get the cops over there. Better not; she didn't want to spook Cord—or Roper—into doing something rash. His was a slow-acting scheme; that was obvious. She didn't even dare leave a message on the machine; if he knew that *she* knew, he might act precipitously. Better to sneak up on him.

Geneva tried Josh's cell phone again, then Maggie's. "I'm on my way home now. Don't go anywhere, especially with . . ." She hesitated—the guy had superior technical resources; he surely would be able to hack into voice mail. "Just stay there. I'll explain when I get home."

Geneva grabbed her coat and went out to her car. The street was shrouded in icy mist; she could barely see the outdoor security lights, let alone the streetlights. Anyone or anything could be out there, watching. Waiting to pounce, waiting to devour, some dark spirit pacing the alley.

"Now who's the religious freak?" she mumbled to herself. She got into the car and turned on the wipers, dismayed to see that the mist covering the windshield had frozen. It was a night like this that Mum had died. It was almost three o'clock in the morning—the sanders wouldn't be out until dawn. Maybe she should wait here until then.

No. She didn't dare. Her priority was to secure her home, and if that had to include Maggie, so be it. Her sister-in-law hadn't been that obnoxious lately, mostly because she wasn't around much. She had found something that worked for her in that Safe Haven place.

Geneva wished they had had something like that for Josh when he was young. He used to go home after school, lock the door, and play with his magic props until she got home from work.

I took good care of him for you, Mum.

She drove automatically, taking the narrow streets of Raven with some care, then opening it up when she got to Route 1A. Heavier traffic meant drier roads; she could do almost fifty without worrying. Why hadn't Josh picked up the phone? No doubt he and Maggie were either arguing or making up. Either way, they would have turned off the phone in the bedroom.

"God help me," Geneva said, her teeth chattering even though the heater was on full blast. "If You're there . . ." Easier to deny than to desire what she had never known—the safety to love and not lose the ones you loved.

Okay, so if You're there . . . why did You leave it all up to me?

Geneva took the turn into Hawthorne, automatically despising the rich people who owned these stately houses. Now that she and Joshua had become like them, she would have to reevaluate this instant dismissal of everyone who had something that they didn't. Maggie had a point when she said Geneva was a stubborn old dog, but Geneva knew her own character; she didn't need Maggie to tell her.

She tapped the brakes, carefully taking the turn to Hawthorne Neck. The streetlights were out on the causeway. The spray shot up and over the rocks, the wind driving it into the rain. Maybe power was out to the whole Neck, which might explain why no one answered the phone out at the estate.

This was a nasty stretch of road. She couldn't understand why they hadn't installed guardrails, especially on the south side where the rocks tumbled down to the water. The snobs on the Neck probably protested that safety rails would detract from the view.

She crept along, then increased her speed. So close now, she just wanted to get home.

Geneva . . .

She instinctively jammed on the brakes. The Lexus fishtailed, then straightened out as she regained control.

"Steady girl, steady," she told herself.

Geneva . . . The voice came from the backseat, a woman's voice, crusty with smoking and hard work.

"Shut up. I ain't buying it."

She was coming to the last turn now, then it would be straight to Beach Road and the estate. Geneva pumped the gas lightly to take the turn when—a woman jumped out in front of her car!

"Mum!" Geneva screamed as her car hit the rocks and rolled over and over into the water.

Charlie woke up screaming before Amy could answer the phone.

He clung to her, all bones and tears in his Bart Simpson pajamas. The person on the other end tried to tell Amy something in a high-pitched and breathless voice. She didn't catch a word of it. "Hold on."

She placed her hand on Charlie's forehead. "'Now may the Lord of peace Himself give you peace at all times and in every way.' Amen."

Charlie stuck his thumb in his mouth and shut up.

"Good boy." And into the phone, "I'm sorry, who is this and how can I help you?"

Amy listened for a second. "She's not here. I don't—wait a minute." With Charlie clinging to her, she duckwalked to the window and looked out. "The camper is here. Can you wait while I get her . . . Beth, you said your name was?"

Beth told her not to waste time but to give Maggie a message.

Amy dialed as she walked downstairs. "Patrick, can you get up here? It's an emergency."

She settled Charlie in the den and went out to the driveway to tell Maggie the tragic news.

Forty-eight

Maggie didn't need to be a doctor to know that Geneva was dying.

Joshua and Amy were with the doctor now, requesting that he lessen her medically induced coma. "I want to tell her good-bye," Joshua had said, choking back tears. His sister had been heavily medicated so she wouldn't struggle against the ventilator.

Maggie kept vigil, holding Geneva's hand.

The door to the cubicle slid open. Amy came in and pulled up a chair next to Maggie while Dr. Potter fiddled with Geneva's IV.

"Where did Joshua go?"

Amy motioned Maggie away from the bed. "He's composing himself. Listen . . . there's not much time left. She's bleeding out."

"Give her blood, then. There must be something . . ."

"There's not. Her coagulation is all screwed up. Once it goes bad, it doesn't reverse."

"Amy, help me." Maggie bowed her head.

"Dear Lord, have mercy." That was all Amy prayed—what more could she say? Geneva was in God's hands now.

Joshua stood against the wall, waiting for his sister to open her eyes. There was no guarantee, but he had to believe that Sola would show him this one mercy. Mum had tried to warn him—if he had been more obedient, maybe he would have seen this coming. A simple phone call to tell Geneva that it had gotten icy on the Neck and she should stay in Raven would have spared her this. But he had been too preoccupied with Maggie's resistance to believe what was right before their eyes.

Terrio and Bowse had already come by and made sympathetic noises. A crime scene was set up on the causeway, though no one could prove this was anything but an accident. It was slippery, late, and some punk with a .22 had shot the lights all along the road.

"Punk shoots better'n me," Bowse had said to Terrio on their way out.

Maggie had rushed over to the hospital, babbling to him about God's mercy. It ran off him like surf on sand.

"Joshua, look," she said.

Geneva's eyes fluttered.

"I'm here, Gennie," he said. "You're going to be fine."

She narrowed her eyes, tipping her head to the side. *No.*

Her gaze shifted to Maggie, struggling to say something around the ventilator tube. "Geneva, I know it feels strange. But don't fight against it. You need it to breathe," Amy said.

Geneva groaned and forced her lips around the tube.

"We can't take it out. You need it. Do you understand?" Amy's voice was gentle. Joshua had resisted Amy's presence, but now he was grateful he had someone to help navigate all this medical stuff.

Geneva stared at Maggie. "Ba ba."

"I'm upsetting her," Maggie said. "I'll wait outside."

"Na na na . . ."

"You want Maggie to stay, Gennie?" Joshua asked.

She looked at him and nodded. Her gaze shifted to Maggie, then back to him. "Ba pa ba pa."

"I can't understand you, Geneva," Maggie said. "What can we do to help you?"

Geneva slapped the back of her hand against the bed rail. Joshua stared, watching her index finger tremble with effort to lift out of the IV setup.

"She wants something," Amy said.

Joshua grabbed the belongings bag. Inside were Geneva's clothes, drenched with blood and saltwater. "There's not much here. Geneva, is it your purse you want? They couldn't find it—it must have fallen out of the car, into the water."

Geneva grimaced. Joshua's heart ached, seeing her reduced to a broken body tangled with wires and tubes. With incredible effort, she again pointed her finger.

"Your coat? Is that it?" Maggie asked. Terrio had brought her coat when he had come; they had found it in the floor of her Lexus after the tow truck dragged it out of the water.

Geneva's eyes widened.

"Is that it, Gennie? Your co—" Joshua stopped.

His sister's eyes had rolled back.

"What's happening? Is she—?"

"No. Not yet," Amy said. "She's just . . . reached the limit of what she can do."

"Gennie?" Joshua rubbed her hand, but he couldn't rouse her. He looked to Amy, panicked. "Is this it?"

"Soon," Amy mouthed.

Too soon, Joshua thought. *Over too soon, and what do we really have to show for it but broken bodies and broken hearts?*

Mum, I tried.

SHE KNOWS.

I can't leave.

YES, YOU CAN.

He needs me.

HE NEEDS ME.

I don't know . . .

I DO.

I love him—

I AM LOVE. WILL YOU LET ME?

Yes.

Forty-nine

MAGGIE DROVE THE CAMPER WHILE JOSHUA STARED OUT THE window. His face was mottled and scruffy with day-old beard. It had been a tough weekend—keeping watch over Geneva, then going to the funeral home to make arrangements. The press had caught up to them there. He hadn't even blinked as the flashes went off in his face.

"Where's Ben?" he asked.

"Yesterday was Saturday. His day off."

"He never takes a day off."

"I told him to take it off. We're going to need him double-time for the next few days," Maggie said. "He'll meet us at home in a while."

Joshua straightened up, stared at her. "So tell me, Maggie. Where is home?"

"Where would you like me to take you? The estate, the office, the studio? If you'd prefer, I can book you a lovely suite in a hotel, get you some privacy."

"You won't come with me if I go to the house?"

"I'll be close by, in the camper."

He took her hand. "Then I'll stay here too."

Maggie drove in silence for the next twenty minutes. When they crossed the causeway, they could see the broken brush where Geneva had skidded off the road. Joshua didn't say anything; he just clenched Maggie's hand.

News trucks were parked outside the estate. Joshua slid down in the seat while Maggie used her remote to open the gate, then drove onto the grounds. She turned off the engine, pocketed the keys.

Joshua opened the door. "Coming?"

"Wait. We need to talk."

"No more talk. I just want to sleep with you holding me."

Maggie covered her face. How could she do this at a time like this? Yet how could she not? If she truly believed Joshua was in danger—and she did—then being firm would honor Geneva more than letting him have his way.

"I will stay close to you and watch out for you and hold you as you mourn," she said. "But as long as you talk with these spirits and do the show and have anything to do with these witches and astrologers, we have to live apart."

He looked at her through bleary eyes. "You promised you'd never leave me."

"I'm not leaving you. But I can't be your partner in any of this. If you'll walk away from it all, I'll be at your side all the way. But as long as you keep on with this stuff—"

Joshua's cell phone buzzed. He patted his shirt, confused.

Maggie found the cell phone in his jacket. She flipped it open, listened for a moment, then looked at him.

"It's Ben. He drove to D.C. overnight, but he's almost back to Raven. What do you want him to do today?"

"Tell him to round up the staff and bring them to the estate."

"It's Sunday."

"With Geneva and Dane gone, we're shorthanded. We've got a show to plan."

Maggie pressed the phone against her chest. "Don't do this."

He grabbed the phone. "You do what you have to do. And I'll do what I have to do."

Maggie straightened the camper, doing everything she could to ignore the ache in her chest. She would think her heart had been broken—losing Geneva, now losing Joshua—but had her heart ever really been whole?

LET ME.

"I *am* letting You! It's not like I have any choice, is it?" Maggie yelled.

She rustled through boxes of props, items that had been so familiar and essential less than a year ago. Forgotten now, traded in by the magician for what—a new set of illusions?

Someone knocked on the door. Maggie peered out, then opened it. "Ben. Come on in."

"I am so sorry, Maggie. Is there anything I can do for you?"

"Talk some sense into my husband?"

He shook his head. "They're going full bore over at the house, planning the next three shows. Maybe it's for the better. These deaths have hit Mr. Lazarus very hard." He looked down, twisting his fingers. "I've been asking myself if somehow it's my fault."

"Your fault?"

"I'm in charge of security. Primarily Mr. Lazarus's, but Dane and Geneva were part of his universe."

"I don't know what to tell you," Maggie said. "Terrio and Bowse aren't saying much, but it looks like Dane may have killed Annette Donaldson. There's some indications that they were having an affair. He wasn't a bad guy, Ben. Just a bit of a jerk, but I'm sure he didn't mean Annette any harm. It's just . . . these Hollywood types always live on the edge. And with Geneva . . . the road was so bad. She had to be exhausted, coming home so late. So I don't know that there's anything you could have done."

"There is one thing. I went to D.C. yesterday to visit an old buddy at the CIA. I told him about these visitations that Mr. Lazarus keeps having. My pal was so intrigued he lent me some equipment so sophisticated, the technology hasn't been released to the public yet."

Maggie felt a spark of hope. If Ben discovered something—anything—maybe Joshua would abandon his delusions. "When are you going to scan everything?"

"I already did, at least the house. I'm going over now to do the office and the studio."

"What did you find?"

He looked past her shoulder as if he was afraid to meet her gaze. "It was clean. I'm sorry, Maggie. I've tracked down terrorists and criminals, but I don't know how to track down a ghost . . ."

She couldn't speak, just waved her thanks. He nodded and left.

Maggie sank into the passenger seat, Amy's words knocking the inside of her head. *He's hearing demons.*

She bent over, her face to her lap.

. . . *demons* . . .

She shuffled her feet, trying to will herself to get up and do something. Something rustled under the seat—she looked down to see the Patient's Belongings bag from the hospital. After they had taken Geneva's body out of the room, Maggie had stuffed the coat inside with what was left of her clothes. She had carried the bag around mindlessly as they signed the forms at the hospital, then met with the funeral director.

Geneva's last conscious act had been to point at her coat. Maggie took it out and put it to her face, breathing in Ivory soap and mints. Something crackled in the pocket. A sheet of paper with a name on it: Hillary Martin, followed by a phone number and address, then another phone number. Probably someone wanting a ticket or maybe to book a private reading.

Maggie tossed the note.

A minute later, she retrieved it from the trash. It probably meant nothing, but since there was nothing else in the jacket, Maggie owed it to Geneva to follow up.

She opened her cell phone and dialed the number that was in Geneva's handwriting.

A Mrs. Martin answered and had confirmed that Geneva had called there in the middle of the night Friday. No way were they going to let a stranger talk to their daughter at that time, or maybe not at all. "Who are you? Her secretary? That woman was downright rude," Mrs. Martin said.

"My sister-in-law. Geneva was hurt in an accident Friday night. She died a few hours ago."

"Oh," Mrs. Martin said.

"It seemed important to her that someone get in touch with Hillary."

"Well—I just don't like strangers talking to my daughter. She's only nineteen, had a tough year."

"Please," Maggie said.

"Maybe if we met you face-to-face . . ."

"Give me directions," Maggie said. "I'm on my way."

This was all unreal. Joshua Lazarus's wife—a pretty woman named Maggie—sat in Hillary's living room. Her father looked on, stone-faced. Her mother had served diet cola and cheese and crackers, trying to make up for yelling at the woman who had died.

"I've been trying to see your husband for months," Hillary began.

"Can you tell me why?"

"Because my friend committed suicide."

"I'm so sorry," Maggie said.

"We were best friends forever." Hillary went on, telling how they had been to the show, what happened the next day, and how Tanya's father disappeared after the funeral. "I've been so worried that he killed himself too."

"Hillary, we hired a private detective," her father said. "The guy vanished without a trace."

She looked at him, stunned. "You did? But you said—"

"Never mind what we said. We didn't tell you because we thought you were carrying too much guilt as it was. For no reason, Mrs. Lazarus; I hope you understand that." He turned back to Hillary. "We loved Tanya too, and we were very concerned about Penn going missing."

"I don't understand," Maggie said. "Who is Penn?"

"Why, Penn is Tanya's father, of course. Penn Roper." Hillary went to her bedroom and came back with a picture of herself, Tanya, and Mr. Roper in Bermuda. "He's a nice man," she said, handing the picture to Maggie.

"Lord, have mercy," was all Maggie Lazarus seemed to be able to say.

Jennifer babbled as she loaded the tray with drinks and snacks. "This stalker kept trying to get in to see Joshua, and Geneva kept throwing her out. Some sad-eyed girl—they're all sad-eyed, aren't they? Hillary something or another."

Penn, more focused on the conversation in the living room, suddenly snapped to attention. "What did you say?"

"Hillary. That was the stalker's name. Like from New Hampshire or Vermont or one of those ski-slope states. What if she, like, drove Gen off the road or something?"

Penn carried the drinks into the living room, his mind racing. He had rid himself of Geneva. That had been the plan all along, anyway. Make Lazarus pay, one person at a time. Would someone in the office make the connection between him and Hillary? He put down the tray, then turned to leave.

"Ben, please stay. We value your input," Lazarus said.

"I want to check out the studio and office, make sure no one is poking around there."

Lazarus waved him away with a grateful smile.

Penn went out to the Lincoln and booted up his laptop. While it initialized, he instinctively scanned the environment. The safety lights framed the house, garage, front and back lawn.

The camper was missing.

Maggie had probably gone to Safe Haven for the night. He clicked on his locator program to check the transponder he had attached to the camper. The icon was static—the camper wasn't moving. But where was it?

He typed in a command, then waited while the signal went out to the satellite and bounced back. The GPS came back with Vermont—still processing to retrieve the exact location, but Penn didn't need that, not when he knew Hillary Martin's address as well as he had his own.

In all his planning he hadn't even conceived that sweet-natured but empty-headed Hillary would be tenacious enough to pursue an answer about Tanya.

Penn needed to head north and intercept Maggie.

Fifty

PENN ROPER. BEN CORD.

Maggie should have called the police right then and there, but all she could think of was getting home. The thought of a murderer being at the right hand of her husband had blinded her to all rationality.

She had mumbled thanks, jumped into the camper, and turned east. By the time common sense took over, she was in the mountains, where cell reception was terrible. No stores were open in the middle of the night up here either.

Maggie finally passed a closed gas station with a dimly lit public phone outside. She got out and punched in her calling card number. The account was denied. She shook out change and finally got through to home. It rang and rang—even the answering machine didn't pick up. She was about to dial 911 when she saw a car pass on the highway, going west.

A silver Lincoln Town Car—now squealing into a sharp U-turn.

Maggie jumped into the camper, thankful she had left it running. As she jammed down the gas, she tried the cell phone again. Nothing. Ben must have somehow tampered with their accounts so they didn't have service.

The limo pulled up behind her. How far was it to the next town? She'd drive through the front window of the nearest bank if she had to, just to get some police attention.

Slam! The camper was rammed from behind, throwing Maggie forward. The seat belt yanked her back with rib-bruising force.

The Lincoln pulled out to her left, trying to come alongside. She swerved to the middle and blocked him. The road was narrow enough here to do that, but they were fast approaching a rise. Up there the road widened into a third lane to allow passing—Ben would be able to get alongside her and push her off the road.

Maggie swerved as hard as she dared. She felt the camper shift and shudder—she was close to toppling it. She grasped the steering wheel, trying to block Ben without overturning herself. The rise seemed endless, and the road was too wide and too well paved to block him for much longer.

Oh, Lord, tell me what to do!

Maggie was gutsy, trying to push that wreck faster than the powerful Lincoln. Then again, what did she have to lose? She knew now that she was running for her life.

He'd catch her soon enough. And then, out here in the New Hampshire woods, he could give her what she deserved. Lazarus would just have to see it all on tape, a fitting irony—Lazarus's brand of entertainment had ripped Penn's heart out, and now Penn would reciprocate.

Penn pulled into the passing lane, about to bump Maggie from the side. Lights came over the rise—a car approaching from the other direction. He could force Maggie into a head-on collision, but no; he wanted hours, not seconds for her demise. He slipped back in behind the camper, watching with amusement as Maggie waved her hand out the window, trying to signal for help.

No way, sweetheart, Penn thought. *You look like a drunk teenager.*

The road narrowed to two lanes as they came down the hill. They'd be to the outskirts of Keene soon—Penn had to make a move.

Maggie floored the camper. Penn cursed—she used the descent from the hill and the weight of the camper to gain speed. She pulled out of sight, but he'd catch her soon enough.

Seconds later, he spotted the camper on the side of the road. He jammed the brakes, skidding in behind it. The driver's door was open. Had she fled into those dark woods?

He'd know soon enough.

Maggie held her breath and prayed.

Ben was inches away from her, pulling boxes aside, dumping the big crate, scraping the cot across the floor.

The curtain to the palanquin opened. A sliver of light crept across Maggie's feet. *Don't move, don't breathe, don't even sweat.* Penn Roper was a predator; he would smell fear. Maggie stood still, counting, praying, remembering that last show at the Sea Breeze, when Geneva had gotten stuck in the trapdoor.

Tap.

Ben tested the wall. He wouldn't see the latch—the false wall was toe-triggered. But he could hear hollow spots.

Maggie leaned her body against the wall, praying that Ben wouldn't tap high or low where she couldn't absorb the sound with her body.

Tap. She felt it now, against her heart.

Another tap. Then another.

Silence.

More tapping, this time of footsteps. Ben bought her ruse and hopefully was going out into the woods. How long should she stay in here? Too quick and he'd see her. Too long and he'd be back.

Her mouth itched to scream. *Give me something to hang on to, Lord!*

Charlie's face rose in her mind, so clear that she could smell the Doritos on his breath, feel his buzz cut, touch his bony shoulder. She drifted along the dining-room table at Safe Haven—Dawna and her cocoa curls; Pedro and his charming bluster; Natalia with her sharp eyes and a tongue to match; Manny who insisted he was heading for the NBA. Amy looked up at her, grinning. "Go for it, Maggie," she whispered.

Maggie opened the trapdoor.

Darkness lay beyond.

Ben had left the back door open. Biting cold air rushed in. She crept on hands and knees to the window.

Where was he?

She spotted a flashlight beam in the woods. Not in deep enough to give her time to get a big head start. She was still too far from Keene; even if she roared away, he'd catch up in plenty of time.

Then she heard another engine, this one purring.

It had been over twenty years since Penn had tracked human prey.

There was no movement in the woods except for the wind in the barren branches. He turned the flashlight back on and slowly swept his perimeter. Maggie had had only seconds to gain a lead—she could not have gone far.

He listened for that tiny crack that signaled a branch being stepped on, that high, faint squeal that meant she breathed through clenched teeth. He sniffed, his nostrils flaring like a dog trying to catch a scent. Salt for exertion, bitterness for fear.

Nothing.

Penn held still; his body remembered before his mind the years before Tanya when he could be stone for an hour at a time. Days when buddies were killers and killers were buddies. Secret medals and commendations for service to his country when he was only really serving his lust for adventure.

All given up so quickly and forever—so he had thought—when he saw a tiny form on ultrasound, felt little fingers close around his for the first time. Picked up again in an instant when he closed his daughter's eyes for the last time, his hands and chest and face soaked in her blood.

You will not escape, he mouthed to the night.

An engine roared. Penn whipped his head around just in time to see the Lincoln blast away.

Taking the keys to the camper would only gain her half a minute. Ben would be able to hot-wire the engine; half the kids Maggie grew up with could do that. She also left a little surprise with no guarantee it would work—the props had sat in the boxes for months, with no maintenance.

She spotted headlights now, coming too quickly. Ben had no regard for his own life. He would push the camper until he drove up her back. She held the steering wheel with one hand, searching for a cell phone with the other, pushing the Lincoln as fast as she dared. This was a forty-mile-per-hour road with curves and banking. She hovered at seventy, the steering wheel gripped in her hand.

She felt the whomp before she saw the headlights. He battered her, this time with the heavier camper. How much could the Lincoln take? It was faster, but the camper was heavier.

He came at her from the side, sideswiping the Lincoln and sending it into a spin. She struggled with the steering wheel, trying to regain control, watching as the car turned toward the woods, then completely around so it was nose to nose with the camper.

She grappled for the gearshift, trying to reverse. She flashed on her high beams, trying to blind Ben and steal a few seconds.

He waved, then floored the camper with a mighty roar.

She punched the gas, the Lincoln shooting off backwards, trying to hold the steering wheel steady, the camper bearing down on her. He was almost on her and then—

A sudden flame erupted in the front seat, startling Ben and sending the camper bouncing off the road and into a ditch. She had set a flash pot with a timer on the floor, unsure after all this time if the powder would ignite. Miraculously it had.

Ben jumped out of the camper and ran down the road after her, raising something, a gun—Maggie pushed down on the gas, skidding now as she tried to keep the Lincoln away from the embankment and the woods, hearing a crack, feeling glass shatter against her face, praying to keep on the straight road, remembering a verse Amy had read to the kids about making straight in the wilderness a highway for our God. *Lord God, I need a straight highway now*—and now it was straight and she could go in reverse two hundred yards or more until the camper's headlights were distant and Ben Cord just a shadow in the night. Maggie squealed into her own U-turn, racing to Keene to find the police and to call Joshua and tell him they no longer had to fear spirits or Penn Roper or anything because God had delivered her.

Fifty-one

"THIS GUY WAS ONE SERIOUS SPOOK," BOWSE SAID. "AND I'M NOT talking about the two-bit, moneygrubbing witches in this town."

"His résumé reads like something out of an action flick. Military covert ops, on to the CIA, then to private industry as a defense contractor," Terrio said. "Roper—whom we all knew as Cord—had tricks that we couldn't even guess at. Microsized cameras and speakers, some remotely triggered, some hooked via optical fibers you couldn't see unless you were wearing coke-bottle glasses."

"What about the ghostly apparitions?" Peter Muir said. "How did he generate those?"

Terrio shrugged. "The brainiacs are still tracking that down. It can be done, but it'd be blasted expensive. Which wasn't a concern to Roper, we're finding out. After his daughter's death, he cashed out everything. Sold that company for pennies on the dollar, converted retirement accounts, his kid's college fund. The guy had money, contacts, and the skills to pull off any show he set his mind to."

"The NYPD stood by his references," Peter said. "What was that about?"

"If they know who vouched for the Cord alias, they ain't saying," Bowse said. "The Agency is playing dumb too. They don't want to lay claim to any devices Roper might have used or any people who might have fronted him."

"All that skill, driven by the oldest motive in the book—revenge," Terrio said. "His daughter, Tanya, had been to *The Other Side* show the night before she killed her mother and herself. Roper must somehow be blaming everyone connected to the show."

Peter fisted his right hand, punched it into his palm. "These people turn the occult into entertainment, suck in the innocent and unsuspecting, then laugh all the way to the bank."

"The Lazarus crowd, you mean," Terrio said.

"Witches, astrologers, psychics, healers, channelers—the list is endless. They open doors to dark places, and people like Tanya Roper are pulled in."

Bowse glanced at his partner. "Beggin' your pardon, Pete, but this ain't nothing new to us. The world turns on greed. People want and want, and when they don't get, they hurt."

"Forget *hurt*. They murder," Terrio said. "And leave it to us to clean it up."

"This is one mess that will need more than the long arm of the law to clean up," Peter said.

Joshua and Maggie had spent the last two nights in a hotel. With police protection and a private firm hired by Peter, they felt secure enough to come back to the estate. Experts had uncovered Penn Roper's devices for eavesdropping and for generating images and sounds.

Even so, Maggie refused to stay in the house. They had come back only to check the computer.

"I have to know why," Joshua had said. "What it was that I said to Tanya—"

They were in the library, booting up the computer. "The shows are all stored digitally now. We've got a huge server at the office—that's what I'm logging on to now." Joshua sifted through icons until he found the New York episode, the first one ever televised.

They watched for a while on accelerated viewing, then Joshua slowed to normal time. "There, I think."

Joshua walked along a row and stopped near a redheaded girl.

"It's difficult to lose someone at any age. But for someone as young as you . . ."

He could have walked away right then and there, Maggie thought. But he stayed, his eyes brimming with concern for Tanya Roper.

"Would you like me to leave you alone?"

Tanya shook her head.

"He's showing me metal. Shiny and bright. Too bright. It was a violent death."

"I thought it was a boyfriend in a car crash," Joshua said.

Joshua touched Tanya's cheek in a gentle gesture.

"He understands about the promises you made that you couldn't keep. He wants you to just let it go. Get on with your life."

"Did it hurt?" Tanya asked.

"No," Maggie said. "Tell me you didn't respond to that." But of course he did. That was his job—his gift, they all thought so many months ago.

"Not for long. He's let it go. He wants you to let it go too. He forgives you, Tanya. And he wants you to know that he will love you forever."

Maggie reached out to grasp Joshua's hand. She looked around, her stomach sensing before her mind could comprehend where he had gone and why.

Joshua ran full-tilt across the lawn, not caring that his chest might explode, hoping it would because it *should*. Guilt shredded him like a pavement cruncher, ripping apart every lie that he had ever believed, every conceit that had driven him, every false hope that had come into his heart and then out of his mouth.

Shiny metal.

A sensitive, lovely teenager, already consumed by sorrow and regret over aborting her baby—and he had made entertainment from it. She believed him too. That was clear by the stunned look on her face, though by then he had turned his back on her, searching out the next mark in the audience.

A violent death.

She must have felt his words in her own bones—her baby shredded to pieces and sucked out into that shining metal basin, imagery so striking that it shattered her heart.

If only Penn Roper would somehow rise out of the ocean and blow his brains out, then perhaps justice would be satisfied. But Penn had chosen a more complete path—instead of simply destroying Joshua's life, he instead had destroyed those he loved. Throughout it all, Joshua had had the ridiculous egotism to believe that he had true power to see past death to what lay beyond.

What you're doing is despicable, Amy Howland had said.

Was there even a word to capture how loathsome he was? No amount of fame or money or even false comfort could compensate for the anguish Tanya had felt when he gave her a message from her own aborted baby. No amount of sorrow could atone for the loss Penn Roper had suffered—for the sake of putting on a show.

One driving impulse remained—the will to get to the cliff. Joshua would just keep running until he met clear air and hung for a miserable eternity before the rocks rose up to break him apart.

If he was shattered into a million pieces, he still would not have gotten what he deserved. A small part of his mind told him to stop now and wait for the hand of vengeance. Sooner or later, Penn Roper would return to claim his revenge. Joshua couldn't allow that because of Maggie—he had to protect her by wreaking vengeance on himself.

"Oh, God, forgive me," Joshua cried, though he knew with every breath that it was impossible to pardon what he had done and even more impossible to forgive what he had become.

He ran faster, close enough now to see the spray as the waves crashed against the rocks.

"Joshua, no!"

Maggie raced to catch up, but he ignored her. She'd never catch him, because he was too fast and too deserving of death. Only a hundred feet now, and then it would be over.

Wait—what was that? Something glittered in the frosted grass, but it didn't matter; he would jump over it if he had to. Time to leap.

Time for it all to be over.

Fifty-two

"I DON'T NEED A SHRINK AND I DON'T NEED A PRIEST. I HAD what I needed and then—" Joshua shook his fist at Patrick Drinas as if he had been personally responsible. "—my wife robbed me of the only dignity I had left."

"You tripped," Maggie said. "Five feet from the cliff and you tripped. Was I supposed to help you up, then push you over?"

"You should have let me die," he said.

He had begged and begged, but Maggie had climbed onto his back and held on until the police came. That was yesterday.

Today they were in the Woodward Clinic, the psychiatric facility where Patrick had staff privileges. A judge's order had confined Joshua for seventy-two hours. After that, he'd be free to walk or, as Maggie thought with a shudder, free to plunge headfirst down the rocks.

Patrick had arranged this family meeting, and at Joshua's insistence, Amy sat in on this session. He said he wanted her there for Maggie.

"Why should Maggie have let you die?" Patrick asked.

Joshua threw up his hands. "Is this some sort of penance, forcing me to repeat over and over what I did to this girl? Or do you enjoy watching me choke on the vomit I've become? Because that's what I surely am. I see that now—I'm disgusting through and through."

"Let's start with that, then," Patrick said. "Disgusting through and through."

"Don't start that Jesus spiel."

"I wasn't going to."

Maggie was almost shocked to see a twinkle of amusement in Patrick's eyes. It was easy to forget that Joshua was just one of many tortured souls whom he treated—and ministered to.

"Then where should we start? How about we start with *me*! Oh yeah, Mr. Self-obsessed, the sun and the moon and the stars, the one that all creation revolves around." Joshua snapped his fingers. "No, wait. Let's begin with my dreams. Fame and fortune. How shallow, huh, especially compared with you candidates for sainthood. Or we could look at my methodology—lying and cheating for the sake of looking like a prophet. Sleight of hand gives way to sleight of mind. Not hard to guess what people want to hear—the other side is a place of beauty and peace where their loved ones get it all together. Oh, and there's that little matter of me being the one who could speak with them there and pass on their good tidings.

"Except I got it so wrong that a girl killed herself. So wrong that I drove an upstanding member of the community to pledge every ounce of his life to avenge his daughter's and wife's death. So wrong that the people around me paid the price that should have been mine alone to pay. How's that for a start, huh, Doc?" He pounded his chest. "It starts here and it ends here, because that's all that's left for me to do—to pay the price I deserve."

Maggie covered her face.

"Oh, shut up, Joshua," Amy said. "You make me sick. You know that?"

Joshua looked at her. "Sainthood isn't good enough—you need to be a shrink too?"

Maggie waited for Patrick to intervene. He squeezed her hand but kept silent.

"I don't have the patience to shrink anyone's head, let alone one as inflated as yours," Amy said. "So how about the voice of common sense? Can I be that?"

"It's not like I can stop you. In case you haven't noticed, they've got me locked in here."

Amy stood up. "You can stop me. Just tell me to walk out that door and I will."

Joshua threw his hands up. "Go ahead—speak your piece. I'll add it to my penance."

Amy tilted her head, touching her index finger to her lips as if deep in thought. "Let me get this straight. You're claiming *total* responsibility for Tanya Roper's despair, her death, her father's raging anger toward you and everyone surrounding you."

"It's about time I did, don't you think?"

"I didn't realize that you were the one who drove her to the clinic to get the abortion."

"Come off it, Amy."

"You didn't sign the papers, you didn't pay for it, you didn't hold her hand and make sure she went through with it."

Joshua pressed his lips together, glaring.

"For that matter, you didn't get her pregnant. And you weren't the jerk who abandoned her to deal with the pregnancy by herself."

Joshua shook his head. "Okay, so that's all true. But I drove her—and then her father—over the edge."

"You're assuming that Penn Roper was *normal* until this tragedy tore his life apart? Spending millions of dollars, murdering strangers just to get back at someone isn't what I call normal behavior."

"Maybe not. But can you blame him?"

"Yes, I can. I blame him for finding no recourse or remedy other than indulging a hideous anger. I blame him for spoiling his daughter—that's what Hillary said, wasn't it? That he gave Tanya everything she wanted and things she didn't even know she wanted. So when the poor girl was faced with something serious, faced with a young man for whom love meant jumping into bed and walking away—when she was faced with a problem that could have become a joy for her or some couple—she froze. From what Hillary said, Mrs. Roper probably bullied her into the abortion because her father had so crippled their daughter by his over-the-top adoration that she couldn't act like an adult."

"Okay, okay. So we're all to blame, then. Tanya and her mother paid with their lives. Penn isn't paying; he's making others pay—Dane and Geneva, this Annette. I'm the only one who's walking away scot-free. I can't do that. No way. Because I can't bear what I've done and what it's done to people I love and was responsible for. To Maggie."

Patrick glanced at Maggie. She nodded but kept silent.

Amy waved her index finger at him, her eyes flashing. "Here we go again—it's all about you, 24/7. There's some responsibility to spread around in your life too. Start with a sister who loved you so much, she smothered you."

"Shut up," Joshua snapped.

"A wife who loved you so much, she clung to you. Hard to walk on your own with two women hanging on you. Add the talent, the good looks, the charm, and it is all about you, Joshua, because the people who loved you best haven't let it be otherwise."

"I won't have you talk about my sister that way. Or Maggie."

"So you're gonna carry all this yourself? From stardom to martyrdom—as long as you're center stage."

"That's enough!" Maggie was on her feet now.

"Pray. Pray and trust Jesus," Amy whispered.

"What's that about Jesus?" Joshua muttered. "He got something to add to your fire and brimstone patter?"

Even with Amy's eyes blazing, Maggie could see the love in her face. "Three simple words," Amy said. "*Come to Me.*"

"Doesn't make sense, Amy. I'm smothered by my sister, my wife, my fans, and now Jesus wants in on the action? When do I get to be a man?"

"When you turn yourself over to Jesus to be loved. He's the only One who can make something good out of this mess. The only One who can lead you to the manhood that He created you for."

The silence was so complete that Maggie could hear the *plop* of his tears hitting the floor.

She took Joshua's hand.

He wouldn't look at her. "How can He forgive me for what I've done?"

"He forgave me," Amy said.

Joshua's smile—shaded with the inevitability of loss—broke Maggie's heart.

"Saint Amy? Not much to forgive there," he said.

"Let me tell you about a girl in nursing school who wanted to be the best nurse ever, wanted to heal every hurting person on this planet."

Joshua chuckled, a joyless murmur. "Yeah, yeah. Like I said—Saint Amy."

"Money was tight. School and work and more work. I took uppers to keep it all going."

Joshua shrugged.

"I became that nurse with the good job; patients who adored me because I adored them. And I truly did, with the love of God. But I had gotten used to the uppers to keep me alert. Which meant I needed something else to get me out of the end of shift. One night, someone gave me some coke. Wow, I thought. I have to pray for an hour to feel this sweet high. Only for a short time, I told myself. Once I get used to the job, I'll stop.

"But you develop a hunger, probably the same kind of hunger a star develops for the spotlight. I kept it up, switched to crack because it was cheaper. Then I made a mistake."

Joshua narrowed his eyes. "What happened?"

"I took a hit while I was on shift, got buzzed, and missed a patient's dose of heparin. Not all that earth-shattering in normal people, but this was a guy with pulmonary emboli—blood clots in his lung. He shot a clot to his heart and died in terrible pain. I wanted to die with him, and I tried to, but my supervisor caught me before I could shoot up with a massive dose of insulin. I was a Christian, Joshua, and I should have known better, but I was trapped in a vicious cycle of sin."

Amy sobbed openly. Patrick put his arm around her, steadying her.

"How did you get through it?" Joshua asked.

"I didn't get through it, not on my own. People who loved me"—she nodded at Patrick—"stood by me. Sent me to rehab, helped me through that terrible two years while my license was suspended. During that time, I worked as a nurse's aide, emptying bedpans and letting God heal me because I couldn't do it myself. He walked by me then and walks by me now. Lots of times I try to fall out of His hand—or leap—but He simply refuses to let go. That's real love, Joshua, and real hope, and it's there for you."

Joshua covered his face. "I don't know. I just don't know."

"Let us help you," Maggie whispered. "Let us pray."

Joshua squeezed her hand and looked inside himself.

The darkness rose to take him. Patrick's prayer was quickly drowned out by the voices. Regardless of whether they had sprung from Penn Roper's rage or some festering abyss, the truth was this: the spirits had found their own life.

We're here to stay. So you may as well just come with us.

The flesh melted from Maggie's hand, and he held dry bones, little more than powder, no flesh, no blood, no life.

No one to help now. And why would you want that, Joshua?

He had been pulled away from the hospital room to this land of gray haze where shadows shifted into other shadows until the only texture was layer upon layer of nothingness.

"Maggie?" he whispered, not wanting to alert anything that lurked here, but the shadows themselves came alive, icy snakes with mouths opening like broad highways to a deeper darkness.

It never ends, Joshua. Might as well hop on.

"Maggie!" he cried again, and then he saw her, praying a thousand miles away, the darkness pushing against her prayers with a foul and carnal laughter, the breath of hopelessness that had sucked him over to the other side. But this place was not of his making—no, this other place was a land of dry bones and sharp rocks, where sky and land and sea had no meaning but all was not all, all was lost, all was naught, all was not that which was from the beginning. There were no words to describe this emptiness because there was no word here to save him.

Don't fight it, Joshua.

Maggie was drifting away, Patrick's voice fading, Amy's breathing next to him like a wisp of air in another universe, but they had none of this, and he wanted none of this, but the darkness leaked into his skin, soaking his heart and blood and bones because it wanted nothing but his soul and that for an eternity of being eaten away until he no longer remembered that he had once been loved.

It's easy here.

He was inside himself now, a world unto himself, a vacuum of self-praise and empty promises. That golden-haired woman had been his last gasp of truth, and she had escaped from this darkness, leaving only a memory that was rapidly becoming nothing, void, abyss, and this one truth was that he was nothing.

All for naught.

Yet there was that tiny spark of gold in the darkness, a beacon so faint that he could hide it in the blink of an eyelash and yet so powerful that it was the Light of Ages.

Though he was nothing, that Light was enough for Joshua. "God help me," he whispered.

Had silence ever been this complete?

Then, a tiny note, pure and vibrant, now growing as the gold grew, crushing the darkness, ringing like a bell, pealing so loudly that Joshua knew it would shatter him and consume him, but he agreed that he deserved destruction and desired grace.

The hand of bones became a hand of flesh, and he held on as tightly as his battered heart could. He saw with an inner eye that had never before seen, and watched as his heart filled with blood, felt as his skin came to life with every nerve ending crying out in tremendous pain, but that was okay, because this was what he was missing, what he longed for, what he would stake his life on because it was no longer his to stake. The gossamer cord that he had tripped over in his headlong rush to the cliff wrapped around his heart now, binding it to the great Light, and now that Light broke through the haze.

"God help me," Joshua Lazanby sputtered. Then he opened his eyes and greeted the day.

Fifty-three

PENN LEANED FORWARD IN HIS CHAIR, STARING AT THE TELEVISION.

The Other Side had been in reruns for a month following what the media called "the stunning revelations surrounding the Lazarus empire." Tonight's show—dedicated to Geneva Lazanby—was live.

Normally a fastidious man, Penn had trashed every motel room he'd been in for the past four weeks, drinking himself into oblivion, forgetting to eat and shower, vomiting wherever he needed to, then moving on to the next hotel room.

The headlines and accusations hadn't fazed him, but what nearly killed him were the pictures of Tanya. As if that weren't vile enough, someone had slipped the media various videotapes—Tanya playing her flute in a school concert, giving a speech for the National Honor Society, holding the Bible when Joanna was sworn in as a state representative.

Penn dropped the Gideon Bible at his feet. It opened at the Psalms, the favorite book of his fellow warriors on the battlefield.

The Lord is my shepherd.

"Not." Penn spit onto the open book.

The familiar theme music came on, followed by hazy smoke, then the title. Lazarus should be thanking Penn big-time—his revenge plot had catapulted him to the pinnacle of notoriety. Geneva hadn't lived long enough to ink her precious network deal. Now all the networks and the pay cable outlets were waving huge buckets of cash at this guy.

Let them, Penn thought. *He'll never get to spend one dime.*

He spit again, then settled back to watch.

Praying was painful—every moment before the throne of grace made Joshua feel like a septic tank being pumped. Tonight he had no choice but to pray. He was about to make three million viewers very angry.

Joshua looked into the camera. "Good evening. I'm going to ask the camera to pan the studio so you at home will see that there is no audience here tonight." Joshua paused, giving Bruce a chance to swing the camera.

"Dear people, I have lied to you. I cannot speak to the departed or for the departed. Some of you are saying, 'Aha, we knew it all along.' Some of you—too many—believe that I really spoke to your friends and family on the other side. I was specific in your readings, giving you names and places and dates. I was compassionate and convincing.

"To perpetuate this fraud, I used your credit-card information and other personal details to hack into your medical records, your municipal records, even your online photo albums. *The Other Side* staff, at my direction, trampled at will—and without conscience—through your lives.

"I will say it again—I am heartsick for what I have done, and I am deeply sorry."

Joshua glanced at Maggie. She smiled her encouragement.

"The news has been filled with the accounts of what happened to Tanya Roper because of this show. I am responsible for her death because I lied to her—all for a night's entertainment, and all because I loved fame more than I valued the truth.

"And the truth is this: only one person has freely crossed between this life and what lies beyond—the Lord Jesus Christ. My faith in Him does not excuse me from the consequences of my actions. There is no excuse for the lie I perpetuated and the harm it has done. I claim faith because, when I was beyond hope, hope found me in the person of Jesus.

"The money I have made through this show will go into a nonprofit foundation called True Sight. This foundation will be administered by a board of directors consisting of local ministers, doctors, psychologists, and educators. Its purpose will be to minister to anyone who has been injured psychologically, emotionally, or spiritually by *any* involvement with the occult. We'll provide contact information at the end of this broadcast. I will move heaven and earth to ensure that no occult practitioner will ever be able to cause the harm to someone else's child that I did to Tanya Roper and to many of you.

Joshua bowed his head. *Oh, Lord, if ever I need the words, it is now.* He looked again to Maggie—her hands were folded in prayer, but her eyes were fixed on him.

"And now I have a word for Penn Roper. Words will never suffice for what you have lost. But I beg you to turn yourself in. I will do everything I can to see that you receive help. It is not too late. God forgave me. He will forgive you."

Tears flowed down his face. "I'll say it again: God forgave me. It's my prayer that you all will too. Good night."

Joshua walked away from the camera, off the stage, and into the arms of his wife.

We are hard pressed on every side, but not crushed; perplexed, but not in despair; persecuted, but not abandoned; struck down, but not destroyed.

2 Corinthians 4:8–9

Fifty-four

JOSHUA GRINNED AS A GROUP OF TWENTYSOMETHING WOMEN walked by, whistling.

"Isn't that backwards?" David Drinas asked. "We're the hard hats. Don't we get to do the catcalls?"

"Woman's lib—taking all the fun out of it."

"So, Laz, how come you're the eye candy while I'm the breath mint? What's your secret?"

"Sleek facial hair," Joshua said. "A killer tan. And we won't mention the muscles bulging from every bone in my body."

"Yeah, well, I'm a balding redhead who can't grow hair on my legs, let alone on my face. I have to wear sunscreen or my skin bubbles, and all my muscles are between my ears. Ouch!" David shook his hand—he hammered his thumb for the first time that day, but it wouldn't be the last.

"All your muscles are in your head, Dino. That's why there's no room up there for hand-eye coordination."

Joshua had pled guilty to Internet fraud. To satisfy his nine-month community service, Patrick had arranged for him to work with his son, rehabbing housing. The hours were long and the work brutal, but Joshua's quick hands had made him a natural, especially for fine finish work. There was something incredibly satisfying in seeing rubble become a home.

"Hey, I'm coordinated," David said. "In a left-handed sort of way."

"In that case, I'll remember to work on your right side."

"No one forced you to work with me. You could have picked up trash on the highway. Or been an orderly over at Mass General."

"Emptying bedpans. Or working with Dino, the left-handed disaster. Talk about a toss-up."

"Oh, shut up, Laz," David said, laughing. "Does your wife know that all the ladies take their lunch hour at our job site so they can drool over you?"

"I tell her every night, but she's not buying it." With the beard and long hair, Joshua wasn't recognizable as the guy who had starred on *The Other Side*. Even so, he still drew a lot of attention. Once it would have gratified him, but now it dismayed him.

"You miss her, huh?"

"Oh man. Don't get me started. Did I ever tell you how we met?"

"Um . . . only four hundred and six times, Laz."

"The thing is, Dino, after we met, we were never separated again until I signed on for this gig. Saturday nights take forever to come, and then, before I've taken two breaths, it's Sunday night and she's back in Raven."

"Dad thought it would be better this way."

"Your dad's a smart guy," Joshua said. "Plus, unlike his carrot-topped progeny, he *can* grow facial hair."

"I'm warning you, Laz. I can exchange this hammer for a nail gun."

"Yeah, yeah. I'm quaking here." Joshua popped open the can of primer and stirred it. Today was Friday; Maggie would take the train into Boston tomorrow night. They'd have supper—either a pizza or baloney sandwiches, which were all they could afford, then go to their weekly counseling with Patrick. After dark they'd crawl into the camper, listen to music, hold each other, and if it wasn't too hot, share a sleeping bag. On Sunday morning they'd worship. Afterward they'd stroll in the public gardens or along the Charles. In the evening, they'd attend a praise service somewhere. Then came that long kiss good-bye until next Saturday night.

The separation is not penance, Patrick Drinas told Joshua, though it hurt enough to be. These months apart were to allow each of them time to grow in their faith before resuming a full-time life as man and wife.

He missed Maggie during the week, but the hard work kept him busy. David and his volunteers worked as late as their aching muscles and daylight allowed, which was ample in June. Maggie was busy as well. She waited tables at a diner in Lynn, volunteered with Amy at Safe Haven late afternoons, then babysat Charlie overnight while Amy worked at the hospital. During the day on Saturday, Maggie took college courses. It would take a good seven years, but she was determined to be a teacher.

Joshua met with his mentor on Tuesdays and his Bible study, on

Wednesdays. The other nights were spent writing letters on behalf of the True Sight Foundation and training with the counselors so he would be able to counsel others who had been sucked into the occult.

All the money that *The Other Side* had accumulated, plus the Town Car, expensive clothes, and high-end computers, funded True Sight. The only thing held back was the house on Admiral's Row that housed the show's offices. He had owned that jointly with Dane; Julia Madsen refused to sell her half, so it stood empty. "I just don't understand," she said. "Jesus or Sola—is there really a difference?"

A life and death difference, Joshua tried to tell her, but she felt betrayed. A year ago, they had been in New York City, filming the first *Other Side* show, Dane and Geneva right at his side. Tanya Roper was alive, as was her mother.

A year ago Penn Roper had been a productive member of society. Now he was a murderer on the run. Last winter, the FBI had tracked Penn through Mexico to Prague and then lost his trail. Joshua hoped that he feared prosecution enough to stay out of the country.

But he didn't believe that. Penn had gone to amazing lengths to bring vengeance down on them. As long as Joshua and Maggie drew breath, they would be in danger. If not this day or this year, Joshua knew that someday they would come face-to-face with Penn Roper.

Theo twirled the poker in the fire. The initiate stood motionless, face slack as if the glowing tip held no interest for him. Cord had joined them after Leonine's untimely passing. Any suspicions Theo had only served to increase the worthiness of this particular initiate. The Coven must be at full strength, because it was only a matter of days before the Vortex would be triggered.

Thus the flame, the symbol of what was to come. Astarte would rise in her glory, crowned with fallen stars. The Astaroths who survived the Vortex would stand as her honor guard. Theo would offer himself as her mate.

Cord had been tattooed two weeks ago. He had insisted on having the lines intersect his eyelids, something even Theo hadn't dared. Cord hadn't cried out once.

No one could bear the hot iron without howling—a foreshadowing of the magnificent cries that would shatter Astarte's bonds and carry her into this world. She visited Theo almost every night now, churning his heart with urgency. So little time, so much work, such great glory.

"Are you ready?" Theo asked.

Cord smiled. Initiates were allowed to specify the location of their brands. Theo's was along his jaw. Many of the others had chosen their foreheads, expecting less pain and scarring there. What would Cord choose?

"I offer you the shadow of Astarte, to be burned into your skin as a foretaste of what is to come. Will you accept?"

Cord nodded.

Theo rotated the poker one last time.

"Where would you have Astarte's mark upon you?"

Cord pointed to his lips.

"What?" Theo wasn't sure Cord understood what the brand would entail.

Cord pressed his lips together and pointed again.

Theo lifted the poker from the fire. The point had been hammered into a tiny star, signifying the stars in their Mistress's crown. His eyes met Cord's as he pressed the brand to his mouth.

Cord uttered no cry, even as Theo took the poker away, pulling burnt tissue with it.

"Open your mouth quickly," Theo said. "Before it fuses."

Cord smiled, then opened his mouth. Only then did he howl.

Even Theo's blood chilled at the sound.

Penn envied Theo his insanity, a madness so complete that it came with its own theology. He envied the rest of Astaroths their drug-addled slavery, their willingness to blindly obey as long as Theo kept the epena coming.

There was something in the initiation that had intrigued him. A last hope, maybe, that there *was* something beyond his rage and loathing, something greater than himself that would reach up and take his pain to itself—*herself*, if Theo's insanity was to be indulged.

He had endured the rites of passage for weeks on end: cleaning up disgusting messes; taking verbal and physical abuse; suffering emotional harassment. The final stage included truth telling, induced by large amounts of epena. Penn had used Theo's trick of coating his mouth with wax, then mineral oil to prevent large-scale absorption of the hallucinogen. He shared nothing of his heart, where his precious Tanya still reigned.

After the truth telling, Penn had been tattooed. It was a permanent disfigurement, as was the burning, but permanence had no relevance to him.

It was all a waste of time, but time was his ally—the more time that passed, the less likely Lazarus would be protected. After the incident in New Hampshire, Maggie had spent a month out of Raven before returning to Safe Haven. Lazarus had been in Boston this entire time but was plenty visible. The time was coming when they would all be brought back together.

Joshua Lazarus had sworn off speaking to the dead but very soon, Penn would make sure that the dead would be all Lazarus could speak to.

Fifty-five

Amy sat on the front step of Safe Haven, enjoying the fragrant honeysuckle bush that David Drinas had planted. The new grass smelled lush and damp. He had insisted they have a lawn, even though their front patch of dirt was only about ten feet square. "Maggie and I are too busy to mow," Amy had protested.

"I'll mow it every week," David had promised, his face turning almost as red as his hair.

Maggie had taken the camper to Boston to see Joshua. Charlie was asleep, exhausted from his Little League game and an afternoon at the skate park with Manny and Natalia. Amy knew she should climb into her own bed—she had to work tomorrow night—but the sweet breeze had pulled her from her office and out to the porch.

The street was quiet tonight, so still that she could hear the peepers from the tidal flats a half mile away. Usually midnight was the witching hour for the Astaroths, the time they fired up their bikes and raced around the Beak. But they were staying in tonight, and that could not be a good thing.

Amy sipped her iced tea and stared at Theo's house. Candlelight flickered against the closed shades. Was that moaning drifting over the road, or was it just a distant wind coming up the river? Sweet spring in the air and sick souls in the houses around her. So many strange sounds leaked from the four Astaroth houses—nothing surprised her anymore.

Five *houses*, Amy thought, mentally correcting herself. That madman Theo Marks owned the very steps she sat on. But his darkness would never come against these children, not with Amy sitting in the night as the guardian of Safe Haven. She knew that she was inadequate to the task, but—*You will tread upon the lion and the cobra*—she had never been called to be adequate. Just obedient.

Theo was lighting the torches in his basement when he heard something move behind him. Was that an animal? No, the breathing was too controlled, the scent too familiar. He held up his candle, trying to see beyond the shadows. "Who's down here?"

Cord stepped into the flickering circle of light.

"What are you doing?" Theo said. "You know the rules. You are not allowed." Cord was an intruder in this sacred place, an acolyte with no value other than to fuel the vortex. This place was where his mistress came to him, whispering promises, showing him things that no man had ever seen, or even imagined.

"Get out. Now." Theo drew courage from the familiar smell of musty brick.

Cord grabbed Theo's shoulders. He tried to back away, but Cord's grip was like granite and just as cold. "You're just like the rest of them, you know."

Theo cleared his throat, trying to sound assured. "What are you talking about? Like who?"

"Your friends across the street. That crowd dispensing Bible verses and bad advice with their cookies and fruit punch."

It was clear now—this was one last test before Theo was to trigger the vortex. He had long suspected that Astarte had placed Penn Roper—Cord—in his way as a trial. He would not fail. "Astarte knows who I am and what I believe."

"Don't you get it, Theodore? It doesn't matter if your god tumbles off a cross or rises out of a garbage heap. It's still all an asinine fantasy."

"My name is—"

Cord jammed his arm against Theo's throat, flattening him against the wall. "Your name is Theodore Stanley Marcillewich, and you're nothing but a two-bit psycho with an overactive imagination and a talent for body art."

The deep shadows cast by the torchlight made Cord's face look skeletal, his eyes empty. Fear curled around Theo's spine. "What is it you want? The acolytes give me things, Roper. Is it money you need? I have plenty. Or women—beautiful ones throw themselves at me. Any drug you could want. Just tell me."

Cord smiled slowly, his mouth split by the brand he had received last week. "I want your precious vortex."

"I can't give you that. Don't even ask. Astarte would not forgive me."

Cord leaned so close to Theo that his lips brushed Theo's face. "I'm not asking, Theodore. I am *taking*. So be on your way. And be sure to say hi to Astarte for me."

Fifty-six

The first day of summer—the summer solstice. The occultists in Raven, Salem, and throughout the world would celebrate the high pagan holiday in many ways, some silly and some dangerous.

The kids of Safe Haven needed to be off the street tonight.

Patrick's church sponsored a full-day outing at a water park. "Make the kids too exhausted to do anything but sleep," Amy had said. The bus took the kids right to their doors, then dropped Maggie, Amy, and Charlie at the house.

Charlie ran to peel potatoes for their supper. He had become quite the cook since being officially placed with Amy in foster care. "Do you mind supervising our magic chef, Amy?" Maggie said. "I need to brush these tangles out of my hair. Too many slides down the Screaming Cyclone."

Amy laughed. "The benefit of frizzy hair—nothing can move it from its course."

Maggie climbed the stairs, lost in her thoughts. Joshua would still be at work; they stayed at it as long as there was daylight, which was almost nine o'clock now. She missed him most of the time but not all the time. Patrick said *that* was a sign of health, that they needed to be apart until they clung to God instead of each other. There were still times of deep depression for Joshua, but David Drinas had a handle on who Joshua was and a heart for where God would take him.

The Astaroths had been quiet this week, staying off their motorcycles and in their houses. Ramping up for tonight, if Amy was right. Maggie mentally shrugged—after facing Penn Roper, Theo was little more than a rat to be shooed away. From the hall she could look into Charlie's bedroom, which was neat and orderly, and Amy's room, a chaos of books and clothes. She opened the door to her room at the front of the house, wondering if she had a clean pair of jeans to put on.

Her heart stopped.

Oh Lord God help me, is that an animal, no not an animal, who would do that to a human, help him but too late, oh Lord God, what are all those snakes doing on my bed and on the floor, and the spiders and scorpions, please give me the voice to scream, too much blood, the feet to flee, the strength to close my eyes and make this all go away oh God help help help help . . .

Maggie felt Amy's hands on her arms, pulling her back, slamming the door, then Amy screaming but cutting off her own howl as Charlie ran upstairs, potato peeler in his hand.

"Get downstairs," Amy snapped.

"But what—? Why is Maggie yelling like that?"

"You need to stop!" Amy pressed her hand to Maggie's mouth, then turned Charlie to the stairs with her other hand. "Down! Right to the front door and stand there."

Maggie and Amy stumbled down the stairs, hands clasped tightly. They found Charlie in the foyer, his eyes wide.

Penn Roper stood next to him, a gun to Charlie's head.

Penn hadn't counted on the kid.

He hadn't sealed the house yet; he couldn't until Lazarus got here. He could toss the kid outside, but the boy would run for help. That would take this long night away from Penn. Tie the kid up and put him . . . where? The Astaroth houses were already rigged for their part in this drama, all the acolytes so deep in la-la land that even the end of their world might not wake them up. Maybe dope him up with epena, hide him somewhere in the yard, and give him some chance of surviving what was to come?

"Let him go," Maggie said.

"Is that what you want?" Penn said.

"You have no quarrel with Charlie. Or with Amy, for that matter. Let them go."

"Is that true, Amy? That I have no quarrel with you?"

"I'm irrelevant. Forget me, but let Charlie go." Amy's face was a deep red. Was she going to have a heart attack? More likely biting her lip—she had a temper and a mouth.

Penn waved the gun at her. "You. Tie up Maggie."

"What?" Amy said.

"I can't have her tie you—she'll know some magic trick or something." He handed Amy the rope he had cut for this purpose, then pressed his gun into her spine. "Maggie, sit." He motioned to the metal desk chair. "Amy, tie each hand to the arms of the chair."

Amy did as she was told, her hands shaking.

"It's okay," Maggie whispered.

"Dream on," Penn said, laughing. "Now the kid." Once those two were tied, he would tie Amy himself.

The kid was stick thin, his shoulders shaking but his eyes bold. "I know who you are," Charlie said. "You were on *Most Wanted* a month ago. Penn Roper."

"How exciting for me and clever of you."

"You got the tattoos now. You with the Astaroths?"

"It's more like they're with me."

The boy mumbled something.

"What?" Penn said against his better judgment. He *had* to stop talking to the kid. He knew from hostage negotiation that the way to soften a hostage taker was to remind them of their humanity. He needed to stay on task here, forget he had once been a little girl's papa.

"I said, Maggie and me pray for you every night. We pray for your soul, Mr. Roper."

"Too late for that, kid," Penn said. "Too late."

Fifty-seven

JOSHUA WAS BEING SUCKED BACK INTO THE ABYSS THAT HE HAD created with his own egotism and disbelief, but *Dear God, not Maggie, not Charlie, not Amy. Put it* all *on me, God. Put it all on me, but show them mercy . . .*

"Don't call the cops," Penn Roper had said when he called. "If anyone but you shows up at the back door, I will skin your wife alive and make the boy watch."

Joshua had asked, begged, then manhandled the car keys away from David. Joshua duct taped his friend and left him in the kitchen where they had been working. "The box cutter is in the far side of the basement. It'll take you a couple of hours to get down there and get free. By then this will be over. Dino, I beg you not to call the cops. Maggie's life depends on your not doing that."

Joshua had rushed for the door, then turned for a last glance. "Dino, pray. Pray and don't stop." Then he was gone, bruising his way through the traffic mess heading north out of Boston. He tried to pray, but Penn Roper loomed between him and God like a black hole swallowing all light.

Joshua was close to losing his mind by the time he got to Safe Haven. The front door had been boarded with heavy plywood and pasted with a notice: "Property condemned by order of the board of health." Joshua raced around the side. The downstairs windows were barred and secure—iron grills there to protect Amy and the kids, now a trap.

The back door was ajar. He ran in, praying—*Dear God*—to find everyone still alive. The first one he saw was Maggie, tied to a chair. Amy was a few feet away, and then little Charlie was also bound to a chair.

Only then did he turn his gaze to the man whose life he had helped turn into a nightmare. Penn's face was disfigured and tattooed, his head shaved. But Joshua knew those eyes. "Do whatever you want to me—"

"No!" Maggie cried.

Penn pointed him to a chair. "Move and I'll blow your wife's face off."

No match for a gun, Joshua let his hands be tied, hoping that once he was secured, Roper would release the others. The others were tied only by their wrists, but Roper bound Joshua's feet as well.

"Let them go," Joshua pleaded. "This isn't their fault."

"And it wasn't Tanya's fault, what happened to her."

"Hold it there a minute, Mr. Roper," Amy said.

"Not now, Amy," Maggie hissed.

"Whose fault was it that Tanya got pregnant? You can't lay that on Joshua."

"Tell that idiot to shut up," Penn said.

"Amy, please. Let it go," Joshua said.

"Let it go? What, like this guy has *let it go*? We all need a dose of the truth—you've certainly had yours, Joshua—so why not Mr. Roper? You've lived in your misery for a long time, Penn—and it was dreadful despair, none of us deny that—but you've held on to it for so long that you've forgotten that you had a hand in this."

"Amy, you don't know him. Please," Maggie whispered.

"That's right, Amy. You don't know me," Penn said.

"I know the fruits of your life, and they are appalling," Amy said. "But it's not too late. God can work miracles, make something meaningful out of your pain and your loss."

Penn pointed the gun at Amy.

"No, please, she can't help it. She has a big mouth," Joshua said.

"I know a great way of shutting it," Penn said.

Charlie and the guys had talked a lot about what they would do if they ever looked down the barrel of a gun. "A .44 would be a piece of cake," Pedro had said. "Now an AK—"

"You guys don't know." Manny knew because his cousin had died in a drive-by. "You just want to wet your pants, is what you want to do. So you don't do nuthin' because anything will make you lose it, and that's the worst thing in front of some dude holdin' a gun. Worst thing. 'Cuz they want you to lose it, man. They want you to wet those pants."

Charlie knew he was going to lose it, especially once Amy started mouthing off and that crazy Penn Roper turned the gun on her. You steered clear of the guys with empty eyes—even the players on the street swung wide of them. You just had to hope they killed themselves before they took out a bunch of your guys. *Oh, God, You can't let me wet my pants, because he might shoot me too. But, God, don't let him shoot Amy. I can't lose her too.*

Charlie felt that warm touch on his heart, the touch that had kept him together all those long nights when Ma worked, those nights after Ma died. He heard God's whisper right here and now, even with a gun pointing at Amy. God said it was okay for him to go ahead and lose it, that it might even be a good idea.

He started to cry.

"Stop crying or I will put a bullet in big mouth's head here."

Charlie sucked back his tears, his sobs filling his cheeks like a tomato about to burst its skin.

The man put down the gun, then opened up a tin of what looked like chewing tobacco. He stuck a big chunk onto duct tape.

"I beg you to let me help you. It's not too late," Amy said.

The guy slapped the tape over her mouth. Amy started to choke, then she went silent, her eyes rolling back in her head.

The sobs exploded out of Charlie again.

"Don't hurt him," Joshua said. "Please."

The man bent down to him. "Just relax, little boy. You'll be okay."

He rubbed the tape over Charlie's mouth. Charlie wanted to puke with the gross stuff that was pressing into his mouth, but he couldn't, not with his mouth covered like this.

"It's sweet, isn't it?" the man whispered.

It was sweet, but Charlie still fought it until he felt a hand he couldn't see, a hand no one could see touching his forehead, then his eyelids, and then leading him into sleep.

Maggie knew that Amy had tried to tie slipknots. It took all Maggie's strength not to test the rope—she had known Joshua was coming, and she didn't want to break free too early—if for the first time ever, Amy had actually tied them right. Now he was here, tied hand and foot. Amy and Charlie were out cold—*Dear Lord, let it not be poison but something merciful.*

"I love you," Maggie whispered to Joshua.

"I love you," he said.

Penn was in the back hall, hammering plywood over the door—making the whole downstairs a trap. Maggie was about to pull the rope free when Penn met her eyes, then pointed the nail gun at Joshua's face. "You move and I'll put a hundred nails through his skull."

In Your time, Lord. But please, soon . . .

"May I ask a question?" Maggie said.

"Why not? I'll be happy to entertain questions from the floor—as long as you do not refer to my family. You cross that line and I will cut out your eyes and shove them down your throat. Are we clear?"

Maggie nodded. "Why did you kill Theo?"

Penn laughed. "He was going to die today anyway. If Theo's insane theology was correct, he is now in the arms of that tramp Astarte, queen of the flippin' underworld. More likely he's burning in hell. I am not a cruel person, Maggie. The rest of his crowd—his little coven—are dying a slower, happier death than our friend Theo did."

"What are you talking about?" Lazarus asked.

"Tell him," Penn growled.

"He hung Theo upside down over my bed. Dumped all his snakes and spiders in the . . . his throat must have been cut because . . ." She choked, unable to finish.

"So you see, Joshua, I do mean business. Any more questions, or shall we get on with it?"

"Why Dane and my sister?" Joshua asked. "Why not just me?"

"Dane came up with the whole concept for *The Other Side.* Geneva worked her tail off to make it happen. Maggie never stopped you . . ."

"She tried to," Joshua said. "I swear, she was against it."

Penn sighed dramatically. "I lived your miserable lives with you, heard almost every pitiful word. Maggie was against the show *once* you heard the spirits. By then she'd already implicated herself. But even if she was totally innocent, she would have to die."

"Why?" Joshua said.

"Because Tanya was totally innocent and she died."

"I am truly sorry for your pain. I am going to spend the rest of my life atoning for my part in that," Joshua said.

"The rest of your *short* life. Which is about to seem like an eternity, because Maggie goes first."

"I don't care! Maybe I do deserve it. But please let Amy and Charlie go," Maggie said.

Penn laughed again. "What will you give me if I let them go?"

"Anything," Joshua said. "We can get you money, safe travel out of the country. A psychiatrist, a priest. Anything. Kill me, fulfill any homicidal fantasy you want, but let the rest of them go."

"How about this? I will let Charlie go in exchange for Maggie's eye. Fitting, isn't it? An eye for an eye."

"No!" Joshua roared.

"Okay, okay," Maggie cried at the same time. "Do it. Just let him go!"

"Take my eyes then," Joshua said. "Cut out my heart if you want, but leave her alone!"

Penn waved them quiet. "You see how it is? Too complicated. So I'm going to stick to my original plan. What will be . . . will be."

He flipped open a BlackBerry, tapped a couple of keys. "No doubt the Feds had a field day with my laptop. But this baby is more than sufficient to manage the grand finale. Which, by the way, was Theo's idea. I just refined it."

"I don't understand," Maggie said.

"Oh, you will."

Penn clicked a key on his BlackBerry and the world around them exploded in flames.

Fifty-eight

DAVID DRINAS WAS SAWING THROUGH THE DUCT TAPE WHEN HE heard his father's voice. "Down here, Dad. Hurry!"

Patrick hustled down the stairs. "Are you all right? Where's Joshua?"

"I'm not sure. He taped me up, took my car, and left an hour ago. What are you doing here?"

Patrick ran his hand through his hair. "I got a call from the Raven police. Someone blew up Safe Haven."

Fire filled the windows. The houses on all sides were engulfed in flames.

"Like it?" Penn said. "Theo wanted to use dynamite, but I had access to so many toys. You might say that we struck a devil's bargain."

"Were people in those houses?" Joshua asked.

"Depends on how you define people. Theo was insane, but at least he had a goal. The rest of them were so hooked on drugs, they were only fit as a sacrifice, and a pitiful one at that. The houses front and back are burning too, as are three vans that are parked on your front lawn. Theo's vortex, which indeed is a work of art. This house is meant to be the center of it."

"That's crazy. Why did you go along with it?" Joshua asked.

"I needed time—and the cover—to accomplish what I want to do with you two. Starting with Maggie."

She was about to try the slipknot when he pulled out a razor-sharp hunting knife. Now was not the time, with that knife slicing her shirt, brushing by her ribs, her throat.

"You'll notice that I placed Maggie in a metal chair. A wooden chair might burn too fast."

"Please, don't. Penn, do anything you want to me—"

"Joshua, be quiet," Maggie said. "I don't care what he does to me, if he'll let Charlie go."

"Dear Maggie, you won't suffer forever," Penn said. "Just minutes—though those minutes will seem like forever. It's only appropriate that you experience the suffering I have for a year now."

Bursts of vicious orange flames licked at the windows from outside. The stockade fence separating Safe Haven from its neighbors was burning, as was the old oak tree near the back door. Penn must have seen the hope in their eyes when they heard fire trucks approaching. "I hacked the records in the Board of Health, 'condemning' this house. No one will be coming to help anytime soon."

Penn had put down the knife, picked up the gun again. Despair gnawed at Maggie—what if Amy had gotten the quick-release wrong? She was a wonderful youth worker but a terrible magician.

"Skin me alive if you must, but leave Maggie alone." Joshua struggled against his bonds.

"Skin you alive? Well, that's almost a decent analogy for burning. The skin goes first—turning red and bubbling. As it blackens, it curls away from the tissue underneath. The smell is horrible, but you'll get used to it. We won't be rushing through this."

Maggie slumped in her chair, her chin on her chest.

"The dear princess has fainted?" Penn said. "No matter. She'll come to, soon enough."

"Do me," Joshua begged. "Take as long as you like, but do me first. I can't bear to watch."

"And I couldn't bear to see my daughter lying in her own blood, dead on my kitchen floor. My precious baby . . ." Penn's pain was raw and explosive. "But I was a man; I sucked it up long enough to make you pay. You will curse the day you were born, Joshua Lazarus, and you will curse the long moments you watched your wife die."

Penn lifted the chair with Maggie in it and brought it into the dining room. She stayed limp as Penn positioned her next to the inner wall, praying God would tell her when to get free and go after Penn.

She heard a tiny tap, peeked long enough to see Penn touching a key on his BlackBerry—and Maggie felt fire explode out of the wall next to her. She felt the flames near her arm, knew it was only seconds before they caught the old, dry wallboard and burst against her body. Maggie's entire focus was her thumb and forefinger of her right hand, trying to find the slip. Amy had left it deliberately short so Penn wouldn't notice, but it was too short and her fingers were too constricted.

Joshua bellowed with anger and fear. She heard his chair knocking against the floor—he must be trying to hop into the dining room. She couldn't react, had to let grace keep her perfectly still, except for those two fingers that seemed impossibly large. The rope seemed impossibly tight, except *nothing* is impossible with God, and so she kept working to grasp the slip between her fingertips.

When the flame touched Maggie's arm, she threw back her head and screamed.

Joshua screamed with her, hopping his chair to get to her and in his haste, tipping over. He tried to roll to her but stopped when he saw Maggie miraculously rise. She slammed Penn with the chair, knocking him against the burning wall.

Penn's back caught fire. He screamed, throwing his arms up, sending the gun spinning. It came to rest in the doorway between the dining room and kitchen. Joshua opened his mouth to call Maggie, but if he alerted her to where the gun had tumbled, Penn might get to it first.

Joshua summoned every ounce of energy and muscle—*God, please help*—and rolled himself and the chair over, then over again, howling with pain as his stomach muscles strained and ripped. The inner wall of the dining room was engulfed. The craft cabinet had begun to smolder. All the paper in there—if that caught, the whole house would soon follow.

Penn was on his hands and knees, his back a mass of charred skin. The pain was unbearable, but he crawled away from Maggie, who kept coming with that chair. Penn crept under the table, then stood up on the other side. He smiled like a wolf with prey clamped in its jaws—holding up the BlackBerry.

Joshua had rolled to the doorway now, kicking against the frame so he could turn to grab the gun. This was an insane idea—he should call to

Maggie, but Penn could get to him just as fast, and maybe that was the right thing to do, to just take a bullet and be done.

But there was Amy and there was Charlie.

Lord, You gave me good hands. Help me.

"No," Maggie was saying. "Please, it's not too late. Help us to pull off that plywood and we'll all go out into the yard. You can get away, start a new life. Please, Penn . . ."

"Don't be ridiculous. Whatever would I have to live for?"

He fumbled with the BlackBerry. Joshua groped for the gun, praying that God would guide his hand.

A sharp blast brought Penn to his knees. Bright red blood blossomed from his side, and he slumped to the floor. Maggie instinctively moved toward him.

"Leave him!" Joshua was side down in the chair, the gun in his hands. "Hurry up, untie me. We have to get out."

Maggie sliced through the rope on his right hand with Penn's knife. She handed him the knife so he could do the rest. There was a *whoosh*—the dining-room curtains caught fire. The smoke in the kitchen thickened; at this rate, they would asphyxiate before they burned to death.

Maggie untied Amy and pulled the duct tape from her mouth. Her skin was gray and she breathed raggedly, remaining unconscious. Joshua was up now, putting Amy over his shoulder like she was a sack of potatoes. She did the same for Charlie, who didn't even rouse. Joshua pushed by her, trying to get to the back door, forgetting that they had watched Penn board it shut.

They moved quickly to the front door, but it wouldn't budge either. "I forgot—he boarded this one from the outside," Joshua said. "Are all the windows barred?"

"Downstairs, they are," Maggie said, choking. "We can open the upstairs ones, but it's so high, Joshua."

"There must be a fire escape."

"There's a rope ladder in the bathroom."

"Go up and check," Joshua said. "These two are too heavy to drag up there unless we know for sure."

Something crashed from the dining room. Sparks flew, smoke billowed, the hall smoldered now.

Maggie raced up the stairs, choking in the smoke that had pooled up in the stairwell. She ran into the bathroom. The rope ladder was gone. Penn had hung Theo with it. He must have done that brutal act while they were at the water park, then waited for them to come home. Was it only a few hours ago that she was laughing with the kids, sliding down water chutes, so cool and clean?

Now the world was on fire. The houses on each side were fully engulfed. Flames forty feet high ringed Safe Haven. Maggie hung out the window, trying to spot sections of the lawn that weren't burning or where Penn hadn't parked a van. Even if she could find a way through the fire, they'd never survive the fall from this high up.

Penn had hemmed them in completely with hell on earth.

Penn lay face down on the dining-room floor, unmoving, facing an ignoble end for a man who had lived nobly most of his life.

He had fought and killed for his country, then provided products that would enable others to fight and kill. He raised a daughter, loved her with his whole being, saw her die. He didn't know if he would bleed to death or burn to death; he did know he had the will and strength for one last act, to lift his finger one last time.

He pressed the function key on the BlackBerry.

The wall exploded, blocking the stairs with a wall of fire.

"Maggie!" Joshua spotted movement at the top of the stairs.

"I'm okay."

"The stairs are burning. We can't come up, not now. You get out!" Penn had rigged his explosives well; Safe Haven was burning methodically.

Maggie disappeared, then came back, wrapped in a wet blanket.

"No! Go out the window!" Joshua yelled, but she disappeared into the flames, then hit the floor with a thud. He pulled her face to the floor where the air was still breathable.

"I've got to break through that plywood on one of the doors," Joshua said. "Are there any tools in here?"

"Maybe the basement," Maggie gasped. "Oh, Joshua, there's a tunnel down there, but David boarded it up."

"Let's get down there. See what we have to work with."

He lifted Charlie, then together they dragged Amy off the floor. With the blanket over their heads and upper bodies, they shuffled through the kitchen and into the back hall. Joshua handed Charlie to Maggie, then lifted Amy. He kicked at the blanket, stuffing it under the door to keep out the smoke.

They raced down the steps; there was no fire here and still good air to breathe. The basement was alive with sound, flickering, popping, snapping from above. The house was old and the wood like tinder now that the fire had gnawed through the horsehair plaster.

"Are there any windows down here?" Joshua asked.

"No. The tunnel—"

There was a horrendous *whoosh,* and Joshua felt the dining-room floor come down on him, surrounding him with burning beams.

"Joshua!"

"I'm okay, okay." The heavy oak table had come straight down, sheltering him. For one panicked moment, Joshua thought he saw Penn looking at him through the flames, but that couldn't be. Penn was dead; his body either burning above them or in the mass of timber and wallboard that had just come through the floor.

As Joshua crawled out from under the table, he saw that the heating duct had been brought partway down, exposing the plywood David had used to close the tunnel.

"The house is caving. We've got to pull that off, try to get out that way."

"I don't see any tools down here! And David said it would take a bomb to get through," Maggie gasped.

Joshua dashed up the stairs with Maggie crying, "Don't, don't." He pulled the blanket out from under the door, wrapped it around himself, and went back into the inferno.

The house was fully engaged now with angry flames, intense heat, and impassable smoke. Joshua had seconds at best to find the gun. He crawled across the floor, a sudden sharp pain in his knee when he moved through melted vinyl. Crawled further, prayed harder, holding his breath until he could hold it no longer. Taking in smoke, feeling the lights go out, his life go out. And then, for the second time, the gun miraculously was in his hand.

He rolled back to the stairs, stuffed the blanket back into the door, then stumbled down.

Alarm filled Maggie's face. "Joshua, what—"

He steadied his hand, then aimed the gun at the plywood, near where David had driven in the bolts.

Blat blat blat. Through the smoke, he could see Maggie cover her ears. *Blat blat blat . . .*

Joshua shot until the ammunition ran out, riddling the plywood with bullet holes. He leaped, grabbed the water pipe over head, and kicked, again and again, splintering the plywood.

There was an abrupt *pop,* and suddenly his foot was through. He kicked a few more times to batter out sharp pieces and to make a hole large enough for them to squeeze into. "Maggie, come on. Get Charlie up here."

The tunnel was just below ground level, putting it about six feet up in the basement. Maggie heaved Charlie over her head with superhuman strength.

"No, you have to go first," Joshua said. "You need to pull him through. You can't push him through."

"What about Amy?"

"I'll put her through."

"How will you get her up if you're in the tunnel?"

"I don't know, don't know! God *has* to provide. Just get going."

Fifty-nine

HE WAS DEAD AND BURIED.

What else could Charlie be, wrapped in darkness and damp dirt? He wanted to yell for help, but his throat was tight and his mouth stung. It was hard to breathe here, but if he was dead, wasn't he done with breathing? How did this all happen? The man with the flat eyes had stuck tape to his mouth, and he got really happy, and then—

He must have died.

But if that was so, where was Jesus? He was supposed to carry Charlie through this dark part until he came out into all that light and singing and dancing and seeing Ma and all the people he had never met who loved him.

The ground under him moved, but no, it was him who was moving. Was it supposed to be this hard to get to heaven? It was too cold here, too wet—*Oh, Jesus, where did You go?*

I AM RIGHT HERE.

Charlie leaned back in Jesus' arms and let himself be dragged. It didn't matter where he was going, because Jesus would be there; he knew that now and that was fine with him.

This was insane.

What did that matter? The whole night was insane, and at least for a moment, they could breathe and not be burned. Maggie inched backward in the dirt, dragging Charlie. How would Joshua get Amy up into the tunnel?

She was still unconscious, and the entry was almost six feet off the floor. Where did this tunnel lead? If it hooked into one of the other houses, they'd be dead anyway. Where else could it go? Maybe into the street, she thought. David Drinas had said these old cities were riddled with sewers and old foundations and even root cellars.

Maggie had known darkness in her life—huddling under the trailer while her parents trashed it in a cocaine-addled fit; hiding under the bleachers at school because she was pretty and the boys pawed at her; curled up in the trunk on stage, waiting for Joshua to stick swords into it while she backed into that tiny compartment; living apart from her husband while he chased spirits and fame.

MY LIGHT SHINES IN THE DARKNESS.

No more darkness, because now she knew Light.

"Get up, Amy, get up!" Someone nagged at her through the darkness, but she couldn't get up because a lie had taken her so high that she had lost her footing.

"Stand up. I need you to stand up!"

Deception had robbed Amy of her arms and legs, but she could still feel. There was not enough air but too much heat, and she knew, under all the silly dreams, that she could burn and die, right here but not like this, with her head too high on a lie—*Please, God*—she needed to be delivered from this—

Her legs straightened and she felt herself pushing up, scraping her back on the wall but no pain, only that incredible urge to—

STAND YOUR GROUND.

Her knees were weak, her feet lame, but somehow she kept rising.

"I got her!" Joshua called. "We're coming. You okay?"

"Yes. No. I . . . don't know where this tunnel is leading." Maggie's voice was muffled, a good sign, Joshua decided. She must be at the far end.

Amy had somehow stood so he could grab under her armpits, lift her with only his arms, and wrestle her into this tunnel. If he hadn't worked with Dino all spring, he wouldn't have had the strength to lift her. He pulled her along, and she helped by pushing with her feet, even though she was still incoherent.

Joshua felt something behind him—Charlie's feet. "Maggie, can you see any end to this?"

"No. Joshua?"

"What?"

"There's water coming in."

"It must be seeping through the ground. They're pouring water on the fires."

"What if the tunnel collapses?"

"It can't," Joshua said. "It won't." But he was in the water now, tiny trickles quickly increasing to a steady stream. This tunnel had been built almost two hundred years ago, with walls of stone and brick and board, constructed to deliver runaways, but now it needed to deliver them—*Please, God*—it was never meant to withstand a flood like scores of fire hoses would deliver.

A brick popped out, hitting him on the back. He felt mud now, cold and slimy, then another brick.

Bowse and Terrio had arrived to find the entire block ablaze. Fire trucks jammed the road. Hoses snaked from hydrants and water trucks. Fire personnel wielded hoses up ladders while policemen pushed people back and waved more emergency equipment through. The scene roared with raging fire, spouting water, revving engines, shouting people. It was hard to hear, hard to see through the smoky chaos.

Bowse tried to help Dr. Drinas hold his son back, tried to get them to see reason. "Roper blew up the whole block," he said. "Don't see how anyone can survive this."

An earsplitting thunder and a hurricane of sparks sent everyone instinctively ducking for cover. It was a full minute before they could see what had happened.

"The last house collapsed," Bowse said.

"No." The young Drinas struggled to his feet, intent on getting back to the scene.

His father tugged at him. "Maybe they're out already, somewhere in the yard trying to shelter from the fire."

Bowse wanted to shake them, tell them to see reason, but that wasn't his job. His was to protect and serve, not to mourn when the ones they served got buried by fire and rubble—at least that's what his head told him.

His heart was another matter.

Joshua had the weight of the world on his back as the tunnel pressed down on him.

Maggie and Charlie inched along in a steady stream of water, but at least up there the tunnel held. He needed to get Amy into that section with them, give her a chance he no longer had. Her skin was still slack; it was only by the grace of God that she pushed enough to move forward. If he shifted, the tunnel would collapse onto her.

"Amy, you have got to wake up!"

She groaned, then choked.

"Amy, you have to slide under me and catch up to Maggie."

No response. He pinched her cheek once, then again. "Come on, girl. Charlie needs you. He's scared."

She inched toward him, groaning. He straightened his back, feeling intense pain as the earth and bricks pressed into his spine.

Amy stopped moving. He couldn't hear her panting anymore. The water and mud had sealed them in; the fire had eaten up all their air.

There was a thundering roar, then water and stone and earth swallowed them in a mighty gulp.

The street collapsed.

Trucks roared, trying to maneuver away from the growing sinkhole. Chief Monroe screamed through a bullhorn, "Back, back, everyone back!" but the fire screamed louder.

David broke away from Patrick. "I see something! Help me, I see something."

Terrio rushed after him, followed by three firefighters.

Halfway down the sinkhole—a morass of mud and pavement—Patrick could see a sliver of blue cloth.

David scrambled down, slipping toward the bottom where a pool of water formed, soon to be a pond, covering that little scrap of cloth. The firefighters swung into action, dropping ropes down the side of the sinkhole, one for David to hitch to, the others to lower more rescuers down. They pushed mud away with bare hands while someone else came down with shovels and tried to dig. It was like trying to push through the center of the earth.

Terrio had seen some amazing and horrific sights in his career, but this topped the list. Rescue personnel had pulled three Astaroths out alive, and the rest—calculated at ten if the coven had been complete—would have been consumed by the fire.

And now this, going over the top of *amazing*.

Joshua Lazarus, pulled out of the mud, gasping.

Amy Howland, slack and gray but not crushed.

A little boy, gasping and then screaming when he found enough air. Then the cracked pavement shifted, sliding toward the rescuers who had to shimmy up out of the way.

Even so—three miracles. Amazing.

With his father fighting him, David Drinas threw himself back into the morass. He lay on a piece of pavement, digging his hands into the mud, breaking a finger on a submerged stone but not minding, knowing his pal Laz would not live without Maggie, so David had to at least try to find her.

It had been over two minutes, past hope now, but he could not give up. A firefighter came back down, then his father, the cop Terrio, all reaching into the mud, hoping to come up with one last body, one last *living* body—*Please, God!*

Joshua tumbled toward them, sliding on his back. "Get him back," David yelled, but all hands were in the mud, searching, searching.

"Please, God," Joshua said, over and over.

David felt something. Not stone or brick or wood or pavement. An arm.

David and Joshua dragged her up together and then let the EMTs take her. When they wiped away the mud from Maggie's face, her lips were still black.

"Asphyxiated," someone said.

Someone else forced a tube down her throat, pumped a bag, and suddenly Maggie's chest rose. Like magic, David thought, all his energy going into that one thought. But life was not magic; life was a gift.

Please, God.

They whacked at Maggie's chest, hurting her, he feared, then he prayed yes, make it hurt, because that would mean she could come back. Charlie cried in someone's arms—his father's, he realized. Amy had been whisked away in an ambulance—*Father God, go with her and bring her back; bring her back to me.*

A doctor bent over Maggie, then looked up at the EMTs, the gloom in their eyes betraying them.

"No!" Joshua screamed, shaking David like a rag doll.

"Wait," the doctor said. "Quiet." She put her stethoscope to Maggie's neck, listening against the tide of fire and water and people. The doctor looked up at the crowd, searching for the right face. When she saw Joshua, she smiled.

Joshua collapsed in David's arms.

We always carry around in our body the death of Jesus,
so that the life of Jesus may also be revealed in our body.

2 Corinthians 4:10

Sixty

CHARLIE WALKED DOWN THE AISLE, HATING THAT HIS SHOULDERS shook. People would think he was a big baby. He was dressed in a suit for the first time in his life and hated it, but it had to be done. "A solemn occasion," Laz had told him. "We'll get through it together."

He joined Laz at the front of the church. Pedro gave him a little thumbs-up, but Dawna was crying. *No,* Charlie wanted to shout. *You cry and then I'll cry and we'll all cry and the whole day will fall in on us.*

A door opened at the side, and Dino came out to stand with them. Charlie had been warned to call him David, even if it was just for today, because it was a solemn occasion. When Dino had pulled him out of the mud and had been the first face he saw, Charlie asked if he was Jesus, and he said, "No, just a friend of His."

There was movement at the back of the church, lots of heads turning. Maggie came in, looking beautiful, but Charlie knew she had wiped away tears. Tears were worse than the stomach bug—easier to catch and harder to shake.

The organ blasted into high gear, making him jump. He felt Laz's hand on one shoulder, Dino's on the other. Maggie stood across from Laz. Her eyes found Charlie, and he felt *so* okay.

The organ switched songs, a bright tune that seemed to make the back door open on its own. And then Amy came in.

A solemn occasion, but Charlie had to smile—almost laugh—because in her white dress and her shining curls, Amy outshone everyone in the whole place, even Maggie. When Amy smiled at him before her eyes found Dino, he knew that they had spoken the truth and there was plenty of room for him too.

David and Amy today—and tomorrow, Mom and Dad. Charlie started laughing, expecting Laz to poke him, but they all laughed with him and life was good and right. *Thank You, God. Thanks a bunch.*

"Ouch!" Maggie yelped with pain.

"Your thumb again?" Joshua called.

"I dropped a can of varnish on my foot."

"Mags, I love you, but I need Dino back."

"You gonna kiss my toes and make it better?"

"How about I kiss you and make me all better?" he said, sweeping her into his arms.

"You're getting paint all over me," she complained, but she hugged him even tighter. They stood cheek to cheek, looking at the half-painted walls.

"A year ago this place was so bad, even the rubble was condemned," she said.

He kissed the top of her head. "And now look."

A developer had wanted to buy the burned-out block on Dunstable Street and turn it into a dance club. Julia Madsen stepped in and outbid him. She sold the estate, then she and Joshua sold *The Other Side* offices and poured the money into this recreation center where Safe Haven had once stood. Children would be in all day, until the evening when the teens would take over. The empty lots where the Astaroth houses once stood would be a playground and two basketball courts.

Enough donations poured in to pay for two full-time staff members—David and Amy Drinas. Members of the neighborhood were being trained to oversee the outside facilities. Volunteers would run the many activities for toddlers through teens.

"I'm going to miss this place," Maggie said.

"It'll always be home."

"The camper's home," Maggie said.

"Good thing you didn't blow it up," Joshua said, laughing.

They were doing inside work on the facility until the newlyweds returned. Then Joshua and Maggie would take to the road again. They had developed an interactive magic act that taught kids to look beyond the illusion to find the underlying truth.

"I can't help but think about Penn," Maggie said. His body had never been found, but that wasn't a surprise—the devastation had been profound.

"I still ache for what I did to that poor man."

Maggie squeezed him. "God will redeem that ache and a whole lot more."

"Amen," Joshua said, kissing her with every ounce of his life.

"Back to work," she said finally.

Back to work.

The Art of Love

You used to have a way with my heart
and there was mystery conveyed in the art
of your love, of your love.
An honest face, the look in your eyes
would speak the charms and hypnotize
for my love, for my love.
You've chosen gold and you're looking for fame.
Sincerity isn't part of your game.
Where is love? Where is love?

CHORUS
For love, time revealed a healing.
For love has found the meaning
of the deepest magic before the dawn of time,
for your life and for mine,
for the art of love.

Now I see this ace of spades
would take on so many different shades
over love, over love.
And when you go to the other side,
do you see? Do you hear how I've cried
for our love, for our love?
I've asked for truth that I'd understand.
and though you've slipped out of my hands
I found love. I found love.

Where do we go from here?
Where do we go from here?
Tell me, where do we go from here?
Where do we go from here?

Acknowledgments

I OWE A HUGE DEBT OF GRATITUDE TO CHIP (JERRY) MACGREGOR of Alive Communications who answered all my questions on magic and the occult with patience and humor. Chip's book, MIND GAMES, written with Andre Kole, was a major research tool for me. I recommend this book highly to parents, pastors, and youth workers.

I am grateful to friends who used their talents for my behalf: Victoria James for writing a song to characterize the book, the touching Art of Love; to Toddi Norum for coining the phrase "Christian Chiller," and for all her tireless efforts on my behalf; to Beth Confrancisco for being my first reader that offers the firm but loving hand; and to Marj Overhiser for long talks that helped clarify scripture and topics in this book.

Many thanks to my home church, the Evangelical Congregational Church of Dunstable, for providing me a spiritually-safe place to write some of the more difficult sections of this book; to my sister Janice Freeman for allowing me to take over her home and write without distraction; to my husband Steve who supported me fully by not complaining when I packed my computer and left for days on end to write; to my sister Mary for providing comfort; to the Rev. David Rinas for guidance on pastoral counseling; to the members of my Writers' Group, fine writers all: Beverly McCoy, Robert Sanchez, David Daniel, David Harrison, Patty Thorpe, Lee Duckett, Kathy Duckett, Joan Pena, Kate Bergquist, and Dave Tuells for helping me keep the faith; with an additional thank you to Judy Loose and Toni Causey. I am so grateful to Victoria James and Steve Bell for providing marvelous music to write by.

As always, I am indebted to my agent, Lee Hough of Alive Communications, who truly guides me with wisdom and kindness. I am blessed by my editor Jenny Baumgartner, who cheers me on, reins me in, pushes me higher.

I thank God for the wonderful privilege of putting words to paper and pray that this book will honor His light that shines so brightly in the darkness.

Look for
Kathryn Mackel's
next book
OUTRIDERS